THE MOST WONDERFUL TIME

This Large Print Book carries the
Seal of Approval of N.A.V.H.

THE MOST WONDERFUL TIME

FERN MICHAELS
STACY FINZ
SARAH TITLE
SHIRLEE MCCOY

WHEELER PUBLISHING
A part of Gale, Cengage Learning

GALE
CENGAGE Learning

Farmington Hills, Mich • San Francisco • New York • Waterville, Maine
Meriden, Conn • Mason, Ohio • Chicago

GALE
CENGAGE Learning®

LIBRARY OF CONGRESS CATALOGING-IN-PUBLICATION DATA

Names: Michaels, Fern. Christmas passed. | Finz, Stacy. A Glory Junction Christmas. | Title, Sarah. Moonshine and mistletoe. | McCoy, Shirlee. An Apple Valley Christmas.
Title: The most wonderful time / by Fern Michaels, Stacy Finz, Sarah Title, Shirlee McCoy.
Description: Large print edition. | Waterville, Maine : Wheeler Publishing, A part of Gale, Cengage Learning, 2016. | Series: Wheeler Publishing Large Print Hardcover
Identifiers: LCCN 2016041692 | ISBN 9781410478009 (hardback) | ISBN 1410478009 (hardcover)
Subjects: LCSH: Christmas stories, American. | Large type books. | BISAC: FICTION / General.
Classification: LCC PS648.C45 M67 2016 | DDC 813/.0108334--dc23
LC record available at https://lccn.loc.gov/2016041692

Printed in the United States of America
1 2 3 4 5 6 7 20 19 18 17 16

CONTENTS

■ ■ ■ ■

CHRISTMAS PASSED

FERN MICHAELS

■ ■ ■ ■

PROLOGUE

Brandy Heyers viewed the stacked boxes in her garage, dreading the thought of opening them. This would mark the third Christmas without Jeff, her husband of twenty years. The third Christmas that she had refused to allow her son, Matthew, and her daughter, Keira, to haul out the artificial Christmas tree and the boxes of decorations she and Jeff had collected during their marriage. It just hurt too much, and she didn't really see the point.

Christmas was just another day now. She'd been telling herself this since the beginning of November, when all the Christmas hoopla began. Same as last year and the year before that. Matthew was twelve when Jeff died, and Keira fifteen. Now at fifteen and eighteen, they weren't so easily convinced to back off where the holidays were concerned.

Yesterday, Keira reminded her that Christmas had been Dad's favorite time of year. She'd reminded her how much he enjoyed taking each ornament out of the boxes and how each one had a special story. She also reminded her just how much her dad enjoyed putting up the lights, dragging the old, faded, plastic Santa and his reindeer out of the attic. Every year, he'd tell them it was time to retire the old guy and his crew, but every year he would find the perfect place for the plastic decorations to hang out until after the New Year.

Three years. It seemed like a lifetime to Brandy. Taking the ornaments out would hurt. All of them. Maybe they would take a trip to Disney World, another thing she'd avoided as it was plagued with memories of Jeff. Maybe they could take a ski trip instead. Or possibly go to New York City, see the Rockettes. Something that had no memories of her life with Jeff. For the past two years, they'd stayed home, and Christmas was just another day to her, and she'd tried to convince the kids it was, too, but they weren't buying it this year.

A little voice whispered in her ear, *"Maybe it's time to move on."*

Her mother had been telling her this starting three months after Jeff died. Brandy hadn't had much of a relationship with her since. While it saddened her, they'd never been close. Her father had died when she was ten, and she was an only child.

How could she possibly move on? Her life ended the day Jeff died. He'd been diagnosed with pancreatic cancer, and within three months, he succumbed to the horrid disease. There was no time to prepare, as if one could ever prepare for such a devastating loss. Shock, extreme sadness, a loss like no other; Brandy lived in a fog those first few months. She'd been a stay-at-home mom, so there was no career outside the house to focus on. Jeff had been a music teacher at Lee County High School. There were a few benefits remaining, and his life insurance paid the bills, but that wasn't going to last forever. In fact, she had enough money to get them through the next few months. After it ran out, she was in trouble. She and Jeff never discussed what would happen to her and the kids if he didn't survive. They never discussed how she would support them when he passed. Brandy had no formal training in any profession other than raising her family. She would have to find a job, a way to support herself and the kids. Like most young, married couples, they hadn't given much thought to their financial future, telling themselves there would be time for that later. When the kids were in high school, they would start a college fund, maybe try their hand at online investing, anything to secure their financial future. And like most young couples, Brandy and Jeff thought they were invincible and had never gotten around to investing for their future.

When Jeff was diagnosed, they'd both gone into a state of semi-shock for a few weeks. They'd decided to wait and tell the kids when the doctor gave them a chemo schedule, and what they should expect over the next few months. Sadly, Jeff hadn't made it through his first round of chemotherapy. Both Keira and Matthew were stunned when she'd explained the reality of their father's health just weeks before he died. Keira, a daddy's girl from day one, rebelled when he died. Her normally shiny blond hair was now a deep reddish burgundy with one side shaved. She'd pierced her nose, and one eyebrow, and wore thick, black kohl eyeliner on her eyes. She looked scary, but Brandy knew this was her way of coping with her loss. Not long after Jeff's death, she'd started hanging with a new group of kids, who dressed in black clothes and had so many piercings on their bodies that they resembled pincushions. Matthew, on the other hand, had become withdrawn and no longer bothered attending his music classes. He was as musically gifted as his father had been. He played guitar, piano, and the trumpet. His dream was to attend Juilliard. Since Jeff's death, he hadn't touched an instrument. Brandy constantly worried about him, feared what would become of him and his talent if she couldn't pull him out of his grief.

An extremely close family, Jeff had always taken the lead, always knew how to resolve whatever crisis the kids were going through. He was the perfect parent. It was thoughts like this that made her wonder if the kids would be suffering this much had she been the one to die. Hating herself for such thoughts, she turned her back on the neatly stacked boxes labeled CHRISTMAS ORNAMENTS.

Maybe next year.

CHAPTER ONE

"We're not skipping Christmas again, Mom. If you want to, that's your choice, but Matthew and I want to celebrate Christmas. It's been almost *three years,*" Keira said, putting extra emphasis on the last two words. "Dad would be so pissed!" she added before racing away.

Brandy took a deep breath and looked at the stack of boxes. Jeff *would* be pissed, but he wasn't here. He'd left her with this . . . *life,* and she almost hated him for doing so. How could he? Hadn't he felt sick? Had he taken all the vitamins she so carefully measured out for him day after day? What did it matter now, she thought as she closed the door leading to the garage. He was gone. She wasn't. He had no life, and though she was here in the physical sense, she hadn't had much of a life since he'd died. Tears filled her eyes just thinking the words *he died.* Still, after all this time, she wasn't over

15

the loss. She didn't want to be. In an odd way, her grief was comforting. Like a child with a pacifier. It was horrible when it's first taken away, but when they got used to another form of security, they forgot all about the pacifier. She was in limbo. She couldn't forget and didn't want to forget. Twenty of the best years of her life. It was wrong even to think about moving on. The kids were young. Their grief had diminished over time. That's what the grief counselor explained to her a few months after Jeff's death. The young were resilient. Their lives were focused on the here and now. Not the past. Their futures were ahead of them. They would grow old, and their father would be nothing more than a faded memory. The family she'd spent so much time caring for was gone, or at least the core no longer remained. Now they all simply existed, and Brandy knew this wasn't good. She had to do something, but Christmas?

She wasn't sure what to do.

She stepped inside the kitchen, where Keira was chatting on her cell phone with one of her friends. Matthew was in his bedroom, doing who knew what. Brooding, and most likely listening to rap music on his iPod. It was Saturday, and Brandy hated weekends. The atmosphere in the house was morose, miserable. She supposed she should ask the kids if they wanted to see a movie, then go out to dinner afterward, but again, that was lame. That's really all they ever did together as a family, and she could count the times they'd done this on only one hand. Jeff would be spinning in his grave. But he wasn't, and she was tired of worrying about the state of her life.

The house phone rang, and she took a deep breath. She still received sympathy calls after all this time. She hated them then, and even more now.

"Mom, are you going to answer that?" Keira asked in a smart-alecky tone.

"Yes," she said curtly, and picked up the phone. "Hello?"

"Brandy, it's me," said Linda, her best friend since middle school. "Are you busy?"

That was the joke of the century!

"No, just moping around the house. What's up?" She knew she sounded about as enthused as dirty laundry, of which she had three giant heaps waiting in the laundry room.

"I just left the library. They're looking for someone to work part-time, three days a week. Knowing how much you love books, I thought of you."

She paused a few seconds before answering. "Is this your way of saying it's time to get off my rear end and look for a job?" She knew she needed to find something, but her heart just wasn't in it. However, her dwindling bank account told her it was time.

"You know me better than that. I just know how much you love books. I thought it would be perfect for you. If you're interested, I can put in a good word for you."

Linda's father-in-law was superintendent of the county libraries. If Linda put in a good word, she knew the job was hers.

"I don't know, Linda. The holidays are coming, I need to stay home with Matthew and Keira."

"Why? So the three of you can mope around the house together? You need to move on, Brandy. It's time. It's been almost three years. You're young, and you have the rest of your life ahead of you. Why don't you at least give it some thought? I'll tell George you're interested and to hold off hiring anyone."

Linda tried so hard, but she still had her husband, Dylan. Her nice little family, three girls and two dogs, plus one parakeet, which equaled the perfect family. She didn't have to go to sleep at night worrying about the future, at least her children's future. She really should look into this. "I'll do it," she said before she changed her mind.

"That's excellent! I'll call George, and tell him."

"You don't think I can get the job on my own merits?" Brandy asked. She hadn't worked in public since she was in her teens, and she would like to believe she was employable. She knew the library system front to back.

"Of course I do. A little help isn't going to hurt, Brandy. You need to take what's being offered." Linda's tone was serious.

"Okay, tell me what to do, and I'll do it." The kids needed her, and especially this time of year, as Jeff had passed away December twentieth. Holidays were tough, but Linda was right. It was time she started acting like a big girl.

"Fantastic! I'll call George as soon as I hang up. So, did you do it?" she asked.

Brandy knew what she referred to. She'd discussed this Christmas tree–decorating issue with her last week. Again. She said she wasn't ready, but the kids were past ready. Maybe it *was* time to at least *think* about pulling out a few decorations. She wasn't sure how far she could go with this whole Christmas thing, but she would try. And she knew this would make her children happy.

"I looked at the boxes stacked in the garage," she said.

"Brandy! You need to open them up and see what's inside. That's a start. And it would be even better if you took a few ornaments out, maybe let Matthew and Keira help."

"I know. Keira is ticked at me now. She told me she and Matthew were not going to skip Christmas this year, so I'm sure they'll be thrilled if I act like I'm excited about celebrating. That was always Jeff's thing. I'm just not sure if I can. I'm afraid of" — she stopped and took a deep breath — "the memories, and how much it's going to hurt."

"Are you still going to grief counseling?"

"No, I stopped that after the second appointment. I really didn't see any point in continuing though the kids went for a few months. I think it helped them to begin the healing process. They've got their whole lives ahead of them. It's hard for them to understand that I had spent the past twenty years of my life with their father, and I just can't wipe those memories out with a few grief-counseling sessions."

"Of course you can't, but Brandy, it's time. Jeff would want you to move on with your life. He would have, had it been the other way around."

True, she thought. Jeff liked being married, and he wouldn't have grieved this long. He would certainly have remarried by now. Maybe even had another child.

"I know, but it doesn't make it any easier. What am I supposed to do, Linda? Do I just wake up tomorrow and forget that I was married to Jeff for twenty years? Forget the three months of pure hell we, *he* went through? If you have a solution, or some . . . magic words, please tell me. I really don't like feeling this way, and if I'm honest, I don't really like the person I've become. I'm so . . . miserable, Linnie. I swear the kids hate me, and I don't blame them."

In a soothing tone, Linda said, "Calm down; don't be too hard on yourself. I haven't walked in your shoes, so who's to say how I would react? I just want you to be happy again."

Brandy raked a hand through her hair. It was so long, too long for a woman in her midforties. She'd neglected all personal grooming, other than the basic necessities, and had even been somewhat neglectful of those the past week. She hated December and all that it entailed. She wished she could hibernate and wake up after New Year's.

But she had to be a realist. Before she

changed her mind, she said, "Can you call your hairdresser and make me an appointment? And as soon as possible."

"Sure, I can. I'll send her a text message now. Hang on a sec," Linda said. Brandy heard the lilt in her friend's voice. She smiled. Linda had been her best friend since eighth grade. They'd shared all the normal experiences two young girls could share. Grief, however, had never entered into any of their late-night phone calls. They'd both wanted to get married and have children and would spend hours discussing how they would live next door to each other, how they'd take turns babysitting so they could have date nights. And most of the things they talked about in those late-night conversations had come true. Except Jeff's death. They'd never gotten that far, and looking back, they were too young to even think about dying.

"Emily can see you in an hour," said Linda. "She had a cancellation. The girls are at soccer practice with Dylan. Pretty up, and I'll drive you. Maybe we can even go into one of those nail salons for a manicure and a pedicure. We haven't done this since . . ." She paused. She didn't want to continue talking about Jeff. Brandy would never move on if she did, so instead she said, "Forever. My nails look horrid. So, are you game?"

If Brandy were going to apply for the job at the library, it only made sense that she "pretty up." However, she felt guilty treating herself to such silly things when Jeff couldn't. Plus, there was no one to appreciate her attempts at "prettying up."

"Brandy, yes or no?" Linda persisted.

"Give me twenty minutes. Just toot the horn when you get here. I'll run out, no need for you to get out of your car."

"This is a good sign. I'm proud of you. Now let me get off the phone. I'll see you soon."

In the early years, they had lived next door to each other, but Linda and Dylan had moved into a newer, fancier neighborhood when he made partner at the law firm where he worked. They'd both cried for days, but Brandy had insisted it was part of the lifestyle when one was married to an up-and-coming defense attorney. Though when she'd said this, Jeff was still alive. And she lived only a few minutes away from Linda. While their late-night ice-cream binges weren't as frequent, they'd still managed to sneak away from their families at least a couple times a month. Brandy couldn't remember the last time they'd done this.

She raced to her bedroom, the room she and Jeff had shared for so many years. She grabbed a pair of dirty jeans off the bed and a navy blouse she'd worn at least a half dozen times. Not only was she turning into a person she didn't like, she was turning into a total slob. That was one of the reasons she hadn't invited Linda to come inside; it was easier to run out the door and meet her in the drive. She'd never liked keeping a perfect house, but she'd never, *ever* been ashamed to invite her best friend inside. As soon as she changed, she ran a brush through her hair, then twisted it into a topknot, securing it with a claw clip.

"Keira, Matthew, I need you both in the living room. Pronto!" she shouted, and none too kindly.

Keira was still in the kitchen on the phone, and Matthew walked out of his room with earbuds crammed in his ears. He wore a pair of his father's boxers, his favorite pair, with the musical-note pattern. A silly Valentine's Day gift she'd given Jeff years ago.

Brandy's throat tightened, and she felt a flash of unfamiliar rage. "Take those off right this minute! How dare you take something that doesn't belong to you! You have no business being in my room!" She could feel her heart rate increase, a loud pounding in her ears. This wasn't good. Her and Jeff's bedroom remained unchanged since his death. She hadn't touched any of his personal items. His toothbrush was still in the holder next to hers.

Matthew yanked the earbuds out of his ears and threw them on the floor. "Here, take these. They belonged to Dad, too." With that, he turned around and went to his room, slamming the door behind him. Two minutes later, the boxers in question came flying out of his room, landing at the edge of the hall where she waited.

She reached for the boxers, clutching them to her chest. She felt violated in an odd way. Brandy always kept her bedroom door closed. She'd made it clear to both kids that this was her personal space and asked that they respect this. Apparently, Matthew had decided to take matters into his own hands and rummage through his father's chest of drawers. Gritting her teeth, she stomped down the hall to his room. She pounded on the door but didn't wait for him to invite her inside.

It had been awhile since she had been in his room and what she saw when she entered shocked her. Matthew had always been a very neat kid, almost to the point of obsessiveness. His bed was always made neatly, his clothes put away, books and DVDs had a place on the floor-to-ceiling shelf opposite his bed. Now, however, his bed appeared as though a tornado had swooped in and twisted the sheets and comforter into a tight knot. Clothes covered the floor. His once-cherished music books and his first-edition Harry Potter and Hunger Games novels were opened and tossed across the room as though he'd been using them for a Frisbee, or a boomerang. The odor of stale sweat permeated the darkened room. He sat in the swivel desk chair in front of the desk that she and Jeff purchased just a few months before his diagnosis. He now wore gray sweats, no shirt, and a scowl.

Brandy inhaled and slowly exhaled. She needed to calm down. The last thing she needed was to suffer a heart attack or stroke. Not wanting to sit on the filthy, unmade bed, she leaned against the door frame. "We need to talk." She cleared her throat. "No, *I* am going to talk and *you* are going to listen. You getting this?" she asked, raising her voice a few notches above normal. When she didn't get a response, she shouted, "Listen to me, dammit!"

That must've gotten his attention. Instead of staring down at the mess strung across the floor, he looked at her. His bright aqua eyes were shiny with unshed tears.

"When I told you my room was off-limits, I wasn't joking. That's *my* private space, and you can't just come and go as you please." She was shaking but didn't care. She needed this fifteen-year-old giant of a kid to understand the rules. And the main rule since their father died: Her room was her private space and off-limits. He looked past her, not daring to meet her gaze.

"Do you hear me?" she persisted when he failed to answer.

Before he had a chance to respond, Keira practically shoved her way inside the room. "Matthew, could you give us some privacy?"

He immediately stood, and, in three giant leaps, was out of the room.

"Sit down, Mom," Keira said in a tone that wasn't so much snotty as it was authoritative.

"Look, Linda is picking me up, I don't have time for your crap either, so make it fast." She wasn't going to give her eighteen-year-old daughter the satisfaction of sitting down. Besides, there wasn't a clean place to sit even if she wanted to.

Keira took Matthew's vacated seat. "You really don't have a clue, do you? You're so full of yourself and your grief, that you've forgotten how to be a mom! I can't wait until school starts so I can get out of this diseased house."

Here we go again, Brandy thought.

"Me either!" she yelled back in her best Mom-is-ticked voice. "I am sick of you and your brother. Me, me, me, that's all I hear from the two of you! What more do you want from me? I cook your meals, I see to it that you have a roof over your head. I even bought you a car, which I couldn't really afford! Tell me, Keira, what's wrong with that? Would you rather I not? If so, have at it. It's about time you and your brother learned how to cook your own meals and do your own laundry. I'm rather sick of this" — she made air quotes with her index fingers — " 'diseased' place myself. Now, if you have something important, tell me now. I'm getting my hair done in thirty minutes. Linda will be here any second."

Keira just stared at her and shook her head. "No, Mom, you're right. Just forget whatever I said."

A horn tooted in the driveway. Brandy hurried from the room and grabbed her purse, leaving the two selfish little brats to themselves for a while. She really did need a break.

CHAPTER TWO

Grateful for the unexpected escape, Brandy sank into the luxury car's plush leather seats.

As always, Linda looked like a fashion model. Her shoulder-length chestnut hair was styled in the latest bob, her makeup was perfect. She wore Seven jeans and a bright yellow silk blouse. If she weren't her best friend, Brandy would be jealous. However, Linda was as beautiful on the inside as she was on the outside, and Brandy loved this about her the most.

"If you don't mind my saying, you look like poo warmed over." Brandy smiled. "And you don't smell so swift either," she added, but her tone was anything but playful.

"I know. I meant to take a shower last night, or the night before, but I was busy. Sorry to stink up your fancy car." This hurt her feelings a little, but Linda was right.

She did smell a bit ripe, and her clothes were dirty.

Linda drove through the neighborhood and made a few comments about those who'd moved away. "Do you still feel safe here?" she asked Brandy.

"Yes, I do. As a matter of fact, I rarely give it a thought. Why? Does Dylan know something I don't?" Brandy knew that Dylan, being a criminal-defense attorney, dealt with a lot of petty criminals. If there'd been any vandalism or other problems in the neighborhood, he would know.

"Not that I'm aware of. He'd tell me if there were. I miss this place sometimes," she said, a trace of sadness in her voice.

"I bet you do," Brandy added with a bit of sarcasm.

They approached a traffic light, and Linda turned to look at her.

"What's wrong, Brandy? If you don't mind my saying, you're acting kind of mean. What gives? And don't tell me it's nothing. I know better. Now spit it out, or I'll have Emily shave your head."

"I've been into it with Keira and Matthew this morning. They think they know everything. Little know-it-alls, nothing new there. Sorry to be such a downer."

"What's going on with them? They're

good kids, Brandy. That's not like them."

"Yeah, well, you should spend a day with them. I promise you'd change your mind. Matthew hasn't touched an instrument since Jeff died. Keira looks like something out of a horror movie. She's shaved the side of her hair off since you last saw her. Oh, and did I mention this week's hair color? Burgundy. Matthew's becoming a pig. His room smells like dirty socks, and his sheets are gray and they're supposed to be white. And to top that off, he's been prowling around in my room. I told both kids my room was off-limits. Apparently, he didn't get my message, so we had words right before you arrived. No, I talked, and he pouted. Then Keira marches in and tells me I need to sit down and listen to her. Starts to spout off, and you arrived. Thank you. I couldn't stand another minute in that 'diseased' house. That's how Keira referred to our home — can you believe that?"

"I wouldn't know. Actually, I haven't been inside since the day of Jeff's funeral. I suppose you have your reasons for not inviting your best friend inside your house." Linda paused. "I think you need to tell me what's really going on. *Really.*"

Brandy slumped farther down in her seat. "Just the same stuff."

Linda turned into the shopping mall where Emily's salon was located. After shutting the engine off, she positioned herself where she could see Brandy's face. "Explain. And we're not getting out of the car until you do. So, start talking."

"Look, there isn't anything to explain. Both kids have turned into people I don't know anymore. I've told you this more than once. They go to school and come home. Keira hangs out with that group of Goth kids, and Matthew's friends don't want to hang around him anymore. I heard one of them call him a douche bag the other morning when I dropped him off at school. I'm sure his friends think he's turned into a weirdo. He's a musical prodigy. And he wants to throw it all away."

Brandy shook her head. Tears pooled in her eyes, but she didn't let them flow. She looked out the window so Linda wouldn't see them. "And that, my friend, about sums it up in the Heyers household."

"Brandy, has it ever occurred to you that they're seeking your attention?"

She looked at Linda as if she wore blinders. "Good grief, they have my undivided attention twenty-four seven. You of all people should know I *never* leave the house other than to go to the grocery store or take

Matthew to school. I think I'm going to have him take the bus from now on. I'm sick of getting up at five o'clock in the morning. He's big enough to set his alarm clock and walk two blocks to the bus stop. Everything I do is centered around those two. It's not easy being a single parent. But you wouldn't know that because you have Dylan. Dylan's there when you need a break, Dylan is there to run the girls around. It's just me, Linda. I have to do it all. And now, I have to get a job. I've got enough of Jeff's life insurance to get me through another three or four months, and after that, well, again, it's all on me."

Linda looked at her watch. "Let's go inside. We're talking more later. And I'm not going to listen to your bull." She opened her car door, not giving Brandy the opportunity to continue with her excuses.

Brandy followed Linda inside the salon. The second she saw the giant Fraser fir lit up with dozens of sparkling white lights, she wished she'd stayed home.

CHAPTER THREE

Ryan Rogers, principal of Pelican Elementary School, heaved a heavy sigh of relief, glad that it was Friday. Only two more weeks to go before the Thanksgiving holiday break. And did he ever need a break.

His calendar for the upcoming week was packed. Monday was Lily's eighth birthday. Since her special day fell on a workday, they'd decided to postpone her party until the following Saturday, which just so happened to be the sixth anniversary of his wife, Anna's, death. It would be a tough day, but he would manage. He always seemed to get through this day without too much difficulty; though it was tough the first few years, time had softened the hard edges of his grief.

Fortunately, Lily had been barely two years old when Anna, at thirty-two, collapsed from a brain aneurysm. Ryan had stayed by her side until the doctors declared her brain-dead, which was only three days after she'd been rushed to the hospital.

He'd been so stunned by the sudden loss, he had lived in a fog for months after losing her. Anna's parents, Phillip and Nan, had helped care for Lily. At first, she'd asked for her mommy constantly, then after a few months, she suddenly stopped asking. It was as though her memory had completely wiped out all traces of Anna. At the time, Ryan wished he could do the same, but as time passed, his grief became more bearable.

He'd established somewhat of a routine with Lily with the help of Anna's family and Anna's best friend, Marlie, who conveniently lived across the street and worked from home. For a few years, she became Lily's second parent. Last year, she had sold her house and moved from Florida to California because she'd met the man of her dreams. She had been sad to leave them, and frankly, Ryan was more than a little sad himself to see her go though not for the reasons Anna's parents had hoped. They thought he and Marlie were romantically involved, and they'd given him their approval. But to him, her moving away was losing a good friend and another piece of the life he'd shared with his wife. Lily asked about her all the time when she'd first moved. She wanted to know why her mommies left her. Was she a bad girl? Did they want a new little girl? Each time she asked this, his heart broke a little more.

It was the main reason he hadn't dated since Anna's death. Fearful Lily would get too attached, he reasoned it would be best to remain single and celibate until she was older. Lately, he'd questioned his decision. He was a busy man during the day, given his duties as principal. In the evening he made dinner, helped Lily with homework if she had any, and if not, he'd made it a habit to get involved with a puzzle project. She'd become as addicted to puzzles as he was. He cherished these times, but often he thought about how lonely he was and wondered how much longer staying home doing puzzles of Maps of the World with a soon-to-be eight-year-old would substitute as a social life for a forty-four-year-old. Not that he didn't enjoy this time with Lily. He of all people knew that life could change on a dime. He cherished the time with his daughter, but after he put her to bed, the nights were long and becoming quite lonely. It wasn't that he needed "a woman" as some of his guy friends teased. No, he needed adult-female companionship. Someone to spend time with and enjoy whatever they chose to do. Maybe it was time to start thinking about dating again. He would just keep it quiet. There was no need to tell Lily.

No, for now, he would keep these thoughts to himself.

He filled his briefcase with the paperwork that he needed to attend to over the weekend, patted his pockets for his keys. "I'll see you all Monday," he said with as much cheer as he could muster to the three ladies who comprised his office staff.

"Have a good weekend, Ryan," Bea, his personal secretary, said as her bright pink nails danced across her keyboard.

"Thanks, I plan to." He didn't, but she didn't need to know that.

Bea's two assistants, Chloe and Ruth, waved as he passed through the front office. He gave a friendly two-finger wave in return but didn't say anything. They were engrossed in whatever Bea had assigned them. She was almost seventy. He dreaded the day she retired. It would be difficult functioning without her. But, again, he had experienced loss, and the loss of a secretary could and would be dealt with when the time came.

He exited the building through the staff door. Greeted by bright sunshine, and a tinge of a breeze, Ryan hoped they'd have a bit of cool weather for the upcoming holidays. Florida during Thanksgiving and Christmas was not conducive to throwing one into the holiday spirit.

He tossed his briefcase in the backseat, cranked over the engine on his nine-year-old Ford, and was backing out of the parking space marked PRINCIPAL ROGERS when his cell phone rang. He looked at the caller ID. "Yes, Bea, what did I forget?" he asked.

"Nothing. I just wanted to remind you that tonight's your turn to host the session at the library. Seven o'clock."

"Thanks, I'd completely forgotten about it," he said, and wished he hadn't made the commitment. He was always true to his word, so he'd go, and maybe tonight he would tell the members to take him off the volunteer list.

"You're supposed to bring the snacks, too. I went ahead and ordered three dozen cupcakes from Cream Cups for you," Bea said.

"You're a real doll, Bea. Thanks. Have a good weekend," he said, then clicked off.

Since Lily was spending the weekend with Phillip and Nan, they'd picked her up an hour ago, which gave him time to drive the three blocks to the bakery, so he wouldn't have to backtrack later. With the house to himself, he would read through the paperwork he'd been avoiding, then prepare himself for tonight's session.

Thirty minutes later, he placed three boxes of cupcakes on the table, dropped his briefcase on the kitchen floor, and headed to the master bedroom to shower and change.

When he finished, he dressed in faded jeans and an equally faded burgundy-and-gold Florida State T-shirt, his alma mater, and hopefully one day Lily's, too. He grabbed a can of Coke from the fridge, then removed the papers from his briefcase.

He took them out to the lanai and read them three times. He'd questioned this idea for months, and now he had to make a decision. Once he signed the papers, it would be final. There would be no turning back.

However, he was only forty-four, still reasonably young. It was time to move forward. Before he changed his mind, he took a pen and signed all the papers, then went inside and faxed them to the real estate office.

When the last paper slid through the machine, he lifted his can of Coke in the air, toasting his bravery.

The home he and Anna had shared was now officially up for sale.

CHAPTER FOUR

Brandy started her new job at the library the Monday after Thanksgiving. She'd been nervous at first, but George and the rest of the staff knew her and treated her as though she were an old friend, not a new employee on her very first day. She knew them from her many visits over the years.

"You know this place inside and out, Brandy," George explained. "Just follow Andrea, and she'll show you what your job entails." He patted her on the shoulder. "You'll do just fine. I was thrilled when Linda told me you were interested in the job. Now, welcome to our little family."

"Thanks, George, this means a lot to me. I'm going to like working here, I can feel it," she said, as a way to convince herself. She thought that she would, but she was still frightened. She'd never had a *real* job, had never been the breadwinner. She had to work now. It wasn't a choice. The pay

40

wasn't as much as she needed, but George assured her that after her ninety-day probationary period, the pay would increase. She'd breathed a sigh of relief when he told her this. What little bit of money she had left from Jeff's insurance would now be her and the kids' nest egg. Unless it was absolutely necessary, she wouldn't use another dime of it.

"So can I. Now let Andrea show you the ropes. I'll see you later," George said, then headed to his office.

Andrea was short and round, with bright blue eyes and a headful of bouncy red curls. Brandy guessed she was somewhere between fifty and sixty. It was hard to tell. "Follow me, hon. I'll get you the list of December's events, and let me tell you, it's a long one this year."

Brandy nodded and followed Andrea to the back of the library. She felt good today. She wore a black pencil skirt with a dark green silk blouse. With low heels and minimal makeup, she felt as professional as one could, given her circumstances. Linda had pretty much told her to get off her duff and start living again or else. She hadn't asked what the "or else" referred to, but assumed it was drastic. Her feelings of happiness could be as fickle as the weather. She'd had brief moments of happiness before. But as soon as she thought about Jeff, she was back to that dark, sad place where she'd existed for so long and wasn't sure she'd ever leave. But in order to survive, she had to allow herself a few moments of respite from her grief, though doing so gave her a massive bout of guilt. She hoped that Jeff would understand. In the meantime, all she could do was cross her fingers and offer up a silent prayer that he was okay with her focusing on her new job. She would return to her grief tonight.

"Brandy, are you all right?" Andrea asked her.

Startled, she said, "Uh, yes. I was just in awe of all the books we passed." She tried to sound light and teasing, but from the look on Andrea's face, she hadn't been successful.

Andrea's friendly face showed concern. "Are you sure?" she asked. "We can have a cup of coffee in my office if you'd like. Give you a chance to get used to working here." Andrea smiled. Brandy knew her as a library employee, but now she was also her immediate supervisor.

"No, I'm fine. Truly. It's still hard, you know." She let the sentence hang. Everyone at the library knew she was a widow. She hated being called a widow. It made her sound old and ugly. But she reminded herself that she wasn't a young babe in the woods anymore, either. And ugly, well it depended on what one thought of as ugly. She actually smiled at the thought.

"You know we have grief counseling sessions here. Every Friday at seven o'clock. You should attend. I went for a couple of years after my husband passed away. They really helped me to move on with my life."

"I'm sorry. I didn't know" was all she could come up with.

"Howard had been ill for a long time. In a way, it was a relief. He suffered for so long."

"I suppose it's for the best, but it's still hard, you know?" Brandy said.

Andrea nodded. "It took me a couple of years to decide to live again, but when I did, my life now is so much better since I changed my attitude.

"I know Howard isn't suffering, and he would want me to be happy. We talked about this before he passed away. We even discussed the fact that I might even meet someone and fall in love again. I told him that was highly unlikely for someone my age, but you know, I was wrong. I have a boyfriend now." Andrea's eyes lit up like stars. "He's the best thing that ever happened to me, too. You'll see. One day, you will also find another special someone."

"I don't think so," she said sternly. She thought Andrea was a bit crazy. How could she just forget her husband? And a boyfriend? It seemed like a betrayal, but she would keep that to herself. She didn't want to start off on the wrong foot, especially not with the woman who was her supervisor.

A bit hesitantly, Andrea asked, "Surely, you and your husband discussed this sort of thing?"

Brandy could feel the heat rise to her cheeks. What right did she have to ask such a personal question? They stood like two statues in front of what Brandy assumed was Andrea's office.

"It's too personal. I'm sorry. I can't talk about this now. Just show me what my job entails. I came here to work, not discuss my future dating habits," she said. She knew it came out all wrong, but it was too late to take it back.

Andrea threw back her shoulders, gaining an inch in height. "Of course." She turned and walked inside the office. Brandy trailed behind.

She removed three large stacks of papers from a filing cabinet. "These are the requests we have for use of the meeting rooms. Since this is the main branch, we schedule for all Lee County's libraries. Here is a master list of the requirements for the applicants. Most of the forms are returned to us by fax or e-mail."

Brandy had thought she would be working at the main desk, checking out books, interacting with the public, discussing their favorite books and authors. She wasn't sure she could do this. Maybe it was a mistake taking this job. She could find something else. She preferred to work from home. She should let someone else who needed the job take over.

What am I thinking? I need this job.

"I can manage that," she forced herself to say. "Is there more to the job than scheduling?"

"Oh yes. Much more. You'll be reserving computer times for those who've put in a request. Then there is the homework-assistance program. You will need to match the volunteer to the student, that sort of thing. And story times for the preschool children. When at all possible, we like to have a children's author as a guest reader. I have a list of authors who regularly read to the children. You'll need to familiarize yourself with the children's books, then set up the story times, which almost always stay the same unless something drastic happens. It's all quite simple. Just a matter of being organized. Now" — she came out from behind her desk and held the stacks of papers out to Brandy, who took them — "I'll show you to your office. Give you time to read through the applicants. Just use the master list as your guide and schedule according to the event. It's all laid out for you." She motioned to the stack of papers she held, and said, "You'll get the hang of it in no time. Oh," Andrea added, "one more thing. You will also be responsible for organizing the Christmas-decorating committee volunteers. Actually, you should start that first. The holidays are just right around the corner. We're usually completely decked out by the first of December." Andrea smiled. "I hope this isn't too much for you."

Brandy took a deep, miserable breath. "No, it's not. I can't wait to get started," she replied, and knew that Andrea knew she was lying.

"There's a list of Friends of the Library who always volunteer to decorate. It's somewhere in that stack of papers. You'll want to contact them today."

"Of course," Brandy said, trying to display more enthusiasm than she actually felt. "I'll get started right away."

She followed Andrea through a zigzag of rooms she hadn't known existed. "This," Andrea said as she opened the door, "is your new office."

A room not much bigger than her closet held a utilitarian gray desk, a chair, and a desktop computer. There were no windows, no plants, and not a single book. She wanted to toss the papers and run, but she swallowed hard and shook her head. "I love it."

And now she was turning into a liar.

CHAPTER FIVE

"Daddy, that was the best birthday party ever. Lisa, Cara, and Joy said so today in school. They said they wanna have fairy princess parties, too," Lily said as she swirled a spaghetti noodle around her fork.

Ryan smiled. She looked exactly like him. Black, curly hair, deep brown eyes, and, from the looks of it, she would be tall as well. Hopefully not as thin as he was, but he thought her perfect. He only wished Anna could've lived to see what a little angel they'd created, but it wasn't in the stars.

"I agree. Fairy princesses are the best," he said as he sat across from her. He'd made her her favorite dinner. Spaghetti and meatballs. Iceberg lettuce with ranch dressing and garlic bread.

She nodded. Red sauce circled her mouth. He pointed to his mouth with his index finger. She reached for her napkin and wiped her mouth. They were on the same wavelength. She was such a sweet little girl. Well behaved, smart, and beautiful. Right this moment, he thought his life was as close to perfect as it was going to get, at least for now. That made him smile.

"What's so funny, Daddy? You look silly when you grin that way," she said, and giggled.

"I was just thinking how lucky I am to have such a beautiful, intelligent, and very well-mannered daughter. I smiled because you make me happy," he replied honestly.

She appeared to contemplate his answer. "Did Mommy smile at me a lot when I was a baby?" she asked as she continued to eat her spaghetti, carefully winding the long noodles around the tines of her fork as he'd taught her.

About to take a bite of spaghetti, he lowered his fork. It had been a very long time since Lily had mentioned anything about Anna. "Mommy smiled at you all the time. She, too, thought you were an amazingly smart little girl." That was all he could come up with though it was the truth. She'd just caught him off guard.

"Did Marlie smile at me a lot?" Lily asked.

He laughed out loud. "Of course she did. You remember her, don't you?"

She placed her fork at the top of her plate

as he'd taught her. "Kinda, but not real good. Her face is kinda fuzzy. I just forget 'cause I was small, right?"

"Of course. We can get out the pictures after dinner if you want," he suggested. Sometimes he did this just to let her know she had a mother and that Marlie really existed. Though she spoke to her on the phone at least once a month, Lily was becoming almost shy when they talked. He should take her out to California for a visit this summer, but he wasn't sure if this would do more harm than good. It could trigger the loss all over again. After Marlie moved, Lily cried herself to sleep every night for almost three months. He couldn't risk that again.

"Nope, I don't wanna. They're too old," she said. "I want to get the Christmas stuff out. You said we would. Please. Please. Please," she added, then gave him her best smile. She'd lost her two bottom teeth, and she stuck her tongue through the space where they belonged. It always made him laugh in delight.

Kids. He loved his daughter so very much. Someday, he hoped to meet a woman who would love Lily as much as he did, but he knew he had to wait until she was old enough to understand what a relationship between a man and a woman was all about. Maybe when she was a teenager, he'd meet someone. She would need a woman's influence then more than ever. Nan was great, but Ryan knew from experience that when girls reached a certain age, they didn't want to hang out with their grandmother. But, he could be wrong about that. Lily loved her grandparents very much, and he would never take that away from her. He loved them, too. Recently, they'd started dropping hints that it was time for him to move on with his life. They didn't come out and say, "It's time to start dating," but he knew what they meant, and he agreed.

He had more news, and he knew he couldn't put off telling them much longer. He planned to tell Lily soon. And he hadn't planned on putting up the Christmas tree.

At least not in *this* house.

CHAPTER SIX

Linda had insisted that she and Brandy meet for dinner tonight. Brandy didn't want to. All she wanted to do was go home, take a hot bath, make a pot of tea, and read the latest novel she'd brought home. Her fourth day at the library had been much tougher than she really wanted to admit.

But her longtime best friend had been very persistent and wouldn't take no for an answer, so here she was in Molly May's, sitting alone in a darkened restaurant on a Thursday evening. She checked her cell phone to make sure she hadn't missed a call. Maybe, *hopefully,* Linda had called to cancel, but there were no missed calls or voice messages. Molly May's, one of the few fine dining restaurants on the Cape, had several artificial Christmas trees, with soft white lights entwined throughout their fake branches. Christmas tunes played quietly in the background. At least they hadn't gone into overboard mode as far as the decorating went, Brandy thought as she waited for Linda to arrive.

She was about to prepare to leave when Linda came rushing over to the table. "Sorry I'm late. Dylan was delayed getting home, and I hadn't lined up a sitter. I thought if I called, you would just beg off, so here I am," she said, then pulled out the chair across from Brandy.

As usual, Linda was impeccably dressed. She wore navy slacks with a navy-and-cream pinstriped blouse, low heels, and always-perfect hair and makeup. Where she found the time with three girls, Brandy hadn't a clue. Despite her shortened hair and fancy manicure, Brandy still felt dowdy beside her.

"What's so important that we have to have dinner? You could have called. I'm exhausted," Brandy said, her tone grudging.

Linda squinted her eyes when she looked at her. "Are you serious? Can't two girls have dinner together? Two *best friends*? Do I need a reason to invite you?"

Brandy shook her head side to side. "No. I'm just tired. We're putting up that twelve-foot tree at the library, and everyone who agreed to come in and help decorate canceled. Andrea told me I would have to do it myself. So that's why I'm so cranky. I've been lifting boxes and climbing up and down a ladder all day. I hope you and George aren't behind this."

Linda smiled mischievously. "Whoa! I guess this calls for a celebration." She waved to a passing waiter. "We'd like to see the wine list."

Incredulous, Brandy asked, "You think my aching back is cause for a celebration?"

"No. I think the fact that you're actually participating in something Christmasy calls for a celebration. A good bottle of wine, and your aches and pains will be history." Linda took the wine list the waiter gave her, choosing a bottle of 2009 Lang & Reed North Coast Cabernet Franc.

The waiter brought the wine to the table. He poured a small amount into the glass. Linda took a sip, then nodded. He filled both their glasses, then stepped aside. "We need a few minutes," Linda explained.

"We do?"

"Yes, I really didn't bring you here to eat. Well, eventually, but first we need to talk." She took a sip of her wine.

"Okay. Shoot," Brandy uttered, her lack of interest apparent.

"Keira called me today," Linda informed her in a serious tone. "She was upset."

Brandy rolled her eyes. "What now? I let

them put the tree up the day after Thanksgiving. They took out every single ornament Jeff and I had collected. I told them that was okay. I even let Matthew drag out that old plastic Santa that Jeff used to put in the front yard. Is that what she's upset about? Please, tell me it's something new." She took a sip of wine.

Linda hesitated before speaking, as though weighing her words. "She never mentioned Christmas or anything connected to the upcoming holiday. What she did tell me worries me. She was concerned about Matthew."

"I'm concerned about Matthew myself. I've tried talking to him, and all he does is shake his head, yes or no, or give me that darned shoulder shrug. And lately, the kid hardly ever wears any clothing. If I see him in those gray sweats again, I just might be tempted to toss him along with the sweats into the washing machine. He's becoming more of a slob than I am," Brandy confessed.

Linda traced the rim of her wineglass with a manicured finger. "That's what I want to talk to you about."

"Matthew's sloppiness?"

"No. You said he hardly wears clothing anymore. Doesn't that strike you as odd?

Being a Floridian, I know we can virtually run around half naked most of the year, but that's not the case with Matthew."

Brandy rolled her eyes. This conversation was getting old already. "What are you trying to say, Linda?"

Her best friend took a sip of her wine before she spoke. "The reason Matthew is running around half dressed all the time is because the kid has outgrown his clothes. Keira said he's been borrowing jeans from a friend of hers and sneaking into Jeff's clothes. When you're not around, of course. She said you practically chewed him a new rear end a couple weeks ago when you saw him in a pair of his father's boxer shorts."

Brandy felt as though she'd been struck by a giant fist. She pressed both palms over her lips to hold back a cry. Tears filled her eyes, and she didn't try to hide them. Shaking her head from side to side as though she *had* been physically hit by a giant hand of disbelief, with a trembling hand, she reached for her wineglass, brought it to her lips, and downed the contents without tasting any of it. "I didn't know," she said, her words barely audible.

"That is why I invited you to dinner," Linda stated.

When Brandy felt she'd absorbed the

enormity of her obliviousness, she realized just how neglectful she'd been of Matthew. Yes, she'd provided a roof over his head, three meals a day, and a ride to school, but now she realized that anyone could do those things. What mattered most hadn't even entered her head. Three years, and she hadn't noticed the changes.

Riddled with disbelief by her own lack of parental awareness, she finally found her voice. "I don't know what to . . . say, *do*." She met Linda's gaze.

"I'd start with a trip to the mall," Linda advised. "The rest, well, you're on your own since I'm not a grief counselor."

The waiter chose that moment to return. Linda quickly ordered salads for both of them. Food was the last thing on Brandy's mind. As soon as he stepped away, they returned to their conversation.

"No, you're not. Every Friday the library has some kind of grief session. It's on the schedule as long-term. They use the main room every Friday night."

Linda raised her perfect eyebrows, a slight smile lifting the edge of her mouth. "Maybe you should consider going."

"I will. Tomorrow night. I . . . I am a terrible mother, Linda! I've been so self-centered since Jeff died. The kids have been

57

trying to tell me this, in their own strange ways, and I haven't paid attention. Keira's changed her hair, gotten the piercings, not to mention the new attitude. Matthew's giving up on his music. They probably hate me by now."

"Possibly, but they'll get over it," Linda replied confidently.

"Thanks."

"Hey, I'm not here to sugarcoat the situation. This is serious, Brandy. You need to — no, forget I said that." She held her palm up as if to stop whatever she'd planned to say. "I am not going to tell you what you *need* to do, I'm going to let you figure that out for yourself, but if you can't, then I'll do whatever is in my power to see to it that you get the proper counseling."

Brandy nodded. "How long has it been since I told you what a good friend you are?" She grinned. "Forget I said that. I don't even want to know. Seriously, Linnie, I appreciate your doing this." She motioned to the bottle of wine, the quiet restaurant. "You could've chosen to do this in front of the kids, making me appear more of a jerk than I am already, but you didn't. So, thanks." For the second time that evening, her eyes flooded with tears, and again, she allowed them to flow freely.

Linda reached across the table and patted her hand. "That's my girl."

CHAPTER SEVEN

"There's a swimming pool?" Lily asked, her excitement spilling over the next morning as her father prepared her breakfast.

Ryan had spent the night narrowing down the homes he was considering purchasing. All three had swimming pools, so he felt it was safe to tell this to Lily.

He grinned. "There is," he said as he took the bagel out of the toaster. "And one of the houses has a hot tub, too." He slathered strawberry jam on the bagel before placing it on a small plate in front of Lily. He poured two glasses of orange juice and refilled his coffee cup before sitting in the chair across from her.

Between bites, Lily asked, "What's that?"

Of course she didn't know what a hot tub was. "It's a cross between a little swimming pool and a giant bathtub. It has jets of water." He stopped. She wouldn't understand this. "I'll show you a picture of one, how about that?"

"Okay," Lily said.

He took his iPad out of his briefcase, made a few finger swipes across the screen. "This is a hot tub," he said as he adjusted the stand in order for Lily to get a good view.

She squealed, her childish excitement on overload. "Could I take a bath in my swimsuit?"

He laughed. "Well, you can wear your suit in the hot tub if we buy this house. I'm not sure this is the house for us."

Lily took a drink of her orange juice. "How's come?"

Ryan shook his head. Lily would ask questions all day if he let her. He really didn't have an answer for her. "I'm not sure. Why don't we look at this house after school?"

She nodded. "Okay. What about Grandma? It's Friday."

Every Friday Lily spent the evening with Nan and Phillip while he attended the grief sessions at the library. He decided tonight would be his last night attending. He'd learned how to handle his grief, and if he were totally honest, he was finished mourning Anna. He would always have a special place in his heart for her, but he knew she would want him to move on. He would

61

make the announcement tonight at the meeting. He'd take Lily to her grandparents' after they looked at the house with the hot tub.

"It's okay. We have time to see the house before I drop you off. Now," — he returned his iPad to his briefcase — "if you're finished, it's time to go. The principal can't be late for school," he teased. "I wouldn't want to have to give myself a tardy slip."

Lily snickered. "Daddy! You can't do that."

"Of course I can. I have to be on time, too. Remember, principals set an example for the students?"

"But what if you're sick or . . . break your leg? Or die? Like Mommy. You won't get a tardy slip, right?" Lily asked as she put her saucer and glass in the dishwasher. "Are you dying soon? 'Cause I don't want to stay with Grandma. I want to stay with . . . someone else whose house doesn't smell like a cat box."

Ryan felt as though he'd been sucker punched. How did one answer such a question, and to an eight-year-old who was wise beyond her years?

"Lily, that's not a nice thing to say about Grandma" was all he could come up with. He did not want to talk about dying. Not today, when he'd just made life-changing decisions affecting both of them.

"Sorry, Dad. Let's go, or I'll be late," she said.

A typical eight-year-old. One minute they're talking about dying and smelly cat boxes, then she's worrying about getting to school on time. For once, Ryan was glad of his daughter's ability to switch topics before he even had a chance to formulate an answer.

"Yep, we can't be late. Grab your book bag," he said as he clicked the dishwasher on.

Fifteen minutes later, they arrived at school with plans to see the house with the hot tub.

"Dad, if we like this house, what are we going to do with our old house?" Lily asked, as they entered the school.

"We will sell it to another family. It's a great house."

"Then why are we moving? Is it because you want that hot tub? I do," Lily said in her matter-of-fact way.

He laughed. "It's time we had a pool. You're going to want to have pool parties when you get older, and I decided I'd better start looking for a house with a pool before they're all gone."

"Dad," Lily singsonged. "If there aren't

any houses to move into, you have to build one. Cara's mom said they are building a new house because she's sick of the repair bills. Is that why we're moving?"

Inside, Ryan took the keys to his office from his pocket and unlocked the door, motioning for Lily to enter. They still had fifteen minutes before the buses and car riders were due to arrive. Lily didn't always come to his office with him, but today he felt like they needed some privacy so he could continue this conversation. He didn't want her to tell Mrs. Pellegrino, her first-grade teacher, about the upcoming move for fear the entire staff would find out. Mrs. Pellegrino was a superb teacher but she loved to discuss private things with some of the other teachers. He wanted to make it clear to Lily that this had to be their special secret for a few days.

He was brief and direct. "Lily, we have to keep the house a secret. We can't tell anyone yet."

"What about Grandma and Grandpa? Can I tell them?" she asked as she re-arranged the things on his desk.

"Yes, but I want to be the one to tell them. Do you think you can keep this a secret tonight when you visit?"

"Dad! Of course I can. I am not a tattletale. I didn't tell on Cara for taking Lisa's blue pencil case." Her dark eyes widened, and she placed a hand across her mouth. "I won't tell Grandma or Grandpa."

Ryan nodded, aware that she had just revealed a secret. He decided to let it go. All little girls shared secrets. Didn't they?

CHAPTER EIGHT

It was a miracle that Brandy didn't have an accident on her way home from Molly May's. It wasn't the one glass of wine she'd had. No. She couldn't stop the tears from blurring her vision. Crying had become normal for her, yet her tears tonight were hard, and almost cleansing. This time her tears had nothing to do with Jeff. In fact, she hadn't thought much about him the past two hours. All she could think of was Matthew and how terribly she'd treated him. And Keira, too. How self-centered her grief was.

When she pulled into the driveway fifteen minutes later, Keira's car was parked haphazardly, which seemed a bit odd. She rarely stayed home in the evenings since getting her driver's license. She and her new group of friends met at Starbucks, the library, and sometimes, they'd meet at the Barnes & Noble in Fort Myers. Brandy never questioned her daughter's whereabouts or asked her about her social life, other than asking her if she'd had anything to eat. She supposed caring for her daughter's appetite earned her at least a couple brownie points in the mothering department. She didn't ask Matthew this because all he did was eat and listen to music on his iPod.

She shut the ignition off and just sat in the driveway. There was simply no way she could make up for the past three years of neglect. However, she could start acting like an adult, the mother of two hurting teens.

Brandy walked in the house she had shared with Jeff for most of their marriage. While it appeared to be the same as it was when Jeff lived, it wasn't. The light was gone. The heart and soul that gave the house life was gone. At that moment, she realized it was up to her to bring back the light, the heart and soul, to their home. Without it, they would continue to let the darkness of their grief consume them. Her grief, as she felt Keira and Matthew had moved forward. It was she who'd kept the sadness and darkness alive, with her inability to focus on her life as it was now.

Renewed, at least for the moment, she shouted to the empty living room, "I'm home." Not expecting a response, she was surprised when both kids shuffled out of their rooms.

"Did you bring anything to eat? We're starving," Keira informed her.

"Hello to you, too. And no, I didn't bring food. Why don't we call out for a pizza," she suggested, something they all enjoyed but rarely took the time to do anymore. "I had dinner with Linda." She directed her gaze to Keira. "We had a long talk."

Keira almost smiled. Matthew hulked beside her.

"And?" Keira pushed.

"And, we can order a pizza and sit down together, as a family, and discuss how oblivious I've been since your father died." There. She'd said it. Now she had to back up those words.

Matthew spoke. "I'll order the pizza. Can we get a bottle of soda, too?"

"Of course," Brandy replied. Had she been so out of touch that her children had to ask for such simple things as a bottle of soda? The breezy, free lifestyle they'd all been so accustomed to had slithered through the hard edges of her grief, and now, it seemed as though they were strangers living beneath the same roof, strangers who knew nothing about one another. She blamed herself for this. She'd wallowed in grief and self-pity much too long.

She kicked off her shoes and made her way to the dining-room table. In the past, this had been the gathering place, not only the place where they shared meals but where they told one another of their days, of what was happening in their lives. She intended to reestablish her family, no matter what it took. No, it wouldn't be the same, but she was going to try. She thought of that old cliché, "Better late than never."

Keira plopped down in the chair her father used to sit in. Brandy had never allowed this in the past. She knew her daughter was testing the waters, and though it hurt to see Jeff's former place at the head of the table occupied by her daughter, in her heart she knew Jeff would want this. She wasn't going to call attention to Keira's behavior as there was no point.

"What kind of pizza do we want?" Matthew called out.

"Get whatever you both want," Brandy said. "I had dinner with Linda." They hadn't asked why she'd been so late, but she needed them to know she wasn't out . . . what? Meeting up with some *guy*?

"Thanks, Mom," Matthew replied a bit sheepishly.

"You're welcome," she said. "And when

you've finished, would you mind having a seat? I really need to talk to you."

Keira rolled her eyes. "What's with the mom act? Linda hit a nerve or something?"

Her normal reaction would be to snap at Keira, but it was time to get real. "Actually, she did. When Matthew finishes, I'll explain."

They waited while Matthew finished ordering the pizza. He sat in his normal chair and placed his elbows on the table. Before she had the chance to ask him to remove them, he did. Well, she thought, he had been listening to her all these years. She smiled.

Clearing her throat, Brandy felt more relaxed than she had in a very long time. And she knew it wasn't the single glass of wine. "I know I haven't been the most attentive mom since we lost your dad, but as of now, I promise I am going to do my best to change that. I know it's hard to comprehend" — she paused to see if either would speak; when they remained silent, she continued — "why I've been so neglectful. I really don't understand it myself, so I don't expect you to, either. Your father and I were young when we married. Most of my adult life was revolved around him. Then you guys came along, and I loved, *love* being your

70

mom more than anything in the world, but somehow I lost track of that. I know this doesn't excuse my behavior, but I am going to try my best to make it up to both of you. If you'll give me the chance." She wanted to cross her fingers, but didn't.

"So Linda told you about Matthew's issue?" Keira said.

He perked up. "What are you talking about, Keira? What did you tell Mom?" Matthew seemed flustered.

"Matthew, it's okay. I know what your 'issue' is, and there's no need to get upset." She made a point to look at his clothes. He wore a pair of faded Levi's that she knew she hadn't purchased, nor had they belonged to Jeff. And as usual, he was shirtless and shoeless.

He seemed embarrassed by her scrutiny. "Saturday morning, let's go to the mall. I think it's time we all did a bit of wardrobe updating. What about it, Matthew? Keira?"

"That'd be great, Mom," Matthew said.

Brandy thought she heard relief in his words.

"Keira? We can go to Hot Topic if you want." Brandy wasn't so out of touch that she didn't know where her daughter's clothing of choice was sold. She remembered seeing that store in the mall on one of her

71

shopping trips when Keira was in middle school. They'd both commented on the strange clothes.

"I'll go shopping, but I don't want to shop *there,*" she said. "Why would you assume I'd want to anyhow?"

Brandy knew her daughter wanted to start an argument, but she wasn't going to take the bait. Yes, she'd been neglectful. And yes, she probably deserved Keira's scorn, but she was her mother.

"Okay. Where would you like to shop? Anyplace in mind?" she asked her.

"I'll think about it. I just want some food right now. And speaking of food, you need to get to the grocery store. Since you started that stupid job, we've been out of milk and bread. There's hardly any food in this place."

Brandy wasn't going to let Keira continue. "Okay. Make a list of what you want. You too, Matthew. Then when we finish shopping at the mall, you two can go to the grocery store. I'll just give you my debit card. I have a few things I need to do around here." She waved behind her. "This place is in need of a major cleaning."

Keira's black-rimmed eyes almost doubled in size. "You want *me* to take Matthew to the grocery store? Tell me I just imagined what you said. 'Cause there is no way I am going to do your job! You get our attention for five measly minutes, then the next words that come out of your mouth, you want us to do your dirty work. Well, Mom, thanks, but I have other plans! *You* can go to the store. Take Matthew. See if you even remember what *he* likes to eat. We're both sick of frozen dinners and premade salads." She stood up and stormed out of the room, calling behind her, "Come and get me when the pizza arrives."

"Keira, get your rear end back in here, now! And I am not playing games," Brandy said. She raised her voice but only so that she could be heard.

Feet stomping in the hall, then stopping, let her know Keira was returning to the dining room. Brandy was not going to utter a word until her daughter sat down.

"I'm here, what did you want to say? You want me to clean the house, too? Do all the laundry that's been piled up for weeks? What?"

It was time to stop playing games. "Sit down, Keira. Now. I will take your car away. And don't you dare smart-mouth me!" She must've hit a nerve.

Reluctantly Keira sat in her father's chair. "What?"

Brandy knew this was a turning point in

their lives, and it would affect all of their futures. "Matthew, I want you to listen to this, too." Might as well go for the gusto and lay it all out on the table.

"From this day forward, I have to work. Your father's life insurance is almost gone. I'd like to save what's left so we have a nest egg for the future. When I pass my ninety-day probationary period, I'll be earning more and will start adding a little each month to our savings." She took a deep breath. Both Keira and Matthew stared at her. "Your dad and I didn't plan for the future. We were young, and death was the last thing on our minds. We'd just started talking about saving for college for both of you. I know we should've planned our finances better, but we didn't. The house is paid for, that's in our favor, but there are still taxes, utilities, and all kinds of expenses you two are unaware of. If your father were here, I doubt we'd be having this talk, but he isn't, so you both need to know that our family situation isn't that great. At least financially.

"Keira, I've allowed you to come and go as you please, and I can't stop you as you're eighteen now. A legal adult in the eyes of the law. This is your last year of high school. I would love to see you attend college, but I won't be able to pay for it. I'm thinking that instead of your hanging out with your friends after school, you might want to start thinking about a part-time job. A little cash to replace what I am not going to give to you but will place in a bank account for your future. It won't be much, but I've been giving you at least a hundred dollars a week. I will pay for one tank of gas per week, enough to get you to and from school, plus I'll continue to pay for your lunches as I've been doing.

"This doesn't mean I don't want to do all those things for either of you, but it does mean it's time for you to pitch in." Brandy hadn't said this many words at one sitting in ages. It felt good to get it out, to form a life plan of sorts, even if she was ad-libbing. This had been Jeff's department. Now it was hers, and it wasn't going to be footloose and fancy-free. Both kids needed to learn to be responsible. She and Jeff had pampered them too much, and while their intentions were good, she realized that the kids were spoiled. She was, too. She'd never wanted to work outside the home. All she had ever wanted to be was a wife and mother. She hadn't picked her new and different life, but she had to learn to live with it, and they would, too.

"Matthew isn't old enough to work. You have to be sixteen to get a job in Florida," Keira said, her tone hateful.

"It's okay, Keira," Matthew interjected. "I can find something."

"Matthew, Keira's right. You aren't legally old enough to get a job, but you're old enough to kick in around here. I've decided to stop the lawn service. We have a perfectly good mower in the garage. From now on, that will be your job."

He nodded and seemed okay with his new chore. "Might have to get the blades sharpened. Dad used to have them sharpened a couple times a year. And the weed whacker's broken."

"We can take care of that. How did you know the weed whacker was broken?" Brandy asked.

"Dad told me."

"Oh."

"Couldn't you have waited to spring this on us until after Christmas? Or is this just another way for you to make the holidays miserable again?" Keira demanded.

Brandy took a deep breath in order to keep her temper in check. Now wasn't the time. "I'm sorry, Keira. You're right. I should've waited. I just want our life to be normal again." Tears pooled in her eyes. She didn't try to hide them or make excuses for them.

Right now, all she wanted to do was to crawl into bed and sleep. When she awakened, maybe she'd realize she'd only been dreaming.

CHAPTER NINE

The real estate agent sent the code to unlock the "hot tub house" in a text message. Lily was so excited, she could barely contain herself on the ride over. "This house doesn't even need a key?"

Ryan laughed. "There's a special lock real estate agents have. I'll show you." He pulled into the circular driveway and shut the engine off.

"Is this it?" Lily asked.

"Yep, this is it. What do you think?" he asked as he unhooked Lily's seat belt.

"It's so pretty, Daddy! It's got a zillion flowers!"

It was a beautiful home. More than they needed, but he was thinking ahead. Lily really would want to have pool parties in a few years, but that wasn't the only reason he'd looked at homes much larger than their house. What if he met someone and had more kids? What if he met a woman with children? At his age, it was highly unlikely he was going to meet a woman without kids, so he thought long and hard when he'd narrowed his search down to three houses. Four bedrooms, three baths, a pool, and of course this place had the hot tub, plus so much more. The lawn was a dream. Though it might not have a "zillion" flowers, the landscaping was colorful, and the hibiscus were in every shade of the rainbow. There wasn't a weed to be found in the plush green grass. Ryan liked tinkering around with plants and cutting grass. It would be a challenge to maintain this lawn, but he was up for it. The big bonus — direct access to the Gulf of Mexico. He'd wanted a boat forever, and maybe now he would buy one. He was in sound financial shape for a man his age. Good investments with the money from Anna's life insurance policy ensured Lily's education was paid for, and he would be able to live life as comfortably as Anna's parents. They had insisted they buy life insurance shortly after they married. They'd been a bit creeped out at the time, but Phillip, a former investment banker, had explained to them in great detail why it was worthwhile. Now he was glad he had taken his father-in-law's advice.

He helped Lily out of the old car and

thought maybe it was time to think about a new car, too. Taking his daughter by the hand, he led her to the main entrance. "This," he said as he punched the code into a boxlike lock on the door, "is a special kind of lock. When real estate people can't come to the houses they're selling, they give clients the code, and the potential buyers can get in. But when a person or a family buys the house, this comes off and the new owners receive a set of keys."

He pushed the heavy doors aside and let Lily enter first. She pinched her nose. "It kinda smells funny, Dad. Like the laundry room at home."

"It's the chlorine in the swimming pool," he explained to his daughter. "You think it's too bad to finish the tour?"

Lily let go of his hand and ran to the sliding glass doors that led to the pool. "Let's get this house, Daddy! Please, please, please?" Once they were outside, she raced around the pool, and before she fell in, Ryan grabbed her arm.

"Careful, Lily. This pool isn't like the plastic kiddie pool in our backyard. You have to learn how to swim."

"Oh, but will you show me how?"

"We will make sure you have swimming lessons," he replied, now wondering if a house with a pool was a good idea. Lily could've fallen in. He was getting negative, and he did not like negativity. They would simply have to get lessons and take the proper precautions until she learned how to swim. All this, and he hadn't even bought the place. He smiled. This *was* a great house.

"This," he said as he removed a large plastic cover, "is the hot tub."

Lily peered inside. "Wow, Dad. This really is like a giant bathtub." She poked her finger in the water. "It's cold though."

"It has a heater. When you want to get in, you have to turn it on to heat up the water." He played with a few switches, turning the hot tub's power on. The jets spit and spewed a bit, then created tiny bubbles on top of the water. "These are the jets I showed you in the picture. Put your hand here." He carefully guided her hand to the jet. She yanked it back.

"That tickles." She grinned. "In a good way. I want to get in now, but I know I can't. It's too cold."

"Smart girl. Now let's see the rest of the house. I want your opinion."

He really wanted her to like the house because he guessed they would stay for a long time in whatever house he chose to purchase. Most likely, it would be Lily's last home before heading off to college.

They went down a long, brightly lit hallway. "This," he said, opening the door, "would be my bedroom." The room had doors leading to the pool and a private bath.

"It's as big as our house."

"Pretty big, but not quite that big. Let's look in the other rooms. You can tell me which room you would like for yourself if we buy this house."

They went through the other three bedrooms, the two baths, and the kitchen. Lily didn't care about the dining room or the four-car garage. She told him this, and he couldn't help but laugh.

"So, which room would you pick?"

"I think I want the one next to yours. Just in case I needed to pee during the night. Your bathroom is the closest." She said this so matter-of-factly, that he busted out laughing.

"You're a smart girl, you know that?"

"I do. So, if we move here, could I have that room?" she asked.

"Yes, you can. So, do you want to look at the other two houses Saturday? You might like them more than this one," he explained as he led her out the front entrance. He replaced the boxlike lock and reset it so the code could be activated for the next potential buyer. Though something told him this was the house for him and Lily. It had everything he'd ever dreamed of, and more. It was in his budget, and close to school, and even closer to Phillip and Nan's house.

"Not really. I think we should move in here. Before Christmas. We could put the Christmas tree by those big doors. And we could put lights on that big-screen thing around the pool. Lots of people do that at Christmas. Grandma and Grandpa's neighbor has lights on their screen thing now."

Yes, he agreed that it would be the perfect spot for a giant tree, but even if he did buy this house, could they actually move in before Christmas?

Back in the car, he buckled her seat belt. "Let's talk to your grandparents later and see what they have to say. But not tonight; for now, this is our secret, remember? Deal?" he said as he hooked his own seat belt.

She held out her little hand to shake his. "Deal," she said. "Dad, what about Mommy? Do you think she'll see us from Heaven if we move?"

He took a minute to form his next words. "Lily, no matter where we go, Mommy will always be watching over us. If we moved to

Timbuktu, which we're not, but if we did, Mommy would know, and she would be happy for us."

"Okay. I just wanted to make sure she doesn't lose us is all," she said. Childlike but serious as though she, too, knew this move was more than just another house. It was a new beginning for both of them.

Minutes later, they arrived at Phillip and Nan's. Anna's parents were sitting on the front lawn beneath the one shade tree when they pulled up. Lily unhooked her own seat belt and raced out the door. "Daddy's getting us a new house." The words came out of her mouth so fast, she didn't have time to think. She looked at her dad, realizing that he had asked her to keep their new house a secret. Tears spilled from her chocolate-brown eyes.

"What's wrong, sweetie?" Nan asked, taking Lily in her arms. She was still a very attractive woman in her late sixties. Silver hair cut short, and a slim figure courtesy of an active walking group, she looked at Ryan, questions in her bright blue eyes.

He hadn't wanted to break the news like this, but it didn't really matter. He'd already listed his and Anna's house; there was no turning back. They'd been after him for months to move on, and now that he had started the process, he wasn't sure how they would react.

Sighing, he had no choice. Lily had been excited, and the words just tumbled out of her mouth. He shouldn't have asked her to keep such a big secret. There really wasn't any reason to, so he explained his plans. "I put the house on the market. I think it's time," he said. By this time Phillip had gotten wind of their conversation.

"Personally, Ryan, I think it's smart. The housing industry is starting to pick up. You'll get a fair price," he said.

How could a man be so lucky? Most parents wouldn't want the husband, the widower of their daughter, to move on. They were supportive of every decision he'd made since Anna had passed.

"Thanks. I wasn't sure what your reaction would be. I asked Lily to keep it a secret, but she's too excited." He told them all about the house and its location. The other two homes weren't even mentioned.

He'd make an offer on the Seahorse Lane house first thing in the morning.

"There's one other thing I want you all to know. Tonight's going to be my last night at the grief sessions."

He waited for them to say something, but they just nodded, and Nan said, "It's time,

Ryan. You're ready to move on."

And he was. Truly.

CHAPTER TEN

Brandy finished putting the last ornament on the tree and stepped back to view her work. Though the tree was artificial, it was stunning, if she said so herself. She'd spent hours adjusting the red and white lights, making sure they were perfectly aligned on each layer of branches. The bright red poinsettias clipped onto the branches looked real even though they were totally plastic. If she hadn't put them on herself, she'd never know they were artificial. The Friends of the Library, at whom she was ticked at right now, had created some of the most beautiful handmade ornaments she'd ever seen.

Some were glass, some were made from seashells, and others were little books, many of them classics. Jane Austen's *Pride and Prejudice,* Louisa May Alcott's *Little Women,* and Charles Dickens's *A Christmas Carol.* She liked those ornaments the most. There was even a book ornament depicting the cover of Clement C. Moore's "The Night Before Christmas," her very favorite Christmas story of all time. The Friends had really taken great care in choosing the titles of the little book ornaments, she could tell, but she was still mad at them for not helping her decorate the giant tree.

She laughed at herself. No, she really wasn't. At first she was, but not now, not after she saw what she'd created. She realized this was the first time she'd ever completely decorated a tree, top to bottom, all by herself. Add that to her ever-growing lists of accomplishments.

Now, she had about thirty minutes to put away the boxes, freshen up a bit, and prepare to attend a grief session. She really dreaded doing this, but if she wanted to move forward, she knew this was a good place to start. She'd been grieving and sad for so long, she wanted to find a way to help herself so that she could be a better mother and a nicer person. She hadn't liked herself much the past three years. The third anniversary of Jeff's death was right around the corner. Instead of spending that day alone in her bedroom looking at old photos and crying and wishing he were here, she had a plan. This year she would try something new.

Last night's attempt to direct the future for her and the kids hadn't been particularly successful, at least not where Keira was concerned. But Matthew was thrilled at the prospect of going to the mall to shop. *Poor guy,* she thought. He'd always been such a sensitive child. How had she totally ignored his growth spurt? Three years was a long time. He'd gone through puberty, and she hadn't so much as noticed that he'd started shaving though there wasn't much to shave. Still, she should have paid attention to the changes he was going through. He was now much taller than his father had been. And if she were honest, much more handsome. Jeff had been cute, with thinning brown hair, a tad too long for a music teacher, but it was because of this that he got away with his whimsicalness. A free spirit, totally devoted to his passion. Family and music. Maybe in the opposite order. Jeff always dreamed of playing in a band, and he did occasionally. But sometimes his dreams were unrealistic. She'd never thought of this when he'd shared them with her, but with hindsight, they were. He wanted to be the next Axl Rose of Guns N' Roses, but he wasn't quite as talented. Teaching music was his calling, she thought. The students loved him, and he was good at it, but his true passion was to become a famous rock star. Sadly, he hadn't lived long enough to pursue the dream, and, what was even sadder, Brandy knew in her heart of hearts that he wasn't quite talented enough.

She sighed and had picked up a few boxes to take to the storage room when a man's voice startled her. She dropped the boxes and whirled around to see a tall, dark-haired man carrying what looked like cake boxes.

"Can I help you?" she asked apprehensively.

"I think I should be asking you if I can help you." He nodded to the pile of boxes she'd dropped. "I must have startled you."

She followed his gaze. "Yes. I mean no, you can't help me. Yes, there's quite the pile here. I need to put them away before tonight's grief session. Is there something I can assist you with?" she asked in what she hoped was a professional voice. She didn't know this man. He could be another volunteer. Maybe one of those Friends of the Library who'd canceled on her.

"You could help me with these cupcakes," he said.

"Sure," she replied, taking the top box, and when she did, their hands touched briefly. Brandy's hand felt like she'd stuck her finger in a wall socket. His dark eyes met hers, and when they did, she quickly looked away. "Where do you want these?" She assumed they were for tomorrow since it was so late.

"The main room. They usually have a table set up. Frankly, I haven't a clue who's responsible for the preparation, but someone's set up the Keurig and all the stuff that goes along with it." He looked at the tree. "Best I've ever seen it. Did you do all the work?" he asked.

She headed to the main room before it hit her. Again, she felt out of her realm. This was the room where the grief sessions were being held tonight. Of course they'd serve snacks or cupcakes. Was she supposed to set the room up? If so, Andrea had failed to tell her so. One week on the job, and she was already neglecting her duties.

"I guess not," the tall man said to her as he followed alongside her.

"Guess not what?" she asked stupidly.

"That you're not responsible for decorating the tree."

"Oh," she said. Again, she felt silly. "Actually I did. The Friends of the Library were supposed to help, but they canceled at the last minute."

"That's unusual. They're usually on top of everything the library needs," he said, sounding a bit perplexed.

"Well, this year, all twenty-three of them apparently had other things to do," she said, as they entered the main meeting room.

"Odd."

When the man turned on the lights, Brandy saw that someone had set up the table with the Keurig coffeemaker and all the little extras. Paper plates, napkins, and plastic utensils were placed beside the powdered creamer and packets of sugar.

"I've never seen you here before. Are you a new volunteer?" the man asked as he opened the boxes and began placing the cupcakes on a platter stacked beside the coffee machine. She barely even noticed them. For that matter, she'd hardly noticed anything except the man's long, tapered fingers, the lingering scent of his cologne, and the beginnings of a five o'clock shadow, which happened to look exceptionally attractive on him.

"No," she said.

"Are you here for the grief session? Dr. Farough is speaking tonight. He's quite good," the man added.

Feeling an overwhelming sense of relief, then a sense that she'd missed out, though on what, she hadn't a clue, she couldn't find her voice for a few seconds. She raked her hand through her newly cropped, shoulder-length hair. Had she worn makeup today? Yes, thank goodness, but she hadn't had time to freshen up as she'd planned. She'd dressed in plain black slacks with a matching blazer and red blouse. Truly, she hadn't planned on caring if she freshened up, what she wore, but she had the thought, so it must mean something. She was attending the session so she could be a better mother to her children, more focused on her life as a widow and a single parent. She hadn't allowed herself to use those words, *widow* and *single parent,* too much, but it was the cold, hard truth, and she had no choice but to acknowledge them as facts.

It was a good thing, she thought. A sign that she would get through this. She'd had almost three years. She'd spent three years crying over the loss of her husband, the father of her children, the heart and soul of her family; but now it was time for her to step up to the plate and meet her responsibilities. She was going to do her very best to make up for lost time.

And she had vowed that she would start now.

"This is my first week working at the library. Yes, I thought it would be good to sit in on the grief session. I hear they're very . . . helpful."

"Since we're the only ones here, what would you think about sneaking one of these cupcakes before the others arrive? They're the best, and there won't be any left if we don't have one now." He grinned, and Brandy felt her heart thump in a way that it hadn't in a very long time. She found herself smiling back. A real, genuine smile.

"I think it's the best idea I've heard all day," she said, reaching for a chocolate cupcake with red frosting. He handed her a paper plate and a fork. She shook her head. "Cupcakes weren't meant to be eaten with a fork." She bit into hers and closed her eyes. She'd deprived herself of all desserts for so long. She took another bite and another, then took a second cupcake, not caring that the man watched her. This time, she chose a red velvet cupcake with cream cheese icing sprinkled with red sugar. She bit into this one and smiled. The sugary concoctions were heavenly. She wanted a third but refrained.

"I take it you like sweets," the man said.

She nodded, wiping her mouth on a paper napkin. "I haven't had anything sweet in almost three years. Those are divine."

He still held his on a paper plate, then when he saw she was watching him, he devoured his in three bites. "Lily would have a fit if she saw me eating like this, but she isn't here, so no harm no foul."

She nodded and wondered who Lily was. He must've recognized the curious look on her face.

"Lily is my daughter. She's eight and thinks she's twenty." He laughed. "And she would not like the fact that I haven't introduced myself. Where are my manners, she'd say. I'm Ryan Rogers." He held out those tapered fingers.

Dare she shake his hand? She did, and again, felt a bolt of desire shoot straight from her hand to her belly and down to places that hadn't been touched in so very, very long.

These thoughts caused her to blush, and she hoped this man, Ryan Rogers, didn't notice. Quickly, before she embarrassed herself further, she said, "I'm Brandy Heyers, it's nice to meet you." Good grief! It wasn't *nice* to say this at a grief meeting.

"Yes, it is," Ryan said.

Suddenly feeling awkward, Brandy made herself a cup of coffee. As she waited for the cup to brew, Ryan stood next to her. "How long for you?" he asked, and she had no idea what he was referring to. Sex? A relationship? Then it hit her like a brick.

"Three years on December twentieth," she told him. Expecting tears to fill her eyes as they almost always did when she said the date out loud, she was surprised when she remained dry-eyed.

"It's been six years for me."

"I'm sorry," she said. "It must be very difficult for you." Not that it would be anything but difficult, but six years was a long time to grieve. Wasn't it? She'd been grieving for three, but it hadn't seemed that long.

"Actually, I'm good. Or rather, I've accepted my loss. I'm over mourning Anna. She would want me to be. Now I go to these sessions more for the company than the counseling. Six years is a long time. Actually, I've decided that tonight is my last night. It's time to move forward."

He seemed so confident, so *finished* with mourning his wife. Would she feel this way after six years?

Being candid was new to her, but she felt the situation called for it. "Why tonight?" Why did she feel a tinge of sadness that he wouldn't be attending meetings in the future?

"I'm not sure, really. No, I'm not being honest." The soft murmur of some people entering the room made him lower his voice. "I've decided to purchase a new home and move on with my life. I've learned that it's okay to move on and be happy. For the first year after Anna died, I felt like I was living in a bubble. Lily was barely two years old when her mother died, and I was sure I couldn't go on, but I did. Then one day, I realized that an entire day had passed without my thinking of her, then another, and there I was, living my life with my daughter. Working helps. With eight hundred kids to focus on, I found myself busy, content with my life, and well, it just continues to go on. Grief passes in time. Not the loss, but the pain lessens. Anna was only thirty-two."

Brandy listened intently while he spoke. They'd wandered over to the group of chairs when the room filled up. They sat side by side. "Jeff was forty-two."

"Then we've both lost our partners at a young age. Do you have children?"

Brandy smiled. "Yes. A boy and a girl. Keira is eighteen, and Matthew is fifteen." It was so liberating to speak to someone who knew what she had been going through. She remembered she was moving forward and had to move forward in her thinking as well.

"Kids can be trying at that age," he said, but he was grinning when he spoke.

She laughed out loud, then realized some of the other attendees were staring at her. She lowered her voice to a whisper. "I shouldn't be laughing, and here of all places, but you said 'trying.' That's putting it nicely. How is it you know so much about teens when your daughter is only eight?"

"I'm the principal at Pelican Elementary. In my profession, I'm around kids of all ages."

"My husband was the music teacher at Lee County High. Maybe you knew him? Jeff Heyers?"

"The name sounds familiar. We probably ran into each other at one school function or another."

Suddenly, their conversation became stilted, as if they'd been caught talking about something they shouldn't. Like their dead spouses.

The speaker, Dr. Farough, stood at the dais, introduced himself, and began discussing the different stages of grief. "There are five stages of grief. Denial. Anger. Bargaining. Depression. Acceptance. There is no order for these emotions. We're all individuals with different coping skills."

Brandy tried to focus on Dr. Farough's words but found herself more focused on Ryan Rogers, who seemed to listen intently as the doctor continued explaining the different stages of grief. She knew them all. Very well.

As she halfheartedly listened, she came to the conclusion that she was tired of death, tired of grief, and tired of feeling guilty the few times she'd managed to feel several moments of happiness. A good book. A movie that made her smile. All of her focusing on her grief had alienated her from her children.

It truly was time to move forward. So deep in thought, she almost jumped out of her skin when Ryan whispered in her ear, "Are you game for coffee when this lets out?"

Is he asking me out on a date? At a grief session?

"I am," she said.

For the first time in three years, Brandy Heyers felt hopeful about the future.

CHAPTER ELEVEN

It was after midnight when Brandy finally climbed between the cool sheets. Physically, she was exhausted, but mentally, she was as alert as ever.

She'd looked in on Keira and Matthew before going to bed. Both were sleeping soundly. Kids — they were very resilient. They would be fine, she thought. Yes, they were going to go through some rough patches, but this would happen whether Jeff had lived or not. Maybe he would've been better equipped to deal with them when they came, but she would be, too. She had to be. She was here, and he wasn't.

She rolled onto her side, peering out the window. The sky was a midnight blue, and the stars glistened like tiny white diamonds. Often, she wondered what lay beyond them, but tonight she simply admired their beauty. The quietness of the night. Occasionally, a frog croaked, and a wild bird swooped across the sky, its wings creating a soft, rippling sound across the water. Tonight, she listened to this and realized that she couldn't recall the last time she'd actually focused on something other than herself and the grief she'd carried around for so long. Too long, she'd told Ryan. And it hurt to admit this, but it was true. Her grief had been through four of Dr. Farough's stages numerous times. Now it was time to allow herself to move forward to the fifth stage.

Acceptance.

She accepted that Jeff wasn't coming back and accepted that her life would be different but reminded herself that different isn't always a bad thing.

She closed her eyes and drifted into a soft, dreamless sleep.

A tap on her bedroom door jolted her awake. She jumped out of bed, tripping over the clothes she'd had on yesterday.

Was she late for work? She glanced at the bedside clock. Eight thirty! They'd fire her!

"Mom?" Matthew called from the other side of the door. "What time are we going to the mall?"

Relief washed over her. It was Saturday! She opened her door. "Come on in, let's chat." She plopped down on her bed, motioning to the spot beside her. She and Jeff had always had an open-door policy. When their door was closed, that meant the children were not allowed to come in, or that they had to knock unless it was a life-threatening emergency. Those rules no longer existed. Her policy had been complete isolation in this room. No more.

Hesitantly, he entered her room. "You sure?" he asked timidly.

"Of course I am."

He sat on the edge of the bed. "So what time should I be ready to leave?" he asked.

The mall didn't open until ten, but she knew he was as anxious as ever to go.

"Why don't we go out for breakfast first? We haven't done that since —"

Matthew interrupted. "Mom, can we stop?"

"What?"

"Every word that comes out of your mouth, well not *every* word, but close enough, always has to do with Dad. Before he died. After he died. What he liked, what he didn't like. Can't we just live like now? Without, you know, always saying that stuff."

Brandy saw Matthew's eyes. They were full of tears, and he struggled to keep them at bay.

"I know," she said as she brushed the hair

102

from his face. "I have a long way to go, but I promise to try my very best."

"What's going on in here?" Keira stood in the doorway. Her burgundy hair was back to its original shade of blond, and had been cut into an adorable pixie style.

"Keira, you look like an angel!" Brandy said, and motioned for her to join them. "How, rather when, did this happen?"

Keira gave up a grin. A real Keira grin. Her blue eyes were minus the thick black eyeliner she'd caked on for three years. "Linda took me to Emily's last night after dinner."

Leave it to Linda. She had three daughters, one two years younger than Keira. She must've said the magic words because Brandy had moaned and groaned about her hair and makeup, and Keira just caked on more. Whatever Linda said, she owed her big-time.

"Emily did a great job. You look like," she almost said "your father" but didn't. Instead, she said, "you."

"Thanks, Mom. I know I've been a real witch lately. I'm sorry. Linda told me some things, and well, I know it's time for me to get serious and stop acting like I'm twelve."

No doubt more of Linda's parental expertise. Her children had turned into little cherubs. Overnight. Later, she'd ask Linnie what sort of threats she used. She wanted to borrow them for the future. Just in case.

Matthew's stomach rumbled so loudly they all heard it. "Mom, are we still going out for breakfast?"

"Yes, and from the sounds of it, we'd best get a move on. Keira, do you want to come along?" Brandy decided to treat her daughter like an adult. Maybe this was the key to getting their relationship back on track. She was willing to try anything.

"Yes. Give me five minutes," she said, then gave her mother a quick hug, poked Matthew's shoulder, and practically skipped out of the room.

Brandy looked at her son. "What was that all about?"

He sighed, and smiled at her. "She's decided she didn't like the Goth look? I don't know. Whatever it is, I think she should stay this way. She's nicer without that makeup and purple hair. She's been pretty nice to me, though."

"Whatever the reason, I am not going to push my luck by questioning it. She's herself, and we are going to eat breakfast. Give me a couple minutes to get ready."

"Sure." Matthew seemed to stand taller, his shoulders squared, more confident.

In the master bath, she took a two-minute shower, then slipped on a pair of jeans and a T-shirt. She let her hair frame her face, deciding she liked the shorter version better. She appeared more youthful, less dragged down. Before she changed her mind, she added a few swipes of mascara, blush, and a soft pink lipstick. Spying her favorite Lancôme perfume, Miracle, she spritzed it on her neck and the insides of her wrists. Saving perfume for "that special day" was ludicrous. Every day was special, a gift to be taken advantage of. She knew life could change in seconds. And she also knew, she was going to cherish every moment from here on.

Hurrying now, she entered the kitchen. "Here you go," Keira said, handing her a to-go cup of coffee. She had one for herself as well.

"Starbucks. I'm addicted," she said before Brandy had a chance to ask her when she'd started drinking coffee. Apparently, this was just one more thing she'd missed.

"Thanks," she said, and took a sip. "Yum." She grinned, and her daughter grinned back. *Truly a miracle,* she thought, as they walked out to the car. "Let me drive, Mom. Save your gas."

Brandy was so shocked at Keira's sudden

about-face, she was almost suspicious. Was she playing games? No, no, no!

She had to stop questioning every single action, every motive of those she loved.

"Okay, I'm game," Brandy said, piling into her daughter's white Toyota hybrid. It was then that she realized she'd never actually been a passenger in her daughter's car. Yes, she had allowed her to drive when she got her learner's permit, but it had always been in *her* car, and on *her* terms. She sat in the backseat. "Matthew, you sit up front. You're way too big to fit in the backseat."

"Thanks, Mom. Keira makes me sit back there sometimes, but it's okay."

Keira poked him with her elbow. "You're the little brother. You're supposed to ride in the back," she quipped, but in a teasing way.

Her daughter fastened her seat belt, adjusted her rearview mirror, then her side mirror, then hit the start button. The car hardly made any sound at all. She reversed down the drive, then wound her way through the side streets that led to the main road. "Where to?"

"You two pick," Brandy said.

"There's this cool place that just opened," Matthew said. "It's called the Starlight Diner. They have musicians. Could we go there?"

Brandy's heart fluttered as though a bird were trapped inside and struggled to get out. In three years, well, almost three years, this was the first time she'd heard Matthew mention the word *music.* She caught Keira's wink in the rearview mirror.

"I've heard they have the best breakfast in town," Keira said. "Starlight Diner, here we come."

Overnight, her kids had returned to normal, and she'd turned over a new leaf. Maybe Christmas was a magical time. She wasn't going to question these changes. She was going to enjoy the moment.

Chapter Twelve

Ryan spent the rest of the night filling out the papers that would give him ownership of the house on Seahorse Lane. Phillip and Nan were still awake when he'd returned to pick up Lily last night. He was on cloud nine when he arrived, telling them all about Brandy. He truly was like a kid at Christmas.

Not only was he purchasing his dream home, he was really starting to look forward to the possibility that he could share his and Lily's life with another woman. And maybe that woman was Brandy. They'd spent three hours talking nonstop, and he hadn't ever been as attracted so quickly to a woman. Not even Anna. Their relationship was slow and easy. No need to rush, they'd said. They had their whole lives ahead of them. They couldn't have been more wrong.

Brandy told him how she'd grieved, and how she'd just come to the realization that her kids were strangers to her, and she to them. She told him about her son, Matthew, and how tall he'd become. How he'd had to borrow clothes to wear. He never met the young guy, but he felt sorry for him. He remembered those incredibly awkward years when he had sprouted up like the Jolly Green Giant. He'd outgrown his clothes in a matter of months. His mother, bless her heart, had done her best, but he, too, knew what it was like to wear borrowed clothes and hand-me-downs. His mother had passed away before Lily was born. She would've adored her, and Lily would have adored his mother, her namesake, too. But, he'd managed to get by, and because he'd studied hard, like his mother told him, he had received a full academic scholarship to Florida State University, where'd he'd earned his bachelor's degree as well as his doctorate in education. He knew life could be tough, but he also knew you really could make lemonade out of lemons.

He'd fallen asleep at his desk and almost jumped out of his skin when Lily spoke. "Dad, are you awake?"

"Yes, I am now. What's up, sugar bug?"

"Daaaddd, you said you'd stop calling me that, remember?" she reminded him.

"Sorry." Yes, he remembered that she'd asked him to stop calling her that last summer when Cara was over. Lily told him Cara said it was a baby name. And, of course, he'd done his best, but he still had an occasional slipup. He was just a dad. He raked a hand through his hair.

"I dreamed about the house with the hot tub last night," Lily said. "Me and Cara and Joy and Lisa were swimming, and this giant frog jumped out of the lake, and jumped in the pool with us. He wasn't scary. He was nice. He said he wanted to be our Lily pads. Isn't that funny? A frog wanting to be a lily pad?" She giggled in her eight-year-old way, and Ryan laughed with her.

"That was some dream," he admitted. "Now, I think it's time I had a cup of coffee. What about you?"

She giggled and wrapped her hand around his waist. "I don't drink coffee, silly; that's for big people."

He lifted her up on his shoulders, and they raced through the house, pretending they were being chased by a purple horse. Why this, he had no clue. Lily had come up with this when she was around three, and ever since, when he hoisted her onto his shoulders, they were being chased by a purple horse.

"Dad" — she placed her hands around his neck — "can we have breakfast now?

110

I'm really hungry."

He lifted her off his shoulders and gently put her on the floor. "Yes, we can. You want pancakes?"

"Yep! Daddy, think we'll get the hot-tub house? I really, really would like to live there. I want a Christmas tree in front of those big windows." Lily sat in her chair at the table in the kitchen, hands folded, cupping her heart-shaped face. "A real one. Not a fake one. Can we get a real big one? And can we go to the mall? I want to see Santa and tell him what I want for Christmas. Can we, Daddy?"

Lily talked nonstop as he made pancakes with crispy bacon. He sipped his coffee while he cooked, listening to her. She was so full of life. Her Christmas spirit was catching. "I think a real tree would be perfect. They smell really nice."

"Not like a cat box?" she teased.

He turned to look at her. "What's up with the cat-box thing?"

"Grandma is cat sitting for her neighbors' cat. I love the cat. He's old, his name is Clovis. But that box he goes to the bathroom in stinks. Grandma said all cat boxes stink, and that you get used to it after a while. I don't think I want a cat. I like Clovis, but I would like a dog. Can we get a dog? I want a dog for Christmas. Do you think Santa would bring me a puppy if I promised to take care of it?"

This had been her request for the last two years. A puppy. At first, he'd thought she was too young, and the novelty would wear off once she saw the work involved, but now, he thought it was something to consider. "We can ask Santa, I suppose." He put a plate of pancakes in front of her.

"So does that mean we're going to the mall?" she asked.

The kid knew how to play him. He laughed out loud. "I guess it does, but first we have to stop by that real estate office so we can get the keys to our new home."

Lily's eyes sparkled like a million bright lights. "Really and truly?"

He nodded. "Really and truly." What he didn't say: how he'd spent the night negotiating a cash offer, how he'd been on pins and needles as he waited for the e-mail telling him that his offer was accepted. At 6:18, his computer pinged that an e-mail had come. The owners had accepted his offer, and he could pick the keys up today. He'd never acted so out of character in his life. He always played it safe, by the rules. Looked to the future, but cautiously, and when he had seen Lily's eyes light up yesterday, he knew this house had to be their home. So he'd spent the night doing his best to make it happen, and it had. He couldn't wait to tell Phillip and Nan.

"Why don't you call your grandparents and tell them we're moving?"

"And getting a dog, too?" she added.

"I wouldn't tell them that yet."

He dialed their number and handed her his cell phone. "We're moving. And going to the mall to get a Christmas tree that's real. And Dad says maybe a dog because we don't want a bad cat-box smell in our new house."

He could hear Nan laughing.

"Let me speak to Grandma," he said, reaching for the phone. "Finish your pancakes."

He washed the skillet he'd used to fry the bacon in while he spoke. "Let me clarify a few things. We are going to the mall. To see Santa, of course. And if Lily is a really good girl" — he spoke extra loud because he knew she was hanging on his every word — "we might ask Santa for a puppy. But first we have to stop by the real estate agent's office to pick up the keys to our new house."

After listening to Nan for a minute he said, "Thanks, I'm thrilled." He spoke for a few more minutes, then clicked off.

"Why don't you get your teeth brushed and find something to wear while I finish cleaning up? I need to take a shower myself." He raked a hand across his stubble. "And shave," he added to no one in particular.

Hadn't Brandy mentioned something about going to the mall? He was sure she had. Picking up his pace, he tossed the remaining dishes in the dishwasher and raced to the shower.

Fifteen minutes later, they were in the car heading toward the Thomas Edison Mall. It would be packed with shoppers. Sale signs would be posted in all the windows. Christmas was definitely around the corner.

He made fast work of picking up the keys to the house on Seahorse Lane. Lily hopped from one foot to the other while he finished signing the rest of the papers.

"Thank you, Mr. Rogers. It's been a pleasure."

He shook hands with the agent, then led Lily out to the car.

"Now, are we going to the mall?" she asked.

"Yes. Let the Christmas countdown begin," he said cheerily.

CHAPTER THIRTEEN

Matthew ordered three scrambled eggs, bacon, and hash browns, with a side of biscuits and gravy.

"I'll have the same," Keira said.

Surprised, Brandy said, "Make it three."

The Starlight Diner was a tribute to music of all genres. Rock. Pop. Soul. Country. Pictures of famous bands and singers lined the walls, and, for a moment, Brandy was reminded of Jeff and his dreams of becoming a rock star. Somehow, in this environment, they didn't seem as childish and unrealistic as she'd thought only yesterday. But Jeff was gone, and that wasn't going to happen. At least not in this life.

Before she started brooding over the past, Brandy asked Matthew, "Have you been here before?"

He looked at Keira, who kicked him beneath the table. "Go on. Tell her."

She looked from one child to the other.

"Tell me what?" Good grief, was he in trouble? Had he been kicked out of school? Did he have a girlfriend? And was she pregnant? A million thoughts swirled through her mind in less than a nanosecond.

"You look like you've seen a ghost," Keira said, then, realizing her words, said, "You know what I mean. Not a real ghost. If there is such a thing, which personally I don't believe in, but to each his own." Keira was truly her old self. Talking a mile a minute. Brandy wanted to leap over the table and grab her in her arms, but she didn't want to humiliate these kids who she'd just rediscovered were the coolest on the planet.

"If you don't tell me what's going on, I am going to . . . I don't know what, but, please, don't keep me in suspense any longer." She looked at her son.

His eyes were shiny, his cheeks had a healthy glow, and she knew whatever he had to tell her was important, and whatever it was, it made him happy. And right now, in the precarious life she had, they had, it was all that mattered.

"I've been playing guitar with this band here on Saturday nights. For three months."

She didn't say a word.

"I didn't want to tell you. I thought you might get mad at me, and, well, it's the kind of music I want to play."

"And," Brandy prompted.

"And that's it. I just wanted you to know. I get twenty dollars every time we play. I've saved it all. So when we get to the mall, I can buy my own stuff so you don't have to."

"Matthew Heyers! How did you keep this from me? I thought you'd lost interest in your music. You don't attend lessons anymore, and I just . . . Well, whatever I thought, I was wrong. I'm thrilled for you." She reached across the table and squeezed his hand.

"Tell her the rest of it," Keira encouraged.

"The rest of what?" Brandy asked.

Their waitress set their plates in front of them then. There was enough food to feed a horse, Brandy thought after thanking her.

"I stopped going to music lessons because . . . because Mr. Wyatt said he had to get paid." Matthew dug into his food, not meeting her eyes.

Had she really been *that* self-centered in her grief that she hadn't even paid for her son's music lessons? Matthew was a gifted musician with a bright future, with dreams of attending Juilliard in New York City. Had her negligence cost him his education? Mr. Wyatt had always said Matthew had a very good chance of being accepted into the prestigious school and would most likely earn a scholarship.

Had she unknowingly ruined his chances for a career in music?

"We tried to tell you, but . . ." Keira shrugged.

"There is no excuse for this. Death or not, I should've paid more attention to you. Both of you," she said, and reached for Keira's hand, too.

"It's cool, Mom, really. In a way, I'm glad — because I . . . I really don't want to go to Juilliard. I want to stay here. I want to teach music. Like Dad."

She truly didn't know her children, the young adults they'd become while she had spent her days and nights in her room crying for a life that was over the minute Jeff drew his last breath. She had ruined so much; she wasn't sure if she could ever make it up to them, but she would do her best to try. And from now on, Jeff would always be in her heart, but now, he could no longer exist in her day-to-day life.

"I don't know what to say. 'I'm sorry' seems downright dumb, but I am sorry. For both of you. I'm sorry you lost your father, but I'm even sorrier you lost me when I needed to be here. In the present. With both of you. Would it be too much to ask you two to forgive me? Just a little?" Her eyes filled with tears. She dabbed at them with her napkin. These weren't tears of sadness, they were tears of regret, tears of renewal, and tears because her kids were so darned mature and cool and all that other gobble-dygook stuff.

"I'm okay, Mom, really," Matthew insisted. "I've been a jerk, too. Spending all my time in my room. I just wanted to listen to my music and escape."

"I understand," Brandy said.

"So, we're all good now," Keira asked. "I am so through with being Goth. Just so you know. I think I kind of like the Taylor Swift look. I'm going to get a tube of bright red lipstick at the mall."

They all looked at one another and cracked up laughing.

Brandy knew in her heart they were going to be perfectly fine.

CHAPTER FOURTEEN

Christmas carols filtered through hidden speakers throughout the mall. Shoppers carried the familiar red shopping bags from Macy's. Store windows were decked out in the latest holiday theme, which this year seemed to be a return to the classic Christmas decor of the early fifties. At least this is what Ryan thought of as classic Christmas stuff. Sleighs and fake reindeer. Snowmen and mugs filled with hot chocolate. Warm sugar cookies scented the air, tempting the shoppers to forget about their diets. A little taste wouldn't hurt.

There were about fifty or so people in line ahead of them, and he knew it would move slowly. Santa had to listen to each and every child's request and their promises to be good.

Santa sat in a large, red, velvet-covered chair. Several elves danced their way through the long lines, passing out candy canes if the parents allowed. What parent *wouldn't* allow their child to have a candy cane while waiting their turn to see Santa? He scanned the line. Most of the kids who'd been approached had candy canes. Good.

"Dad, what are you gonna ask Santa to bring you for Christmas?"

He chuckled. He'd just spent a small fortune on their new home. He thought that enough, but knew this wasn't the answer she wanted to hear. "I think I need a new wallet." He told her, knowing she would tell Nan, and together, they would shop for a new wallet so Lily would have a gift for him come Christmas.

He'd splurged last night and bought Nan and Phillip a two-week Caribbean cruise for Christmas. They never took vacations like they had when Anna was alive. He knew for a fact the only reason they didn't was so they would be there for Lily and him. While he'd waited for the real estate agent to send his offer to the homeowner, he'd scoured the Internet, not really looking for anything in particular, just something to kill time while he waited. When he saw the cruise package, he'd decided on the spot this would be his gift to his in-laws. Before he changed his mind, he'd booked the cruise, and now he hoped that they would enjoy themselves.

The line moved faster than he thought, and it was finally Lily's turn to crawl up onto Santa's lap and tell him what she wanted for Christmas. While he watched her, he couldn't help but grin. She was talking the poor guy's ear off. Probably telling him about the cat box.

"Sir, would you like a photo?" a young girl dressed as an elf asked.

"Absolutely," he said, and handed her his credit card. As soon as business was taken care of, the photographer posed Lily, and she grinned. Snap — the flash from the camera capturing another moment in time.

Lily stood next to him as they waited for their picture. The attendant placed her picture in a Christmas frame and placed the frame in a plastic bag.

"Can we get a cookie?" Lily asked. "They smell sooooo good."

"Get me, buy me, take me, I want. Yack yack yack," Ryan teased, as they headed over to the Cookie Factory. "You are one spoiled little lady, but you already know that, right?"

"Grandma says I'm spoiled, too, but in a good way. Is she right?"

"She is. So what did you ask Santa to bring you this year?" Ryan asked.

"I thought if you tell, it won't come true, so I can't tell you."

"It's okay to tell. It's the birthday wish you're supposed to keep secret," Ryan said, as they waited their turn in line.

"Okay, Dad. I'll try to remember, but if I don't, tell me again, okay?" Lily replied. "I asked for a puppy."

His daughter brought such joy to his life, all he could do was shake his head and grin. Maybe a pup wasn't such a bad idea after all. Their house was too quiet at times. A pup would certainly liven things up a bit. He would visit the local shelter as soon as possible.

"Can I help you?" the barista asked when it was his turn to order.

"Four sugar cookies and two large cartons of milk." Ryan dug a twenty-dollar bill from his pocket and handed it to the teen. Feeling charitable, he said, "Keep the change."

The big tip brought a smile to the kid's face. "Thanks," he said, and handed him four of the largest sugar cookies he'd ever seen.

They sat at one of the tables in the center of the mall. Ryan watched the people as they raced about with cell phones glued to their ears and shopping bags stuck in their grip.

The mall was crowded. He didn't see any of his teachers or students, which was unusual, as it was a small town and he was the principal of the only elementary school in town. Not that he minded. He enjoyed watching the people as they went from store to store.

He had no more had the thought when he spotted a familiar face. He lit up like a string of bright Christmas lights. His heartbeat increased, and he felt like a kid at Christmas. Ryan was about to stand up and call out to her when she spotted him sitting at the table.

She waved, and he stood up, motioning for her to come and join them. He wanted her to meet Lily. And he wanted to meet Keira and Matthew, too. She had talked so much about them last night, he felt he knew them a little bit.

"Brandy, great to see you," he said, and took her hand in his.

"Ryan, uh, hi. I didn't realize you were going to the mall today," she said, and instantly wished she hadn't. She sounded like a young girl with a crush.

"I didn't either until Lily asked to go this morning." He looked at his daughter, whose mouth was covered in cookie crumbs and a milk mustache. "This is my daughter, Lily."

Lily smiled and waved.

"Hi, you want some of my cookies? They're way too big, and Daddy made pancakes for breakfast this morning, so I am very full. I asked Santa Claus to bring me a puppy for Christmas."

Everyone laughed.

"It's a pleasure to meet you, Lily. Your dad has told me a lot about you." Keira and Matthew lingered in the background, each laden with bags from their favorite store. She suddenly remembered they were there. "This is Keira and Matthew."

"I'm Ryan, and this is my daughter, Lily," Ryan said, and held his hand out for them to shake.

"Aren't you the principal at Pelican Elementary?" Matthew asked. "I think I remember you from when I was a student there," he said.

"I am, and you look a little familiar to me, too, though I have to be honest, I see hundreds of kids who used to go to school there. Some I really remember because they spent most of their time in my office. I don't recall ever seeing you there."

Keira laughed with Matthew. "He was the perfect little student," she explained. "Me, on the other hand, well, I might've been in the office a time or two, but you weren't the principal when I attended Pelican."

Ryan looked at Brandy. "Why don't you all have a seat? I can get you something to drink. A cookie?" He looked at Keira and Matthew when he invited them to join him and Lily.

Lily had been quiet for almost a full minute. She motioned for Keira to take the seat next to her. Keira grinned and sat down. Matthew sat beside Brandy, who sat next to Ryan.

"Would any of you like something to drink or eat?" Ryan asked. "These cookies are pure bliss."

"I'll have one," Matthew said, surprising Brandy. His sullenness had lifted like a rain cloud. His former shyness was now nonexistent.

Ryan looked to Keira, then at Brandy. "No, thank you," Keira said.

Again, Brandy was stunned by the total and complete about-face her kids had made. After all the crying, pouting, and shouting from days ago, their change was still a bit of a surprise. Sure that Linnie had had a hand in this, she would ask her, but later. Now all she wanted to do was soak up the holiday atmosphere and get to know Ryan and Lily, and she could only hope that they wanted to get to know her family, too.

"So you have a boyfriend?" Lily asked Keira.

Everyone laughed.

"Lily, remember what I told you about asking personal questions?" Ryan said, a bit too seriously. He didn't want Keira to feel embarrassed. He knew how teenagers were.

"No. I forgot," she answered, and again, they all laughed.

"It's okay, Ryan. I don't mind. Lily, I do not have a boyfriend, but I am always on the lookout for one." She ruffled the little girl's hair. "Do *you* have a boyfriend?"

"No, but Cara does. She's my best friend. She likes Tyler Banfield. He picks his nose. Cara isn't in Mrs. Pellegrino's class, so she doesn't see him. It's so gross. I don't like boys," she said firmly.

"Lily! Where are your manners!" Ryan softly admonished.

"Sorry, but he does pick his nose, ask Lisa," she insisted, refusing to back down.

"Matthew, let's leave these girls alone and get some more cookies. Something tells me Lily will keep your mother and sister entertained."

Matthew laughed. "She's a cute kid." He followed Ryan back to the Cookie Factory.

"Mom, tell me how you know Ryan. When in the world did you meet him? He's a total hunk," Keira asked.

Brandy's face turned beet red. "Keira!" She directed her gaze to Lily, who was listening to their conversation.

"I know what a hunk is. All the teachers at school say Daddy's a hunk. He is sad sometimes at night. I hear him."

"Oh, sweetie," Brandy said. "Of course he's sad. He lost your mother." She knew it was okay to say this because over coffee last night Ryan told her Lily really had no memory of her mother other than photos and what he told her.

"I know, but that's not why he's sad. Grandma told me that he needed to find someone to love again, so he wouldn't be so lonely."

Brandy's heart skipped a beat. So there was hope after all.

"My mom does, too," Keira added. "She needs to find someone, too." Her daughter never took her eyes off her while she said this. Was this her way of telling her it was okay to meet someone? To possibly fall in love again?

She didn't have a chance to question her about it because Ryan and Matthew returned with a pile of cookies, cups of hot coffee, and cartons of chocolate milk.

For the next half hour, they munched on

the cookies and talked about the upcoming holiday. "Lily and I were going to search for a live tree today. If you don't have any plans, why don't the three of you join us?"

"I have to go to band practice this afternoon," Matthew said.

"I'm meeting some friends at Starbucks," Keira offered.

"I wanna go with you, too, but only if Brandy comes? Will you go with us? Please, please please!"

If Brandy didn't know better, she would think she was being fixed up by an eight-year-old.

Ryan looked at her, and in the sweetest voice he said, "Please?"

At that moment, the ice surrounding her heart began to melt.

EPILOGUE

December 20

It was going to be the most amazing day this year, yet the strangest. For the past three weeks, she and Ryan had spent as much time together as possible. Their kids were thrilled, and they were, too.

She thought she might be falling a little bit in love, but how could she when such a short time had passed, and she'd been in full-blown-grief mode when they had met.

Almost.

Tonight, she, Keira, and Matthew would celebrate Jeff's life. With Ryan and Lily. They'd made plans to go to one of Jeff's favorite restaurants for dinner, and afterward planned to go to the beach for a short ceremony in Jeff's honor.

When that was over, they were all going back to Ryan's new home, which just so happened to be two blocks from hers. He said he wanted her to meet Lily's grandparents, who she knew were Anna's parents, but he'd assured her they weren't uncomfortable at all. Since it was to be a celebration of sorts, she'd asked if she could invite Linda and Dylan. He agreed.

She'd told him of her friendship, how much Linnie meant to her, and how she'd changed her kids' life in one night. Brandy had begged Linda to tell her what magic she'd performed that night when she'd taken Keira and Matthew to dinner, but she'd promised them that she wouldn't discuss it, and Brandy knew for a fact that Linda always kept her promises. Someday, maybe Keira or Matthew would tell her, but it really didn't matter. They were the best kids in the world, and Lily, too. She and her kids had fallen in love with the spirited little girl the past few weeks.

They met at Sakura's, Jeff's favorite Japanese steak house.

Brandy wore a new dress she'd purchased last week. Dark green and clingy in all the right places without being too obvious that she was showing off her figure. She'd asked Keira to do her hair and makeup. When she looked in the mirror, she realized she didn't look like the woman of a few weeks ago. Her eyes were brighter, her cheeks glistened, and her attitude was totally changed. She reeked positivity. Even her coworkers at the library had commented on the change.

"You look ten years younger, Mom," Keira said as she applied her own lipstick.

"And you are the most gorgeous girl in the world," Brandy said, giving her a hug.

"And Lily, too," Keira added. "I've become quite attached to that little minx. I've always wanted a little sister."

"Really? I never knew." Brandy was thrilled with this information. She loved Lily, and knew as time passed, she would come to love her as much as she loved her own children. She looked at her watch. "If we're going to make our seven o'clock reservation, we'd better get a move on."

Keira dropped her lipstick in her purse. "Then let's get out of here."

Matthew was waiting in the living room. He wore khakis and one of his father's shirts. Brandy enjoyed seeing him like this. She was sorry that she hadn't allowed him access to his father's things sooner. Two days ago, she'd cleared all of Jeff's clothes, books, and belongings out of her room. She'd donated some and kept things that would hold a special memory for the kids. She had put all of Jeff's clothing in a giant tote in Matthew's room. He could keep what he wanted, and after the holidays, they all agreed they would donate the rest of his possessions.

Thirty minutes later, the five of them were seated at the hibachi grill, where their chef delighted in entertaining them while he prepared their dinners.

He made a giant heart with a mound of rice, then slid a metal spatula beneath it, then slowly made it rise so that it looked like a beating heart.

In a heavily accented voice, he told Lily, "This is good for you."

She smiled. Someone, presumably Nan, had fixed her long, brown hair into a French braid, securing it with a bright pink ribbon. She wore pink leggings with sparkles, and a silver shirt with little pink hearts on it. Brandy's heart melted when she saw her.

"Brandy, is that stuff really good for me?" she asked her.

"Yes, it is, but between us, brown rice is much healthier."

When Brandy was around, Lily asked her questions all the time. She knew that the little girl was crazy about her, and the feeling was mutual. Keira and Matthew adored her, and recently they'd started referring to her as their adopted little sister. Neither she nor Ryan had objected when they'd heard

133

them explaining their relationship to strangers.

The chef spent the next half hour flipping shrimp tails through the air, tossing eggs so high, the group caught their breath when they'd disappeared from sight, then landed on the chef's steel spatula.

"Jeff loved it here," she said to Ryan. "Whenever we had a chance to splurge on dinner, this is where we came. Lots of good memories here."

Keira and Matthew told Ryan about the time one of the chefs had tossed an egg high in the air only to have it land smack-dab in the inside of their mom's new purse, one she'd just bought that day.

The food was fabulous, but the company was out of this world, Brandy thought, as they made their way back to their cars. She had yet to visit Ryan's new home, and she was excited yet a bit nervous about meeting Anna's family.

The trip to the beach was a bit somber. Brandy and the kids wrote Jeff's name in the sand and then they all stood back and watched as the incoming waves slowly washed it away. But when Jeff's name in the sand was slowly smoothed over by the lapping waves, Brandy felt like something in her had been released.

"Are you two okay?" she asked the kids as they headed back to the car.

They both nodded, and Keira said, "We've been okay for a long time, Mom. You're the one who wasn't okay. Until now." Brandy wrapped her arms around both of her children and realized how blessed she was to have them.

The spirit of Christmas had taken on a whole new meaning for her. She would never take anything or anyone for granted, ever again. And, now that she had finally admitted her scheme, she would always be grateful to Linda for calling every single member of the Friends of the Library to tell them it was imperative that they cancel. Though Linda hadn't planned on her meeting Ryan, she knew that Brandy decorating the tree by herself would start her on the road to healing.

When they pulled into the grand, circular drive on Seahorse Lane, they were somewhat taken aback. The house was five times the size of their own. Christmas lights in red, green, and white were strung on the gutters; the windows, and the giant palm trees in the front yard were trimmed in white and green lights. Giant tubs of poinsettias flanked the massive doorway.

Just as she raised her hand to ring the

doorbell, the door was opened by an older woman with short, silver hair and a welcoming smile. Lily stood next to her.

"You must be Brandy; I'm Nan," she said gracefully before turning to the kids. "And this must be Keira and Matthew, who Lily can't seem to stop talking about. It's wonderful to finally meet all of you. Please come inside."

"I told you she was pretty, didn't I?" Lily said to her grandmother.

"You certainly did, and I agree one hundred percent," Nan said.

Nan led her to the living room, where a live tree, at least ten feet tall, stood by the giant glass windows. Ryan hurried across the room to greet them. "So, what do you think?"

Brandy was overwhelmed, then she saw Linda and Dylan chatting with an older man who she knew had to be Phillip. Linda practically leaped across the room.

"Well, don't you look like someone who's just jumped out of a bandbox." She kissed Brandy, then hugged the kids.

"Lily, why don't you show Keira and Matthew around," Ryan said. "Excuse me, but I have something I need to take care of. And quickly."

Brandy nodded and followed Linda to

where Dylan was in deep conversation with Phillip. After the introductions were made, Brandy found herself feeling beyond happy, and it showed.

"Why are you two here already?" she asked Linda, who handed her a glass of white wine. "I thought you were coming later."

"We've known Ryan for years. The girls go to school at Pelican, and Dylan and Phillip used to do business together."

"And the world keeps getting smaller and smaller," Brandy said, smiling.

Ryan came back in the room with a box that seemed to have a mind of its own. "Nan, could you ask Lily, Matthew, and Keira to come inside for a minute, or else I'm not sure about" — he looked at the box — "this."

When everyone was inside, they gathered around the Christmas tree. They all had a drink of some sort when Ryan said, "I would like to propose a toast." They all gathered as close as possible and clinked their glasses together. "To the newest members of the Rogers and Heyers family!"

He stooped down and opened the box.

Three yellow Lab puppies jumped out of the box. One peed on Linda's shoe, another ran into the glass window, and the third plopped on top of Brandy's feet.

"Merry Christmas!" Ryan said to Lily, Keira, and Matthew. "The shelter found them abandoned by their owner. I had to take all three of them," he explained with a grin.

Brandy picked up the little puppy and then, not caring that her children and Anna's parents were in the room, she kissed Ryan for the first time.

And he kissed her back.

"Now *that* is the best Christmas gift I've ever received," Ryan said before wrapping her and the little pup in his arms.

"Merry Christmas, everyone! I got three puppies," Lily squealed with delight.

Their future was so bright, they all sparkled and shone like the brilliant glow emanating from the Christmas tree. It was truly a Merry Christmas.

■ ■ ■ ■

A Glory Junction
Christmas

STACY FINZ

■ ■ ■ ■

CHAPTER ONE

Hannah Baldwin peered out the window across Main Street to the river. They'd been working on that ancient gazebo all day. Hammering and sanding while their fingers must be frozen to the bone. With only three weeks until the wedding, she supposed Chip and Valerie didn't have the luxury of waiting for a warm day, especially in December.

At least the bride and groom would save on decorations. The entire downtown was decked out like a winter wonderland — no one did the holidays quite like Glory Junction, California. Luminarias lined the rooftops of the old-timey shops, ginormous colored balls dangled from the trees, garland draped every streetlight, and a menorah made by a famous sculptor shared the town's stage with a nativity scene courtesy of Glory Be Catholic Church.

After the ceremony Valerie and Chip were holding a reception for two hundred guests at Winter Bowl, one of the fancy ski resorts at the summit of the mountain.

Hannah was pretty sure she was the only one in town who hadn't gotten an invite, not that she blamed the couple. It would've been awkward, given that Chip was her ex-husband.

"Did you hear the news?" Deb, Hannah's best friend, came bursting through the door of the shop and stopped short. "You redid the whole store . . . Again!"

Deb gazed around Glorious Gifts, letting her eyes fall on a collection of candles that Hannah had stacked in the shape of a Christmas tree next to an arrangement of dreidels, then focused on a colorful display of hand-knit sweaters.

There were talented knitters — some even raised their own wool — in the area, and Hannah liked to promote local goods as much as possible. Near the woolens, she had an array of Delaney Scott handbags, casual wear, and party dresses. The Los Angeles fashion designer now lived a few miles away. Hannah had even managed to persuade Tawny Rodriguez to stock a few pairs of her custom cowboy boots in the store. Tawny had grown up with Hannah in Nugget, a small neighboring town, and now made boots for celebrities.

"This is my busiest time of year," she told Deb. "I've got to make the shop pop."

Deb let out a breath. "Is that it? Or are you doing the manic thing because you're depressed?"

"I'm not depressed." Hannah began to re-arrange the Christmas ornaments on the counter.

"There's nothing wrong with you having a hard time with this wedding. You may not be in love with Chip anymore, but it's still got to hurt. You should take some time off, go on a trip, and use some of the money Sabine left you."

Two months ago, Sabine had died from ovarian cancer after being diagnosed eight months earlier, right after Chip had an-nounced that he wanted a divorce. In one excruciating year, she'd lost the two people she was closest to. This would be her first Christmas alone in the shop and in Sabine's Victorian cottage, the other prized posses-sion her aunt had bequeathed her.

"I'll go in January," Hannah said, and shivered as she watched the bundled-up passersby. "Maybe a tropical beach."

Deb nudged her head at the window with the prime view of the gazebo. "That sort of defeats the purpose, don't you think?"

"I can't go now, not during the Christmas

rush. Who'll run the store?"

"I could do it for you."

Deb had good intentions and was the kindest person Hannah knew, but responsibility and work ethic . . . not exactly strong points. Deb could barely hold down her waitressing job. Skiing, river rafting, and mountain biking were her first priorities. Like a lot of people in Glory Junction, Deb lived to play. Work just paid for the equipment.

"Thanks, but Sabine would want me to be here for her first Christmas away from the store." Hannah knew it would end any further argument from Deb, who like everyone else in town had loved Sabine, too.

"You should at least get out a little. I don't think you've had a day off since the funeral. And leave the store alone, it looks great. You're just making yourself crazy. Tonight we should go to Old Glory, have a couple of beers, and shoot pool."

Hannah let out a groan. "That's Chip's hangout."

"Not anymore."

Chip was a recovering alcoholic. Sober 394 days, the first ninety in rehab. When she'd gone to pick him up from Napa Meadows, he'd been wearing a suit. In all the time she'd known him, barring his high school graduation and their wedding, he'd never worn a tie, let alone a jacket.

She'd helped him load his luggage into the trunk and wrapped her arms around him. When she went to kiss him, he pulled away, giving her a weary smile. "Thanks for coming to get me."

At the time, Hannah thought it was a bizarre thing to say. She was his wife; of course she'd pick him up. "I'm so proud of you, Chip."

They'd gotten in the car, Chip in the passenger seat. He turned to face her, his eyes wet, and said, "I'm sorry that I was a drunk and that I let you down. I'm sorry that I stole the entire nine years of our marriage."

He'd already apologized profusely many times. It was part of the program — making amends.

Taking the Silverado Trail from the rehab center to the highway, they passed winery after winery, tasting room after tasting room where the region's famed cabernet, merlot, and chardonnay ran freely. The irony wasn't lost on Hannah.

"We'll start fresh, Chip." She reached for his hand.

The silence stretched long as the country road when Chip finally replied, "I've done a lot of thinking in the past three months and the thing is . . . I don't love you. Not the way I'm supposed to."

Perhaps she should've been prepared for that. There had been all kinds of signs during rehab. He'd refused to take her calls, to let her visit, and his e-mails had been filled with trivialities: the weather, what he and the other "inmates" had been served for dinner, or inanities about a television show he'd watched. Never once had he said he missed her or loved her. She'd managed to convince herself that in his new sober state he was deeply ashamed. That it would take time to rebuild their relationship.

Yet, the words "I don't love you" made her throat close up and she swerved to the side of the road. "Chip," she said, turning to face him. "What are you saying?"

Pausing for what seemed like an eternity, he finally said, "I'm sorry, Hannah, I want a divorce."

There it was, out in the open, everything she'd come to suspect but was too afraid to admit to herself. Still, it didn't stop her from wanting to scream, sob, even slap him. After all those years of finding him passed out on the floor, cleaning up his vomit, making excuses to their friends and families, lying to everyone they knew, he was finally sober. The new and sober Chip didn't love her

146

anymore. And she knew why. He was in love with someone else.

Hannah was too hurt to realize she was relieved. That would come later. For so long she'd been hiding from the truth — just as she had with Chip's drinking — that their passion for each other had expired a long time ago. Still, a divorce . . . Nine years. Nine freaking years.

Too afraid that any little outburst would drive him to the bottle again, she drove the three hours home in silence, dying a little more with each passing mile.

"Well?" Deb said, bringing her back to the present. "Old Glory, you up for it?"

"All right." *What the hell?* "I'll meet you there as soon as I close the shop."

"It'll be fun." Deb played with one of the hand-knit infinity scarves, looping it around her neck in the mirror. "How long before you open?"

"Twenty minutes. When does your shift start at the Morning Glory?"

"Same time. Felix has a new cook. He wants me to help out in the kitchen and cover the counter." The diner couldn't seem to keep cooks.

"Ten seems kind of late for the breakfast shift."

"He has me on lunch today. I'm hoping

to get on the slopes by four. That should give me two hours before it gets dark." Deb grabbed one of the Delaney Scott dresses off the rack and held it against her. "What do you think?"

"That it would look amazing on you." Deb had the kind of body guys drooled over. Only one man was immune, and of course he was the one Deb wanted. "You look at the price? Even with the whopping discount I'd give you, it's a lot of tips."

She found the tag and her eyes grew round. "Jeez, people can actually afford this stuff?"

The tourists could for sure and nowadays even the locals. While it would not have been the case years ago, the town residents had changed from ski bums and back-to-the-land hippies to professional athletes and tech moguls. They were much more affluent now. There was even a landing strip so San Franciscans and Los Angelinos could zip up in their private planes for a weekend in their ski condo or lake chalet. Otherwise it was a three-and-a-half-hour drive from the Bay Area and seven hours from SoCal.

These days, Glory Junction boasted a Four Seasons Hotel, a couple of high-end restaurants closer to the ski resorts, and three Starbucks, which seemed excessive for a town with a population of only ten thousand. Hannah thought all the glitzy growth was kind of nauseating, though her cash register didn't complain.

Then again, she came from a working-class railroad town half the size of Glory Junction, and even Nugget had a posh bed-and-breakfast now. Hey, it was California. Expansion was inevitable.

"Try this." She pulled another dress from one of the racks and handed it to Deb. "It's a quarter of the price and you'll rock it."

Deb examined the label and scowled. "It's not a Delaney Scott."

"Nope. That's why you can afford it. Slip it on before your shift starts at the diner."

Deb disappeared behind the dressing-room door and came out a few minutes later.

"What do you think?" She did a little twirl.

It hugged her curves and accentuated her long, shapely legs just like Hannah knew it would. "It's got your name on it."

"Can you hold it for me until payday?"

"You can take it. It's my gift to you."

"Hannah." Deb put her hands on her hips. "Don't give me stuff."

"Call it an early Christmas present. I know you want it for the Garners' party —"

"Oh my God, that's what I came in to tell

149

you. Josh is home. They're having a big pancake breakfast for him at the VFW. I signed us up to be servers."

Hannah had already heard from Mary Garner that her son was returning from Afghanistan. She was happy for the Garners, who were like a second family to Hannah. But there had always been weirdness between her and Josh. In fact, she suspected that Josh, Chip's best friend, blamed her for enabling her ex's addiction. Whatever the reason, Josh had always been cold to her and she hated how much it bothered her.

"You should've asked first," Hannah said. At this point in her life she didn't need Josh's righteous indignation.

"Since you're a member of the Glory Junction Chamber of Commerce, I thought you'd want to be involved. Josh is a war hero."

His leg had been shattered in a roadside bombing while he tried to save other soldiers. Despite the tension between them, the idea of him being injured made her ache. And the uncomfortable truth was she wanted to see him.

Hannah looked at her best friend knowingly. "You signed us up because Win will be there."

"So?" Deb shrugged. "It doesn't mean I

don't want to show Josh support . . . I can't imagine how difficult it's been for him."

Hannah couldn't argue with that. He'd always been so strong and athletic — and reckless. Not surprising since the Garner family was in the extreme sports and adventure business. Before Josh had gone off to college and the army, he'd worked for his parents, leading rock-climbing tours, ski expeditions, and river-rafting trips. For as long as Hannah could remember, Mary and Gray's four sons had spent their weekends, holidays, and summers working in the family business.

Deb checked her watch. "I've got to get." She dashed back into the dressing room and came out a few minutes later in her black waitressing clothes.

"Take the dress," Hannah called to her. "I need to make room for new inventory."

Deb handed it to her. "Keep it for me until tonight. I don't want it to smell like a deep fryer. See you at Old Glory at around seven."

After Deb left, Hannah wrapped the dress in tissue paper and put it in one of her new Glorious Gifts canvas bags. Last year, the town had outlawed plastic bags and required shop owners to charge ten cents for paper. Hannah upgraded to canvas and just gave them away. What the heck? With her logo emblazoned on the front, the totes were free advertising.

She unlocked the front door and turned the sign to OPEN. A few minutes later, Win, the youngest Garner, strolled in, carrying a green protein shake from the Juicery.

"Can I hide in here for a few minutes?"

"Of course," Hannah said. "Who you hiding from?"

"Rita Tucker. She's been chasing me all over town . . . wants me to be in her porn calendar."

Hannah laughed. "It's a good cause." Every year, Rita photographed the local hunks in provocative poses to raise money for the volunteer fire department. The calendars sold like hotcakes.

"She wants me to be Mr. December in nothing but a Santa hat and a piece of mistletoe covering my you-know-what. First of all, there's not a mistletoe plant on God's green earth large enough for that. And second of all, it's exploitation. I've got a brain and feelings inside all this brawn, you know?"

She stifled a laugh, since Win ran around in nothing but board shorts all summer long. "Tell her you want to wear something more modest."

"Everyone wants a piece of this." He ran his hands down his impressive chest, flashed a cheeky grin, and wandered the store, picking up various items here and there and generally making a mess of her displays.

"I hear Josh is back."

"Yep. You going to the shindig on Saturday at the VFW?"

"Deb signed us up to be servers," Hannah said.

Win came back to the front counter and downed the rest of his protein shake. "Good. He could use some pretty women making a fuss over him."

As long as Hannah had known Josh he hadn't needed anyone making anything over him. Even at sixteen, he'd been overly confident and aloof.

"I heard about his leg."

Win got quiet, his eyes growing distant. "He's having a rough time. But Garners are tough. We'll get him back."

Two middle-aged women opened the door, letting in a rush of cold air as they deliberated on whether to come in. One of the women lasered in on the Delaney Scott handbags and made a beeline for the display.

"I'll catch you later, Hannah," Win said.

She watched through the plate-glass window as he crossed the cobblestone street to the Riverwalk, where he greeted Chip.

"Let me know if you ladies need any help," she told the customers who had now moved on to the knitwear.

"You have some lovely things here," one of the women said. "We're up from the Bay Area."

"Are you staying at one of the ski resorts?" There were five in total. From Main Street you could see the chairlifts and gondolas going up and down the mountainside. Some called Glory Junction the Western equivalent of St. Moritz without the hefty price tag.

"Winter Bowl," she said. "Neither of us ski but our families do."

Hannah didn't ski either. Even though her hometown was only thirty minutes away, kids there couldn't afford the luxury of lift tickets and rental equipment. Since Nugget was largely a ranching community, the young folks there entertained themselves horseback riding, competing in junior rodeo, and participating in 4-H.

"There's plenty to do in town," she told the ladies. "Good restaurants, too."

"We heard there were horse carriage rides."

"They don't start until a week or so before Christmas." Although Hannah had heard chatter that the company might start tacking on a few extra weeks with so many more people visiting right after Thanksgiving to see Glory Junction's holiday displays. "You may want to check in with Garner Adventure next door. They do various tours that might interest you."

The women perked up and the one who'd been doing most of the talking said, "We'll do that. Thanks for the suggestion."

Forty minutes later, they left, weighed down with shopping bags. If the day kept going like this, Hannah would make her daily sales quota in no time. At noon she called in an order to the Morning Glory Diner and closed the shop for ten minutes to run across the street to fetch her lunch. She ate a tuna melt and fries in her tiny office, keeping an ear to the front door. Customers trickled in throughout the afternoon — all in a buying mood. The holidays tended to loosen people's wallets.

At six, Hannah locked up, put the till in the safe, did a little remerchandising, and ran a vacuum over the hardwood floors. She got to Old Glory early and snagged a window booth overlooking Main Street so she could watch for Deb.

Every inch of the bar's wall space was covered in American flags. Even the unisex bathrooms had Stars and Stripes wallpaper. There were big barrels of peanuts, and patrons were encouraged to drop their shells on the floor. On weekends there was live music and on Wednesdays open-mic night. Although mostly popular with locals, tourists had started to discover the bar because it had thirty microbrews on tap and served excellent pub food.

While she waited, a couple of guys she'd never seen before asked if they could buy her a drink. More than likely they'd come down from one of the resorts. None of them had the look of a local. Their North Face and Patagonia jackets were too shiny and their snow boots too new. She politely declined and they moved on, ordering a round of tequila shots for their table.

Gazing out the window, Hannah watched as little by little the Christmas lights and luminarias flickered on. Although the last snow had been cleared from the streets and sidewalks, patches still covered the eaves of the buildings. The town really was one of the most picturesque places she'd ever seen.

Under the streetlight, in front of the bar, a truck pulled up and a man got out of the driver's seat. It only took her a second or two to register that it was Josh, though she hadn't recognized him at first. He'd always been tall, maybe six-two. But now he carried himself differently, like a warrior, she supposed. And while his face was still handsome, its soft boyishness had been replaced by sharp angles, and a carved jawline. He locked the Ford and slowly moved toward Garner Adventure. That's when she noticed the pronounced limp. Hannah had assumed he was in a wheelchair.

He must have felt her gaze on him because he stopped, turned, and held her stare through the window, then quickly looked away. Even as he vanished inside his family's store-front, Hannah's heart hammered. Way back when, before he'd decided to ignore her, she'd seen more than interest in those piercing blue eyes. She, too, turned away, her chest squeezing. What was it about him that always got to her?

CHAPTER TWO

Saturday morning Josh Garner went with his family to the VFW hall on the outskirts of town. He looked forward to the event about as much as getting a tooth pulled. But the good veterans of Glory Junction wanted to give him a hero's welcome and it would be disrespectful to stand them up.

"You need help, bro?" Win opened the passenger-seat door and offered him an arm.

"I've got it!" Josh growled.

"No need to get surly, dude." Win moved out of his way.

"Just go inside with Mom and Dad." His brother TJ was already here and Colt was supposedly on his way. He was Glory Junction's police chief so there was no way to predict whether he'd get caught up in an emergency.

"There's nothing wrong with letting someone help. But fine, do it yourself." Win threw his arms in the air and strode toward the hall.

Because it was Josh's right leg that had suffered the damage, passenger-side seats were tricky. At least on the driver's side he could get out using his left leg without having to put weight on his right. For this he'd have to do some maneuvering and he didn't want an audience. It was bad enough he walked like a goddamn cripple.

He'd nearly lost the leg completely in a series of IED explosions that had killed three and injured seven soldiers in his squad as they crossed a footbridge during a routine patrol in Nevay-deh. He and another Ranger had managed to carry the survivors to safety. But Josh's leg had been torn and mangled and doctors had proclaimed it beyond repair. They'd wanted to amputate. But one brash surgeon had insisted on stitching together enough of his blood vessels to save the leg long enough to get him to Germany. There, they'd reconnected his bones with plates and rods and mended his wounds with muscle and skin from other parts of his body.

He should've been the Bionic Man, except he had trouble walking, let alone running.

Josh managed to get out of the truck and hobble to the VFW door. At least he could eat his damn pancakes sitting down. He was just about to go inside when Colt pulled into the lot and ripped his siren, calling attention to both of them, the asshole.

He got out of the cruiser wearing a big-old grin. "Want me to carry you over the threshold?"

Josh gave him the finger but waited, leaning against the wall to catch his breath.

"How you doing, little brother?" Colt draped his arm around Josh's shoulder in a show of brotherly affection but Josh knew he was really propping him up. This time he didn't resist.

They went in that way and the crowd burst into cheers. Josh thought he heard a couple of *hooahs* and couldn't help but smile. Then his grin quickly turned grim.

"I didn't know she'd be here?"

"Who?" Colt said, looking around the room.

"Hannah Simmons."

"She's back to using Baldwin now." She was putting syrup on the tables. "She came to welcome you home . . . and she's looking hot. You got a problem with that?"

"I'm not sure coming here was such a good idea," he said, grimacing.

"Nah." Colt nodded at a few guys waving at them. "They're proud of you, Josh. We're all proud of you. Now smile pretty, chicks love a guy in a uniform."

It hadn't been his idea to wear the dress blues or the tan beret; it had been his father's. A few of the older veterans came over to greet them as they made their way through the crowd. Josh's leg was killing him and all he wanted to do was sit. Colt must've sensed it because he steered Josh toward their parents' table and deposited him in a chair.

"I'll get you some pancakes." He took off toward the kitchen, leaving Josh to make small talk with a few of his parents' friends.

The whole time, he kept his eye on Hannah, who stood with a clique of women. He'd seen her at Old Glory the previous night. It didn't seem possible but she'd gotten even more beautiful than when they were kids — or on her wedding day when she'd taken his breath away. Chip, of course, had been three sheets to the wind. As his best man, Josh had to practically hold him up at the altar.

She spotted him, paused, and hesitantly walked over. Shit! He tried to stand but his leg locked. It did that sometimes, especially when he overworked it.

"Hi," she said, standing over him.

It seemed rude not to get up. She saved him the trouble, though, by taking the empty seat next to him.

"Hey."

"I saw you last night on Main Street. I don't think you recognized me."

They both knew that was a lie. He hadn't wanted her to see him dragging his leg down the sidewalk.

"Anyway, I just wanted to say that it's nice to have you home," she continued. He thought she seemed nervous. "I'm glad you're safe and sound."

He was hardly "sound" but nodded out of politeness. "Thanks. I was sorry to hear about Sabine. I would've sent something. . . ." But he'd been at Landstuhl Medical Center, getting put back together again. "You running the store now?"

"Mm-hmm. She left it to me, along with her house."

He had this outrageous urge to touch her hair. It was blond, lighter than he remembered, and fell past her shoulders in soft curls. It framed the face that had gotten him through many a bad night. Instead, he kept his hands stiffly at his side.

"She'll be missed," he said lamely. Sabine had been one in a million and with all the death he'd seen, Josh should've been more adroit with condolences. "What about you? How've you been?"

She let out a breath. "Chip and I got divorced."

"Yeah, I heard. I'm sorry." More platitudes. This time, though, he wasn't sorry at all. "I also heard he's sober now."

"Val staged an intervention and got him into a program." Her eyes didn't quite meet his when she said it.

"Yeah, she e-mailed me in Kandahar . . . wanted me to come." He couldn't of course.

"She did?" Hannah reeled back in surprise. "I didn't realize you two knew each other."

"We don't. I figure she was covering all her bases."

"Are you . . . the best man at their wedding?"

He could tell it pained her to ask. "Nah. Just a guest. Chip and I . . . we kind of fell out of touch." Not just because Chip had been a drunk but because Josh's feelings for Hannah were complicated.

"I didn't know that. Now that you're back, maybe you'll reconnect." She darted a look around the hall. "I should probably pitch in some more. It was nice seeing you, Josh."

"Likewise." He watched her walk away as a dozen guys' appreciative gazes followed her across the floor.

"What did Hannah have to say?" TJ

slipped into the seat she'd left empty.

Of all Josh's brothers, TJ was the serious one. Their parents were the founders of Garner Adventure but TJ ran it. He was the chief bean counter, hiring director, and marketing guru rolled into one. And although he was eighteen months younger than Colt, people always thought he was the eldest — and the smartest, which he probably was.

"Nothing," Josh said.

"Nothing, huh?" TJ rolled his eyes.

Colt finally returned with Josh's pancakes. Josh drenched them in syrup and took a big bite. A couple of old high school friends stopped by to say hi and soon every person in the place came over to welcome Josh home. There were speeches and accolades and the Glory Junction High School band played "The Army Song."

Someone called Josh to the stage and he slowly made his way to the other side of the hall. When he got to the stairs Colt was waiting to help him up.

"I've got it," Josh hissed. *Rangers lead the way.*

The mayor gave him a key to the city and a proclamation, claiming December fifth to be Josh Garner Day. Josh said a few words and managed to get off the stage without

164

his leg buckling. His recovery required excruciating months of physical therapy and possibly more surgeries. Still, doctors didn't know if his leg would ever work properly again.

"You ready to go home?" Win, who'd disappeared, was suddenly at Josh's side.

"Yeah." Sweat beaded on Josh's forehead from the exertion of getting up and down the stage.

"Mom and Dad are sticking around to represent so we're good to go." Win pulled truck keys from his pocket and led the way to the door, stopping every once in a while to gab with someone he knew. Everyone thought Win was the most charming of the Garner brothers. Josh didn't see it but he thought his younger brother was definitely the cockiest.

At long last they made it outside and a blast of cold air hit Josh in the face. He managed to hoist himself up into the passenger seat and ten minutes later, when Win pulled into their parents' driveway, he gingerly got out of the truck and limped straight to the kitchen. He grabbed a handful of ice packs from the freezer and made it to the family room before collapsing in their father's recliner.

Win followed him in and turned the TV

165

on to the Cal Bears game. "You okay?"

"Yeah." He tilted the chair back as far as it would go and applied the ice packs. "You mind getting me a couple of painkillers?"

Win got up to go in search of the ibuprofen. The doctors had given Josh a prescription but he refused to take anything stronger than over-the-counter.

Win returned and handed Josh a few pills and a glass of water. "Here you go. How's it staying with Mom and Dad?" Josh was the only one of his brothers living at home.

His folks had an en-suite guest room on the main floor. "Good . . . for now."

That was the thing, he didn't have a clue what his future held. It's not like he could lead tours, or even nature hikes. His plan had always been to come back to the family business. Then a shitload of shrapnel happened. TJ had talked to him about taking bookings, which amounted to a receptionist job. If his leg didn't kill him, boredom from being a phone jockey surely would.

Win got up and turned on the lights on the Christmas tree. His mother always did the holidays up nice. Stockings, wreaths, garland, the whole nine yards. He was pretty sure if he inspected the tree he'd find more than a dozen homemade ornaments he and his brothers had made in grade school.

Macaroni angels and bottle-cap snowmen.

The doorbell rang and Win got up to see who it was. Josh wasn't in the mood for company and hoped it was UPS. His mom got a lot of deliveries this time of year.

Win came back in with Chip on his heels.

"Hey," he greeted Josh. "Sorry I missed the breakfast. Wedding crunch."

Josh forwarded his chair into a sitting position and started to get up.

"Don't bother, man. Stay comfortable."

"You get that gazebo done?"

"Yup. Just have to paint it, but I'm watching the forecast."

"I'm taking off," Win said, and grabbed the jacket he'd dumped on the couch when they came in. "I'll catch you later, Josh." He turned to Chip. "If you need any help with painting let me know."

After he left, Josh and Chip sat in silence for a while, staring at the tree.

"You see Hannah at the VFW?" Chip asked.

"For a few minutes. Why?"

"I just figured she'd go is all. Val would've gone too but she had her last fitting. I'd like you to get to know her . . . she's the best thing that's ever happened to me."

No, Hannah had been the best thing that ever happened to him and he'd made a mockery of their marriage.

"Were you seeing Valerie when you and Hannah were still together?" Despite the fact that they'd been best friends since kindergarten, it was none of Josh's business. Still, he couldn't help asking.

"Not like that. We'd become good friends, though." According to Josh's brothers, Val worked with Chip at the California Department of Fish and Wildlife. "I guess, to be honest, I'd started falling in love with her while Hannah and I were still together. I never acted on it, though."

Who was Josh to judge? He'd been in love with Hannah the whole time she'd been with Chip. But Chip's behavior still gnawed. He finally got himself sober and the first thing he did was dump his wife for his coworker.

"Val saved my life," Chip continued, sounding too damned defensive to Josh's ears. "She got me into that program."

Josh didn't say anything, his disapproval clear, which agitated the hell out of Chip.

"You can quit with the condemnation," he spat. "Hannah's free now . . . for you. The funny part of it is she always thought you couldn't stand her. Little did she know you were dying to have her for yourself. I knew, though. So don't act so holier than thou."

"Is that why you came over, Chip? To give me your blessing to go after your ex-wife? Or is it because your guilt is killing you?"

"Maybe a little of both." Chip got off the couch and walked out, leaving Josh to brood.

He didn't need Chip's permission, not now that Hannah was single. From the first time they'd met he'd been infatuated. It'd been at a football game between their rival high schools. She'd been standing slightly apart from a group of chattering girls, secretly reading a paperback hidden in her purse. Josh had peeked over her shoulder, wondering what was so good that it had drawn her away from the party. She'd caught him curiously trying to read the text.

"I'm almost at the end and am dying to know who did it," she'd said. "I'm pretty sure it's the crazy, jealous wife but inevitably it's always someone who makes a two-second appearance in the story. I hate when writers do that . . . it's lame. Anyway, I had to know."

Josh had started to ask her the name of the book but Chip had slipped in, working his drunken magic. Back then the booze had made him funny and charming. Later, just a buffoon. In any event, Chip got Hannah and Josh couldn't bear to watch him ruin both their lives. So he went away to college in Southern California and was recruited by the army.

Ironic that he and Hannah were back in the same town again, this time both available. But sadly, Hannah wouldn't be any better off with a cripple than she'd been with a drunk. He couldn't even take her on a winter stroll without hobbling, let alone rescue her from Sawtooth like he'd done all those years ago.

He didn't want to be . . . couldn't be . . . the guy who sat helpless while his woman clung to a cliff.

So it didn't change anything that Hannah was free and that there'd been a time when he'd wanted her more than anything in the world. It didn't change the fact that he was only half a man and wasn't sure he'd ever be a whole one again.

CHAPTER THREE

"Is something wrong?" Hannah quickly climbed the stairs of her front porch, anxious at finding the police chief there. Though Glory Junction was a relatively safe town, recently there'd been a few burglaries.

"Not a thing." Colt stood up from Hannah's swing. "Lancer said you bought a tree and didn't have a way to get it home."

She didn't have a rack on her car and planned to borrow Deb's truck.

"You brought me my Christmas tree?" She beamed at him, relieved and enormously touched.

"It's a sorry-looking thing."

She could see that he'd propped it against the side of the porch. "What are you talking about? It's a silvertip."

"I don't know what it's called but it looks like one of those Charlie Brown trees. Scrawny as hell."

"You come back when I have it all decorated. Then tell me it's a Charlie Brown tree. What do I owe you for the favor?"

"Cup of coffee if you got one."

"I can make that happen," she said, and unlocked the door.

He hefted the tree in behind her. "The place looks good." The last time he'd been here hospice had set up a bed for Sabine in the middle of the parlor.

She dumped her purse on the phone table and told him where to place the tree.

"Lancer said you had your own stand."

"I'll get it." It was in the mudroom, where she'd wiped out the dust and cobwebs from last year.

Within a few minutes he had the tree in the stand and centered inside the bay window.

"Looks great." She smiled. "That was a nice ceremony they had today at the VFW for Josh."

"Yep. He enjoyed it."

She fixed him with a look. "Liar."

"He was hurting some. But he appreciated the sentiment."

"Come in the kitchen."

She found coffee in the cupboard and made a pot. Colt leaned against the doorjamb, letting his shoulders fill the entryway.

"It's weird not having Sabine in this kitchen," he said. "She used to make that damned fine pecan pie."

Hannah let out a sigh. "I sure do miss her."

"You going home to Nugget for Christmas?"

"Not this year. My parents are taking a cruise." She laughed because it was so out of character for them. Their last vacation had been a doll convention — her mother was an avid collector — in Irving, Texas. After Sabine died, Hannah had pleaded with them to do something special for the holidays. In part, she wasn't ready for a big family gathering. "My brother's going to his wife's family. Same with my sister."

"Why don't you come to our place? There's always room at the table."

"I'll probably do something with Deborah but thanks for the invite, Colt."

"I just thought it would be nice for Josh to have some of his friends around."

Apparently, Colt hadn't gotten the memo that she wasn't one of Josh's friends.

"You're coming to the party, right?" Every year the Garners held a Christmas Eve open house at their adventure company for the community. They had it catered and hired a DJ.

"I wouldn't miss it."

The coffee was done and she poured him a cup. "You want cream and sugar?"

"Nah, black is good." He sat at the breakfast table and she joined him.

"Are you off duty?"

"Yeah, but I'm on call. I plan to have supper over at my folks' house. You're welcome to come too."

Colt was full of invitations today. She couldn't remember him being this attentive. "I'm gonna pass. I'm looking forward to a nice quiet night in." Perhaps tomorrow she'd have a few people over to trim the tree.

"The store doing okay?"

"Mm-hmm, this is our busy season."

"I hear that crazy clothing woman, Delaney Scott, is selling things in your store now."

Hannah gave him a questioning look. She'd found Delaney to be quite sane, delightful, actually. "She's not crazy."

Colt shrugged, and drained the rest of his coffee "She's not exactly cut out for mountain life and should get herself back to LA."

Hannah supposed there was a story there but before she could ask, Colt rose and took his mug to the sink.

"I better get going."

"Thanks for bringing my tree." She walked him to the door.

"No problem. Pop in at Garner Adventure Monday and say hi to Josh, wouldya?"

"Sure. Is he working there now?" She couldn't imagine him leading tours, not with his leg.

"Yeah. He's starting on Monday so say hello." He pulled her in for a hug before striding down her walkway to the street, where his police cruiser sat, leaving her to wonder what that was all about.

On Sunday, much to her surprise, Josh came in the store. At first he didn't say much, just limped around, thumbing through the postcards and T-shirts. Eventually he tested a new glider she was selling, moving it back and forth. She suspected he just needed a place to sit and rest his bad leg.

"Where did you get this?"

"A Nugget furniture maker named Colin Burke makes them."

"Nice," he grunted. "I need a gift for my mom."

Ah, that explained why he was here. "For Christmas?"

"Secret Santa. All the employees at Garner Adventure draw names. I got Mary. I'm out of time and you're the only game in town."

She sat on the glider with him and ignored his gruffness. He made it sound like he'd rather be anywhere else but here, which she suspected he would. "Does your leg hurt?"

"A little," he said, and she thought that probably meant a lot. "It's sore right now from therapy and the cold . . . it hurts worse in the cold." It had snowed overnight and they continued to get a few scattered flurries.

"You go to therapy on Sundays?" That surprised her.

"Mondays, Wednesdays, and Fridays. I do it myself the rest of the time."

She wondered if he was supposed to do that. "In the gym?" Garner Adventure had a nice workout space with a rock-climbing wall and a lot of fancy equipment.

"Yep," he said, and paused for a second, looking out the window. "It must be hard for you, watching them work on that gazebo."

The statement threw her, it was so blunt — and out of the blue. "Not really, why would you think that?"

"Wasn't Chip the love of your life?"

"No. What, you think I'm still pining for him? I'm not. But for the record, he left me." She didn't want Josh thinking that she'd dumped her husband for having a drinking problem. She'd stuck to her vows. *In sickness and in health.* "And it wasn't like I didn't try to make it work."

"I'd never suggest that you didn't."

"But you were thinking it. You've always thought it. But I have news for you, Josh, Chip struggled with alcoholism long before he met me."

"I know that."

She jerked her head, startled. "Why didn't you say something?"

"Like what? Your boyfriend's a lush? I thought it was pretty evident."

It had been obvious that Chip liked to drink. To someone as naïve as Hannah she thought it was a choice, not an addiction, and that he could quit whenever he wanted. By the time she realized her mistake it'd been too late. They'd already gotten married — and she'd loved him. Boy, had she loved him.

There had been so many wonderful things about Chip. Like the time she'd gone to a gift show with Sabine in San Francisco for five days and he'd surprised her by refinishing the hardwood floor in their kitchen to seamlessly replicate a picture she'd cut out of a magazine. Or the time he sold his prized Yamaha dirt bike to take them on a romantic trip to Hawaii because she had never been and had always wanted to go. It was those sweet, considerate moments that had kept her clinging to the hope that he'd sober up and they'd have a life that was good.

"Whatever you might think, I tried to get him help. I tried every damned day." Her eyes misted and she got up so he wouldn't see.

He followed her, propping his hip against the counter for support. "I never blamed you for his drinking, Hannah. Chip had a sickness. I tried to get him to stop too and had about as much luck as you."

"I guess Val is special." Hannah knew the comment was petty but couldn't help feeling like a failure. It hurt knowing that Chip loved Val so much that he got sober for her but couldn't do it for Hannah.

The door jangled and the UPS man carried in two big boxes. "Morning, Hannah. Where do you want 'em?"

She pointed to a spot on the counter and thanked him as he left.

Once he was out the door, Josh continued, "I wasn't judging you, Hannah. I just simply wanted to know," he hesitated again, "if you were still in love with him."

She got the sense that there was more to

the question than he was letting on but didn't press. "I'm not in love with him. In all honesty, the love was gone before he left." She surprised even herself by admitting that.

Grabbing a box cutter, she opened one of the cartons, lifted out a stack of sweaters, and scrunched up her face. "This isn't what I ordered."

Josh chuckled. "Glad to hear it because they're ugly."

"Hideous is more like it." And she laughed too, especially at the 3-D Christmas tree one with blinking lights. There was another one that played "O Tannenbaum." She couldn't imagine walking around with her chest singing.

Hannah came out from around the counter, rushed to the door, and looked down the street for the UPS man. Gone. "Shoot. I would've sent them back."

"There has to be like twenty in these boxes," Josh noted, going through the pile she'd taken out and holding up the particularly heinous ones.

"Well, I'm definitely not keeping 'em." She refolded the ones Josh had looked at and packed them back into the box. "I'll take them to UPS on my way home."

"Maybe I should give one of them to my

mom." He started to grab a sweater from the box but she stopped him.

"Uh-uh. No way would I let you do that to Mary. I know what she wants."

"Oh yeah, what's that?" He bobbed that strong jaw of his at her and once again Hannah realized how good-looking he was. Too bad he was so often sour. She preferred him like this.

She made her way across the shop to the woolens and showed him an angora cowl. "This."

He followed her, holding on to a few of the racks to steady himself. Josh filled her roomy store like a giant.

Peeking at the price, he said, "We're only supposed to spend twenty bucks."

"Well, you're in luck. This just went on sale." She walked back to the counter, found a Sharpie pen, scribbled out the old price, and wrote "$20." "Would you look at that?"

He shook his head but his lips curved up. The first smile she'd seen from him. "Don't do that, Hannah. I've got to play by the rules. I'll get her the scarf . . . or whatever it is . . . for Christmas at the real price. But help me find a twenty-dollar secret Santa gift. Maybe a snow globe or something."

"Ick, not a snow globe." She pawed through a large basket by the socks. "What about these slippers?"

Josh rocked his hand back and forth. "Meh. How about a Glory Junction cap?"

"Uh, yeah, that would certainly be original," she said. "If you want something with 'Glory Junction' on it, how about a phone case?" She walked over to a rack and passed him one of her new acquisitions from a company that did custom orders. "We just got them in. Yay or nay?" she asked, ready to move on to the next item.

"Yay," he said, and handed her back the case, letting his warm hand linger in hers. "I'll take one too. Show my hometown spirit."

"Okay." She gazed up at him and he was staring at her mouth, his head slightly tilted like he wanted to kiss her. It would've been an audacious thing to do right there in the middle of the store, where anyone could see. Furthermore, he didn't even like her, so the notion that he wanted to kiss her had to be Hannah's imagination. Crazy as it was, though, she wanted to feel Josh Garner's lips on hers.

The door chimed. "Do you by chance carry batteries?" someone asked.

"Nope, try the hardware store," Josh said, and they continued to stand there frozen until they heard the customer's retreating footsteps and the door click closed. Josh snapped his head up and backed away.

"I'll get the other case for you." Just like him, she gathered some distance and went over to the rack to grab another one. "Want me to wrap your mom's?"

He checked his watch, seemed torn, but finally said, "Sure."

She swiped two pretty holiday gift bags from the card aisle and some tissue paper from behind the counter, and packaged up the phone case and the cowl.

"Colt says you're starting work tomorrow at Garner Adventure."

"I'm answering phones," he said, his voice terse.

"Nothing wrong with that. I'm sure as your leg continues to heal you'll take on more."

His eyes fell to the counter and he didn't say anything.

She walked around the cash register and handed him the bags. "There you go."

"Thanks."

He made his way out of the store and she could tell he was struggling for a normal gait. Despite his churlish behavior, it made her chest squeeze into a tight ball watching him try so hard.

■ ■ ■ ■

Josh didn't know why he'd listened to TJ. He could've just as easily driven to Reno to get the goddamn secret Santa gift for his mom. Hell, he probably would've found something at the hardware store or even the supermarket — a cooking gadget from the baking aisle.

But TJ had insisted, practically pushing him into the store. Josh would've looked foolish protesting, since Glorious Gifts was the obvious place to buy a present. And if he wanted to be honest with himself, he'd been curious. About the store . . . about Hannah. In Sabine's time, Glorious Gifts had been a cluttered hodgepodge. Now, it was organized . . . and high-end. It reminded him of one of those shops you'd see in downtown Aspen or Vail, filled with expensive clothing and furnishings, all artfully displayed.

Going in there, though, had been a bad idea. If the battery guy hadn't walked in, he would've kissed Hannah sure as day and she would've let him. He'd seen it in her face. Longing. Why, was beyond him. What would she want with a cripple, especially one who'd never been that nice to her? Even today, he'd been up in her grill, asking hyperpersonal questions. *"You still in love with Chip?"* It was none of his damn business.

"You get it?" TJ asked as Josh shambled into Garner Adventure.

Josh held up his bags. "You finish your work?" Dumb question since his brother, a workaholic, was never finished.

"Just have to return a few calls. How's Hannah?"

"She's at Glorious Gifts, why don't you go over there and ask her?"

TJ brushed off the sarcasm, sneaking a look at Josh's leg. "You up for lunch at Old Glory?"

"Sure. Why not?"

"Let me just close out the computer."

To kill time, Josh watched out the window as the noon crowd bustled into the restaurants and shops along Main Street. Hannah exited her store and headed down the sidewalk, Josh presumed to grab lunch. He noted that she was a single ray of sunshine in an otherwise dreary day.

CHAPTER FOUR

On Tuesday, Hannah called Deb after work to see if she wanted to meet at Old Glory for a drink but got voice mail. Probably for the best. Hannah's house could use some TLC. She'd gotten down the Christmas decorations from the attic and they were strewn across her living room. Yet, the tree was still bare.

As usual, Hannah stashed the cash box in the safe — she'd have to do a bank run tomorrow morning — grabbed her purse and coat, and locked up. On her way to her car she noticed that Garner Adventure still had its lights on, which was unusual. By five, the place cleared out like a bank. The Garners did offer night tours but they typically met off-site for those adventures.

All the shopkeepers looked out for one another so Hannah searched inside the windows to make sure everything was okay. It was a big space but she could see all the way to the back, to the gym and simulated rock wall. There, she spied a lone figure working with leg weights.

She didn't know what got into her but she rang the after-hours bell. Josh wouldn't appreciate her interrupting his workout, yet she couldn't seem to help herself. A few seconds later he answered the door in nothing but a pair of exercise shorts, his chest and six-pack glistening with sweat, his arms popping with veins.

"I just wanted to make sure everything was all right," she said. "The lights were on and I got worried."

"All good here," he said, and started to close the door.

"What are you doing?" she blurted, and immediately realized the stupidity of that question. "I mean, can I come in?" Hannah couldn't remember ever being this pushy.

He moved out of the way, ushered her in, and shut the door. Then, without another word, he walked back to the gym and resumed his exercises. Some kind of leg curl on an exercise ball. She sat on one of the weight benches and watched him. Josh seemed to know what he was doing and she wondered if these were calisthenics he'd done as an Army Ranger or exercises recommended by his physical therapist.

Next he did deadlifts with dumbbells. Each time he did one his face scrunched up in pain.

"Maybe you shouldn't do those," she said, and realized her mistake as soon as the words left her mouth, because he glared at her.

"If you want to stay, no talking." He didn't say it meanly, just made it clear that this took all his concentration and that he didn't appreciate any meddling.

When he completed the deadlifts, he moved on to the leg press machine. By now his entire body was drenched, and with each press, both legs trembled like a newborn foal's. She couldn't tell how much weight he was using, though it looked like a lot.

Again, she wanted to say that maybe he was doing too much, but didn't dare.

He switched to a series of seated calf raises. At this point she really wanted him to stop. The agony etched on his face told her he'd gone beyond breaking. Still, he kept pushing himself until she thought he would pass out. Finally, he finished with a set of barbell hip thrusts and just lay on the exercise bench, breathing hard, perspiration running into his eyes.

If it hadn't seemed so excruciating for him, Hannah would've appreciated watching a man as fit and ripped as Josh perform feats of strength. For a person who had been gravely injured, Josh was in better shape than anyone she knew. Just watching him, she was struck with the certainty that he wasn't someone you wanted to physically tangle with. Even with his leg, he'd win.

"Did you need something, Hannah?" Josh had apparently caught his breath.

"I was just curious. That's an extremely rigorous workout you do."

"In the Seventy-Fifth Ranger Regiment that would've been considered a Mommy and Me class."

"I think you're being ridiculously hard on yourself," she said. "Most men wish they had the kind of strength and stamina you have."

"I'm not most men."

"No, you're not. Most men wouldn't have overcome the injuries from that explosion or have saved as many men as you did. The way I see it you were one of the lucky ones." She got up to go when his arm reached out to grab her.

"No one knows better than I do how lucky I am. I was there, Hannah, with a front-row seat to the carnage. The things I saw . . . There's nothing wrong with me trying to get back to who I was before the bomb."

"As long as you don't kill yourself doing it."

"Ever hear the proverb: 'What doesn't kill you makes you stronger'?" He sat up.

"I suppose it's good to have goals as long as you don't reinjure yourself."

"I've gotta goal." His lips slid up into a conspiratorial grin. "I want to ski Royal Slope on Christmas Day."

Hannah looked at him like he was nuts.

Even experienced skiers found the steep, narrow trail with its hairpin turns challenging. Only the Garners dared to bomb down the slope like madmen every Christmas. And every year, the town formed a pool on which Garner would wind up in the hospital. For someone recovering from a significant leg injury, skiing Royal Slope would be suicidal.

"Now I know you're certifiable," she said, and folded her arms over her chest.

"I used to do it."

"And I thought you were certifiable back then but for God's sake, Josh, give your leg at least a year to heal first. What you're talking about . . . it's sheer lunacy."

"I don't have to go down fast. I just have to make it to the bottom." He said it like that somehow made it more rational.

"Does your family know about this?"

He didn't say anything, just took her in from head to toe, and a hot wave of sexual awareness passed between them.

"Josh?"

"It'll be their Christmas surprise." He got up and although he tried to hide it, she could see that he'd put all his weight on his good leg. "I've got to shower." He started for a small locker room at the other end of the gym.

Hannah walked past him on her way to the door.

"You don't want to wait for me?" he called over his shoulder.

"What for?"

"I'll buy you dinner," he said.

His offer surprised her. Although there had been a noticeable softening in his attitude toward her, she still got the sense that something about her bugged him. But there had been that moment in the shop when she could've sworn he wanted to kiss her. So in spite of her reservations, she got comfortable in the seating area near the reception desk and waited.

Josh rested his forehead against the shower tiles. The cold felt good against his skin. Everything else felt out of control. Being home, his leg, Hannah. He didn't know why he'd let her stay for his workout or why he asked her to dinner, just that he couldn't seem to stop himself. She'd always been his weakness. That's why he'd left in the first place.

After the shower he found an ice pack and strapped it to his leg, then dressed in everything but his pants. He wrapped a towel around his waist and walked out to join Hannah on the sectional. The towel didn't cover all his scars and he wondered if he was consciously trying to test her.

"You mind if I ice my leg for a while before we eat?"

"Not at all," she said, and took in the knee wrap that went more than halfway down his leg and at the lines that crisscrossed his fibula like a spiderweb. "Does it hurt?"

"Nah, I just need to ice it after I work it like that." He continued to watch her but she didn't seem repulsed. "How was your day . . . the store?"

"It was all right. Busy." One of the ice packs slid off his knee and she carefully put it back in place.

He gazed outside the window at Main Street. "Glory Junction has changed a lot. It's more crowded with lots of fancy homes in the hills. I guess that's good for your business."

"Yep, and yours. There was a building boom after you left. A lot of folks telecommute to their jobs in the Bay Area and Sacramento."

"I guess they need infrastructure. That new chain supermarket still blows me away. It has a freaking wine-tasting counter and a chocolate fountain."

She smiled, those pale gray eyes of hers twinkling. Josh had missed those eyes. "When it first opened I swore I'd never go in there. But between you and me, I love it. It's so big and clean and everything's so fresh. Sometimes I spend an hour in there just walking around, looking at the food displays."

Grocery stores didn't excite him that much but he liked listening to her . . . looking at her. She sparkled, always had.

"Where do you want to eat?" she asked.

"TJ likes that new Indian place. I've never been, have you? Or if you want we can go to Old Glory and grab pub food. I'm open to anything."

"Old Glory is fine."

"Let me just put on my pants." He grinned because it was a funny thing to say.

"Shouldn't you keep the ice on for longer?"

Yeah. But it was getting too intimate sitting alone with her. "I'll do more when I get home but I'm starved."

In the locker room he put on a pair of clean jeans and his boots, and returned to the front area. "You ready to go?"

They walked the half block to the bar and he found them a table in the back. It was still early for the rowdy crowd — at least you could hear yourself talk. He ordered Hannah iced tea, got himself a Sierra Nevada on tap, and a basket of peanuts to share. A couple of guys from the fire department came over to say hi and stood around a little while shooting the breeze.

The guys left when a pool table became available, and he turned to Hannah. "You know what you want?"

"A burger and fries."

He flagged a waitress over and ordered for both of them. She started to say something but Chip and a woman — Josh figured it was Valerie — wandered in and took a table not far away from theirs.

Hannah whispered, "I don't think it's a good idea for him to be in here, do you?"

"Nope. But it's not your problem. Are you uncomfortable?"

"Not like that," she said. "I'm having déjà vu of when he used to insist that we come in here and the whole time my stomach was tied in knots over whether he'd drink too much and make a fool of himself. One time he passed out and three guys had to help me get him home. Another time he got into a fight over karaoke and then proceeded to sit on the stage and sing through everyone else's song."

Josh laughed, then abruptly stopped, "I know it's not funny. Sorry."

"I just think it's weird that Val would allow him to come in here. It's too much temptation for a recovering alcoholic."

He shrugged. "Maybe it's part of the program, like a trial or something."

"Maybe. But you're right, it's not my problem." She leaned across the table. "Let's talk about you."

"I'm boring."

"Boring? You're a war hero. If the rumors are true, you saved seven men."

"Yeah, I don't want to talk about that."

She looked suddenly contrite. "I'm sorry; I didn't mean to bring up anything sensitive. I guess I don't know what's taboo in a situation like this."

"Nothing to be sorry about. I just don't want to spend our time discussing war." It was shitty dinner conversation.

"I understand," she said. "We'll talk about something else. You're up-to-date on me but how about you? Were you . . . are you . . . involved with anyone special?"

"In Afghanistan?" He laughed. "Nah. Not a place particularly conducive for picking up women. What about you . . . dating?"

"After Sabine got sick I didn't have time. And now . . . it's nice with it just being me."

Just her. Single. Man, how he'd wanted her before he'd left. Afraid that the whole world would see how much, he'd gone out of his way to ignore her.

"I can understand that," he said, because in a lot of ways she was recuperating from a trauma too. It couldn't have been easy taking care of an alcoholic . . . or an aunt with cancer.

The waitress brought their food and for a while they sat silently eating; every now and again he'd sneak a peek at her. Looking at her had always done him in. It wasn't just her physical appearance but a quiet dignity that had drawn him to her. She'd hung out with a giggly group of boy-crazy girls. And while Hannah had outshone them in beauty, she'd always been reserved and serious like Josh. Two people standing outside their raucous clique, while Chip had been the center of it.

"How's it being back at Garner Adventure?" she asked.

"Awesome." His voice dripped with sarcasm, which he knew sounded ungrateful. He was fortunate to have a family business to fall back on. Hell, he was fortunate to be alive. "I booked a skydiving trip for a group of seniors . . . you know, bucket list."

"Skydiving, huh?" She feigned horror. "People actually find jumping out of a plane entertaining?"

Josh couldn't help but laugh. "Don't knock it until you've tried it."

"Never."

He laughed again. "You still afraid of heights?"

"I don't know." She took a bite of her burger. "I never go higher than the second floor of my Victorian."

"Hannah, I've got a newsflash for you. These mountains we live in are nearly six thousand feet in elevation."

"As long as I'm on flat ground I'm okay."

He knew they were both remembering hiking up Sawtooth in their junior year of high school. She'd gotten stuck midway up the mountain and he'd been the one to get her down. Not Chip, who'd complained that he had sunstroke. Josh had always suspected that it was really a monster hangover.

"I can't move."

"Yes you can." Josh held his hand out to

her. She grabbed it, looked down, and promptly turned green.

"I think I'm afraid of heights."

"Good time to figure that out, Baldwin." Thank God they'd taken the easier saddle trail instead of the rough scramble, which he preferred. But they were still a hell of a ways up.

"Go ahead and be an ass. But how am I supposed to get down?" She looked scared enough to throw up.

"I'm gonna help you. You trust me?"

She didn't hesitate. "I do, even if you are the spawn of Satan."

But she wasn't looking at him like he was the spawn of Satan. No, she was looking at him in a way he'd never seen her look at Chip, like he was her hero. Like he was everything.

They finished their meal and Josh paid the bill. A tight fist of panic welled up inside him as he walked Hannah the short distance to her car. If he wasn't careful, he'd wind up kissing her and wouldn't be able to stop.

"Thank you for dinner," she said, and stood there for a few seconds . . . waiting, considering. "I'm having a few people over tomorrow evening to help me trim my tree. Would you like to come? It'll be casual. Deb and Foster . . . you remember Foster, right?"

Josh had gone to high school with him.

"Yeah, I remember Foster. How is he?"

"Good. He owns Sweet Stems now and is killing it. All the resorts have him do their floral arrangements."

"That's great." He zipped up his jacket, thinking they'd probably get more snow overnight. "I'll try to stop by; it'll depend on my leg."

"I hope you make it," she said. They were so close the toes of their shoes touched.

He opened her car door, jammed his hands in his pockets, and watched her get in the driver's seat. It killed him to do it but he watched her drive away, then limped across the street to his own truck.

CHAPTER FIVE

Oh boy, what had she gotten herself into?

Hannah got as far as her driveway and called Deb. "We're trimming my tree tomorrow tonight. I need you to bring that cheeseball dip you make."

"No can do," Deb said, and it didn't sound like she was alone. "I've got a thing."

"What thing?"

She heard Deb moving on the other end. In a muffled voice she said, "I'm with Jeremy."

"Jeremy who?"

"A guy I met. He's only here for another day, skiing."

"I invited Josh." Hannah puffed out a breath.

"Josh Garner?"

Like what other Josh could she possibly mean? "Yes, and I told him you and Foster were coming."

"So? Just tell him I had something else to

do. What's the big deal?"

"He'll think . . . I don't know what he'll think. But he hardly even knows Foster."

"Oh my God, you like him. You like Josh Garner." Hannah could practically see Deb jumping up and down. "And why should I be surprised? You had a thing for him in high school, don't say you didn't. I can't wait for asshole Chip to find out. He was always jealous of you two."

"Stop being ridiculous. He's a friend . . . was the best man at my wedding. He doesn't even like me."

"Make up your mind. Either you two are friends or he doesn't like you. Which one is it?"

Hannah wasn't sure. Up until recently she would've said the latter but he'd taken her to dinner and they'd had a lovely evening. "We're frenemies."

"Straight guys don't do frenemies," Deb said. "Look, if you're not into him why are you worried about me not being there?"

"I'm not. Fine, don't come. Have fun with Gerome and I'll see you tomorrow."

"It's Jeremy and you better have something good to report."

As soon as Deb hung up, Hannah called Foster.

"Sweet Stems," he answered. "How can

we make your day beautiful?"

Gag. "You can make my day beautiful by coming over tomorrow night to help trim my tree."

"Is that code for sex? Because as gorgeous as you are, Hannah, I swing the other way."

"I invited Josh Garner and told him you and Deb were coming. Deb can't make it."

"Well neither can I, honey. I've got a wedding this weekend."

"So, you've got plenty of time."

"They're spending three thousand dollars on flowers, which is a lot of arrangements to get done in four days. Kiss Josh for me. Gotta go."

Hannah felt a surge of anxiety. It would look like a setup. Josh coming over to an empty house. Just him and Hannah, like she was trying to seduce him. *Oh God.*

Once in high school they'd wound up seeing a movie alone. It was supposed to be a double date, except Chip and Josh's girl had canceled at the last minute. After that night Josh had grown even more distant. Hannah remembered the incident like it was yesterday.

"Hey, Garner, where's Robin?" she asked as they wound their way around the velvet ropes into the small theater's old-time lobby.

"She has a history final tomorrow . . . had to cram."

"Chip has the flu," she said. "It's going around."

Josh's brows winged up, dubiously. "I guess it's just you and me then."

Wordlessly, they headed to the snack-bar line.

"Don't sound so thrilled."

"Believe me, Baldwin, I'm not." He stepped up to pay for Hannah's popcorn.

"What are you doing? I can afford my own food."

He got a second bucket for himself and she noticed his bulging biceps. Hard to miss in the white T-shirt that stretched across his chest. Most of the boys she knew, including Chip, were still filling out. Josh, though, looked like a man. Tall and built and rugged. She supposed the muscles came with his job, working for his family's business. Lord knew he showed them off every chance he got.

"Jesus, Baldwin, don't get so touchy. You can buy the sodas." But while she fumbled through her wallet he grew impatient and got those, too.

They went inside the theater, which had already gone dark. He managed to hold his popcorn and soda in one arm and palm her elbow so she wouldn't trip. His hand was big, strong, and steady. And although it was just her sleeve he touched, a little quiver went through her.

"Right here," he whispered, and grabbed them two seats and helped her get situated with the snacks.

At one point in the show their legs rubbed together and Hannah's belly dipped. They sat thigh to thigh for the rest of the movie, making it hard to concentrate. At the end, when he moved his leg away, she instantly felt bereft of his body next to hers, like she'd lost something integral.

"You staying at your aunt Sabine's tonight?" he asked as they made their way to the parking lot.

She nodded and he said, "I'll follow you home."

"Uh . . . No . . ."

"Why not? Chip would want me to."

"It's okay, I'm going to his house first," she lied, having no intention of seeing Chip that night. But for some indiscernible reason she felt guilty about spending time with Josh, even though they hadn't done anything wrong.

"Fine with me, Baldwin." He turned on his heels and spent the summer snubbing her.

Josh nearly turned back three times on Wednesday before pulling up in front of Sabine's house . . . Hannah's now. His leg hurt like a bitch and for a guy who was trying to stay detached he was failing miserably. Dinner the previous night and now Hannah's home. He was setting himself up. Hannah might want him — as teens there had always been this sexual charge between them — but he was pretty damned sure not in the same way Josh wanted her. He took solace in the knowledge that he wouldn't be the only guest at this gathering.

Her street hadn't been plowed yet and Josh cautiously got out of the truck, afraid that his bum leg wouldn't hold him if he slipped in the snow. He made his way to the passenger side and grabbed the bottle of wine he'd bought at the market.

It had been a long time since he'd been here. Sabine's two-story Victorian had always reminded him of something out of a storybook. He took her walkway slowly, struggled to climb the stairs, then took a few minutes to collect himself.

It was too cold for loitering so he finally rang the doorbell. Hannah answered in a pair of skinny velvet pants and a sweater that clung to her breasts. Yep, this had been a colossally bad idea. He'd bug out as soon as possible.

"Come in," she said, and he handed her

the bottle of wine.

She told him to make himself comfortable in the parlor while she put the wine in the kitchen. A fire was blazing and a couple of platters of munchies had been laid out on the coffee table. Stockings hung on the mantel and garland swung from the staircase banister. Everything was designer perfect. Except for the tree, which looked anemic.

"What's wrong with your tree?" he called to her.

"Nothing." She came into the living room, holding two mugs. "I heated some cider. But if you'd prefer I could open the wine."

"Nah, this is great." He wondered if because of Chip she had a thing against drinking. "Where is everyone?"

She let out an audible sigh. "Foster had to work. He's got a wedding this weekend. And Deb . . . she made other plans. It looks like it's just us."

"That's too bad." *And dangerous.*

"Dig in." She pointed to the food. "I probably went overboard."

"I didn't have dinner so probably not." Right then his stomach growled and she grinned.

They both sat on the sofa and Josh filled a small plate with what his mother would've called finger foods. Pretty, but not very filling.

"That's one skinny-ass tree," he said. Next to it were crates of decorations.

"Colt said the same thing. What's with you Garners? You've never seen a silvertip before?"

"We always go with a Douglas fir . . . nice and fat."

"The ornaments get hidden in those trees. When this one is decorated you'll see how elegant it is."

Josh wasn't really into elegant but whatever. "The house looks good. Did you move in after you and Chip broke up?" They'd purchased a place together right before the wedding. It'd been a small cottage but Josh remembered Hannah being over the moon about it.

She nodded. "Chip bought me out. It turned out to be for the best because after the diagnosis Sabine needed me. There were a lot of bad memories in that cottage anyway."

Chip had always been a happy drunk but Josh couldn't help but wonder whether he'd become abusive in the later phase of his alcoholism. Josh knew it wasn't uncommon.

"He wasn't physical with you, was he?"

"Chip? Never."

She got up, sorted through a box of clear lights, and began wrapping them around the tree. Josh joined her, taking over on the top half.

"I had a thing for you in high school, you know?" The words slipped out before he could call them back.

"What are you talking about?" She laughed. "You couldn't stand the sight of me."

"I couldn't stand the sight of you with Chip. But he had dibs and I abided by the guy code . . . never poach on your best friend's girlfriend."

Her face registered surprise. "I think you're reinventing history. You thought I was a wimp. Remember how angry you were with Chip for spending too much time with me on the bunny slopes instead of flying down the double black diamond trails with you?"

"You misinterpreted anger for something entirely different."

"Like what?" She stopped what she was doing and crossed her arms over her chest, which only helped accentuate those perfect breasts of hers.

"Jealousy. Look, I'm only telling you this because I know I wasn't always nice to you and I feel crappy about it."

"No, you weren't. But I assumed you were irritated that I took Chip away from you and all the fun things you both liked to do . . . and later that I wasn't a good wife."

"He was a bad husband. You? You were . . ." *the world.* He shrugged. "Water under the bridge but I wanted to explain . . . apologize."

At first she didn't say anything, just stooped down to grab another ornament and hung it on a branch. "It explains something I always wondered about."

"What's that?" Josh finished with the lights.

"In the beginning there seemed to be electricity between us, like you were interested. Then, suddenly . . . ice cold. Because of Chip." She let out a sigh. "You ever wonder what would've happened if you and I got together?"

Every goddamned day. "We were kids and I went to war."

Something flickered across her face. Disappointment, maybe. It happened too fast for him to tell for sure. But the urge to kiss her was as constant as the throbbing in his leg.

"Can you put the Santa on top? I can't reach."

"Sure." He took the ornament from her

and placed it on the tallest branch when his knee gave out. Grabbing the wall, he stopped himself from toppling over.

"My God, are you okay?" Hannah ran to his side and wrapped her arm around his waist as if she could hold him up. He probably had ninety pounds on her.

"I'm fine," he said, humiliated, and made it to the couch.

"Should I get a heating pad or some ice?"

"It'll be okay in a minute." He wanted her to stop making a big deal out of it. Until a few minutes ago he'd actually felt like a normal man again. He didn't need to be reminded that he was disabled. His leg had done that all on its own.

"How about a throw blanket?"

"Hannah, enough!" he barked, and she flinched.

"I was just trying to help."

"I don't need help. But I do need to get home." He pushed off of the couch, putting all his weight on his left leg, hoping like hell he didn't fall on his face. "Thanks for having me over . . . for feeding me."

"Let me get you to your —"

"I'm good." He raised his voice louder than he should have. But he didn't need her assistance getting to his goddamn truck.

He didn't need anyone's help with anything.

CHAPTER SIX

Thursday morning, Hannah was in the middle of taping up the boxes of ugly sweaters she'd forgotten to ship back when Chip came in the store.

"Can I help you with something?" she asked.

"You don't need to be so formal, Hannah, I just came in to say hi and see how you're doing. It's been awhile."

"Not that long. I saw you in Old Glory the other night with Valerie."

"We were getting dinner. Even though I don't drink they have the best tri-tip in town."

"I was just surprised you'd go into a bar . . . Valerie must be an amazing influence." It was bitchy, but she enjoyed getting a little dig in.

"If there is anyone you should be angry with it's me, not Val."

Strangely enough she wasn't angry with

211

either of them. Just at herself. Not a day had gone by when she didn't blame herself for not being stronger or tougher or giving Chip ultimatums but everything she'd read said you couldn't negotiate with an alcoholic.

"We're all good, Chip."

"I heard Josh was over at your place last night."

Ah, the real reason he was here. Apparently Deb hadn't wasted time spreading the word. She liked to stick it to Chip every chance she got. Deb's loyalty was commendable but Hannah preferred to keep her personal business out of the public eye. For years, Chip's drunken antics had made them a household name in Glory Junction. Just for once, she'd like to maintain a low profile.

"I had a little holiday get-together," she said, because to point out that it was none of his damn business would only make it seem like she had something to hide.

Chip snorted. "He didn't even wait a full twenty-four hours."

"For what?" She had no idea what he was talking about.

"I gave him permission to pursue you, since he's wanted to get in your pants ever since our sophomore year in high school."

If Josh hadn't made his confession the previous night, Hannah would've laughed in Chip's face. Instead, she let him have it. "You gave him permission? Who are you to give anyone permission to see me?"

"Your ex-husband."

" 'Ex' being the operative word."

"Don't go getting yourself all worked up. It's a guy thing. Men don't sleep with their best friend's exes. No matter what."

Chip had dumped her, yet he got to decide whether one of his friends could see her. What kind of crap was that?

"Look," she said. "I'd really appreciate it if you'd stay out of my business. You at least owe me that."

"I was just trying to help."

"Don't! Worry about your own love life." *And staying sober.*

"If it's any consolation, it pissed Josh off too."

She wasn't going to have this conversation with him. Her private life was just that — private. Let Chip think that she and Josh were hot for each other when the last thing Hannah needed in her life was another man who didn't want her help. Just offering to get Josh a heating pad for his leg had set him off. He might not be a drunk, but war had left him embittered and she didn't have the wherewithal to take on another damaged soul.

Chip made a surrender motion with his palms. "Fine."

"Well, now that we have that all settled you can go."

"You kicking me out?"

"Yep." She wrestled the vacuum cleaner out of a tiny utility closet.

"Okay, I can take a hint."

She didn't bother to explain that telling someone to get out of her store was way more than a hint. Next time, she'd just club him over the head with a baseball bat.

As soon as Chip was out the door, she locked up and went next door.

"Hi, Hannah. How are you, honey?" Mary looked up from the front desk of Garner Adventure.

"I'm good. Is Josh around?"

"He's in my office. Go on back."

"Thanks, Mary."

Hannah made her way down the long, narrow hallway and found Josh sitting at his mother's desk, tossing a Nerf ball into a toy net hung over the closet door. Good to know he was keeping busy.

He looked up and she said, "I'm not a piece of meat."

"Okay." He studied her face. "Am I supposed to know what you're talking about?"

"Chip said he gave you permission to date me and he has a hell of a nerve . . . and you . . . you . . . I expected more of you."

"Hannah" — he motioned at a spare chair — "take a seat, would you?" She plopped down. "Now explain to me what exactly I did wrong."

"You and Chip conspired behind my back."

"Conspired?" He raised his brows. "Chip came over, said he knew I had a thing for you in high school, and told me that he and I would be good if I made a play for you. That was it."

"And you don't see anything wrong with that?"

"We had some words over it." She waited but he didn't elaborate.

"Well, I'm not a tradable commodity."

"I never thought you were."

"But Chip did."

Josh let out a long-suffering sigh. "It's a guy thing, Hannah. It was more about our friendship than it was about you. In any event, high school was a long time ago. We're adults now . . . and" — he glanced down at his leg — "you don't have to worry about me going after you. I couldn't catch you if I tried."

"Josh, why does everything boil down to physical prowess for you? For instance, this conditioning thing you're doing to ski Royal Slope. No one is going to be impressed with you doing something idiotic." And it was idiotic. His leg could barely hold him up. And while she didn't have the heart to come right out and say it, there was no way in hell he would make it down. "So why are you putting yourself through this?"

"My family is in the extreme sports and adventure business, Hannah, so yeah, it's about physical prowess. I need to know what I'm capable of doing and what's off the table. Until then I'm a desk jockey, which really doesn't work for me." He looked at her, hard.

"You couldn't do one of the less challenging trails?"

"I could, but if I want to start leading tours again I have to be at the top of my game." Clearly tired of justifying himself, Josh shook his head as if to say: *If I want to freaking climb and ski Denali, it's my business.* "I don't know how we got off track. This was about Chip, remember? About me chasing after you. Like I said before, you've got nothing to worry about, since I'm incapable of catching you."

She returned his same steely stare. "Perhaps you hadn't noticed, Josh, I'm not running." She got out of the chair and went back to her store.

Josh got out of the shower when he heard the door buzzer go off. He tugged on an extra pair of gym shorts and padded out to the reception area to see who was hitting the damn bell over and over again. Hannah.

He turned the dead bolt and let her in. "Back so soon?"

She gaped at his bare chest for a few seconds then blurted, "This Royal Slope scheme of yours is . . . ridiculous. But if it's what you want I plan to help you."

Sure, skiing Royal was borderline insanity. But Rangers did crazy-ass shit all the time. It's what made them stronger and it built endurance. He didn't have to barrel down the mountain. The goal was to get to the bottom in one piece. More important, though, was how the hell did she expect to help him? Hannah wasn't exactly coach material — or a physical therapist, for that matter.

"Could you stop staring at my chest? I'm not a piece of meat." He enjoyed throwing her own words back at her.

She swiftly averted her eyes. "Sorry."

"I need to ice. Are you staying or going?"

"Staying . . . I guess."

He deadlocked the door and went back into the locker room to put on a shirt and get the ice packs. When he returned, Hannah sat on the sectional, typing something on her phone.

"Whaddya doing?"

"My banking."

"Your banking?" He cocked a brow.

"Store stuff." She put the phone back in her purse.

"You over your visit from Chip this morning?"

"I'm done talking about that. I let him whip me up, which I shouldn't have. Besides, I think your involvement was minimal."

"Oh yeah? Why's that?"

"Because you're too honorable to treat a woman like she's a baseball trading card." She glanced at his leg. "Does it hurt? Or shouldn't I ask because you'll get irritable . . . like you did last night?"

He had to stifle a grin. Hannah had spine and he liked a woman with spine. And, he'd been a crybaby. "Not too bad today. What's this sudden revelation that I need help with my workouts? I don't, by the way, but you're welcome to hang out." He suspected she worried that he'd overexert himself and die.

218

"I know you don't. But . . . I need to feel a part of something . . . something bigger than me."

He tilted his head, at a loss. "Why's that?"

"Just humor me, please." She turned away, staring off into the distance.

That's when he got it. "I'm not Chip, Hannah, not even close. I don't need an intervention."

"Of course you're not and of course you don't. I would never compare you two. But you've been through a trauma and you're trying to rebuild, which I totally respect, and it would mean a lot to me to be part of your support system."

Like Val to Chip; she was paying it forward, as Josh liked to say. "Suit yourself. I'm here Tuesdays, Thursdays, and on the weekends." He was tired of talking about himself. "You finish your tree?"

"I'll get to it."

"I should've at least helped you clean up."

"There wasn't a lot to do, Josh, don't worry about it."

He imagined she was used to doing everything on her own. In the time he'd been gone . . . there were so many things he didn't know about her. "Besides the store and taking care of Sabine, what have you been doing all these years?"

"I got a marketing degree at University of Nevada, Reno. Since then, I've taken a few night classes at the local junior college in merchandising, which I love. If the town keeps growing, I'm thinking about expanding the store."

"Ambitious," he said. "Would you carry the same kind of stuff?"

"I'd like to branch out into more furniture, like the glider you admired the other day, and carry a larger variety of local wares. Ceramics, weavings, leather goods, clothing, those sort of items."

"I don't know much about retail but you seem to be good at it." He watched her face brighten from the compliment and something in his chest tightened.

"Thank you." She reached over and touched his injured leg where the skin had turned bright red from the ice. Even through the numbness he could feel the warmth of her hand. "Is it alleviating the pain?"

He couldn't help himself and laid his hand over hers. "Yep."

That's when, despite all the warning bells going off in his head, he leaned in to kiss her. Feather soft at first. Then deeper — going from melding lips to tangling tongues. She felt and tasted amazing, like warmth and comfort and hot sex. And he wanted more. Just a little bit, he promised himself. But when he pushed her against the back of the couch it was no-holds-barred and he devoured her like a man who'd waited a lifetime for this. She banded her arms around his neck, pressed against him until he felt every sexy curve of her body, and made sweet whimpering noises that drove him crazy.

The alarm signals continued, reaching a piercing level that screamed, "Knock it off, now!" Yet, instead of stopping, he changed the angle of the kiss, letting his hands roam over her sweater. She inched under his shirt and he hissed in a breath when her small hands grazed the skin right above the elastic waist of his shorts.

Somewhere in the distance he heard the *snick* of a lock and a door open and close. Hannah must've heard it too because they pulled apart at the same time and looked up to see TJ standing near them, grinning like a loon.

"I forgot my charger," he said, and didn't even have the good grace to go in his office and get it. No, he just continued to loiter with that big sloppy smile on his face.

Josh planned to wipe it off with his fist.

CHAPTER SEVEN

The next morning, Hannah hit the Morning Glory Diner early, hoping to run into Josh during his coffee run. After the Kiss Interruptus, he'd gotten a little squirrelly and she just wanted to clear the air. No harm, no foul, but secretly she'd been living off that kiss for the last thirteen hours. Reliving it in her head and in her sleep a hundred times over. Because, boy, could Josh make her feel things that questioned her sanity. Her life had become so much easier post-Chip. It would be masochistic of her to get romantically involved with yet another man who had more baggage than a Greyhound bus. Being his "sponsor" until the Royal Slope run would be emotional enough.

Still, she couldn't stop thinking about him.

A few minutes later he came in the coffee shop, his limp a little less noticeable. Or maybe there were too many other things about him to look at. The broad width of his shoulders, the way his jeans hugged the best butt she'd ever seen, and his I'm-your-man-in-a-crisis attitude.

He spotted her while standing at the bakery counter, giving his order, and came over to her booth. "This seat taken?"

"It's all yours." She nudged her head at the pink box he carried. "What's with all the pastries?"

"They're for our meeting this morning."

"What kind of meeting?"

He took off his jacket and sat across from her, sipping from his to-go cup. He had on a long-sleeved crewneck that hugged his rock-hard chest and clung to his biceps. Hannah had never been that into muscular men but on Josh . . . oh Lordy.

"We have one every week and they're boring as hell," he said. "Mostly TJ running his mouth, loving the sound of his own voice."

She laughed, then asked pointedly, "You want to talk about what happened last night?"

"Not really. Do we have to?" He leaned back in the red plastic banquette, his lips curving up in a naughty grin.

"I'll just put it out there, then. I'm enjoying this newfound friendship of ours. And I very much enjoyed the kiss." *A total under-*

statement.

"Okay, good to know."

She leaned across the table. "Did TJ say anything?"

"TJ's a loser. He's so hard up he has to live vicariously through others."

Hannah suppressed a laugh, knowing that for all the Garner brothers' ribbing they loved one another like crazy.

"So we're good, right?"

"Couldn't be better," he said. "You still want to come to my workouts?"

"Of course. Why wouldn't I? We're friends."

"Yep. Friends," he said, enunciating "friends" and getting to his feet.

"You're leaving so soon?" *Could he be any more uncommunicative?*

"Got to get these to the meeting." He motioned to the box and put his jacket back on.

"You want to come over tonight and help me finish the tree? I could make us dinner."

"I've got physical therapy in Reno." He paused as if he was about to use his appointment as an excuse to say no. "Yeah, all right."

Why did she get the feeling he didn't really want to come over?

"I very much enjoyed the kiss," Josh mimicked as he drove back to Glory Junction from physical therapy. That kiss had been off the freaking hook, the gold standard of kisses, the one all others should be compared against. He'd be willing to bet his Soldier's Medal that it was the best damned kiss she'd ever had. Josh's leg was screwed up but his mouth worked just fine.

And *"I'm enjoying this newfound friendship of ours"* made them sound like girls at a freaking tea party. Ah, what was he complaining about? It was all for the best. No sense starting something he wasn't in a position to finish.

Yet here he was, going back to her house, wondering whether he should pick up flowers.

Sweet Stems was at the end of Main Street, near the police department, so Josh headed in that direction, convincing himself that it was just plain mannerly to bring something to dinner. It didn't mean anything.

There was a parking spot right in front of the floral shop and he snatched it before noticing Colt standing on the sidewalk talking on his phone. The last thing he needed was an interrogation from his brother. Colt had always been a nosy SOB and by now, news of Josh and Hannah's kiss had likely spread through the Garner clan like a tornado. Too late to leave, though; Colt had already gotten off the phone and was looking straight at him.

Josh carefully got out of the driver's seat and nudged his head in greeting.

"You here to see me?" Colt asked.

"Nope. I wanted to say hi to Foster."

"Foster? I didn't realize you two were such good friends."

"We went to high school together and I didn't get to catch up with him at the VFW breakfast."

Colt smirked. "You went to high school with just about everyone in this town. Who are *you* getting flowers for?"

Josh answered by flipping Colt the bird and hobbled off to the floral shop. But Colt followed him.

"Now I know they're not for Mom," Colt said with that shit-eating grin that never failed to annoy the rest of the Garners.

"Get lost, big brother, and mind your own business."

Colt ignored him and raced ahead of Josh into Sweet Stems like he owned the place.

"Hey, Foster, my brother needs flowers, something real expensive."

Foster came to the counter in an apron, covered in pine needles. "You need them now? Because I closed an hour ago." He eyed Josh. "Who are they for?"

Colt leaned up against the counter, his arms folded over his chest, one eyebrow raised. "Don't keep us in suspense, Josh."

Josh turned around and made his way to the door. "I'll just get 'em at the supermarket."

"Come back here, Joshua Garner," Foster called. "Don't you dare buy any janky supermarket flowers. Tell me what you want."

"Flowers." Josh raised his hands in the air. "Just freaking flowers."

Foster let out an exasperated huff. "If I knew who they were for I'd have a better idea what kind of flowers."

Josh looked at Colt and back at Foster. "How about roses?"

"Cliché," Foster trilled, then waved him off. "Come back in fifteen minutes and I'll make you something fabulous. Something that won't embarrass both of us."

That worked for Josh. He let Colt cajole him into hanging out in the police department, where his brother could harangue

227

him some more.

"You go to therapy and your vet session today?"

It wasn't enough to get pricked and prodded, Josh was also expected to talk about how nearly losing a leg felt, emotionally. He could sum it up in two words: It sucked. "Yep."

"How did that go?" Colt asked as they walked to his office. The room was small and Colt cleared some paperwork from a chair and told Josh to take a seat. He sat at his chief's desk, leaned back in the chair, and folded his arms behind his head. "You didn't answer me, how did the group session go?"

"Fine."

"You sleeping better?"

"I'm sleeping fine, Colt." He'd just spent the last two hours having his leg bent six ways to Sunday and his brain shrink-wrapped; the last thing he needed was the third degree.

"We just care about you, Josh." Colt got up and paced the office. "Mom's worried you're pushing yourself too hard."

"The exercise is good for my leg. I stop when it's too much."

Colt sat back down. "Don't go overboard.

Take the time you need to heal. There's no rush."

"I know." Josh fidgeted with the zipper on his jacket.

"You having dinner over at Hannah's?" When Josh didn't answer, Colt said, "Mom will want to know how many settings to put down."

Which was total bullshit. Dinner at the Garners was a casual affair. Basically, whoever showed up when the food was ready ate.

Josh glanced at his watch. "Would you look at the time. Well, Colt, I'm really glad we could have this talk together."

Colt walked him out and Foster was waiting at the counter in the shop.

"I'll be right back." He headed to the back of the store and returned a few minutes later holding a big red-and-white arrangement. Josh didn't know a lot about flowers but it looked impressive.

"Nice," Josh said, and Foster let out an impatient sound, like "nice" didn't cover it. "What do I owe you?"

Foster rattled off a figure that seemed pretty reasonable to Josh, considering how involved the arrangement was. He pulled out his wallet and handed Foster his credit card.

"Hannah says you're killing it in this place."

"Yep. It's certainly not the same skank shop you probably remember."

Josh didn't remember it at all. Come to think of it, he'd never been in the store before today. Still, he nodded just to appease Foster, who briskly finished their transaction. Josh took the floral arrangement to his truck and secured it in the backseat.

When he got to Hannah's house, he grabbed the flowers and took his time getting to her porch and up the stairs in the snow. She opened the door before he could ring the bell.

"Hi."

He flashed a sheepish smile. "Sorry, I'm early."

"I'm glad. Come in, it's cold out." She pointed to the flowers. "They're gorgeous, are they for me?"

"Yeah." He'd been too busy looking at her and had forgotten that he was holding the vase. "I think you just need to add a little water."

She took the vase and Josh tugged off his gloves and jacket. He hung everything on a coatrack in the foyer and followed Hannah to the kitchen. She filled the vase from the tap and set it on the counter.

"Thank you, Josh. I don't think anyone has ever given me flowers this beautiful."

He wondered if she was just saying that. In all the time they were together, Chip must've gotten her flowers. "You can thank Foster."

"But it was your idea, right?"

"Yup." He went over to the stove. "What do you have going here? It smells good."

"French onion soup, roast, potatoes, and salad."

"You managed to do all that after work?"

"I made the soup a couple of weeks ago and froze it. The roast and potatoes are nothing and the salad is from a bag."

It seemed like a lot of work to Josh. She'd also changed into some kind of sweater dress that skimmed her body like a wetsuit. He was having a hard time taking his eyes off her.

"How was your therapy?" she asked as she moved around the kitchen, checking the temperature of the roast and adding rosemary to the potatoes.

The table had already been set with fancy dishes. Hannah definitely had a flair for doing things up. All Josh had to do was look at her store.

"All right," he said.

"Does it hurt?"

Like a bitch. "Not too bad. The key is to get motion back and work the muscles."

"I guess your Ranger training prepared you for a rigorous rehab."

"That's probably true. The course was sixty-one days of hell. I made it through that, I can surely make it through this." He smiled because she was a rapt audience. "You need any help?"

"Could you open the wine, please?" She gestured at a bottle of red on the counter.

"I wondered if you drank . . . after Chip . . ."

"He was the one with the problem, not me."

"I know that." He took her hand in his. It was delicate and warm and he probably held on too long. "Sometimes certain things cause bad associations. I wasn't sure whether that applied to liquor."

"Chip's drink of choice was Jim Beam. Just the smell of whiskey sends me over the edge," she acknowledged. "Wine, on the other hand, wasn't his thing."

He couldn't help himself and brushed her cheek with the pad of his thumb. "You're really beautiful, Hannah." She looked skeptical, like he was feeding her a line. "Come on, men have to tell you that all the time."

She shrugged. "I'm just trying to get used to the fact that you don't hate me."

He couldn't hate her if he tried. But he needed to knock off the flirting.

"Foster's flower shop looks good." He uncorked the bottle of red, giving it a few minutes to breathe before pouring.

"It does, doesn't it?" She bent over to take the roast out of the oven. Josh used the opportunity to stare at her ass and felt himself grow hard — something that hadn't happened in awhile. He didn't know whether to cry with relief that it was working or from frustration that he wouldn't be using it tonight. To make himself useful he poured the wine and carried the salad bowl to the table.

She bent over a few more times to move things around in the oven, clearly trying to kill him.

"Everything looks great." He grabbed the serving tray of sliced roast off the counter.

"Sit and relax." She took the platter from him.

"Hannah, I can carry a plate." It came out rougher than he intended but he could handle walking and holding a lightweight dish at the same time.

"I have no doubt that you can cart a lot more than a serving tray." She eyed his biceps. "But I'm the host and I take my serving responsibilities seriously."

It was a good save, he'd give her that.

"I'm already impressed." She might act casual about it, but a lot of work had been put into this dinner and he appreciated it.

"Did you eat those MREs overseas?"

He nodded. "And more recently hospital food."

"So the bar's pretty low?" Hannah started to take her place at the table and Josh pulled the chair out for her.

"Nah, I've been eating my mom's food and she's a great cook."

Hannah served him salad, meat, and potatoes. "Dig in and tell me if my meal lives up to Mary's."

He took bites of everything and, yeah, Hannah knew her kitchen stuff. "It's fantastic," he said with a full mouth, and kept plowing through the huge portions she'd served him.

And damned if she didn't glow like downtown Glory Junction's holiday lights. It made him wonder if Chip had been stingy with the compliments. But look at her: She ran her own business, made delicious home-cooked meals, decorated like a pro, and was smart, gorgeous, and sweet to boot. If she were his, he'd praise her until the cows came home. Longer.

"I made Sabine's pecan pie for dessert," she said.

"Seriously? When did you have time for that?"

"I made a couple of pie shells a few days ago and froze them. The filling is nothing. You'll have to take a piece for Colt. He loves her pie."

Josh choked back a laugh. No way would Sabine's pecan pie ever make it past Josh's mouth. Colt could get his own damn pie. "Sure."

Even though he was stuffed, he took seconds on the roast and potatoes. Every time he took a bite Hannah beamed. "Am I making a pig of myself?"

She laughed. "Not at all. I like to cook and it's nice to have someone enjoy it."

"You can cook for me anytime," he said. "Let me ask you something, you still read mysteries?"

"My gosh, you remember that." Of course he did. She was reading one the first time he'd met her.

"I'm addicted to them," she continued, ticking off the title of the latest book she was reading before glancing at his empty plate. "You ready for pie or should we finish the tree first?"

"Tree first. I couldn't eat another bite."

She got up and started clearing away the dishes. Josh tried to help but she wouldn't let him.

"You can help with KP next time, but first-time dinner guests get a pass."

He at least leaned against the counter while she quickly rinsed their plates and stuck them in the dishwasher. Within a short time she had the leftovers packed away and the table wiped clean.

She grabbed the bottle of wine. "Let's go in the living room."

He brought both their glasses, put them down on the coffee table, and topped them off. Next to the tree were the same boxes of ornaments from the other night.

"You want me to keep hanging them?" he asked, nudging his head at the decorations.

"That would be great. I have some ribbon I brought home from the store in the mud-room."

He watched her walk away, getting lost in the sway of her hips, then started hanging small wooden birdhouses off the tree's surprisingly sturdy branches, trying to keep his mind off all the things he wanted to do with Hannah. None of them included decorating a Christmas tree. Although he had to say, he liked it, especially being in this house with her, just the two of them.

"Pretty, right?" Hannah was back, holding up spools of ribbon.

He shrugged. "What's it for?"

"To wind around the tree. You'll see, when it's done it'll look amazing."

"Okay, you're the boss. I like your dress, by the way."

She turned a nice shade of pink. "It's warm and this house is drafty."

"If you're cold I could make a fire." He eyed a small stack of wood by her hearth.

"That's okay, I'll warm up decorating." She brushed by him, her breasts grazing his back, as she wound the ribbon around the tree.

He wanted to be the one to warm her up, take her in his arms, and hold her. The other night had been a mere dress rehearsal for all the things he wanted to do.

"What are you thinking about?" Hannah rehung one of the birdhouse ornaments he'd haphazardly put on the same branch as another one. "You drifted off for a second there, didn't you?"

"You really want to know what I was thinking?" She smelled like rosemary and evergreen and a perfume so familiar . . . His desire throbbed. "I was thinking that my kisses are a hell of a lot better than nice."

"Who said they weren't?"

"You did." He moved toward her, took her around the waist, pulled her into his chest, and smothered her mouth with his.

She melted against him. "Mm. For sure . . . better than nice."

"They sure the hell are." A wall, he needed a wall to lean on so he backed her up against one and caged her in, using his forearms to hold him up. She twined her arms around his neck, never letting go of his mouth. He angled her head back so he could take the kiss deeper, using his tongue to explore. She tasted like wine and her body felt soft and warm snugged against him.

His own body reacted instantly. With his arms holding him up, he couldn't touch her, which he desperately wanted to do.

"Could we move this to a bedroom?" he asked, hoping he wasn't being too presumptuous.

"It's upstairs."

She was worried he wouldn't make it up, which ordinarily would've pissed him off — he was a Ranger, for God's sake — but right now he was of a single mind. Getting her to the closest bed possible. It was impulsive, like yesterday's kiss, and irresponsible, but he'd dreamed about being with Hannah for fifteen years. No way could he hold back now, even if it was just a taste.

"There's the couch," she said, sounding breathless — and hot.

Although he liked her enthusiasm, the sofa was too small for what he had in mind. He kissed her neck, scraped her earlobe with his teeth, and whispered, "Upstairs."

She led the way and he did his best to climb each step, using his left leg as a stabilizer. It hurt something fierce but the reward waiting for him at the top spurred him on. He made it up the steep climb — apparently they didn't have building codes in the Victorian era — in record time and trailed Hannah into what must've been her bedroom. A lot of ruffles, lace, and throw pillows.

She quickly closed the drapes while he sat on the edge of the bed, catching a second wind. When she was finished shrouding the room in darkness, she lit a few candles on the dresser and nightstand. Nice touch, but he would've preferred a few lights so he could see her better. She started fussing with the pillows and he pulled her down on the bed.

"Don't worry about 'em." He touched her breasts through her dress and continued to kiss her. She felt so good that he forgot about his leg and moved over her, pressing himself against her. "This okay?"

"Mm" was her only answer as she rocked into him. "Is it okay for you?"

If it got any better he'd embarrass himself. "Perfect."

"I want to take off my dress. It's getting warm."

Hell yeah. He rolled off her and watched her inch the dress up and drag it over her head. *Holy shit!*

His hands went to her flat stomach as his eyes took her in. She had on a push-up bra overflowing with her breasts, and a strip of lace that passed for panties. "Jesus, Hannah. You take my breath away, baby."

Her hands inched up his Henley. Josh stripped it off, desperate to feel his bare skin against hers. She touched his shoulders and chest . . . his scars from the shrapnel . . . so reverently that he sucked in a breath, afraid he wouldn't be able to hold on. Josh took her hands and held them above her head as he trailed kisses down her neck, over her breasts, and lower to her belly.

"Oh yes," she said, grinding into him.

"You smell good." He continued to explore her body with his mouth while he pulled down the cups of her bra and fondled her breasts.

Hannah sat up, reached behind her, unhooked the clasp, and let the bra slither off. It was the sexiest thing he'd ever seen. He weighed each breast in his hands and sucked on her puckered pink nipples.

Her moans drove him crazy. He worked his way down, finding her wet and so sensitive to his touch that she nearly came off the bed when he put his mouth on her panties.

"Josh, I want you . . . please."

He slid the scrap of lace down her legs and stroked her until she begged. She watched, heavy-lidded, as he undid his belt and shucked off his pants and shorts . . . and came to a screeching halt.

"I didn't bring condoms," he said, and felt woefully unprepared.

"We're okay. I'm on birth control." She pulled him down on top of her.

"You sure?" he asked. She ground into him in response and he spread her legs, entering her tight sheath a little at a time. "This all right?"

"It's been awhile."

He moved slowly inside of her, letting her grow accustomed to him while trying to find the sweet spot.

"Oh," she moaned, and he knew he'd found it.

She put her feet flat on the bed and he was able to go deeper and pump harder.

"Jesus, you feel so good." Josh lifted her bottom and quickened the pace.

"Josh, Josh," she called, and he could feel her clutch around him and shudder.

It wasn't long before he followed, throwing his head back, exploding inside her, and collapsing. Afraid of crushing her, Josh rolled to his side and gathered her up in his arms. He'd never been the cuddling type but he wanted to hold Hannah, even sleep with her for a while.

"How you doing?"

"I think the best I've ever been." She ran her hands down his back. "How about you?"

"Ditto." He kissed her. "Want to take a nap?" His eyes were already closing as he said it.

Sometime around ten they woke up. Hannah went downstairs and brought up pie to eat in bed. Then they made love into the next day.

The sex exceeded his fantasies. And the intimacy they'd shared went far beyond anything he'd ever imagined. She made him forget Nevay-deh, the explosion, and the things he could no longer do that he once took for granted.

But in the light of day, he knew he'd see

things more clearly. Maybe it was just a hookup for Hannah, which was fine. If she needed more from him, though, he didn't have it to give. Since losing most of the use of his leg, he'd become a stranger to himself. Until he figured out his new place in the world, he couldn't fit into hers.

CHAPTER EIGHT

Hannah woke a little disoriented, rolled to her side, and looked at the clock. It was only eight. Plenty of time to get to the shop. She wanted a few minutes to lie there and savor the night, the best she'd ever had.

"Good morning." Josh stood over the bed fully dressed.

"You're leaving?"

"I've got to go home, shower, change, and get to Garner Adventure."

She swung her legs over the bed, realized she was naked, and pulled the blanket up to her chest. Silly, since Josh had seen every inch of her. "Let me make you coffee."

"Don't worry about it. Stay in bed a little longer." He bent down, kissed the top of her head, and started for the door. She noticed his limp was worse than usual and she blamed herself.

"Your leg is hurting you, isn't it? Maybe we shouldn't have . . . you know . . . it was probably too much exertion."

He shrank back like she'd just slugged him. "I've got to go."

"Josh," she called to him, grabbing her sweater dress off the floor and quickly tugging it over her head as she went after him down the hallway. "Wait."

She got to the top of the staircase and looked for him, wondering if he'd already left. "Josh?"

There was a noise and she spotted him sprawled halfway down the stairs.

"My God, you fell."

"I'm fine." He grabbed the railing and tried to hoist himself up only to fall back down again.

"Here, let me help."

"I don't need any help!"

She felt her face pale and wondered whether she should call Colt. Josh grabbed the railing again and she stuck out her hand to assist him.

"Use me for support," she said. He responded by staring daggers at her.

This time, he managed to get to his feet and balanced precariously on his good leg. She feared he'd fall again but he clutched the railing and somehow hopped safely to the landing. He was breathing hard and sweating, perspiration dotting his forehead.

"I'm all right," he said, and stood there for a second, trying to compose himself. "I slipped, no big deal."

She wanted to drive him home but didn't dare suggest it, knowing that he'd go ballistic. "Let me make you that coffee at least."

"Thanks, but I don't have time."

Hannah came down to where he was standing and stared up into his turbulent blue eyes and saw a world of emotion there, shame being right on top. "I've taken a tumble or two down those stairs myself."

He fixed her with a look that said she was full of crap and practically stumbled to the front door. "Thanks for last night."

Thanks for last night? Wow.

He was just mortified by the fall, she told herself. Unfortunately, Josh wasn't the type to accept the things he couldn't change, like a leg that flamed out on him. And she'd already gone that route with Chip, who hadn't been able to accept that he had a drinking problem. An epically bad recipe for a relationship.

A few minutes later she heard his truck start and drive away. She went back upstairs and took a hot shower, dressed, and changed the bedding. The torture of smelling Josh on her sheets was too much. Ever since he came wandering into her shop something had sparked between them. Perhaps *rekindled* was a better way of putting it because truth be told Josh Garner had always heated her blood, even back when she'd thought he despised her.

She made it to the store at exactly ten, too late to get coffee at the Morning Glory. Even though Deb sometimes relieved her long enough to grab a cup, Hannah hoped she didn't drop by today. One look at Hannah's face and Deb would see everything. She was intuitive like that.

"Hey." Win came in, sipping his disgusting green protein shake.

"Who you hiding from today?"

"No one. Just wanted to smell the goodness." He stood over one of the candles, sniffing. "At work I'm stuck snorting my dad's dirty socks."

"He walks around without shoes?"

"It's his new thing, climbing the rock wall in just his socks. Don't ask me why. There's no research that says it's beneficial. Clearly, it's not safe. But this is the guy who decided to water-ski last summer in the nude."

Hannah scrunched up her nose. It's not that Gray Garner wasn't fit. Middle-aged women in Glory Junction threw themselves at him even though he was married. But water-skiing in the nude? Ew.

"What do you have here?" Win pointed at the cartons by the door.

The ugly sweaters she kept forgetting to return. Soon it would be too late. "I was supposed to take them to the UPS office. The company sent me the wrong order."

"Want me to load them into your car?"

"You wouldn't mind?" He was still bundled up in his down jacket.

"Not for you." He winked. The man really did think he was God's gift to women and unfortunately he was, despite an ego the size of the Pacific Ocean.

"Just put them in my backseat, the trunk's full. And could I coax you into getting me a cup of coffee, too?"

"What's in it for me?" he teased.

"I'll give you one of those candles for Garner Adventure."

"TJ would probably fire me. *Candles are against company policy,*" he mimicked. "You want cream and sugar?"

"Just cream, please. And thank you, Win." She handed him her car keys and a five-dollar bill for the coffee.

"Your money's no good here." He shoved the keys in his jacket pocket, hefted the boxes with ease, and imitated Arnold Schwarzenegger in *The Terminator:* "I'll be back."

Good to his word, he returned to the store less than fifteen minutes later with a steaming cup of coffee. She took a fortifying sip but still wasn't ready to greet the day. If she had her druthers, she'd go home and stick her head under the covers, even though she should be walking on air after the best sex of her life.

"What's bugging you?" Win asked, pulling her from her thoughts.

"Nothing."

"I heard through the grapevine that Josh didn't come home last night. You wouldn't happen to know where he was?" His lips curved up into a knowing smile.

"Don't you need to get to work?"

"I'm taking a couple of extreme skiers up in thirty. We're meeting next door, so no rush. Back to Josh . . . you don't know where he was?"

"Shut up, Win."

He smirked and gave her a big hug. "And here I always thought it would be us. But Josh is a good second placer."

She didn't want to talk about Josh, especially with his brother. "What about Colt and TJ?"

"They're tied for last. You'd be better off with a mutant." She muttered that they were too competitive and refolded a couple of

T-shirts. Outside, it looked like Chip and a few friends were painting the gazebo. Risky, since there was more snow in the forecast.

Win saw her watching the men work. "I always thought you and Chip were mismatched."

"Really? Why?" Other than Chip had liked to drink himself into oblivion and she hadn't.

"I don't know. I just always thought you and Josh would be better suited. You're both goal-oriented people, whereas Chip is more laid back."

It was true. Even when Chip wasn't drunk, which was basically never, he didn't have a lot of aspirations in the world. Ski, fish, inner-tube down the Glory River, those were the bulk of his ambitions.

"How did you ever come up with Josh and me? Back then we didn't even like each other."

"Exactly." Win bobbed his head, smirking. "You two were so hot for each other you fought like cats and dogs. We all used to laugh, it was so comical. And then it wasn't, you know what I mean?"

Because she'd married an alcoholic and Josh went off to war. Yeah, not so comical.

"I better get going." He gave her a quick peck on the cheek. "I'm rooting for the two of you this time around."

Based on the way Josh had acted this morning, they didn't have a skosh of a chance. She didn't need another man who wouldn't accept her help. This time around she wanted someone who'd be a true partner in every sense of the word, not someone so prideful he refused to take a hand when he was down.

That's why, later that day, she interrupted Josh's workout by ringing the bell at Garner Adventure. When he answered the door she brushed him aside and pushed her way in.

"Let's get last night out of the way so we can move on." She plopped down on the sectional. "What's the deal with us, Josh?"

He let out a long sigh and said, "Yeah, I guess we should probably talk about that." He sat next to her and gently lifted her chin. His eyes were filled with what looked like regret. "Last night was truly amazing, Hannah. The best thing that's happened to me in a long time. I'm sorry I ruined it by making the morning suck." Another long breath. "I'm frustrated and angry at having to learn to live with a body that's foreign to me and I lose it sometimes. It's not an excuse for acting like a dick. I shouldn't have taken my fall out on you."

No, it wasn't and no, he shouldn't have.

But she could understand how difficult that explosion had made his life. "Okay, we'll just forget about . . . the whole thing."

"Ah, Hannah, I'll never be able to pretend our night together didn't happen. But I don't have anything to offer you. If not for my family's business I wouldn't even have a job. I'm not good boyfriend material, not like this."

"What is this?"

"Disabled." He had trouble even saying the word. "I don't know if my leg will ever be normal again. And after everything you've been through you deserve a whole man."

She winced. "You are whole. You were hurt in an explosion, you have a limp, yet you're acting like you only have a few months to live."

He stared openly at his leg. "I have to figure out my future, Hannah. All my life I've been active. It's how I made my living. How I served my country. Now I have to figure out where I go from here."

"Silly of me to think I could have been part of that."

He didn't say anything, just sat there still and painfully quiet. She pulled away, feeling sad and alone.

"You're right, I do deserve more," she

said. "I deserve a man who leans on me as much as I lean on him and someone who doesn't measure his worth as you do — as if anything short of physical perfection is shameful. Maybe we can work on our friendship because it seems to me that you can use a good friend, one who can remind you that you're more than an imperfect body."

She waited for him to say something encouraging — *"I want to be more than friends, Hannah"* — and when he didn't and just nodded, she wanted to be angry. But how could she be? He'd at least been honest. For someone as alpha as Josh to have admitted that he felt like only half a man . . . well, it was sad . . . and warped. It made her want him to see that he was every bit a whole man and then some.

But that couldn't include sex. They had too much history, too much chemistry, too much respect for each other. Not to mention that that kind of intimacy, without a true partnership to go with it, would tear her apart.

"I can't sleep with you again," she said. "I don't do casual."

Again he nodded, making her turn away out of disappointment that he'd acquiesced so easily.

What could she do? Nothing but put on her best face, including a phony smile, and point at the back of the room to the exercise equipment. "Get to work," she said.

CHAPTER NINE

On a cold, clear day, Josh attended Chip
and Val's wedding and cut out of the reception early to meet Hannah at Garner Adventure. He suspected that she wanted to pump
him for details on the Big Event, like women
were inclined to do.

"Are you sure this is a good idea?" Hannah sat on the weight bench, watching him
strap his feet into the Nordic-Track ski
machine for the first time. "I've never seen
you use this before."

How she'd become his exercise muse he'd
never know. But her being in the room kept
his mind off the pain and motivated him to
try harder.

"Compared to the weights and the dead
lifts, this should be easy," he told her. "I
just want to see how long and hard I can
go."

"For Royal Slope?"

"Yeah." He glided back and forth. Slow at

first, picking up the pace when he felt certain that the movement wouldn't make his leg buckle. So far, so good. Then again when he did it for real, he wouldn't have a machine holding him up.

"Did you tell your physical therapist about this?"

"Yup." About the NordicTrack, not Royal Slope. "He thought it was a good idea. I do the treadmill with him."

That appeared to reassure her.

"You seem to be holding up pretty well." She studied his bearing as he glided faster and faster.

"It doesn't hurt as much. In the beginning the pain was excruciating." The admission caught him off guard. For months, he'd tried to hide the constant throbbing from his family — or anyone who asked. "In a few months I meet with my doctors to determine whether I need another surgery."

She started to say something but stopped herself.

"What?"

"Don't you think you should see them before doing something crazy like skiing Royal Slope?"

It was a fair question in light of the fact that he'd tumbled down her stairs. Still, he'd never advance without drive. Ranger

School had tested his capabilities until he thought he would break. Perseverance — and admittedly a little bit of crazy — helped him power through. Same would hold true with Royal Slope. It was a mind-set, he told himself.

"Not really," Josh responded.

"Was the wedding nice?" she asked.

He laughed to himself. Yeah, he'd called that one right. "It was nice enough, pretty much your run-of-the-mill wedding, except for being alcohol-free."

"What did they serve instead?"

"Cider, grape juice, soft drinks." He slid her a sideways glance as he took the tension up a notch on the machine. "You really want to talk about Chip's wedding?"

She grinned. "Come on, it's only natural for me to be curious. How did Val look?"

"Fine, I guess. She didn't hold a candle to you." Maybe he shouldn't have said that but it was the God's honest truth. "I can say that because we're friends, right?"

"Absolutely." She smiled but it didn't quite reach her eyes.

"Colt said your folks are on a cruise for Christmas."

"They didn't want to go but I insisted. I didn't want to do the big family thing without Sabine. Not this year."

He nodded. Hannah's parents were nice people. They wouldn't have left her alone unless she'd wanted them to. "You could come to our house for Christmas breakfast."

"I've got plans with Deb and Foster. But I'll come to watch you ski."

"Okay." Although he wasn't too sure how he felt about it. It would be embarrassing if he wrecked. But given how invested she'd become in his progress how could he say no?

He glanced at the clock, realizing he'd done twenty minutes without breaking a sweat. A good sign.

He did another twenty and got off the machine. "Are we gonna do dinner again tonight?"

She deliberated as if to say no, but he pressed, even though it was probably sending mixed messages. But she shouldn't be alone on the night of her ex's wedding. At least that's what he told himself. "Come on. We can go up to one of the resorts." They were spread out enough that they could easily avoid Chip's reception.

She seemed surprised. "Those restaurants are expensive and we'd need reservations."

"Nah," he said. "All I have to do is drop Garner Adventure's name and we're golden."

"I'll pay for my own."

"The hell you will." He might not be able to carry her up a flight of stairs in Sabine's Victorian but he damned well could pay for her meal. "You've fed me twice at your house, my treat."

"I should go home and change."

"What are you talking about? You look great." She had on tight jeans tucked into a pair of knee-high boots and a low-cut clingy sweater.

Hannah stood up and stared in the wall-to-wall gym mirrors. "Too casual, don't you think?"

Josh laughed. The resort restaurants were nicer than anything in Glory Junction proper but at the end of the day they still served a bunch of skiers in fleece and après-ski moon boots. Not exactly high fashion, though he suspected a lot of it was designer and cost a pretty penny.

"You'll fit right in," he said, though she'd also stand out for being the most beautiful woman in the room. "Let me shower and ice, and we'll head out."

And that's how it went in the following days. Hannah would meet him in the gym at Garner Adventure, sit with him while he worked his leg, and afterward they'd have dinner. There were no discussions about relationships and no sleeping together. But they talked about the future: Hannah's shop plans and how Josh wanted to take a bigger role in his family's business, including leading expeditions and adventure tours.

She never suggested that his plans were pie in the sky or it was too soon to be thinking on such a grand level with his leg only marginally functional. Maybe she was just humoring him but he appreciated her tacit approval just the same. His family was more cautious.

"Don't rush things, son. All in good time. Your body and soul need time to heal . . . and you need to find your center again." His father had always been one of those hippie-dippy metaphysical types.

His brothers, especially TJ, were more practical. There would be no assignments until he could prove himself. He was planning on doing just that Christmas Day on Royal Slope. A few times he'd gone up on the mountain just to take it in, listen to the birds, smell the winter air, and feel the earth under his feet. Rangers prepared for combat by knowing their environment. At one time he knew the trail like he knew the back of his hand but it was time to reassess . . . to be mentally ready. He could do this if he truly focused. Nothing fancy, just slow and easy. All he needed to do was make it down the trail.

"Hey." Deb walked into the store wearing the dress Hannah had given her. "You ready to go?"

"I'm having second thoughts."

"You're kidding me . . . because of Josh?" Hannah had given Deb a blow-by-blow of Josh's decision to just stay friends.

She didn't answer, just bit her bottom lip.

"Oh for God's sake. Screw him and all the Garner men. They don't deserve women like us. Besides, you've been his workout buddy all week, why would you miss out on the best holiday party in Glory Junction? It's Christmas Eve and you've got nothing else to do."

"Thanks for pointing out my pathetic life. I'll go for an hour." She didn't want to waste her new outfit. After much hemming and hawing, she'd finally broken down and purchased the Delaney Scott red A-line party dress with the plunging princess V-neck that she'd been salivating over for months. Even at wholesale the dress cost a fortune and this was the only event she really had to wear it to.

"Okay then." Deb twirled around the store. "Let's get this place locked up . . .

and party!"

The usual closing routine got cut short, leaving Hannah time to fix her makeup in the bathroom and slip on the dress in the changing room. When she came out, Deb blew a catcall whistle.

"And I thought I looked smokin'," she said, making Hannah turn for a full view. "You bought it, you little vixen."

"Yep. A bit of an investment but it's worth it, right?"

"Uh, hell yeah. One look at you in that dress and Josh'll swallow his tongue . . . the bastard. You ready?"

"I have to put on my shoes." A pair of sling backs with ice-pick heels Hannah bought after her divorce and had never gotten the chance to wear. She put them on and adjusted the straps. "What do you think?"

"That if you don't get some tonight, both of us are moving."

"Foster is meeting us there, right?"

"Yep." Deb grabbed her clutch and followed Hannah outside.

They walked next door where a DJ was playing and a few couples were already on the dance floor. They found Foster at the buffet, stuffing his face.

"The food's good, nothing like those

Costco meatballs the Canadells serve." The Canadells owned the local insurance company and also held a holiday open house every year. It wasn't nearly as popular as the Garners'. "Don't look now but Josh is at six o'clock, checking you out."

Hannah couldn't help it and turned around. There he was, his shoulder propped against the wall, gawking. Unlike the rest of the partygoers, he'd gone casual. A pair of button-fly Levi's, a flannel shirt, and motorcycle boots. Hannah supposed that when you were the best-looking man at the party you could wear whatever the hell you wanted.

He lifted his chin in greeting, pushed off the wall, and cut a swath through the crowd to get to her. "You look beautiful. New dress?"

"It's old." She did a visual lap around the room. "Big attendance."

"Yeah? I missed last year's so I wouldn't know." Given where he'd been, what he'd seen, this must feel pretty frivolous, she thought.

"You ready for tomorrow?"

He beamed. "As ready as I'll ever be." He pushed a loose strand from her updo away from her face. "You'll be there, right?"

"Unless I can talk you out of it." She tilted

her head to the side. "You really don't need to prove anything, Josh. There's no one in this town who's a bigger hero than you."

"How about I'm doing it just for fun?"

She shuddered. "I can't think of anything less fun."

"If I didn't know you better I'd think you lacked a sense of adventure, Hannah Banana."

He used to call her that in high school and she'd hated it. But today for whatever reason it gave her goose bumps. "I do."

"Nah. You're more of an adventurer than you know."

She didn't know what he was alluding to but didn't have time to think about it. An arm snaked around her waist and suddenly she was being pulled onto the dance floor by Win. Out of the corner of her eye she saw Josh shake his head.

Win could barely keep a beat. He looked like a horse suffering from blind staggers. It was weird because he could spring down the face of a mountain on a snowboard like an acrobat.

"Ah, come on." He tried for a little bump-and-grind action.

"Hey, Win, you're embarrassing yourself."

He laughed, which Hannah had to give him kudos for. Guys as good-looking as Win

Garner usually weren't self-deprecating.

"You coming over for Christmas breakfast?" he asked, whipping her closer to the DJ.

Josh's trip down Royal Slope was supposed to be a surprise so she didn't tell him she'd see him at the crack of dawn — that's when the whole Garner clan met at the mountain. "No, I'm hanging with Deb and Foster."

After Royal Slope Hannah wanted to keep as much distance as possible. It hurt too much to have finally rediscovered the right man only to be rejected by him.

"You should come. Josh wants you to." Win must've sensed that something was up because he added, "He may need a little time to find his place in the world but he cares about you, Hannah. He always has."

Unfortunately, he'd always had a funny way of showing it.

Win returned her to Josh, who was back to leaning against the wall. Hannah wasn't sure if it was because of his leg or because he knew how hot it made him look. Colt was dancing with Deb and Hannah wished her best friend could fall for that Garner instead. Although Colt was probably as much a confirmed bachelor as Win. TJ was huddled in the back of the room with a hotel owner Hannah knew from Nugget. Nate Breyer. He, his sister, and wife owned a cabin resort fifteen minutes away. If Hannah knew TJ he was probably embroiled in a business deal.

"Who you looking at?" Josh asked her.

"Your brother."

He snorted. "Which one."

"TJ."

Josh craned his neck, found TJ in the crowd, and with keen eyes observed his brother in action for a few minutes. "He's finagling something. The guy can't even take a night off."

The party wrapped up around ten. Deb insisted they stay until the bitter end, even though most of the party-goers had left to finish the night off with their families.

"I'll walk you to your car," Josh said.

"It's right outside, in front of Glorious Gifts. Save your energy for the morning."

He ignored her and walked her anyway. It had begun snowing and she worried about his leg on the wet sidewalk.

"You want me to pick you up on the way to Royal Slope?" he asked.

She thought about it for a moment. "It would be better if I came on my own."

Josh started to say something and stopped himself. "You should get in your car before you freeze." He grabbed the keys from her hand, clicked the fob, and opened the door.

"I'll see you tomorrow, Josh."

As she drove the few blocks to her house, snow flurries covered her windshield faster than her wipers cleaned them away. There'd be plenty of fresh powder for Josh's foolish run down the mountain. As she got ready for bed a sense of foreboding hit in the pit of her stomach. Hannah feared that the whole scheme would end badly and it would be her fault for being an enabler, just like she'd been with Chip.

CHAPTER TEN

Hannah's alarm clock went off before dawn. Forcing herself to get out of bed, she pulled her curtains aside to peer outside. It was a white Christmas, perhaps too white. A deep layer of snow not only covered her front lawn but the street as well. If the city didn't plow, she might not be able to get out of her driveway.

She quickly showered, wanting to give herself extra time to get to the resort, and bundled up in the warmest clothes she had, including thermal underwear and snow boots. Downstairs, the smell of coffee filled the air. Good thing she'd set the timer. Hannah filled a thermos, put on her down jacket, scarf, and mittens and slogged to her car, the snow so deep she could barely open her door. In the glove box, she found an ice scraper and got the frost off her windshield while snowflakes stuck to her hair. It was wicked cold so she sat in the car waiting for the engine to warm and the interior to get toasty before heading out. Luckily, she had all-wheel drive but it would still be a trial getting up the mountain.

She managed to maneuver her car out of the driveway and across town, using city streets, to Route 22, a one-lane one-way road that climbed the steep, winding grade to Royal Slope. Even in good conditions the road was not for the faint of heart with its sheer drops off the side. At least reverse traffic came down the other side of the mountain.

Visibility from the snow was so poor that Hannah opened her side window and stuck her head out to navigate the treacherous road. A few times she considered pulling over and phoning Josh to cancel the whole thing. But turning off onto a shallow shoulder seemed even more risky, not to mention that cell reception up here was sketchy at best.

So she continued to inch up the mountain, doing less than five miles per hour, her tires sliding on the icy pavement. With the white-out conditions she didn't even know if there were other cars on the road. If so, their head- and taillights were invisible.

Although she was used to winter driving in the Sierra, the mountains seemed particularly desolate and she turned on her radio just to hear something besides her pounding pulse. All she got was static. She kicked herself for not catching a ride with Josh. This wouldn't have fazed him a bit. She'd read about what it took to be an Army Ranger. Just to make the grade, you had to be able to handle anything. Josh had always been like that. In high school he was the guy who could start a bonfire without matches, the one who stopped Chip from sucking the venom out of Stretch Kandinsky's leg when he'd gotten bitten by a rattlesnake, knowing that the procedure was more fiction than fact. He'd been the one to rescue Hannah when she'd climbed halfway up Sawtooth and suddenly discovered she was afraid of heights.

She took a deep breath, starting to feel claustrophobic from not being able to see the horizon — or anything. There was a curve and she tried to turn into it slowly. That's when she hit a patch of black ice, her car fishtailing out of control. She slammed on her brakes, causing the car to spin and roll down an embankment.

The last thing she remembered was hanging upside down from her seat belt.

"She's not answering her goddamn

phone . . . not her cell or landline." Josh continued to pace across the kitchen floor.

"You think she tried to head up to Royal Slope and didn't know about the road closure?" Gray Garner asked. Even Josh's Zen father seemed worried.

"That's exactly what I think." Josh grabbed his jacket and started for the back door.

"Son, let's talk to Colt." His brother had gotten called out early that morning on weather-related accidents.

"What can he do that I can't?" Josh challenged.

"He can get us past the barriers, for one thing. He also has better equipment."

All benefits of being the town's top cop, Josh supposed. Gray didn't wait for his son to acquiesce, just took the landline away from Josh and speed-dialed Colt.

Win came in the door covered in snow. "Damn, it's as windy as it is cold. She's not home, but there was a fresh pot of coffee made."

"Did you break in?" Josh asked.

"No, Deb met me over there with a key. She's worried sick."

Sick didn't even begin to describe what Josh was feeling. Petrified and guilt-ridden. He'd tried to call her to say the ski outing

271

was off but she didn't answer. Josh figured she'd started off before they closed the road and the goddamn Highway Patrol hadn't bothered to check before putting up their barriers. If she'd made it to the resort she would've notified them by now.

Gray held the phone between his ear and shoulder. "Colt is calling the CHP. If we don't hear anything from them, he'll take us up."

TJ looked up from his coffee. "You want me to gather up the search-and-rescue guys? It might take a little time since it's Christmas."

"Start calling them," Josh said.

Gray got back on the phone and everyone in the room stopped talking so they could hear the conversation. TJ went to grab his cell and Mary started filling thermoses.

"Colt says the CHP has no report of accidents on Route Twenty-Two and nothing coming from area hospitals."

Josh let himself breathe. "Let's go."

"Hang tight," Gray said. "Colt's coming over."

"Why the hell are we wasting all this time?" It was freezing temperatures. If, God forbid, Hannah was stranded in the elements she didn't have much time.

He finished putting on his jacket, grabbed

his keys, and rushed out into the cold.

"Josh," Mary called from the doorway. "At least take a radio."

He turned around, went back, and took the two-way from his mother.

"You should wait for your father and brothers, Josh."

He kissed her on the forehead. "This is what I do, Mom."

"Keep in communication with everyone. The last thing we need is everyone tripping over one another up there on the mountain. And, Josh, be careful."

"I will." He got inside his truck and headed for 22, continuing to call Hannah's cell on his Bluetooth. The calls went straight to voice mail. Not a good sign.

Despite being away for so long, he still knew how to navigate these mountainous roads in blizzardlike conditions. It was a deadly time to be driving and the possibility that Hannah could be out here somewhere, injured, made his gut clench. When he got to the barricade there was a CHP officer rerouting traffic. Josh rolled down his window.

"We've got a missing woman likely trapped between here and Royal Ski Resort."

"Sir, I need you to turn around."

"It's an emergency. I've got —"

"Sir, turn around."

The idiot wouldn't listen. Josh kept trying to explain the situation and the cop, like a parrot, kept telling him to turn around. In another minute, Josh was going to get out of his truck and have a real confrontation with the guy. Except Colt cruised up in his police rig, flashed his creds, and suddenly Officer Moron was all ears.

Next thing Josh knew the chippy moved the barrier. Colt came over to Josh's truck before he could drive through the opening, and banged on his window.

"What the hell you going rogue for? We should be doing an organized grid search, not you going off half-cocked."

Josh knew his brother was right but they were talking about Hannah here. He couldn't wait while the local SAR team put new batteries in their flashlights and pored over maps. He needed to do something. Now!

"I've got a radio," he said lamely. "What channel are we using?"

Colt didn't hide his annoyance but told him the frequency. "Stick to the road, don't go off exploring in this" — he looked up at the snow-covered trees blowing like it was a hurricane — "you hear me? If you see something, radio."

"Roger that," he replied, knowing how sarcastic he sounded. But Colt telling him how to conduct a search and rescue was beyond absurd. And the fact that Hannah had been missing for three hours made him angry at the world.

He took off, trucking up the hill, looking for any signs that Hannah's Ford had been there, hoping like hell she'd discovered that it was too dangerous to continue and had pulled over to the side to wait for the weather to let up. If she had enough gas she could keep the heat running. The problem: There weren't a lot of turnouts and the guardrails on the sheer-drop side of the road were no real protection from heavy impact. It was near impossible to see them with the snow coming down so hard but he kept his eyes peeled, using his headlights to check for damaged rails. If she'd gone over the side . . . ah, Jesus, he didn't want to contemplate it.

At the first turnout he pulled over. Not easy when you couldn't see shit. A pair of NVGs would come in handy about now, though they didn't really work in the snow. He got out of the truck, grabbed a pack he kept in the backseat, and rummaged through it for a flashlight, sweeping it over

275

the roadway. No skid marks that he could see. Next, he checked the guardrails.

"Colt," he called over the radio because his cell was useless. There was a crackling sound and then his brother's voice. "I'm at mile marker forty-seven. I don't see anything up to this point. I'm going the rest of the way on foot, that way I don't miss anything. Warn the guys, would you?" He didn't want to get hit by one of the search-and-rescue team's vehicles.

"We should section it off . . . you can't cover all that ground by yourself. I'll radio you as soon as the SAR folks get here."

"Colt, do me a favor, second-check the territory I've already gone over. She could have slid down the side of the mountain where there isn't a guardrail. The way the snow is coming down the skid marks could be covered by now."

"Ten-four," Colt signed off.

Josh pulled his wool cap over his ears, strapped the pack to his back, and began the trek up the mountain road. His bad leg stiffened in the cold but he continued climbing, undeterred. Every few feet he did a sweep with the flashlight. Nothing looked out of the ordinary. He tried his cell phone again and got zero bars. At least someone at base would continue trying to call Hannah.

With any luck she'd made it to Royal Resort and was sitting next to a toasty fire in the lounge, drinking something warm. But his gut told him it wasn't likely and he had to fight hard to banish the images that kept popping in his head.

At the fifty-mile marker he stopped to rest, the cold cutting through his parka and burning his face. His breath hanging in the air like a puff of smoke. Although Hannah had probably dressed warmly for the outing, she wouldn't have been equipped like someone skiing. If she were lying somewhere, unconscious . . .

He took another sweep of the area and continued up the road, keeping his senses attuned to the environment. Listening, smelling, feeling. The radio crackled with Colt's voice.

"You find anything?" Josh asked, about ready to jump out of his skin.

"Nothing yet. The team is here. TJ and Win are gonna drive the road to the resort, then double back. If you want they'll pick you up."

They were worried about his goddamn leg. "I'm fine. It's better to have boots on the ground."

"All right but listen for TJ's truck. The last thing we need is for you to get hit."

"Will do."

"And Josh, we're gonna find her. Don't do anything rash."

"You and I both know we're running out of time. She's in a tin can of a car, probably wearing some kind of fashion jacket. Can't we get a sheriff's copter . . . cover more area." He was specifically talking about getting light down in the ravines.

"In this storm it would be a suicide mission," Colt said. "We're not even positive she took Route Twenty-Two. Mom's trying her family. Maybe she got called away on an emergency."

"She would've called me, Colt." Not only was Hannah responsible that way but she knew how important the ski down Royal Slope was to Josh. Hell, she'd been sitting through his dull nightly workouts for days. She wouldn't bail without at least leaving him a message. She'd know he'd be worried.

"As soon as the weather calms down I'll try to get a bird up in the air."

Hannah didn't have that kind of time, which only made Josh search harder, paying as much attention to the copse of trees on the left side of the road as he did to the drop side. They were closing in on ten o'clock already. And even with gloves on,

278

Josh's fingers were numb. At least visibility had increased. The wind had let up and with the sun fully out, the road wasn't shrouded in white anymore.

From a distance he heard a car engine and moved as far off the road as possible. TJ's Range Rover crested the hill, slowed down, and stopped next to Josh.

TJ unrolled his window. "Anything?"

Josh shook his head. "Nope."

"Hop in, get warm, and you can hike down when we get to the top."

"I'm good," he said, and started to walk away.

TJ caught up. "Don't be an idiot, Josh. Rest your leg for a few minutes."

"Hannah doesn't have a few minutes."

"We're not gonna stop looking for her."

"You're wasting time." Josh waved them on. "Go!"

TJ banged on his steering wheel but took off up the mountain. Josh crisscrossed the road, looking for any sign of a disturbance. Although it seemed impossible that someone could disappear into thin air, he'd seen it happen many times before in the Hindu Kush.

Colt came over the radio. "You're a stubborn jackass. How good you think you'll be to Hannah when your leg gives out or we have to take you to the hospital for hypo-thermia?"

"What are the searchers doing?"

"They're spread out along the road. We'd like to get down the side of the mountain but with the snow . . . Jesse Phillips is bringing his dogs. They can get down there."

Josh was heartened by the news. Search dogs were good. "You need something of Hannah's for them to sniff?"

"Deb brought a few things from her house."

"I hope he's getting here soon."

Colt must've heard the fear in Josh's voice because he said, "Any minute. Radio TJ if you want him to come get you."

Josh signed off, climbed another mile, and stopped to take a slug of water. Despite the cold, he needed to stay hydrated.

That's when he saw it. . . .

Broken branches, dirt mixed with snow, and flattened bushes just over the edge of the road. Most people would've chalked the disturbance up to the storm but Josh's spidey sense was going crazy.

It wasn't a sheer drop, so no guardrail. He attempted to get down the side to explore, but between his injured leg, the snow, and rough terrain, it took every ounce of strength to keep from going down, headfirst.

He managed to crawl several yards down when he saw a tree with a big chunk of bark missing from its trunk.

He pushed himself farther. Behind a cluster of pines he caught something shiny glinting off the snow, like a foil wrapper. Josh followed the shimmer and that's when he realized it wasn't a wrapper but a slice of bumper — from a car. Despite his leg, he ran as fast as he could through the snow. A little ways beyond the broken bumper he spotted Hannah's Ford. Its wheels were straight up in the air and the chassis was covered in snow.

"Hannah," he yelled as he got closer, a combination of adrenaline and fear pumping through his veins. "Hannah."

By the time he made it to the car his leg was ready to give but through the shattered glass he could see Hannah hunkered inside the roof, her body rolled into a fetal position.

Don't let her be . . .

He reached in through the rear windshield, careful not to cut himself, and started to check for a pulse. Her eyes fluttered and in the faintest of voices she said, "What took you so long?"

His heart rolled over in his chest. "I would've gotten here sooner but you were a little hard to find."

He'd already grabbed the radio from his belt as Hannah started to stir. "Don't move until I check you." When Colt came over the air Josh gave him his GPS coordinates and asked for an ambulance.

"Is she . . . breathing?"

"She's breathing and talking." Josh smiled at Hannah reassuringly. "But I'm concerned about broken bones and a concussion. Her car went over the side and rolled at least a dozen times before landing on its roof."

"We'll get there ASAP."

Josh used his army knife to remove much of the glass and crawled as far into the car as possible so he could examine Hannah. He wasn't a medic but had been trained in basic first aid.

"Anything hurt?" he asked, gently running his hands up and down her back, arms, and legs.

"Everything." She sat up.

"Hannah, honey, I told you not to move."

"I've been moving for hours, how else do you think I stayed warm?"

It was then that he noticed that she was wrapped in those hideous sweaters. She'd layered them over her ski jacket, her legs, even over her head.

He pointed at the sweater she used as foot

warmers. "You never returned them, did you?"

"Nope. I think I have brain damage just from having to look at them all this time."

Josh laughed. Other than a few cuts and bruises, he thought Hannah was probably fine. "Here, drink some water." He pulled a canteen from his pack as well as a blanket to wrap her in.

"Did you make it down Royal Slope?"

"Ah, baby, the road was closed due to the storm. I tried to call you. I can't believe you came out in this . . . you must've been scared as hell."

"No." She shook her head. "I knew you'd rescue me."

"You weren't worried that I wouldn't be able to get to you . . . with my leg?"

"Not for a second," she said.

Right there and then, he forgot himself and their agreement to just be friends. He pulled her close, wrapped her in his arms, and let his mouth take over. She clung to him and there inside her wrecked car he held on to her, never wanting to let go.

"Josh?" she whispered.

"Hmm?"

"Thank you for finding me. I think anyone else would've given up by now. But not you."

"Nope," he grunted. "I'd never give up on you. Ever. Remember what you told me up on Sawtooth when we were kids?"

"That I trusted you to get me down the mountain?"

"Yep. You can always trust me, Hannah."

"So why can't you trust me?" she asked in a faint voice that told him she was fading from cold and exhaustion. "Why do you have to get down the mountain all by yourself?"

He contemplated that, thinking about how she'd been there for him, even though he hadn't made it easy. How she made him feel whole at the lowest point of his life.

"Maybe I've been wrong," he said.

After the hospital, Hannah went home and slept ten hours. Josh had drawn her a hot bath, anticipating how sore she'd be. Nothing like rolling down an embankment in three thousand pounds of steel. Then he'd tucked her in like a baby and snuggled up next to her. Frankly, she was too tired to think about the implications of that and drifted off to sleep, forgetting that it was even Christmas.

The next day bloomed bright and clear with just a smattering of snow. Josh surprised her that evening with a horse-drawn carriage ride. Somehow he'd gotten the coachman to do a personal pickup in front of Hannah's house and they clopped down to Main Street just as the holiday lights blinked on.

At first they didn't say much, just held hands under the plaid blanket, which he tucked tighter around her. Since the accident, he'd been beyond attentive. And sweet. And he'd stopped acting like an island. This morning, he'd actually let her massage and ice his leg. After yesterday it was so stiff he could barely move it.

"This okay?" he asked, pulling her ski cap over her ears.

"Are you kidding?" she said, and scooted closer, resting her head on his shoulder. "This is perfect."

His breath turned white in the cold as he exhaled. "I love you, you know? I have since high school."

Her heart skipped a beat. *Love* was a big word for someone like Josh Garner to sling around. "You sure that's not the adrenaline rush from yesterday talking?"

"Almost losing you knocked a good amount of cold sense into me. But you've gotta know that I've always loved you. So much so that I had to leave Glory Junction."

She closed her eyes, remembering the

past, which had become so much clearer in the last couple of weeks. "I think it was easier for me to convince myself that you disliked me. That way I could block out my own feelings for you." Inappropriate feelings.

"For me it probably started that day on Sawtooth," she continued as the driver lapped the long block. "But when I saw you at the VFW Hall . . ." She took in a deep breath and her throat clogged with emotion. "I love you, Josh."

Josh pulled her in tighter so that she was practically sitting on his lap. "There's no guarantee that I'll ever get full use of my leg again. But, Hannah, I don't want to lose you."

"You think that matters to me? For goodness' sake, Josh, my life flashed before my eyes yesterday. The only thing that kept me sane was knowing that nothing would stop you from finding me. Bad leg or not. But I can't be with you if you don't let me in. I can't do that again . . . not like with Chip. We have to be in this together. You can't let your leg define you or it'll wind up defining our relationship."

He squeezed her hand under the blanket. "I know. After your accident, I realized how damned lucky I was. That by some miracle of fate I didn't lose you a second time. Hannah, I've wanted you for so long. . . ." He scrubbed his hands through his hair. "I don't want to screw this up."

"Then don't." Her eyes filled and she swiped them with the back of her hand. "Let me help you find your way back."

"That's the thing," he said. "I'm pretty sure you already have. Just knowing you were here, in Glory Junction, brought me home . . . gave me hope."

"So we're doing this?" she asked, and could feel a smile a mile wide open in her chest.

"Oh yeah," he said. "We're doing this."

EPILOGUE

On New Year's Day, Hannah took a chairlift up to the top of Royal Slope. The entire Garner clan waited for her so that Josh could ski down the mountain.

She didn't know why he continued to insist on taking his life in his hands. The last week had been wonderful, Josh making a concerted effort to take the limitations of his healing leg in stride. It had been baby steps for both of them. Josh learning how to let Hannah in and Hannah learning how to love again.

And now this.

Looking down from the lift made her queasy. She abhorred heights but even worse was envisioning Josh shredding three miles of steep trail. His leg was getting stronger every day but this was too much too soon. Even his dare-devil family had tried to talk him out of it. But stubborn Josh wouldn't be dissuaded.

She got off the lift dressed in layers and a ski hat pulled over her ears. It was cold enough that, even with gloves on, her fingers hurt. Josh met her at the landing with a coffee thermos.

"You're sure I can't talk you out of this?"

"Nope."

She couldn't believe he was able to move around on skis. Then again he was practically born in a pair. Bum leg or not, Josh Garner knew what he was doing.

"All six of you are going down together, right?" she asked. Safety in numbers.

"Yep." Josh slung his arm around her shoulders and walked her to where the others stood, waving.

Hannah took one look at Mary and knew that Josh's mother thought the same as she: This was beyond crazy, it was dangerous, and ridiculously unnecessary. Josh was making great headway. A bad spill would not only set him back physically but Hannah feared that it would send him into an emotional funk. Josh wasn't a man who had a high tolerance for failure.

"I got this, Hannah Banana." He kissed her, which he'd been doing a lot lately, and beamed like a madman.

She struggled between begging him not to do it and putting faith in him to know his own abilities. The latter won out. But if it turned out badly . . .

"Let's go, Team Garner," Gray called, and the rest of the Garners lined up like tin soldiers. Some kind of signal was given and they took off.

Hannah was heartened to see that Colt and Win skied in formation with Josh, letting him set the pace. TJ and Gray took up the rear with Mary leading the way. He was protected on all sides.

It was beautiful watching the way they traversed down the mountain like a choreographed dance. There were a few other skiers on the slope who stopped to watch. From up high, Hannah kept sight of them until a quarter of the way down. Then their ski jackets blurred into colorful spots.

She used the binoculars Josh had given her to get a better view. He seemed to be holding up fine. Still, she felt on edge, like any minute something terrible could happen. Soon the trail would narrow and Win and Colt would have to leave Josh's side to ski single file in order to maneuver the skinny twists and turns.

They did it in perfect unison, Win first, Josh second, and Colt in the back, winding down so gracefully — and fast — she began to lose track of who was who. Then one of them went down, tumbling headfirst over and over again. It happened in a split second and even though she'd been expecting something like this, it felt surreal. Out of body. The worst part was she couldn't tell how bad he'd crashed. Her tiny slice of view had become obscured by other skiers.

All she knew was that she needed to get down there. Hannah didn't have any skis and to try to walk the trail would be treacherous. Looking around, panicked, she spotted someone wearing a SKI PATROL jacket.

"Excuse me," she shouted, and pointed at the scene below. "There's been an accident. Will you take me down?"

He rode over on a snowmobile, took note of her lack of ski equipment, and told her to hop on the back of his Ski-doo.

By the time she got to the scene a large crew had cut over from another trail and had formed a circle around the downed skier. Hannah pushed her way through, knowing it was Josh, fearing that he would need to be airlifted to the nearest hospital. She worried as much about his spirit as she did his leg.

But as she made her way through the gathering crowd she found Josh sitting against a berm, a giant grin on his face. Another member of the ski patrol was checking him for injuries while the rest of the Garners stood over him like a protective ring of mama bears. He took one look at her face and stopped smiling.

"I'm okay," he said.

She moved closer and sat with him in the snow. "What happened?"

"I ate it." He beamed again, totally confusing her.

"Why are you smiling about it?" She wondered if he'd hit his head . . . got a concussion.

"Come here." He pulled her closer and snuggled her under his arm, his grin growing wider. "You were right; I should've waited until my leg was better healed."

"Uh, okay." She looked at the rest of the Garners, who seemed as thrown as she was. This was not the Josh they knew. Too rational. Not hardheaded enough. "You seem . . . good."

"I'm better than good, baby." He pressed her into the snow and kissed her. "I made it farther than I should've. Next year . . . all the way. But it doesn't really matter because I've got you."

Josh glanced at the growing crowd. "You mind giving us a little space here?" Everyone but the Garner clan dispersed. "You guys, too."

Gray gathered his flock. "Call us when you're ready."

Hannah watched them traverse to the other side of the trail. "Maybe sitting here in the snow isn't such a good idea." She feared hypothermia would set in. "They could probably bring a sled or toboggan to get you down."

He shot her a look. "When I'm ready to go, it won't be on a stretcher. Reach into my jacket, would you?"

She figured he must have a flask in there. Brandy to keep them warm because even bundled up she felt chilled to the bone. She searched in his pocket only to come up with a small velvet box and looked at him, her head angled, hardly able to breathe.

Josh grinned. "Open it."

She wasn't sure if her hands shook from the cold or from anticipation. She popped the lid, and a large marquise diamond glinted in the sun. "Oh, Josh!" Her eyes welled up.

"Will you marry me, Hannah Baldwin . . . make me the happiest man in the world? If you will, I promise you'll never regret it. I'll spend every day loving you . . . worshipping you." His face split into the biggest smile she'd ever seen grace Josh Garner's face.

"Yes! One hundred percent yes." She

threw herself on top of him, kissed every inch of his mouth, cheeks, eye-brows, and chin. Then she pulled off a woolen glove to put the ring on. "Were you planning this . . . up here on Royal Slope?"

"Well, I knew damned well I'd never be able to propose to you while skydiving or mountain climbing or rock scaling. We've really got to work on that fear-of-heights thing you've got going."

And he pulled her down for another kiss.

■ ■ ■ ■

Moonshine and Mistletoe

SARAH TITLE

■ ■ ■ ■

CHAPTER ONE

Of all the ways Emma Fallader imagined she would eventually die, hurtling off an icy cliff in West Virginia was definitely not one of them.

And yet, here she was.

"Sorry," her friend, Liam, said as he regained control of the sliding car.

"Don't apologize, just drive." She grimaced from beside him.

"How you doing back there?" Liam glanced in the rearview mirror, where two of his three passengers were slowly turning green.

Bernie rolled down her window an inch. "Sorry. It's either this or I mess up Emma's nice car."

"Thanks for driving, by the way," Emma said softly.

"Just let him drive," Bernie said as Liam focused on the slick road in front of them. "Whose idea was it to get married at Christmas anyway?"

"That was Kevin," Liam said to the road. "Daniel picked the place, Kevin picked the time. It's their wedding, after all."

"Very democratic," Becky said from the seat behind Emma, where she was clutching the seat belt with alarmingly white knuckles.

"And Daniel finally got all of us to West Virginia," Emma added. "If I didn't know how much he loves Kevin, I might have thought that he's getting married just to make us come visit here."

Daniel was emphatic in his love for his home state, and proselytized its beauty and warmth with the fervor of the newly converted. It was one of the things that Kevin had found most annoying about him, or so Kevin claimed when they were all getting to know each other their first semester in library school. But there was so much to love about Daniel that a little home state obsession was decidedly no big deal.

Sometimes it amazed Emma, how well Daniel fit in with all of them. He was cool. Not nerdy-cool like the librarians, but actual-cool. He was an architect and he wore slim-fit suits and played guitar in a post-punk band. The rest of them were just total librarians. Obsessed with books and equity and access to information. They argued about metadata. They did a lot of bar trivia.

Maybe Emma wasn't being fair. Liam could go toe-to-toe with Daniel on indie bands nobody else had ever heard of. Becky had an artistic streak, though she rarely showed it, working in a corporate law office. Bernie was a social justice warrior in her own right, using her college library for community good.

So maybe it was just Emma who was the nerd.

She was such a library nerd that she was working her way to becoming Doctor Library Nerd. Once she got her PhD, she could teach the next generation of librarians, encouraging them to embrace and improve the small, rural libraries like the ones she'd grown up in. Her research on access and Internet speeds was being published in the *Journal of the Indiana Library Association,* and she hoped it would be a good jumping-off point for her dissertation. Except she wasn't sure if her approach was broad enough. . . .

She had to stop thinking about it. That was what she'd promised her three wedding dates when she picked them all up at the airport in Charleston. But the truth was,

she could really use some more time thinking about work. Lately she just couldn't
seem to focus. She'd sit down to look at her
research or outline her thesis and suddenly
everything else in the world was more
urgent and more interesting. Her dishes had
never been so clean, her bookshelves never
so alphabetized, her dissertation never
so . . . unwritten. At this rate, the only thing
she was going to get her doctorate in was
procrastination.

Of course, none of that would matter if
she went hurtling off a cliff on her way to a
wedding.

Kevin was one of her best friends, so she
supposed imminent death and further
procrastination were worth seeing him happily off into the next chapter of his life. It
was a little sad, too, because every good
thing that happened meant nothing would
be the same. They'd graduated from their
master's program (hooray!), then got jobs
in different parts of the country (boo). That
meant that last Christmas was the first one
in a while that Emma'd spent away from
Kevin's aggressive holiday cheer. As much
as she protested the elf shoes and the
constant glitter, she had really missed it.

And so her other best guy friend who lived
in upstate New York now and was theoreti-

cally better at driving in icy weather was driving her car, full of her two best girlfriends, Bernie and Becky, and more pairs of shoes than was strictly necessary, and they were all slipping and sliding to a long weekend culminating in the gay wedding of their best friends in beautiful, scenic, icy Froggy Rock, West Virginia.

Ho ho ho.

"You got a room all to yourself, as promised. It's booked under the name Abel Zebidiah Tate, Nashville Superstar."

"Ha-ha," Abe said into the phone. Cousins. Hilarious.

"Thanks for doing this, really," Daniel said. "It means a lot."

Abe grunted. He knew what Daniel meant. Still, he and Daniel had always left their unconditional love for each other unspoken. It was easier that way. Besides, the wedding would be emotional enough — all weddings were. They didn't need to start early.

Technically, Abe and Daniel had grown up in separate homes down the road from each other. But they spent so much time together that it was more like they each had two rooms in two different houses. Besides, being poor meant not a lot of toys, so pooling their resources made them feel rich.

They also got into twice as much trouble. At least that's what Granny Sue always said whenever the two of them were together, which was always.

The point was, Abe was as good as Daniel's brother, and of course he would be at the wedding. And of course he would play at the wedding. And of course he would do it for free. There was no need to get mushy about it.

He did have one condition, though.

Abe loved family reunions, but he didn't love the accommodations. He had lots of cousins, and his cousins had lots of kids. That meant lots of kids and cousins piled into tiny rooms, and since Abe was single and allegedly tough, he usually got stuck on an air mattress, usually next to some cousin with undiagnosed sleep apnea.

So Abe agreed to play the wedding, and he'd do it for free, as long as he didn't have to share a cabin with sixteen other people.

"Can't wait to see you, cuz," Daniel said.

"Me too," Abe replied, cutting off the mush. "How's Kevin?" If Daniel wanted to get mushy, let him get mushy about his husband-to-be.

Abe liked the guy. While Daniel was one of the most laid-back people Abe had ever known, Kevin was . . . well, Kevin was not. He liked order and he liked plans and he liked sticking to those plans. Like all good couples, Daniel was mostly blinded by love so he didn't mind that Kevin often got more pleasure out of planning things than actually doing them. When it got to him, though, Daniel would threaten to erase Kevin's Pinterest boards, which was their signal that Kevin needed to step back, take a deep breath, and focus on what really mattered. Which was not stressing about the right napkin-folding technique for the place settings.

"Kevin is good. He's stressed. But we're dealing."

"We'll get some moonshine in 'im. That'll loosen him up."

"Oh, great, that's just what I need. A drunk, weepy fiancé who's trying to fold napkins."

Abe laughed.

"You laugh now, but wait till we get down there and you're pressed into service. There are wedding favors that have to be assembled. And you have dexterous fiddler's fingers, so you'll be great at it."

"Wedding favors?"

"Don't worry about it. I've said too much. Just get down there early, and be careful. I hear the roads are bad."

"The roads are always bad."

"Yeah, but you're a city boy now, so don't get any ideas about muddin' or anything."

"I'm pretty sure the Sentra isn't going to go muddin'."

"Not on purpose, anyway."

"Like Kevin would allow it to rain on your wedding day."

Abe swore he could hear Daniel smiling through the phone.

CHAPTER TWO

"Oh my God, it's adorable! Don't you think it's adorable, guys?"

Becky was the first one out of the car, which was good since she was looking kind of green. But whatever distress her stomach was in seemed to be soothed by the scene in front of them.

"Totes adorbs," said Liam, heading for the trunk.

After a harrowing twenty minutes when the GPS decided that suddenly it had never heard of Froggy Rock and did they mean *Fraggle Rock,* the fictional underground TV show?, they found their way to the Froggy Rock Ski Chalet and Cabins.

After getting out of the car and looking around, Emma thought it was worth it.

The building in front of her did resemble a chalet, sort of. Maybe more like a log building with chaletlike trim. But it was decked out in greenery and lights and what it really looked like was a gingerbread house, and in the gloomy, sleety weather, it felt particularly inviting. Emma thought she might die of the cuteness. The log cabins were spread around the woods, close enough to see but not so close that you could see in. She could just imagine that if the snow that was predicted really started, the whole place would look like an enchanted gingerbread forest.

Gazing out at the little cabins, imagining smoke pouring out of the chimneys and hot toddies by the fire . . . it almost made Emma wish Kevin had booked them into one of those instead of getting them rooms in the main lodge. But the cabins were a little rustic, he told them. And a little drafty. And were basically one room with lumpy bunk beds and a tiny, tiny bathroom. Those were reserved for the various aunts and uncles and cousins with kids. The librarians were sophisticated guests. They got their own rooms.

Luxury!

As she and the sophisticated, overpacked librarians walked into the lodge, Emma let go of all her remaining reservations about staying in a campground in West Virginia for a wedding. It looked just about like heaven. The stone floors were covered in colorful throw rugs. There was a fire crackling in the fireplace, but most of the comfy chairs were facing toward the giant picture windows that looked out over the valley. The large, open space was decorated for the holidays with more green and glitter, but it was subtle and tasteful.

"I guess they didn't let Kevin decorate," she murmured.

"No, but they let him make a schedule." Becky came up behind her with a stack of gridded papers. "Looks like Kevin has a whole weekend planned for us."

"Kevin?" Bernie asked. "Plan every detail with meticulous precision? I never!"

"Do I hear the bitter sarcasm of my spinster friends?"

"Kevin!"

They all turned to the automatic doors, where their beloved, off-the-market Kevin was striding through, looking like good ol' Kevin in his slim khakis and peacoat.

"And Daniel!" they all shouted as Kevin was followed in by his fiancé, still too handsome for his own good, and carrying a cardboard box.

"Why does Daniel get a bigger reception than I do?" Kevin asked, as cheeks were kissed and hugs were given.

"Because I don't call them spinsters,"

Daniel replied, kissing and hugging around the box.

"I can't believe you're marrying this jerk," Bernie said to Daniel.

He just shrugged. "What can I say? I love the jerk."

"Ha-ha," Kevin said, but he leaned in and kissed Daniel anyway. "So," he said, turning back to his spinsters. "Are you settled in? Did you get my itinerary?"

"No, and yes," Liam said. "Well, Becky got one. The rest of us just heard the rumors."

"Well! Hurry up! We've got a cooking lesson planned in twenty minutes!"

"Uh . . ." There was a collective shuffling of feet and general sense of how-to-let-the-poor-guy-down.

"Sweetheart," Daniel said, putting the box on the nearest table and wrapping his arms around Kevin. "Maybe give them a minute."

Kevin looked at his watch.

"No, a metaphorical minute," Daniel said with a smile. "They just drove in from the airport, right, guys?"

"Liam drove," Bernie clarified. "But we all stressed."

"Very helpful," Liam added.

"Let's let them check in, settle down, and maybe meet for dinner."

"But what about the cooking?"

"We can do it tomorrow."

"But tomorrow's all booked up."

"We'll work it out, I promise," Daniel said, then leaned in to whisper something in Kevin's ear that made Kevin blush and made the rest of them look away jealously.

"Okay, fine. Go, check in, be comfortable," said Kevin. "We'll meet up for dinner."

"And welcome to West Virginia," said Daniel, with a huge, victorious grin on his face.

CHAPTER THREE

Abe smiled as he swiped his room key and stepped into what Kevin referred to as his monastic cell. Kevin was obviously used to living on more than a struggling musician's salary. (Ha, salary.) The room was bigger than his living room back home, but at least this one, Abe didn't have to share.

His roommate in Nashville was okay — a singer-songwriter whose primary goal in life was to sell a song to Taylor Swift. Never mind that Taylor Swift wrote her own songs. And that, even if she didn't, she probably wasn't going to suddenly start singing about beer and pickup trucks. Goddamn red Solo cups.

Drake joked that he was craft beer, Abe was moonshine. That suited Abe just fine. He wasn't interested in making big money, in being part of the Big Country Music Machine. But he did want to make a living making music, and he had a better shot in

Nashville than he did in Podunkville, West Virginia.

Or so he thought. It turned out, throw a rock in Nashville and you'd hit a skinny mountain kid wanting to make it in the roots music movement. Never mind that most of the kids weren't from the mountains, and knew more about Mumford & Sons than they did about Hazel Dickens.

He shouldn't be bitter. He was too young to be bitter, as Granny Sue liked to remind him. Maybe Nashville was just too big for him. Maybe he needed Bristol or, God help him, Gatlinburg. Nashville was a place for people with dreams of stardom, selling out arenas and making music videos and owning more than one suit jacket for red carpet stuff and more than one for business meetings. That wasn't him. Abe just wanted to earn enough money making music that he didn't have to deliver pizza or sell insurance or write songs about beer and pickups. He didn't need Graceland, although not having a roommate would be nice. He just wanted to make the music he wanted to make, and to pay his bills. Was that too much to ask? It'd been five years, and so far, that wasn't happening in Nashville.

Dammit, he *was* bitter. Not just because he was a failure, but because he'd fallen for the trick. Like every other dumb kid comin' out of the holler, he thought he was special. He thought because old-time music spoke to him, that he had something to share. Not hardly, said Nashville. You just keep doin' odd jobs and playin' on other people's records, and we'll save the fame and fortune for a guy willing to wear rhinestones.

Damn, he was *bitter.*

"Abe!" The shout made the knock on the door kind of redundant, but it did the trick. Abe woke up out of his stupor and opened the door.

"How're the digs?"

Daniel stood in the doorway, his plaid shirt untucked and his hair a little mussed.

Abe raised his eyebrows at his usually fastidious cousin's disheveled appearance. Then he decided he didn't need to know. Or rather, that he did know, but he would let it go. It was the guy's wedding weekend, after all.

"Luxurious. Come on in."

Daniel followed him into the room.

"Something from the mini-fridge?" If Daniel was paying, the least Abe could do was be a good host.

Daniel shook his head and sat on the corner of the bed. "I think I ate something bad."

"Or you got cold feet."

"If I have cold feet, how come my stomach hurts?"

Abe shrugged. "I ain't no doctor, son. I jes' came for the big hoedown."

He was being a jerk, playing up his own accent to tease Daniel about how his was gone. Still, Abe loved how easily he could slip into his real accent when he came home. It was like pouring molasses over his words, everything was slower and sweeter. Nashville might be the South, but it had nothing on West Virginia for accents.

Daniel looked suddenly serious. He took an intense interest in watching his hands wring together.

"It means a lot to me, your bein' here."

"Of course, man, where else would I be?"

"Like always. You're my brother, man."

"I know."

"Do you know how much that means to me? That you've been by my side, no matter what?"

"Same here."

"Remember when I stole those DuckTales comic books from Henry's?"

"I thought Henry was gonna skin you alive."

"I wasn't worried about Henry. I was worried about Granny Sue."

"I'm not angry, I'm just disappointed," they said together.

"Sometimes I wish'd she'd just get angry," Abe said. "Daniel, what's goin' on? Are you drunk?"

"No! I'm just feelin' sentimental. This is my last day as a free man."

"You've been with Kevin for seven years."

"I know. I just, I never thought this day would come."

Somehow Abe knew that Daniel wasn't talkin' about waitin' on the Supreme Court. "Oh my God, you do have cold feet. I swear, Daniel, if you leave that man —"

"No! That's not it! It's just . . . it's a lot, is all. You're here and Granny Sue will be here, and that's all I ever wanted. But now Mom's comin', and your mama and daddy, and a bunch of neighbors . . ."

"You invited 'em."

"Yeah, but I didn't expect them all to come!"

"It's as if they like you or something."

"That's the thing. At first I thought I would just invite people, and then it would be on them to decide if they'd come or not, you know."

"Cuz you're marryin' another feller?" Abe did a little hillbilly dance.

"Shut up. I know it's stupid. Nobody's

said 'boo' about it since high school, except sometimes Carlene asks me to help with her hair. When have I ever done a woman's hair?"

"Never?"

"I guess I was testing people, and didn't expect them to pass."

"And now you're . . . disappointed?"

"No! I'm happy, okay! God!" He threw himself off the bed and tore his hand through his hair.

"Daniel," Abe said, putting a rough hand on his shoulder. "You're kin, and they love you, Lord knows why. And Kevin loves you. And they love Kevin. And soon Kevin will be kin, officially, and so even if they don't love him, they'll love him, you know what I mean?"

Daniel nodded to the carpet.

Abe squeezed his shoulder. "No more of this, okay? We're gonna practice for the big party tomorrow, and then we're gonna have that big party day after tomorrow, and then you and Kevin will go back to the big city, and nothing will be different but a little piece of paper."

Daniel sighed. He started for the door, but turned on his heel and tackled Abe into a bear hug. "Thanks, brother."

"It's okay. Saves me gettin' out my shot-

315

gun later, that's all."

Daniel laughed, and Abe knew it was all okay.

CHAPTER FOUR

Emma groaned and stretched and flexed her toes. It took her a second to remember where she was — West Virginia, wedding, gigantic bed in a picturesque mountain lodge-y thing. She reached her arms out. Yup. Still couldn't reach the edges.

She smiled. So much better than her cramped one-bedroom in Bloomington. More room, better view — she might just stick around. Then her stomach growled.

Looking at the bedside clock, she realized why. It was after midnight, which meant she had slept through dinner and whatever post-dinner activities Kevin had planned for them. She felt a little bad.

Also, not that bad.

The idea of sitting through meeting all of those people and making small talk — it made her want to get back under the covers. She'd always been like that, ever since she was old enough to make small talk. The only place she felt comfortable talking to strangers was over the Reference Desk.

The joys of being an introvert.

She reached for her phone to see if Becky and Co. had tried to rouse her, but she saw that she still had no reception. Nobody did, except for Bernie, who refused to be beholden to one corporation and so had one of those pay-as-you-go phones. She thought it protected her from Big Brother's Big Data. Liam pointed out that she paid with a credit card, so at least one of the big brothers knew what she was spending her money on. Which led to an uncomfortable yelling fight, with Becky intervening. And now Bernie was the only one with a signal on her phone, and so she considered the argument won.

Emma stood up and stretched some more, and noticed a piece of paper shoved under the door.

We knocked. A lot. So either you've been abducted by aliens or you're taking an introvert's nap. I won't point out that you will eventually have to socialize. Instead, like a good friend, I will let you off the hook. This time.

Unless you've been abducted by aliens, in which case, please take notes so I can

318

be prepared for our new overlords.
— Liam (and Becky and Bernie, who
was insistent that we not save you any
leftovers)

Ha-ha, she thought. *Friends.*

Fortunately, Kevin's hospitality included a small welcome basket, including homemade muffins, apparently made by Daniel's granny. She should probably save one for breakfast tomorrow, she thought as she devoured the first and was eyeballing the second. But by tomorrow it would probably be stale. And the trail mix was probably meant for tomorrow's walk in the woods, but surely someone would share. As she popped a nut in her mouth, she made a mental inventory of the guests she knew who she might hit up for a handout: Liam (no), Bernie (doubtful), Becky (probably). Kevin would be mad she'd eaten ahead of schedule. Maybe that cute guy with the beard she saw checking in behind them. She liked beards. She liked his beat-up boots. She liked the way his jeans hugged his —

And the bag of trail mix was empty. And she was fully awake.

Totally awake enough to be productive.

Totally.

Totally productive.

319

Especially after turning on her tablet and discovering that the Wi-Fi password didn't work so no social media distractions. She could call down to the front desk for it. She should check her e-mail. For productivity. Except the university was closed for winter break and all of her best friends were here in the lodge with her, so unless she wanted to slog through the junk mail that multiplied like little digital rabbits, there was no academic need to check her e-mail.

She opened the first article on her desktop folder, labeled "RBJOYNFYD," which, of course, stood for Review Before January Or You'll Never Finish Your Dissertation. All 126 pages opened in an instant. There were now no obstacles to her reading about "Metadata and the Structure of Information: Subject Headings vs. Folksonomy: A Tale of Two Public Library OPACs."

She put her feet up on the edge of the bed and started to read.

Abe was full. He sure missed home-cooked meals. Not that he couldn't cook. It was just that beans on toast didn't have the same appeal as slow-cooked greens and squash casserole.

Kevin and his librarian friends had ducked out early, but he, Daniel, their cousin Pete, and a bunch of Pete's brothers — the ones who used to run around together causing trouble at the old home place — had closed down the lodge bar. (Abe still couldn't believe the lodge had a bar, let alone a restaurant that appeared to serve more than sloppy joes and bug juice. This place really had changed since he was last here as a young Boy Scout.) Pete, though, was relishing a night off from being a suburban dad and he wasn't ready for the night to end. Once he and Daniel started telling stories — well, it was a good thing there weren't many others staying at the lodge that weekend, because the Tates were taking over.

Abe was just starting to get itchy fingers when Pete told him to go get his fiddle. Pete wasn't even his brother, but he sure bossed him around like he was. Never mind that Abe actually wanted to play. All that reminiscing could definitely use musical accompaniment, especially when their memories had been lubricated by the finest local beer. (That was another thing — there were local breweries in town! When Abe was a kid, there was only a shack where you could buy cheap ice-cream sandwiches, and that wasn't even open in the winter.)

Once Abe got away from the fireplace in the lobby, the rest of the hotel was quiet.

Some clever architect had designed the place so the ruckus in the lobby couldn't be heard where sensible people were trying to get their beauty rest. If it didn't look so much like *The Shining,* it would have been actually peaceful. Dang, Abe was definitely getting citified. He used to crave the quiet, the way it would envelop him and clear his mind. Now he was so used to the noise of an urban apartment complex full of starving musicians, well, a man got used to the constant rehearsing and musical pissing contests.

He opened the sliding glass door and stepped out onto the little balcony. Dang, it was cold. He took deep breaths of sharp mountain air, blew out to watch it crystallize. It was quiet out here, too. It smelled like trees and snow and firewood. He looked up and above the trees, he could see the daggun stars. When was the last time he saw actual stars? This many stars? The only stars the people he knew in Nashville wanted to see wore rhinestone cowboy boots. (Actually, he'd love to see a country star wearing rhinestone cowboy boots instead of the expensive, beat-up-looking motorcycle boots everybody wore now.) (Not that he would ever wear rhinestone cowboy boots himself.) (Well, he might. Depended on the scenario.) (This fresh air was doing something funny to his brain.)

He went back inside, took his fiddle out of its case, and thought about going downstairs. Pete was on a roll, and when that guy got going, he could make walking down a quiet hallway sound like a slapstick epic. Abe had missed that, even though he'd heard most of the stories a hundred times. Heck, he was *in* most of the stories, whether he liked it or not. He took one more look at the balcony. It was so quiet. It might just be quiet enough for him to write something. He hadn't felt like writing music in a while. And there was a chair out there. And his emotions were high. Confused, but high. He was missing his home, but he'd moved to Nashville for a reason, right? The reason was to make music.

Trouble was, he wasn't making music. Sure, he was playing. Open mics like every other idiot, playing parties and weddings, picking up gigs as a set musician at little indie studios. But playing on a bunch of other hopeful musicians' records was not fulfilling his dreams. Sometimes he thought he'd be better off moving home and working at Walmart. At least all of his musical juices wouldn't be sucked out of him by the end of the day.

Ah, screw it, he thought, and grabbed his coat and scarf and the fingerless gloves his mom had made him last year. He set up on the balcony, leaned back in the little chair, put his feet up on the railing, and started to play.

Based on the results, end-users relying on folksonomy fiddled —

Emma shook her head. That wasn't right.

End-users relying on folksonomy achieved similar results to those using subject heading guidance. The efficiency of achieving those results depended on the wail of the high lonesome fiddler —

Emma tossed her tablet on the bed in frustration. *Focus,* she told herself. *Pay attention to the folksonomies, dammit.*

It was quiet again, so she reached for the tablet and sat down heavily in the easy chair. She propped her feet up on the table and started again.

The efficiency of achieving those results varied based on the subject's training. More experienced researchers navigated the subject headings quickly, while freshmen, who we can assume have little experience listening to fiddles cry out over the dark winter trees —

"That's it," she said, and she stood. Maybe she would be able to focus if she stood.

It was two A.M. and she sure wasn't tired — her power nap and protein snack had taken care of that. But she still didn't have enough brain power to focus. Every errant sound was a potentially more interesting distraction. Like the fiddle. Her door was closed. Where was that damn fiddle music coming from? Was someone standing in the woods?

She tried one more time.

Respondents reported a greater comfort level with long, low notes carried off by the wind.

She shook her head. That was definitely not in the study.

If it was, it would make the thing a lot more interesting.

Maybe she should start creating soundtracks to academic research papers. She could make millions! If only it helped actually absorb information.

Or maybe she really was tired, and her exhaustion was just disguising itself as manic late-night genius.

It was late. Who the hell was playing a violin at two in the morning?

Whoever it was, they were entirely responsible for her losing another day of potential productivity.

The more she thought about it, the more she blamed the nocturnal musician for her problems. She would have this study done and another one halfway read if *someone* wasn't so inconsiderate.

She should call down to the front desk and complain. On second thought, she wanted the satisfaction of seeing whoever it was come face-to-face with the consequences of their actions.

If only she could find out where they were playing.

She listened. Of course, it was silent. *Now* he was quiet. Because she had decided that this errant fiddler was obviously a man. Or a ghost. But a man-ghost.

She picked up her tablet.

The music started again.

She put her tablet down.

It stopped.

Are you kidding me? She picked up her tablet again.

Nothing.

She started reading.

Respondents reported

Waa-waa-waa, said the ghost-fiddle with annoyingly precise timing.

Dammit, if she didn't get this article read, she would never finish her PhD and then what was the point of it all? She was on this path for a reason. Just because she couldn't remember the reason right now . . .

She opened the sliding glass door, gasping as the cold air hit her pajama'd front. But there was no time for cold. There was only time for action.

"Hey!" she said weakly. It sounded a lot more forceful in her head. Her inner monologue didn't account for the cold.

The music stopped.

Go me, she thought. *Asserting my authority. Liam was wrong; I totally am tough enough to work in a public library.*

She was just turning to go back to the warmth of her room, when the mysterious fiddler started again.

"Can you stop, please?" This one was a little pathetic. But she felt a little pathetic. And desperate, on account of not finishing her articles and the world falling apart.

The music stopped again. She wasn't going to just turn her back, not this time. Fool me once, etc. She stood her ground, shivering. "Please," she said.

"Are you okay up there?"

She stepped to the edge of the balcony and looked over. No one was on the ground, at least no one visible in the dark of the night. And it was really dark here.

"What?" she asked the mystery man in the dark.

"Are you in some kind of trouble?"

"Who is this?"

"I heard you telling someone to stop. Are you in trouble?"

"Oh!" The mystery man in the dark was just a Good Samaritan. That felt kind of nice, knowing that someone was willing to rescue her, should she need rescuing. "I'm fine, as long as that asshole stops playing the damn fiddle."

She looked down, trying to make out her savior's shape in the dark, when a head appeared. From the balcony below her. It was a man. It was the hot, bearded man from the check-in desk.

"You mean this damn fiddle?" he asked, holding a fiddle aloft.

"Uh," she said. "Yes." It was probably that fiddle. She supposed there could be another fiddle somewhere else in the hotel. But she was too cold to argue. "Do you know what time it is?"

"Time to go inside and shut the door?"

"I did, and I could still hear *Deliverance.*"

"First of all, that's a banjo. Second of all —"

"I don't care! I'm trying to concentrate and your damn fiddling —"

"What are you concentrating on at two A.M.?"

"None of your business!"

"Because if there's a man in your room and he's distracted by a little mood music . . ."

"That's hardly mood music!"

He played something low and slow and something in her gut started heating up.

"You still there?"

She peered back over the edge. He was twisting his neck, obviously trying to look up at her.

"Step to the edge of your balcony, I can't see you."

"Why do you need to see me?"

"I just like to see who I'm talking to."

"No."

"Okay, Mystery Woman."

"I'm not a mystery woman!"

"Just a Mysterious Late-Night Concentrator."

"I'm . . . I'm trying to read." Well, that was embarrassing. He'd thought she was entertaining a gentleman caller, and she was reading. If that wasn't a metaphor for her life, she didn't know what was.

"Ah. You must be one of Kevin's librarians."

Oh God. Now he knew who she was. She should just go inside. She shouldn't stand out in the cold and flirt with a handsome man who was disturbing the peace.

"Okay, Mystery Librarian. I'm getting a crick in my neck, so I'm gonna go inside."

"Okay."

"You should go inside, too. You sound cold."

"Okay."

"You want, I could come up and keep you warm."

The grammar was atrocious, but there was something about the way he said it. Smooth like whiskey. She shivered, not entirely from cold.

"Okay, Mystery Librarian. I had to try. See you soon." He played a few parting notes, then she heard a door slide shut, and it was quiet.

Good.

That was what she wanted.

Quiet.

She sighed, and the lungful of cold air made her cough.

She went inside, where she had no more excuses for not getting work done.

CHAPTER FIVE

Because it was way too cold for a sunrise walk, Kevin had been persuaded to adjust his schedule, or so said the note slipped under Emma's door later that morning. This was good news, as she had slept late, and the walk would have been over and she didn't think her friends would forgive her that much society-avoiding. Besides, she had come all this way, driven all the way from Indiana and risked harrowing mountain roads (with someone else driving), to have a reunion with her friends. She should reunite with them.

It looked like the odds were ever in her favor, as Kevin's note explained the new schedule:

Due to Mother Nature's pernicious stubbornness, the early morning walk has been postponed.

The new schedule is: early lunch, then

afternoon walk to admire the beautiful snow-kissed woods, then rehearsal for those involved, then rehearsal dinner for all. Then early to bed for those who need beauty sleep, then morning ablutions, then watch Daniel become the luckiest man in the world by marrying such an organized and attractive man. Then I don't care what you do because I'll be busy.

Emma smiled at the note, and marveled at Kevin's ability to revise his schedule and get it printed and delivered so early. She wasn't surprised — to know Kevin was to know Kevin's ability to plan and, as Daniel said, "Pinterest the hell out of anything." He had an unending supply of energy to devote to the details.

And monogrammed stationery.

Daniel was the first man Kevin had ever dated who was laid-back. Kevin usually went for fellow type A's, which led to competition and bickering and lots of really uncomfortable silences when they all went out together. Daniel was different. He didn't care about the little things, but he appreciated them. He seemed charmed by Kevin's insanity. And when Daniel teased him for it, Kevin would smile back, not blow up. That's how Emma knew Daniel was The One. They balanced each other out. Daniel made Kevin breathe.

She flopped back on the giant bed, still clutching Kevin's note. She wanted a Daniel. Not Kevin's Daniel — there were more than a few obstacles to that relationship working out. But she wanted the kind of guy who would balance her out, smooth out her frantic edges, help her realize that, yes, she was on the right path and she would be a great researcher in the field of library and information science. And if he looked something like Daniel, she wouldn't complain.

She thought about the Fiddler on the Balcony. He was tall and broad, like Daniel. He wore more plaid and had more facial hair. He kept irregular hours. His social skills were as bad as hers, but differently bad.

Balance.

Her stomach growled. Last night's muffins had been delicious, but she needed real food, especially if she was going to endure a "walk." She'd gone on a "walk" with Kevin and Daniel before. Daniel's idea of a "walk" was any other normal person's idea of a hike that required, like, supplies and gear. Good thing Kevin was a preparer. And that she'd packed long underwear.

She hopped in the shower, and in record time she was clean and layered up for a light, probably-at-least-ten-mile walk in the West Virginia woods.

The hotel felt dark this morning, she thought as she followed her nose to the bacon awaiting her in the restaurant. She looked up at the high windows, and the sky was an ominous gray. Good band name, she thought, tucking it away to tell music-obsessed Liam later. And good thing she'd packed long underwear, even if it did make her jeans feel a little snug.

Snug jeans and growling stomach, and here she was, faced with the fluffiest-looking biscuits she'd ever seen. Good thing her dress for the wedding was forgiving, because she planned on eating the hell out of this breakfast.

The restaurant was more crowded than when they'd checked in the day before. There were definitely more kids running around and people had pushed tables to-gether and were sitting in massive, loud groups, laughing and slapping backs and wearing faces that said they didn't want to be anywhere else.

And Emma didn't know a single one of them.

This was her nightmare.

She was about to turn tail and retreat to the solace of her room, but her growling stomach wouldn't let her go. Plus, when she turned around, she ran face-first into a Wall of Liam.

"Running away?" he asked.

"No," she answered in a manner that was not at all cagey. "I was just going to look for you guys."

"Huh." He turned her around by her shoulders and pointed her in the direction of a small table in the corner where Becky and Bernie sat, enjoying coffee and full plates of food and, if the looks on their faces were any indication, Emma's discomfort.

Hilarious.

She didn't know if she could handle their gentle ribbing on an empty stomach. Fortunately, she didn't have to, and she accepted a plate from an older woman in front of her in the buffet line.

"You here for the weddin'?" she asked, totally dropping her *g*.

"Yes." Emma nodded and lifted up the lid of the chafing dish.

"Mmm . . . sausage gravy," the woman explained.

"Ah," Emma said.

"You put that on your biscuits."

"Oh, right. Biscuits and gravy. Got it."

The woman laughed. "You must be one of the friends from out of town. Are you an architect or a librarian?"

"Librarian."

"The last wedding I went to, I could just ask 'bride or groom' to figure out where people belonged."

Emma braced herself for what she had been bracing herself for as soon as she got the invitation to a gay wedding in West Virginia.

The woman laughed. "Well, this old dog ain't too old to learn new tricks. If it's good enough for the Supreme Court, it's good enough for me. And as long as that Kevin is good to my Daniel, I don't care what kind of plumbing he's got."

Sound logic. Emma was glad she didn't have to make polite conversation with a bigot. She hadn't even had coffee yet. If she had, she would have been more ashamed of her assumptions about old ladies in West Virginia.

"I'm Sue Holstein, Daniel's great-aunt." Emma tucked her empty plate onto her arm and shook the outstretched hand. "Most people call me Granny Sue."

"Okay, hi. I'm Emma."

"Nice to meet you, Emma. So are you the

one who works in the big city?"

Emma shook her head. "No, I'm in a college town, working toward my doctorate."

Granny Sue whistled. "Lotta work."

Emma nodded.

"Better you than me. I'm happy with my little room of books. Of course, if I could get people to bring them back on time, I'd like it even better."

"Room of books?"

Granny Sue pointed to her gray hair swept up in a bun. "Old-school librarian, I think you kids call it. Down in Coral Bottom."

"Daniel never mentioned . . . wait. No. Now I remember. He definitely did. Your storytimes are legendary."

Granny Sue threw her head back and laughed. "That's just us mountain folk. We don't know when to shut up."

"I think you're being modest," Emma said. She was also trying to decide if she had enough room on her plate for the fruit, on account of the biscuits and gravy and bacon and eggs and . . . she'd better add some fruit or she'd probably have a heart attack.

"You hang around here long enough, you'll see how folks love to talk. And there's nothin' we love more than tellin' each other stories, even if we have heard the durned

338

things a hundred times before."

"I'd love to talk to you about your library," Emma said. That was really her dream — to run a small library of her own. But that wasn't a very lofty goal, especially now that she was pursuing her doctorate.

"I'll do you one better — stop in later, if Daniel hasn't killed you on that hike of his."

Emma glanced through the dining room and out the window. "Maybe it'll be canceled."

"You think Kevin would allow something like that?"

Emma laughed. "He might not have a choice if it starts snowing."

"Bless his heart," Granny Sue added with a wink. "You wanna join our table?"

Emma looked toward the table of rambunctious kids waving Granny Sue over.

"Thanks, my friends are saving me a seat."

"That's right, you visit with your friends. I'll catch up with you later and we'll talk shop."

Emma headed to the table, but there were no free seats. Kevin stood and pushed his chair under her.

"Morning, sunshine," he said, pecking her on the cheek. "You came out in public today."

"And I wore thermal underwear," she

added helpfully.

Kevin looked at her.

"For the hike? As much as it pains me to admit it, the hike may not be happening." He gestured to the gray mist hanging over the woods.

"Oh." Becky sounded actually disappointed. "I brought my camera and everything."

"It's supposed to stop raining this afternoon," said a stranger who approached their table and slapped Kevin on the back.

"So Daniel keeps telling me," he said. "Folks, this is Daniel's favorite cousin, Abe."

"Hi, Abe," said the librarians.

Oh God. The hot guy from reception. Emma was stalking him without even trying.

"Abe here's a big fancy Nashville musician."

"I don't know about that," Hot Abe protested.

"What do you play? Anything we would know?" asked Liam.

"Not unless you're really into old-timey fiddle music."

A piece of Emma's biscuit lodged itself firmly in her throat.

"Slow down, there," Bernie said, slapping her back. Emma looked up, watery-eyed, and gave a thumbs-up. Abe was looking at her funny.

Oh God, she thought as she took the glass of water Becky handed her. *He knows. He knows I'm the one who yelled at him and likes reading more than sex.*

"Well, it was nice meeting you folks. I'm sure we'll see plenty more of each other."

"On the hike," Becky said brightly.

Abe smiled and turned toward the buffet, but not before he definitely winked at Emma.

She hoped the warm feeling sweeping over her entire body was her coming down with the flu, and not a full-body blush.

"Damn, it just got hot in here," Bernie said. "Becky, did it just get hot in here?"

"It got somethin'," she said, fanning herself with her napkin. "Liam, do you feel that?"

Liam looked up from his plate of biscuits and gravy, a forkful halfway to his mouth. "Uh . . . what?"

"He doesn't feel it," Bernie told her. "I wonder if Emma feels it. Emma, does it feel hot in here?"

"Okay, ha-ha-ha, I'm blushing, I get it."

"The question is, *why* are you blushing?" Bernie asked smugly, as if she knew that Emma had already made an anonymous ass of herself in front of the most attractive man in West Virginia.

"Yeah, why are you blushing?" Liam asked. His question seemed a little more sincere.

"Shut up," Emma said, and suddenly her biscuits and gravy were the most interesting thing she had seen all weekend.

"Are you okay?" Bernie asked. "You look a little red."

"I'm fine," Emma said. "Just, ah, too much biscuits and gravy."

"I've never heard of such a thing," Liam said, shoveling more biscuits and gravy into his mouth.

Kevin looked toward the door. "Uh-huh," he said.

"Uh-huh what?" Becky asked.

"Uh-huh my hot future cousin-in-law just walked in and Emma is blushing like the house is on fire."

"I am not," Emma insisted, even though she could feel herself getting hotter by the second. "It's just . . . I'm wearing thermal underwear, that's all."

"Yeah, Kevin," Bernie said. "It's just a problem with her underwear."

"I would throw part of this biscuit at you but I don't want to waste biscuit," Emma said, giving Bernie her best menacing glare.

342

Bernie held her hands up in surrender.

"And yet," Kevin said, pulling a chair from the next table and sitting down. Right next to Emma. "And yet, I still wonder why the sight of my hot future cousin-in-law makes you blush."

"He is pretty hot," Becky admitted.

"What are you guys talking about?" Liam asked.

"Eat your biscuits," Kevin said. "Girl talk."

Liam rolled his eyes.

"Hot guys always make Emma blush," Becky said.

Liam turned around, then quickly back to the table. "The guy with the beard? Not bad. Carry on."

"You might as well tell us what's making you blush," Bernie said. "Because right now I'm imagining that you made a late-night trip to the ice machine and he came swaggering up, bearded and shirtless, and asked to carry your ice back to your room and oh my God if that's what really happened I'm going to kill you."

"What? No!"

"Good. Remind me not to fill my ice bucket before I go to bed."

"Why was he shirtless?" Liam asked.

"Because it's my fantasy, and men don't wear shirts in my fantasy," Bernie explained.

"Do I wear shirts in your fantasy?"

"I don't fantasize about you. You're Liam."

"Uh . . . thanks?"

And then Abe was back, his plate almost as full as Emma's had been before she started choking on it. He shifted his plate to one hand and grabbed an empty chair with the other. He twirled it around and plonked it at their table. Right across from Emma.

She felt her face getting redder.

She saw Bernie's smug curiosity.

She focused on her breakfast.

"After all this food, I'm gonna need a nap," Abe said. "Can't I persuade you and Daniel to change the schedule?"

"Daniel wants a hike, Daniel gets a hike," Kevin said.

"Awww," said Becky and Bernie.

Abe muffled a yawn with his fist. "I don't know about you guys, but I didn't sleep too good last night. And I think I actually met one of you."

"Oh?" Bernie said, as the four pairs of eyes that were not Emma's swung in her direction.

"Well, I didn't really meet you. I was fidd-lin' on my balcony last night —"

"He plays the fiddle," Kevin explained.

"And someone unleashed the wrath of the devil upon my innocent head."

"It wasn't that bad!"

Emma realized what she was saying when the words were halfway out of her mouth, but by then it was too late.

"Aha! Mystery Librarian!" Abe said, pointing a biscuit at her with a smile.

"Why'd you unleash the wrath of the devil upon his innocent head?" Becky asked.

"I didn't! I was trying to work and he was making noise, so I just politely asked him to stop."

"Sure didn't sound polite to me."

"You were trying to work instead of coming to dinner?"

"No! This was after. It was the middle of the night."

"Why were you trying to work in the middle of the night?"

"Why were you playing music in the middle of the night?"

"I was kinda drunk," Abe explained. "That's my excuse."

"So that's where you disappeared to," Kevin said.

"I disappeared under the vengeful wrath of the mystery librarian."

"Well, you don't look any worse for wear."

"Nope. I feel great. I feel even better having met her in person. In fact, I feel so great that I'm going to eat my body weight in biscuits and gravy, and then I'm going to hike the hell out of these woods."

And then Abe picked up his plate and left, but not before tossing Emma a parting wink.

"Okay, Emma," Becky said, putting down her fork. "Tell us what really happened."

CHAPTER SIX

They ate, they laughed, they watched the rain turn to snow and then, finally, stop. Emma looked out the big picture window that showcased a beautiful view of the valley.

Yesterday it showcased a beautiful view of the valley.

Today there was a gray, wet mess.

Her toes curled in her wool socks. This was not hiking weather. This was curl-up-by-the-fire-and-read weather.

She looked longingly at the shelf of battered paperbacks next to the fireplace.

"I call dibs on the Johanna Lindsey," Bernie whispered in her ear.

"Oh, I have plenty of reading to do," Emma assured her, even though she had secretly had her eye on it, too. And that was one of the Malorys she hadn't read yet.

"We might still hike," Becky said. "That was meant to sound hopeful. Did it sound hopeful?"

They all shook their heads at her.

She shrugged. "I tried."

"Everyone, can I have your attention?" Daniel was standing on the stone hearth, his hands and his voice raised. "You may have noticed that Mother Nature isn't exactly cooperating with our plans."

There was a mild and general "boo" from behind her.

"But we are hearty mountain people, and we're not gonna let a little mud slow us down."

"We're not mountain people," Bernie pointed out. The boos turned into a hearty laugh.

"Exactly," Daniel said. "I don't want to pass up the opportunity to show you the beauty of my home place."

CHAPTER SEVEN

"This sucks," Pete's kid said.

"Language," Pete's wife said.

"He's not wrong," said Pete.

"I can hear you!" shouted Daniel from the front of the pack.

Despite the clear beauty of the night before, the ground was a mess. The trail was nothing but muddy sludge, and while the warm weather was great, it was also causing the snow to melt. Melted snow begets muddy sludge.

Good thing Abe had dug out his hiking boots.

Also, good thing he'd brought another pair of boots to wear to the wedding. Otherwise, he'd be playing barefoot. And after Daniel told him he wanted his wedding to be "country, but not hillbilly," he reckoned he'd better have a clean pair of shoes.

And yet, nothing could really distract him

from how much he loved these woods. Even the heavy clouds couldn't block all of the light coming through the trees. The muscles in his legs sang as they climbed the familiar path. He wanted to reach down and grab a handful of earth and take it back to Nashville with him.

Well, nothing except that whining kid of Pete's.

Anyway, it was only two inches of muddy sludge. Granny Sue had predicted six inches and begged off the walk. Ha, so much for being a hearty old woman.

He tripped over a rock that stuck out over the sludge. He caught himself, but not before slopping mud all over the librarian behind him.

The five of them were like a pack. He got that they hardly ever saw one another, and that Kevin's wedding was an excuse for a reunion. And he got that Kevin's family was small and not real psyched about Kevin marrying another man — and in West Virginia, no less — and so they weren't here for the whole pre-wedding weekend thing.

He just never would have thought that a pack of librarians would be so . . . loud.

He shouldn't be surprised. Librarians were people, too, and they came in all shapes and sizes and volumes. He knew a librarian in Nashville who was covered in tattoos and spent her free time hacking video games. Heck, you could hear Granny Sue coming from across the holler, even when she was in the library.

Maybe he was just annoyed because he just wanted to get one of the librarians alone.

Why he was tempted by a woman who'd spent all of last night yelling at him from a balcony, he had no idea. She was obviously the stereotypical librarian — uptight, way too serious, and just generally no fun.

Except that every time he snuck a glance back at her — just to make sure she and her friends were keeping up with Daniel's breakneck pace, which they weren't — she was laughing and smiling and shouting with the rest of them. But her laugh and smile and shout, those really stood out.

Unbelievable. He had a crush on a librarian.

Maybe it was just the wedding stuff, making him feel romantic. Or maybe he was thinking too much and he should just go back and talk to her.

"How're you guys doing back here?"

"It's not too late to call off the wedding, is it?" Kevin huffed. "I mean, am I seriously going to spend the rest of my life with a man who thinks this is fun?"

"I can hear you, darling!" Daniel shouted from the front.

"That was the idea!" Kevin shouted. "Also, I love you!"

"I'm just saying, if I see a snake, I'm out of here," the short one said. The blonde threw a rock in some leaves. "What was that?" the short one screamed. They all laughed.

"It's a bit cold for snakes," Abe said. City slickers.

"It's a bit cold for humans," the blonde grumbled.

"Not for our Emma," the short one said. "Since she was smart and wore thermal underwear."

"Sexy," said the blonde.

Abe looked over at Emma, squinting up at the treetops. She had these little crinkles around her eyes when she squinted, and he wanted to kiss each one of them.

That was definitely just the wedding talking.

He turned to admire her hairdo again, since apparently the wedding was transforming him into the kind of guy who admires hairdos.

Suddenly it was just the two of them on the trail. And not in a metaphorical way.

The rest of the group must've gotten a sudden burst of energy and were several paces up the hill.

It was a sign. The woods — and the librarians — wanted him to flirt with the librarian.

Emma caught Abe sneaking looks at her. She surreptitiously wiped her nose, checked for biscuit crumbs on her mouth. But he still kept doing it.

Maybe Liam was right. Maybe he was actually attracted to her.

She tried to wrap her head around that idea, thinking that, yeah, maybe it was possible. Sure, she was wearing an unflattering extra layer under her jeans and she might or might not have had something stuck to her face, but, dammit, she had parts that worked and she deserved to be flirted with. Even if the guy was way hotter than any guy who'd ever flirted with her before.

The thing was, he didn't act like a hot guy. He didn't smile like he knew he looked good when he smiled. When he smiled, it just looked like he was happy.

So that was it. She was being flirted with, and she was going to take it and run because this was a romantic weekend and she was on vacation and she wasn't going to think about work and —

And suddenly she was on her knees in the mud.

The first thing she thought was a particularly unladylike curse that made the whining kid laugh. The second thing she thought was that her knees felt wet. The skin of her knees felt wet through one layer of waffle-weave and one layer of denim, and she already felt so gross that she just wanted to sit down in the mud and wait for spring.

Then, the third thing. She was upright and standing on her own two feet.

In mud.

Not in her own two shoes, though. No, she could tell even without looking that one of those shoes was definitely not on her foot, and she could tell that because the mud was soaking into her sock, and practically squishing between her toes.

Unpleasant.

"Hey, you okay?"

Dazed and muddy, she looked over at Hot Abe, who was clutching her hands and holding her upright.

She gave a thumbs-up. A muddy thumbs-up. Oh God, her hands were a mess. And now so were Abe's.

He looked so serious and she was so embarrassed and the only thing she could do was let out a completely unladylike guffaw that ended in gasping laughter. She couldn't help it. It was the funniest thing she had ever seen.

"Emma!" Her friends came streaming back down the trail to where she had been kneeling, and was now squatting, doubled over in nervous laughter.

"I'm fine! I'm fine." She wiped her cheek, which she immediately realized was a muddy mistake but too late. And that was funny, too.

CHAPTER EIGHT

By the time Emma got down the hill, her pants had dried enough that they were just really, really cold, and really, really heavy with mud. One hand was holding up the waistband of her wet, heavy jeans and the other was holding onto Abe's arm. She didn't really need to hold his arm. Her foot didn't hurt — it was just really muddy and really cold. But he offered and he'd already gotten his flannel shirt muddy trying to dislodge her from the mud, and who was she to deny chivalry?

"Oh, bless your heart, look at that mess!"

Abe was not at all impressed with Granny Sue's concern, especially since it came with a healthy dose of teasing laughter. Poor Emma. She was going to be part of a story, he could tell. The time Granny Sue's nephew got married and that poor librarian got herself covered in mud. Poor thing couldn't handle the West Virginia hills.

Part of Abe wanted to protect her from ridicule, even if it wasn't ridicule at all — being part of a teasing story was a great sign of affection around here. Another part of him was really glad that she would be part of a story, that whenever he saw Granny Sue, at least until he did something else stupid, she would remind him of the time he went hiking and came back with a muddy librarian on his arm.

He liked this muddy librarian on his arm.

But now his muddy librarian was starting to shiver.

"I fell," his shivering librarian said.

"I see that," Granny said. "Looks like you took half the mountain with you."

He felt Emma shrug against his arm. "I wanted a souvenir."

Granny Sue threw her head back and laughed. Now Emma was definitely going to be part of a story. Getting a big laugh like that from Granny Sue meant you were friends for life.

"Well, come away from that door, you're going to freeze. Here, there's a fire going inside. Go on and stand by that."

Emma looked like she wanted to protest, but she let go of his arm and allowed herself to be led away.

And now he was cold.

Well, it was cold out. And he was kind of covered in mud. Oh, nowhere near librarian-level, but he'd done a pretty good job messing up his jeans in his brief rescue attempt.

Hmph. Why wasn't Granny Sue making a fuss over him? He was cold, too, dammit. And he practically carried her down the hill!

"Quit that assy face, mister," she shouted over to him. "Come over here and get warm."

Emma gave him a shy smile, and he felt warm all over. Sure, he'd go stand next to her. He'd even help her get out of those wet clothes if she needed him to.

Chapter Nine

"While your drawers are dryin', you wanna run me over to the library?"

Abe looked up from the ancient dulcimer he was trying to tune for Granny Sue. He didn't have the heart to tell her that the old thing had played its last session, especially since she had offered up her washing machine to him and Emma and their mud-soaked hiking clothes. "Granny Sue, you're supposed to have the day off."

She waved Abe's concern away. "Just for a minute. I promised Miss Elsa Mae I'd bring her books to her. She's older'n the hills; you can't expect her to wait to find out what happens to Jack Reacher."

"The library?"

Emma was in the doorway of Granny Sue's kitchen, Granny Sue's giant wool socks on her feet, her hands wrapped around a steaming mug of coffee.

He'd never been jealous of a mug before.

This wedding stuff was really getting to him.

"Oh, that's right! You're studyin' country libraries, aren't you?" said Granny Sue in a way that indicated to Abe she hadn't forgotten for a second that Emma would be interested in seeing their tiny library.

Abe pulled out his phone to check the time. He was two digits into the four-digit unlock password when the battery gave out. "I guess we have plenty of time," he said with a shrug. Which was a nice way of saying that Granny Sue had made up her mind, so he didn't really have a choice.

Plus, Emma looked like someone had just told her she'd won the Nobel Prize and it came with a pack of fluffy puppies and twenty pounds of chocolate. It was a good look for her. Heck, if visiting a crummy library put that look on her face, what would she look like if she was really excited?

Man, he was in trouble. This wedding stuff was really getting to him.

A library! A real, rural library! Emma knew she should try to keep her nerd flag from flying too high — she'd just met these people, and one of them was really hot and she would probably try to flirt with him later, and no reasonable sexual being should get that excited about the prospect of visiting a library. She just couldn't help it. And if Abe was turned off by her enthusiasm (which was perhaps an understatement) (okay, definitely an understatement), then forget him. She'd rather have a library than a man any day.

Oh God. Was that true? She'd never actually articulated that thought before. It seemed wrong. But it felt right.

Of course, so did Abe's arm, helping her down the hill.

She shook her head. She was not required to make a choice. She was just required to put on shoes (and relinquish Granny Sue's fabulous wool socks), get in the truck, and go visit a library.

A library!

As they bounced over the country roads, Granny Sue explained the history of the area.

"Coral Bottom used to be called Coal Bottom, on account of the coal mines up the road. The county was dotted with company towns, up until World War II, when the men of Coal Bottom all went off to fight, and most of the women left for work in a munitions factory outside of Charleston."

"Everyone just left?"

"Well, not everyone. But enough left that the mine shut down. Least that's the excuse they gave for shutting down the mine. Had nothing at all to do with the lack of coal and the union agitators."

"Don't get Granny Sue started on union agitators."

"Your great-grandfather was a union agitator, and you better be proud of that."

"Yes, ma'am."

"Anyway, the mine shut down, so most people left. Only a few stubborn Tates stayed up in the hills and hollers."

"I don't want to shock you, Emma, but those stubborn Tates are where Granny Sue comes from."

"They're your kin too, Mr. Fancy Musician. And don't you forget it."

Abe gave Granny a quick salute.

"So everyone came back after the war was over?" Emma asked. There were driveways and dirt roads along their route — surely people still lived here.

"Well, yes, everyone but the coal company. But while most of the county was at war, the Communists moved in."

"Communists?"

"Oh, yes. My daddy was blind in one eye — he had a little run-in with the company's union busters — so he couldn't serve his country. I guess some Communists decided they'd try to grow the movement in small places. Though what they expected to get out of a town that, at its peak, had less than a thousand people, I have no idea."

"So this is a Communist enclave?"

"I'm not finished. The Communists came, and my daddy was excited at first, because they had ideas about workers' rights and community property that felt right to his ol' West Virginia heart. We'd been taking care of each other since long before the company moved in, so why not make it official?"

"He was pretty optimistic."

"He was a fool, I don't mind you sayin' so. But the Communists came in, and the first thing they wanted to do was change the name of the town. The people left weren't in a position to put up much of a fight, but they weren't quite ready to support it."

"How'd they just change the name?"

"One morning we all woke up, and all of the signs had an extra letter. At that point, the folks who were left were no fan of the coal companies, though they wouldn't say so out loud. So they figured they'd just let it be. And now we're Coral Bottom."

"Which makes no sense at all," Abe pointed out.

"No, it doesn't," Granny said with a proud smile.

"Coral Bottom, Communist enclave," Emma said in wonder.

"Oh, no, they drove the Communists out by the end of the fifties. But the coal companies never came back, so the new name stuck."

Emma sat back. "This might be the most amazing place I've ever been."

Granny Sue laughed and patted her knee. "Oh, these hills are full of stories like that. You stick around awhile, you'll see."

Hmm, she thought. *Stick around awhile.*

"There's a saying around here," Abe said, pulling in front of a tall carriage house. " 'Never let the truth stand in the way of a good story.' "

"Wait," Emma said. "So it's not true?"

"We're here!" Granny Sue said, getting out of the truck. "Welcome to the Coral Bottom Public Library."

CHAPTER TEN

The placard outside the library indicated that the Coral Bottom Public Library building was once the carriage house attached to the coal baron's mansion that now served as town hall. In 1946, the Communists, with the help of the local Boy Scouts, converted the house into the library. A small addition was added in the 1980s, but other than that, the building was historically accurate.

It was also historically adorable. The trees outside were covered in colorful lights. Inside, it was warm and it smelled like books and firewood and trees.

The tree smell came from the large, decorated tree in the corner, decked out with lights and tinsel and paper flags. Granny pulled one off. "This is a wishin' tree. Lots of folks in need around here, but we take care of each other."

Emma turned one of the flags over: WARM SOCKS, MY LITTLE PONY, HARRY POTTER.

"Folks take one, then wrap the presents and leave them here with the tag. There's no shame in asking for help, but some people don't like to."

"And everyone just takes their own presents?"

Granny Sue shrugged. "Haven't had a problem yet, and we've been doing them for twenty years."

Emma saw Abe flip over a few flags. He pulled off two of them and put them in his pocket. He caught her looking and gave her a wink.

"Well, come on in. Abe, you show her around, I've got to get those books for Elsa Mae."

Emma followed Abe to the middle of the high-ceilinged room. "Well," he said, stretching out his hands, "here's the Coral Bottom Library."

"Impressive."

"You have very low standards."

Emma leaned in to Abe to give him a playful shove that had nothing at all to do with reacquainting herself with the muscles in his arm.

"I spent a lot of time here as a kid. Mostly when I got in trouble. Instead of detention, the principal'd call Granny Sue and I'd have to sit in here after school. Almost made me wish I could have real detention."

Just then Granny Sue returned. "Okay, see you kids back at the lodge."

"What? You're not going back with us?" Abe asked.

Granny Sue just started shuffling a pile of books. "I need to get Elsa Mae her books. Edna and the girls are too busy here to do it."

Edna and "the girls" were old enough to be Granny Sue's mother, and he knew that they could run this library with their eyes closed.

Granny Sue was up to something.

Granny Sue was matchmaking.

She was notorious for saying that what "you young people do is none of my business," then going ahead and making it her business. She might claim innocence, but she was responsible for half the marriages in Coral Bottom. She was always nudging the most unexpected people together in a way that was only subtle to her unsuspecting victims. "Oh, you like *Dune*? You know, Carrie told me she's been a fan of *Dune* since she was in high school." "Oh, you're training to be a firefighter? Well, Janice has always had a thing for firefighters." "Oh, you're going to WVU? My nephew Dale lives in Morgantown — he'd be glad to show you around."

And it always worked. Carrie and Stephen, Janice and Elmer, Loretta and Dale — they'd all gotten married and most of them had a bunch of grandbabies for Granny Sue.

She'd even nudged Daniel in Kevin's direction, all the way out in California.

Come to think of it, she'd never gotten involved in Abe's love life.

So maybe he was wrong. Maybe she really did need to get the books she was holding to Elsa Mae.

Matchmaking or not (because what did he and Emma even have in common? She was getting her PhD, he could barely make rent), there was no arguing with Granny Sue once she'd said her piece. So they said good-bye and he opened the truck for Emma, and they headed back to the lodge.

She was awful quiet in the front seat. She didn't strike him as much of a talker, but the way she'd been asking questions back there in the library, he had a feeling that her still waters ran deep.

"What're you thinking?"

"Oh, nothing."

Oh yeah, real deep.

"I think I'm having an existential crisis," she blurted out.

"What now?"

"You grew up going to that library?"

Abe thought he might get whiplash from the twists and turns this girl's brain was making.

"Yeah. When I was a kid. When I got older, only in the summer. Or whenever Granny Sue dragged me in to be cheap labor."

"What was it like?"

"It was like it is now. Lots of books all over the place, lots of people reading to their kids. Usually there was someone asking Granny for help with property line problems or medical symptoms."

"She told you that?"

"No, only what I would overhear. Granny said she was like a priest, and what people asked her in the library was as secret as confession. Of course, if people asked her at the grocery store or in town, that was fair game."

"But the library was sacred."

"Sure, I guess."

"The sacred reference question. Do you have a piece of paper?"

He reached over and opened the glove box and handed her a napkin from Tudor's Biscuit World. She picked up the pen that fell to the floor and started scribbling and muttering to herself.

"You need a second napkin?"

She didn't say anything, just shook her head.

After a minute, she came up for air. Whatever inspiration had just struck her, it didn't seem to ease her existential crisis any.

"I get that, sometimes," he said.

"Get what?"

"An idea. Something'll just strike me and a song will pop into my head. I've learned that if I don't write it down right away, it'll be gone."

"You write songs? I thought you just played."

"Hey, now. I'm not one of those pretty-boy fiddlers who's just there to look good."

"Do they have those?"

"Nashville's lousy with 'em."

"You know, I've been to Nashville. I don't remember that."

"Oh, what'd you do in Nashville?"

"I went for the Southern Festival of Books."

"Of course."

"And to tour the library."

"Busman's holiday."

"I wish."

"What do you mean?"

"I'm not really a librarian. I mean, I have

my degree, and soon I'll have a doctorate, but I'm not an actual librarian."

"You're a fake librarian?"

"It feels that way."

"So that's the existential crisis."

"Yes. What makes you a librarian? Is it the degree or the work?"

"Or both?"

"That's what I think. Becky and Liam and Bernie and Kevin, they all got their degrees and now they're *doing* things."

"Aren't you doing things?"

She sighed. "You're right. Scholarship is a thing. It's important. It keeps the field going."

"Say it one more time with feeling."

She smiled at him, all crooked and cute.

"So what's the crisis? You're doing important work, but you're mad that you're not a librarian?"

"I'm not mad, I'm just . . . disappointed, I guess."

That gave him massive flashbacks to his misspent youth. It was always worse when his mama would say, "I'm not mad, I'm just disappointed." He came to learn that disappointed was way worse than mad. Come to think of it, his mama probably learned that from Granny Sue.

And being disappointed in yourself? Yeah,

he could relate to that. He'd gone to Nashville with big dreams, like an idiot kid, and now all he was doing was playing on other people's records and getting bitter at other people's success.

It was an ugly feeling. He didn't like it.

But his truck could only hold one existential crisis at a time.

"If you could do anything with your life, what would it be?"

"Anything?"

"Anything."

She looked thoughtful, then answered. "I should probably say save the world or something. But the truth is, I'd be Granny Sue."

Just when he was starting to get a crush on her.

"I mean, I'm not Granny Sue, but I would do what she does. Run a small library like that. That's the kind of library I grew up in, too, but in Indiana. I mean, it looked a lot different. Flat and stuff."

"Sure. Indiana is like that."

"But it had a similar feeling. Like everybody used it, even though the collection was small and crappy and the computers were outdated. We all went there after school to do homework and did the summer reading club. My mom would check out these giant historical novels, and sometimes Ms. Glass-meyer — that was the librarian — would set books aside that she thought my mom would like. I think that might be the only time I ever thought my mom was cool, when I discovered she had an in with the librarian."

He glanced over at her. "You know, your whole face changed when you told me that story."

She put her hands up to her cheeks. "Did it?"

"Your existential crisis was gone. Wait — now it's back."

"Well, I can't do that job."

"Why not?"

"I've come too far to turn back now."

"How far are you?"

"ABD. All But Dissertation."

"So write your dissertation and then go work at a tiny, sad library like the Coral Bottom one."

"Ha-ha. I wish it were that easy."

"If it were easy, they wouldn't give you that fancy piece of paper for it."

She leaned her head back on the headrest and let out the saddest sigh he'd ever heard. She had the face of a woman who was starring in her own country song. "The Saddest Librarian in Coral Bottom."

Even he probably couldn't make that work.

"You're so lucky that you grew up here."

He wasn't sure he had ever heard it expressed quite that way. More like, "You grew up HERE?"

"It's so beautiful. And peaceful."

"And boring."

"You think it's boring?"

"No, but I grew up here. I have fond memories and all that junk."

"So why'd you leave?"

"You can't make a living making music in Coral Bottom. Or Froggy Rock or any of these places."

"Can't you?"

"If I could, I never would have left."

"Even with the Internet? Can't you just, like, make a YouTube video and go viral?"

He was about to launch into his speech about how it wasn't that easy, you had to pay your dues, never mind that no matter how many dues he paid, the price always seemed to go up. And never mind that there were kids who did that, who just got famous like it was easy. He didn't even want to be famous, not really. He just wanted to make a living and get some respect. Not necessarily in that order. If it was easy, he would have done it by now.

But when he looked over at her, he saw that her grin was mischievous. So she wasn't an idiot. That was good.

"I ain't pretty enough for YouTube."

"Oh, you're pretty."

And now she looked red as a beet.

"I mean —"

"No, I heard you. You think I'm pretty. You can't take it back."

"I don't think you're pretty! You're . . . you're handsome."

He snorted.

"You are! In a rugged kind of way. With your beard and your plaid and stuff."

Well, now she had a crush on the Night Fiddler. First she has an existential crisis brought on by a small, well-loved library, then she met a thoughtful, funny, charming musician with a great smile upon whom she made a terrible first impression.

What did it matter? Her life was meaningless! Hopeless! She'd never finish her dissertation and she'd be alone forever! She wouldn't even be able to fulfill any meaningful stereotypes because she wasn't even a real librarian! And Kevin and Daniel were going to be happy forever and then Becky and Bernie and Liam would go home to their fulfilling library careers and she would just rot in her crappy apartment in Indiana and stare at her thesis, which still had not managed to write itself!

"Is it really that painful to admit that I'm ruggedly handsome?"

In all of her angsting, she'd forgotten that she was still in the truck with Abe. And that her anxious inner monologue was causing her to miss out on the beautiful scenery.

And now it was snowing.

"Oh," she said as fat, white flakes dotted the road in front of them.

Abe flicked the wipers on.

"Don't worry, we're almost there."

"I'm not worried, it's just — it's kind of magical, isn't it?"

He looked over at her and smiled. She was surprised the snow didn't melt.

"Wait till you see it in the morning when it's covering the trees."

"I bet it's a winter wonderland."

"It is. It's a daggun winter wonderland."

She giggled, because now she was the kind of person who giggled in the presence of a hot man with a snow-melting smile.

All too soon, he pulled into the parking lot in front of the lodge. "Wait here," he said, and hopped out of the truck and jogged around to her door. He started to pull it open and then —

"Oof," she heard from outside her door as Abe disappeared. Then she heard some other words.

People around here sure knew some very creative curses.

She pushed the door open just as Abe was standing up. "Are you okay?"

"Fine," he said, brushing off the seat of his pants. "Mostly hurt my pride. Careful, it's slippery."

"I see that," she said with a laugh, and set her feet on the ground.

Which promptly slid out from underneath her.

She grabbed onto the door for purchase, but she needn't have bothered, as Abe was right there, catching her by the elbow and holding her up.

"Slippery," she said, a little breathless from the fall. Not at all breathless from the smell of rugged man and woods and winter.

"You'd better hold on until we get inside."

"Mmm-hmm," she agreed, though they seemed to have parked on the only patch of black ice in the whole lot. Still, she had had enough falls today, both literal and figurative. It was better to play it safe. And if playing it safe meant Abe's strong arms around her as she walked into the lodge, well, so be it.

CHAPTER ELEVEN

Kevin raised an eyebrow as Abe walked through the door, practically carrying Emma. She was fine — heck, he'd hit the ground harder than she did — but it felt so good to have her lean into him that he might have held her a little tighter than necessary. She smelled like cinnamon. He loved cinnamon.

Thankfully, Kevin didn't say anything, although that eyebrow said plenty. Abe knew Kevin well enough to know that he would be subject to an interrogation later, but maybe Kevin would be too busy to notice.

And Marshall would beat WVU in the Friends of Coal Bowl.

At least Daniel didn't notice. He was too busy staring out the big picture window, his shoulders looking tense and worried. Abe wondered if this snow would ruin tomorrow's wedding. Kevin didn't seem worried, and if there was something to be worried about, Kevin was your man.

"Thanks for the ride," Emma said, not at all disengaging from his arms.

"No problem. Glad I could help with your existential crisis."

"I'm not sure you helped. You might have made it worse."

"Well, then. Sorry about that."

She shrugged. "It's okay." Her eyes still looked guarded and worried, but at least she was smiling.

"Emma! You're back!" The blond one — Becky, he was pretty sure — skipped up to them. "I heard you got to visit a library!"

And that was what got Emma out of his arms. She waved at him, then hustled off to talk to her friends about the Coral Bottom Public Library.

If she wasn't so cute, he would . . . well, he would probably like her anyway. Hard not to like someone with passion. Especially someone with a smile like that.

"And there's a fireplace!"

"In the library? That sounds dangerous." Bernie was curled up on the edge of the couch with a mug of hot chocolate. Emma had barely unwrapped her scarf before she started telling them about her trip to Coral

Bottom and the people and the library.

"What happened to your pants?" Liam asked.

"Oh." Her jeans were still in the dryer at Granny Sue's. She would definitely need those jeans before she left. But she wasn't worried about it. She kind of liked having an excuse to go back to Coral Bottom.

Maybe Abe would take her.

"And what about this guy? Daniel's cousin?" Becky asked.

"What about him?"

"Um, he's hot," Bernie said into her mug.

"He's okay," she said, even as she felt the traitorous blush heat her face. Why was she pretending? She liked him, and these were her friends. What was the worst that could happen? They'd tease her, she'd blush, but she'd still get to talk about Abe. "Actually, he's really nice. And funny. And he has all these stories about growing up in Coral Bottom."

"And you totally have a crush on him," said Bernie. "Not that I blame you."

"So? I came here for the wedding and the reunion. I didn't come here to crush on the cousins."

Bernie waved her concerns away. "Please. This is a wedding. Single people hook up at weddings all the time, or so I hear. Live the

380

dream!"

"Live what dream?" Liam asked.

"Live the dream of hooking up with the hot fiddler," Becky explained.

"Oh. Yeah. Go on," he said. "Live the dream."

CHAPTER TWELVE

Abe tried really hard to listen to Kevin's instructions as he led them through the rehearsal. But it was going to be a short ceremony, and Abe only had to play while they walked up the aisle, then just sit and listen until they turned around to walk back down. In between, he had a lot of time to think about Emma.

He didn't think he'd ever seen a girl have an existential crisis before. He'd thought it would have been more dramatic. All in all, she was pretty chill about the whole thing, or at least she seemed to relax once she got to Granny Sue's library.

The way her face lit up when they walked into that dinky old building — that was something he wouldn't soon forget. He could tell that she was getting charmed by Coral Bottom, seeing the diamond at the heart of its rough. He liked that about her. Showed she had good taste.

And it got him thinking dangerous thoughts about her hanging around.

Which was ridiculous, because *he* wasn't hanging around.

Maybe she'd like Nashville.

Not that he liked Nashville. Well, not the Nashville life he was living.

By the time Daniel herded them all out of the barn and into the lodge for the rehearsal dinner, Abe had moved Emma into a little house near the Coral Bottom Library, where they spent evenings by the fire, her reading and him playing her some musical accompaniment. It was a pretty picture, but it was also just that — a picture. Why would a woman with her PhD move to the middle of the middle of nowhere to run a library that made Podunk look like a bustling metropolis?

Besides, he hadn't even kissed her yet. Maybe she was a terrible kisser.

His eyes zeroed in on her as he walked into the lodge's restaurant. She sat there, laughing with her friends and with Granny Sue, her eyes lit up with amusement. Who knew what story Granny Sue was telling her. He could only hope it didn't involve him losing his britches.

He was about to head off Granny's story when he was stopped by a hand on his shoulder. "Abe Tate? Sounded real good up there."

Abe turned to find Gary Loshe, host of *Up the Holler,* a world-renowned radio show that featured everything from Southern blues to singer-songwriters to mountain fiddlers. He was also Coral Bottom's most famous native son, and a former paramour of Granny Sue's. He'd always been a supporter of kids learning traditional music, and he'd been a good friend to Abe.

Abe almost hated to run into him.

Because Gary was a nice guy, so he'd probably want to talk to Abe about how he was doing, which would lead to questions about how Nashville was treating him, and there was no way Abe could lie and tell him that it was great and that he was probably going on tour with Taylor Swift next year.

"Have a seat," Gary said, and Abe, being a glutton for punishment, did. "How's Nashville treatin' you?"

Well, that didn't take long.

"Great," Abe said, leaving the Taylor Swift stuff unspoken.

Gary laughed. "You never could tell a lie to save your life, you know that?"

"It's rough, man. But I'm still tryin'."

"I remember. 'Course, I was in Nashville about forty years ago, but I remember it like it was yesterday. I've never felt so chewed up and spit out in my life, and I've been married three times."

"I'm playin', I'm just not makin' much of a living."

"You been there, what, a year now?"
Abe nodded.

"Well, as long as you don't stop playin', something will happen. But, you know, things are happening here, too."

"Yeah, I heard your show got picked up."

"Yeah, now I get to do pledge drives in four different time zones, not just West Virginia."

"Heavy is the head."

"Don't I know it. But, listen, if you ever decide to come back home, I'm working on a few things. Traditional music is having a bit of a comeback. 'Course, you never thought it went anywhere, did you?"

"No, sir."

"I got people from New York and all over interested in learning the old songs. It's the young people. I can't hardly believe it. Just a few years ago, you couldn't get a kid to let go of the remote control long enough to listen to a banjo tune, but now it seems like they can't get enough."

"Really?"

"You sound surprised. I have to admit,

it's a small movement, but it's a movement, and I need people to help me build on that momentum. Show those Brooklyn hipsters where the real music comes from."

"Yeah?"

"Just think about it, that's all."

"Gary, will you quit talkin' my grandson's ear off? He ain't even had a bite to eat!" Before Abe could ask more about music and movements, Granny Sue had him up to his eyeballs in fried chicken and greens.

Before he knew what was happening, his belly was full and those who were so inclined were sittin' around the fireplace, pickin' on instruments and tellin' tales. He'd managed to say two words to Emma (she was doing fine, she reported) before he got swept up in a spontaneous jam session of songs older than the hills. Gary was there, too, pulling his harmonica out of his pocket, and a jar of clear liquid from his bag.

That was the moonshine. Abe took a sip when the jar was passed around. He watched Emma take a sip, too, and laughed as she tried, unsuccessfully, to hide a wince. Yeah, it burned goin' down. But that fire loosened up his fingers and he knew they were in for a long night.

Man, it felt good to be back home.

CHAPTER THIRTEEN

Abe was just toeing his jeans off when his door knocked. Or someone knocked at his door. He shook his head. Whshhhoooh . . . white lightning.

He giggled. Which was another way he knew he was drunk. Grown-ass men do not giggle, he reminded himself. Then his door knocked again. He tripped out of his jeans and opened it.

It was the librarian.

She squinted — moonshine eyes — but still managed to look him up and down.

He looked down, too.

Yup, he was standing in the hallway in his boxers.

He reciprocated the look, and he wanted to say something smart about the pink cat pajamas she was wearing, but she just looked too cute. What was she doing at his door, looking all cute?

"Can I help you?"

She leaned against the door frame, which brought her face awful close to his. "Too quiet," she said.

"CAN I HELP YOU?" he shouted, then doubled over in a fit of giggles.

She shoved at his shoulder. He wiped his eyes. God, he was funny.

"I can't sleep."

"I thought you couldn't sleep when it was loud?"

"No, I couldn't concentrate when it was loud. Now I can't sleep cuz it's too quiet."

Funny, he was thinking the exact opposite. This quiet lodge was the first good sleep he'd had in he didn't know how long.

"And I'm cold." She rubbed her arms and shivered.

"Are you trying to seduce me?"

She shrugged one shoulder.

He brushed her arm as he reached for her waist. "Damn, woman, you really are cold."

"I told you."

He pulled her into his room and kicked the door closed. Before he could even take a breath she was on him, her cold hands around the back of his neck, her sweet lips soft on his. He was surprised, but he caught on real quick. He hoisted her up so she was off-balance and pressed tight to him. He ran a hand into her hair to hold her still so he could get inside that hot mouth of hers. They were both sloppy and gasping, but determined, and he walked them back toward the bed.

But then she tripped over his jeans, and he tripped over her, and they landed in a tangle on the bed.

"Shit." He reached for the back of her head, which had made an unfortunate collision with his elbow.

"I'm fine," she said, blinking hard. "Wait. I might have a concussion. Unless your room is supposed to be spinning?"

He flopped onto his back. Yup, the room was definitely spinning.

"Emma," he said to the spinning ceiling. "This is a bad idea."

He heard her sigh, taking all the air in the room with her. "Okay," she said quietly, and clambered up so she was sitting on the edge of the bed. "Sorry."

"No, hey, no, not like that." He grabbed her wrist and tugged her down so she was facing him. Probably not a great idea with the room spinning and all. But he didn't want her to go.

"So, we're gonna do it even though it's a bad idea?"

Her impish grin made his heart do a little flip in his chest. She should definitely go.

"No."

He really was the stupidest man alive.

"But not because you don't want me?"

"Hell, no." The evidence of that was poking out of his boxers.

"Then why not?"

He brushed a lock of her hair out of her eyes. "Because we're drunk."

"I'm not drunk."

"How many fingers am I holding up?"

She didn't take her eyes off of his. "I don't care."

"Shit," he muttered. He ran his thumb over her cheeks. She shivered. She was still cold.

"Come on." He pulled the quilt down and scooched underneath it. She followed on her hands and knees, and he had to shut his eyes because he was pretty sure that was the sexiest thing he had ever seen in his life. Then she landed heavily next to him, and he remembered the moonshine.

He wrapped his arms around her, then pulled her arms around him. Her hands snaked up his shirt and he yelped.

"Sorry!" she said, but she didn't move them. Instead, she heaved a giant, happy sigh and cuddled into him. "You're warm," she muttered into his chest.

He was burning up. It was his own fault

for being so stupid. But he was just trying to be hospitable. She was cold. He could help her with that.

He lifted his arm, held a protective hand over her head. "Shh," he told her, because if she kept talking, he was definitely going to do something stupid. "Close your eyes and go to sleep."

"The room's spinning."

He closed his eyes. Yup. The room was definitely spinning.

"I'm not tired," she mumbled.

He wasn't either. But it was either go to sleep or take this thing that was between them and mess it up.

He should send her away.

But she felt warm tucked up next to him. And she'd said she was cold before. He couldn't send her away cold. What would that say for his Appalachian hospitality?

"I can't believe I'm cuddling with the hot fiddler."

"I can't believe you're still talking."

"It's your own fault for not making out with me."

All kinds of warning bells went off in his head.

"So, how'd you like Coral Bottom?" he asked, even though he knew perfectly well that she'd loved it. At least, she'd loved the quick visit. She might not love it so well if she stuck around.

Whoa. That was some nuclear-level wedding-induced feelings talk.

Her shoulder rose and fell with her sigh. "I like it here. I never thought I would. But I guess I never thought I'd be going to a gay wedding in West Virginia."

"Hey, now. West Virginia legalized it before the Supreme Court did."

She lifted her head and clumsily brushed the hair out of her face. "It did?"

"Yeah. Like six months before, but still."

"Hmm."

"Why, you thought we were all backwards rednecks who couldn't cotton to a feller kissin' another feller?"

She swatted his chest, then leaned back into him. "No."

He ran his fingers through her hair.

"Okay, yes."

"Ha, I knew it."

When she didn't say anything, he asked, "Are you pouting?"

"No."

"You're pouting because the people you've met so far in West Virginia are not as homophobic as you thought they'd be?"

"No! I'm pouting because I was wrong. There's a difference."

"Mmm-hmm. If it makes you feel any better, not everybody was kind to Daniel when he came out."

"That actually doesn't make me feel better at all."

"I had to kick Bobby Avery's ass because he kicked Daniel's ass because Daniel tried to kiss him in fourth grade."

"You did?"

"Yeah, and Bobby Avery's twice my size."

"But you kicked his ass?"

"I may have exaggerated."

"You didn't kick his ass?"

"Well, technically he kicked my ass, but it was in defense of Daniel's honor, so it still counts."

She giggled into his shoulder.

"Are you laughing at my pain?"

"No! I'm just imagining little Abe, slaying the giant for his . . . what is Daniel to you? Cousin?"

"Yup. His mom and my mom were sisters. So close everyone thought they were twins."

"And you and Daniel are close."

"Like twins."

"You were really fine with him being gay?"

Abe thought back to that time. It wasn't until high school that Daniel came out to him. Abe was ashamed of some of the things he thought when Daniel first told him. But he was hurt, dammit.

"I was more upset that he kept a secret from me. We'd always told each other everything."

"You thought he didn't trust you?"

Abe shrugged, jostling Emma. "I don't know what I thought. I didn't really know anything about gay people, I just knew that something was eatin' Daniel up inside, and telling me seemed to make him feel better."

"Must've been a shock."

"And a relief. That bastard is handsomer than I am. If he was straight, I'd never've gotten a girl."

Getting a girl was too close to what he wanted to do with Emma right now, especially with her laughing that sweet laugh of hers and running her fingers along his collarbone.

"Quit laughin'. We're supposed to be asleep."

"The room's spinning, remember?"

"I bet it's not."

She didn't say anything for a minute, and he stretched to look down at her. With the moonlight coming through the sliding door, he could see that her eyes were closed. Then her breathing got low and heavy, and so did his eyelids. The room stopped spinning, which was good. And soon, he was asleep.

CHAPTER FOURTEEN

Emma blinked her eyes open.

It was really, really bright.

Like, really bright.

She looked out the sliding doors. There was snow on the trees. That must be why they looked a little different from yesterday morning. Also, she was really warm, which was another difference from yesterday. Also, her blanket was moving.

That was no blanket she felt at the small of her back. Then she screwed her eyes shut and shoved her face into the pillow. Oh, my God. Last night suddenly came to her with humiliating clarity. Moonshine. She hadn't drunk that much of it. But then she also remembered Granny Sue telling her she didn't have to drink that much for it to work. Then going upstairs and flopping into her pajamas. Then coming down to attempt to seduce Abe. Then being soundly rejected but somehow managing to fall asleep in his arms.

She wondered if there was a way to sneak out of his room without him waking up.

He stirred behind her. All of him stirred. But that was just a natural biological reaction to the morning. He'd made himself pretty clear last night: It was a terrible idea. She was a terrible idea. Her kissing was a terrible idea.

He wasn't wrong. She was a mess. She had no direction. And she was terrible at holding her liquor.

"Morning."

His voice was like gravel. But, like, sexy gravel. It made her feel all warm and tingly inside.

He squeezed her closer to him, which made her feel even warmer and tinglier.

Damn her body and its stupid natural reactions reacting to his natural reactions.

He leaned over her, and she could not think of a polite way to avoid his eyes, so she didn't.

Warm, melted chocolate. That's what his eyes reminded her of.

She loved chocolate.

"You don't look half as bad as I feel," he said, and brushed a lock of hair out of her face.

Wait, was he flirting with her?

He smiled down at her, all crooked and melty, and she couldn't help but smile back, even though surely the next moments held the potential to be the most awkward of her life.

Tempting the devil, she reached up and brushed his hair out of his eyes. He turned his head so his beard tickled her palm, and kissed her.

"Did I snore too much?" he asked, as if waking up with her after platonically rejecting her drunken advances was the most natural thing in the world.

She shook her head. If he had snored, she sure didn't hear it.

"Good." He kissed her cheek. Then the corner of her mouth. Then her lips.

Then he lifted himself up and looked down at her.

"Are you okay?"

She pursed her lips together and nodded. Yup, totally fine. She was just trying to think of a way to get out of here before she embarrassed herself by thinking that his kissing her was an indication that he actually wanted her, when last night it was clear that he didn't.

He kissed her again, gently.

"Are you sure you're okay?"

She would never see him again, surely. Well, except for tonight at the wedding. But after that, probably never. It wouldn't kill her to be honest.

"I'm just . . . confused." Suddenly the popcorn pattern on the ceiling was really interesting.

"What are you confused about?" He tilted her chin so she had to look at him and those damn chocolate eyes.

"Um. Well, last night you were . . ." She waved her free hand vaguely in the direction of *"last night you made it clear you weren't interested."*

"Last night I was drunk. And so were you, by the way."

And how, she thought. "I only had a few sips of moonshine."

"A few? Dang, girl, you can hold your drink. The first time, usually it takes just one to knock you flat on your ass."

She puffed a little with pride. It was sort of a weird thing to be proud of, being able to drink more moonshine than the average first-timer. But in this super-awkward moment, she was going to take whatever she could.

Not sexy enough to seduce a hot mountain man, but at least she had a strong enough constitution to not pass out from one sip of moonshine.

They could put that on her tombstone.

"How do you feel now?"

"Fine. A little fuzzy," she admitted. But, really, surprisingly fine.

"Then why're you acting like the house is on fire?"

Was she? She was just trying to get out from this totally unwilling man who was obviously just trying to humor her in order to lessen her humiliation.

"I just . . . I should go."

"Oh."

She studied his face. Did he look . . . disappointed?

"I mean, I don't have to go. . . ." she tested.

"You should go if you want to go," he said in a voice that sounded like he was testing too.

"I don't have to go. If you don't want me to, I mean."

"Hell, no, I don't want you to go!"

His vehemence surprised the shame right out of her. "Then why the hell did you shut me down last night?"

"Because you were drunk and I didn't know if you really meant it! And I was drunk, so even if you did really mean it, I'm sure I would have made an ass of myself!"

Oh. "Oh."

She looked up at him. "Are we having our first fight?"

He dropped his head to her shoulder. He was shaking. She hoped he was laughing.

"I did mean it," she whispered into his conveniently close ear.

He stopped shaking.

"Do you still mean it?" he asked her shoulder.

"Yup."

He turned his head, just a little, and then his mouth was hot and wet on her neck. She shivered. That was the spot that always made her shiver.

She felt him smile, then she felt his tongue trail a lazy path around the spot, and she positively squirmed.

CHAPTER FIFTEEN

Sleeping with Emma cuddled soft and warm next to him had been nice. Really, really nice. But having her hot and wriggling underneath him . . . *nice* was not the right word. Hot. Amazing. Right.

He kissed a trail down her neck, then back up to her lips, just to make sure that when she said she meant it, she really did. And then he got lost in kissing her, and in running his hands up her shirt and over her sleep-warm skin, and before he knew it, his shirt was torn over his head and he was flipped on his back and Emma was straddling his hips.

"Is this okay?" she asked as she leaned down into him.

"Mmm-hmm," he said into her mouth. But it wasn't really fair, was it, that he was vulnerable to her ministrations on his bare chest while he was still fighting with her pajama shirt. So he bucked her up with his hips and she squeaked and sat up, looking disheveled and annoyed. *Poor baby,* he thought as he reached for the hem of her shirt. She pushed his hands away, though, and tore it over her head, her hair spilling down around her shoulders and his throat going dry as a bone.

She was perfect. Her skin was like milk and as he explored her with his fingertips, he left a trail of pink blush behind. She raised her arms over her head and he traced a path down her sides and over her hips, down to where her heat met his. She leaned over him, her breath coming faster, her soft smoothness rubbing against his hairy roughness.

To hell with the sweet and melty. He gripped her hair in his fist and pulled her closer for a deep kiss. He felt her gasp, and then her open mouth was his. Her tongue met his, and he would have sworn he heard her growl. Her hands were rough in his hair, and his moved down, down her back to press her closer to him.

"Emma," he said, breathless.

"Abe!" she shouted.

God, she felt good. And she was right there with him, grinding into him, kissing a trail down his chest, and —

"Abe!"

That wasn't Emma. Unless she could shout and kiss and bang on his door at the same time.

Probably not, because she froze, her mouth inches from his stomach.

"Abe, I know you can hear me!"

"Pete," he muttered, not at all amused by his cousin's interruption.

Emma sighed, and it went straight through his chest hair and into his pants.

"Do you need to get that?" she asked.

He shook his head. If they ignored him, Pete would go away.

"Abe, I'm serious! Daniel's missing!"

Emma's head shot up, her face confused, which was probably what his face looked like, since he was confused too.

"Pete, if this is some kind of joke —"

Pete banged on the door again and jiggled the door handle.

Abe shot Emma a look of apology and gently dislodged her from her very comfortable position on top of his hips, and slinked out of bed to answer the door.

He only opened it a crack, but Pete barged in anyway. He only paused for a second when he saw Emma, or at least the Emma-shaped lump scrambling under his covers. "Hey," he said, distractedly.

"Hey," she said, turning bright red.

"Hey," Abe said. "What's the deal, Pete? Is this some kind of joke?"

"No, man. I wish." Pete tore a rough hand through his hair. His face was not the face of a man making a joke. "Daniel stayed in my room last night, you know, to make it special for the wedding, or whatever."

"Okay."

"And when I woke up this morning, he was gone."

"Did you try Kevin's room?"

"Yes, dumbass, I tried Kevin's room. Kevin doesn't know where he is and now he's freaking out too."

"Maybe he just went for a walk."

"Have you looked outside today? Oh, probably not."

"Yeah. Not."

Abe and Pete stood in the middle of the room, staring at each other and trying to pretend that there wasn't a half-naked librarian in his bed.

"So . . . Daniel's not in here?" Pete asked lamely.

"No."

"I'll go."

"Yeah."

"Nice to see you again, Emma."

"Bye, Pete."

When the door slammed behind Pete, Abe

sat down heavily on the bed. Emma crawled over and sat next to him, pulling her shirt on. "Should we go look for Daniel?"

He looked over at her, hair mussed and lips swollen. All he wanted to do was lay her down and finish the mutual ravaging they had started. But here she was, reminding him of the right thing to do.

She was a good woman.

He didn't want to leave her when the wedding was over.

That thought shocked him. What was he thinking? He'd just met this girl. So, she was beautiful and fun and smart and sexy and she seemed to have fallen in love with his hometown, which told him that she had good taste and they had a lot in common. He just didn't quite know what that was. And a weekend wasn't enough time to explore it.

That was it. When the wedding was over, he'd find a way to stay in touch with Emma.

If there was a wedding.

"Yeah, let's go find the groom."

It didn't take them too long to find Daniel, after all. One of the housekeepers was changing the towels in Pete's room when she heard a noise. Her scream had Emma and Abe running down the hall, and there was Daniel, curled up in a ball under the weird hangers you couldn't steal and next to the safe that was impossible to open. It was a minor miracle that he fit. Although maybe he didn't; hence the screaming housekeeper.

"Hey, cuz," Abe said as Emma assured the housekeeper that, yes, they knew this man and yes, he was fine and there was no need to call security.

"Hey," said Daniel. He looked like he hadn't slept all night, or that he had slept in a ball in a hotel closet.

"Why are you hiding in a closet?"

"I'm not hiding."

"You know, people are going to think this is some kind of metaphor."

"Shut up."

Daniel took Abe's offered hand and stood up.

"What's goin' on? Are you gettin' cold feet after all?"

"No! I mean, I don't know!"

Emma's heart sank. If this was really happening, she had to find Kevin. She might punch Daniel first.

Abe took one of her hands, one that she had unconsciously balled into a fist, and gave her a reassuring nod. Then he sat next to his cousin on the bed.

Daniel had his elbows on his knees and he was tearing at his hair. Poor guy really looked like he was in anguish.

Good.

"I love him so much," Daniel said. *Oh God,* Emma thought. He's going to cry. She couldn't stand to see grown men cry. Even standing on the precipice of murderous rage, she knew if Daniel cried, she would crumble.

"Then what's the problem?" Abe put a gentle hand on Daniel's back. Daniel seemed to relax.

"Have you looked out the window?"

They had, briefly. It was snowing. And not a gentle, picturesque snow. No, this was a wet, heavy, blinding snow.

It was predicted to just pass over them, the woman in the lobby had told them. It should stop in an hour or so, and then there would be sunshine for the wedding. Sunshine, and lots of wet snow.

"It's terrible out there! People aren't going to make it up the mountain."

"Daniel, that's hours away. What is this really about?"

"It's not perfect! All Kevin wanted was a perfect wedding and I wanted that for him, and now —"

"And you never learned to control the

weather? What kind of jerk are you?"

"It's just . . . I know there's going to be stuff in our life that is messy and terrible. I just wanted to give him this one perfect day, and —"

"You sound like me, you know."

They all three turned, and there was Kevin in the doorway, his arms crossed over his chest, his feet bare. "I'm supposed to be the one who freaks out about the details."

Daniel stood up, but didn't move toward the door. "I'm scared."

Emma swallowed her shocked gasp. She stood against the open door, trying to look as invisible as possible, but ready to jump into the fray should Kevin need her.

"What are you scared of?"

"What if it's different?"

"When we're married?"

"What if, I don't know, what if we hate each other?"

Kevin looked thoughtful, then walked over to Daniel. Abe slipped away and stood beside Emma.

"We're not going to hate each other."

"We could."

"So, you want to call off the wedding because we might one day hate each other?"

"No! Of course not!"

"You're just freaking out?"

"I woke up and I saw the weather and I just . . . If this is how our wedding is going to be, what's our life going to be like?"

"Daniel, babe. We've been together for seven years. Has our life always been perfect?"

"Yes!"

Kevin raised his eyebrow.

"Fine, no."

"And haven't we always dealt with it? Haven't we gone through stuff together? Haven't we fought and made up?"

"Yes." Daniel reached out a finger and traced a pattern on Kevin's chest.

Kevin trapped Daniel's hand over his heart. "We could just get married right now, just the two of us in our pajamas, and I would be happy."

"Really?" Daniel looked skeptical.

Kevin thought about it. "Well, maybe not in our pajamas."

Daniel laughed. Emma breathed.

"All I need is you, babe. As long as you're here, everything's perfect."

Daniel nodded, then leaned in to kiss his almost-husband.

Abe put his arm around Emma. "Crisis averted."

"We did it."

"Yeah. Now as much as I love these two,

let's go before they really start making out."

"We have a wedding to get ready for."

CHAPTER SIXTEEN

As the receptionist predicted, the snow stopped and the sun broke through the clouds and it was "colder'n a witch's tit," as Pete colorfully said, but it was the perfect day for a wedding.

Emma zipped her boots and stood in front of the mirror. The boots weren't as dressy as her heels, but with her knee-length, dark plum dress, they didn't look bad. Besides, she could dance in the shorter-heeled boots. If she wore heels, she doubted she'd be able to make it to her seat.

Librarian problems.

She was just fluffing out her hair one more time when there was a knock at her door. She cursed her skipping heart — it wasn't Abe, it couldn't be. He had to go down early to the barn where the ceremony would take place. That's what he'd told her when he kissed her good-bye after they solved all of Kevin and Daniel's relationship problems.

411

Well, the problems that were interfering with the wedding, anyway. He'd kissed her and made her promise to save a dance for him — save him a dance! — and she'd come up here, floating and frustrated.

It wasn't Abe, it was Bernie and Liam, both looking polished and fancy in their wedding duds.

Bernie whistled at her. "I know a fiddler who's gonna love those boots."

"Ha-ha," Emma said, and stepped aside to let them in. Bernie's floor-length dress swished against Emma's boots. Liam pulled at the neck of his shirt. "Hold on," she said. "You're messing it up." She slapped Liam's hands away and straightened his tie for him.

"Thanks," he muttered.

Before she could close the door, Becky was panting in the doorway. "Oh, good. I didn't miss you. I thought I was going to have to walk over by myself." She looked absolutely adorable, if a little flustered, in her tea-length dress with a giant peacock feather pattern on it. She slipped into her shoes as she walked into the room. "Can't run in these heels," she explained.

"So how badly are we going to freeze on the way over there?" Bernie asked, sticking a wool hat on top of her formerly fabulous hair.

"It's sunny," Liam offered. Liam, who had no jacket on except the one that went with his suit.

They bundled up and headed outside, waving at the other guests they had met over the weekend. They all huddled together and walked in a freezing bunch over a freshly shoveled stone pathway that led to the big red barn on the edge of the hill.

"God, look at this view," Emma said, pausing to take in the snow-covered trees and the sun streaming over the valley.

"Look at it later," Becky said, squeezing her arm and huddling her into the barn.

"Whoa." Bernie stopped in front of them at the entrance to the barn.

Because it wasn't a barn. It was a daggun winter wonderland.

They walked under an arch of willows spun with tiny white lights. A white runner led up the aisle to a matching willow arch. Votive candles were scattered around the space, making the old wood glow. A few dozen white folding chairs were split between either side of the aisle, and the four of them got the last four seats together in the last row.

Emma looked around in wonder, taking in the lights and the shadows and the music. Her eyes stopped on the band: a banjo and a mandolin player whom she recognized from the night before, and Abe. They sat in a half-moon, picking (or pickin', as she'd learned) a slow, sweet melody as people took their seats. Abe looked pressed and clean, his hair brushed back in a smooth wave, his suit cut perfectly over those broad shoulders.

"Good-lookin' band," Liam whispered to her.

"Mmm-hmm," she said absently, mesmerized by the movement of Abe's bow.

Then the music stopped, and Abe stood. Someone coughed and all heads turned to the back of the barn, where Daniel and Kevin stood, handsome and watery-eyed, ready to walk down the aisle.

They didn't hold Emma's attention long. As soon as Abe began to play, she turned back to watch him, his eyes closed, swaying to the music he made. It was low and slow, full of hope and promises, like a lover's voice carrying over the hills. By the time Kevin and Daniel reached the minister at the front arch, there wasn't a dry eye in the house. Abe dropped his bow arm and wiped his eyes with his forearm, and Emma started tearing up all over again. He caught her staring and crying as he headed to his seat in the front, and he winked at her. *Great,* she thought. Now I'm drooling, crying, and my heart is melting. So much for the eye makeup.

"Dearly beloved," the Unitarian minister said. Kevin wiped a tear off of Daniel's cheek and dammit, there went more tears, then laughs, then vows, then cheers, then they were married and the party could start for reals.

CHAPTER SEVENTEEN

While everyone else was busy watching Kevin and Daniel each become the happiest man in the world, the staff of the Froggy Rock Ski Chalet had been busy transforming the mess hall into a bona fide banquet hall. In true Tate fashion, it took about three seconds for the room to turn into a full-on party. One of Daniel's architect friends was deejaying from his iPad, and before the chafing dishes were even hot on the buffet, people were out on the dance floor. Abe had quickly abandoned his seat at the kids' table and was working the room, getting his cheeks pinched by aunties and lots of back slaps. As he traveled between family and friends, he kept an eye on Emma. She mostly sat with her friends, but she got up to say hi to Granny Sue and to dance to some truly awful nineties pop music.

Before she could disappear into the crowd, he stepped over to her and grabbed her hand. "You promised me a dance," he whispered in her ear.

She turned that bright smile on him and followed him into the fray.

IPad DJ obliged with a slow song, and he pulled Emma close. He wrapped one arm around her back and the other hand held hers close to his chest. She put her arm around his shoulder and swayed in time with him.

"Are you enjoying yourself?" he asked.

She nodded. "The barn looked amazing. I can't believe it was even a barn."

He pushed her hair back and kissed her neck.

"That song you played when they walked up the aisle . . ."

"Mmm-hmm?" he said into her neck. She smelled good. Like cloves and cinnamon.

"I didn't recognize it."

"I wrote it."

She pulled back in his arms. "You did?"

"Don't act so surprised! I am a musician, you know."

"I know, I just . . . wow. It was beautiful."

"Thank you." He pulled her close again and she wrapped her arm around him.

The song was over, way too quickly, and a fast old song took over. He wasn't ready to let her go.

"Woo!" Granny Sue came spinning by, followed quickly by Pete.

"Do you want to —"

"Get out of here?" Emma asked. "Yes, please."

He clasped her hand and practically dragged her off the dance floor. He heard her say good night to her friends. He waved to Daniel. They got out of there.

Emma started to get nervous as soon as Abe unlocked his door. She shouldn't be nervous. She'd done this before. She'd almost done it with him before. She wanted this, maybe more than she'd wanted anything in her life.

It was just that she knew it was going to mean something.

It would mean something, and then it would be over. She'd go back to ignoring her dissertation, he'd go back to Nashville.

Well, they'd always have Froggy Rock.

Besides, once she stepped into the room, Abe had her head between his hands and he kissed her, deep and steady, and she decided the future could wait until the future. Tonight, there was just this. She pushed his jacket off his shoulders and he let it fall to the floor. She wanted him to hold her tight and kiss her lights out, but

418

she also wanted to feel him. She untucked his shirt and felt the smooth muscles of his back. Then she felt him fumble with the zipper on her dress and before she knew it, they were flat on his bed wearing nothing but each other's bodies. She closed her eyes and soaked in every moment, every touch, every breath that skimmed over her skin. She commanded her fingers to memorize the curve of his shoulders, the ridges of his stomach, the muscles of his thighs. As the moon crossed the sky, she memorized the feel of all of him, over her, inside her, around her, and she cried out and held him as he shuddered, and she fell asleep, smiling, in his arms.

CHAPTER EIGHTEEN

They decided to let Liam drive to the airport. (Not that they gave him a choice.) Emma had a long drive back from Charleston, and she wanted to put off getting behind the wheel for as long as possible. Besides, she didn't think she could focus on the road right now.

It was Abe's fault. Waking up in his arms — for the second time — felt so right. Seeing him smile down at her felt so right. Having him kiss her fully awake felt so, so right.

But then she had to pack and take her friends to the airport and go back to worrying about her miserable future in academia. She would so much rather be canoodling with Abe.

She had his number and his e-mail address, and as they came down off the mountain, she saw that she had three texts from him.

Hey beautiful
Indiana isn't too far from Nashville
What are you doing this weekend?

You, she wrote back.

She smiled. This was going to work. They could make it work. Abe was right; they weren't so far apart. A few hours. Not bad for a weekend. Of course, she wouldn't be able to see him this weekend. It was Christmas and she was due at her family's. And then the semester would start, and she had two classes to TA and all those articles to read. . . .

"Emma. Emma! What's wrong!"

"I think I'm having a panic attack." She rolled down her window and gulped big lungfuls of mountain air. "I think I'm having a panic attack. Is this what a panic attack feels like?"

"I don't know," said Becky. "How do you feel?"

"I just feel like I can't really breathe and I'll probably throw up any minute."

Liam looked back. "Do you think you ate something bad?"

Emma shook her head. She pressed her lips together, as if that would keep the tears from ruining her mascara.

"Oh." She leaned forward and Becky

421

rubbed slow circles on her back.

"What's going on?" Bernie turned around in the front seat. "Oh my God, Emma, are you crying?"

"No," said Emma. "It's just . . . It's Abe and . . . last night . . . and he's so . . ."

"Did he hurt you?"

Emma jerked her head up at the anger in Liam's voice. "No, no, it's just . . ." It was hard to get the words out with all the hiccupping. Her mascara was shot for sure.

"It's just that you really like him?"

She nodded at Becky.

"You like the hot fiddler? Dang, what's wrong with that?" Bernie asked.

Emma shook her head. Nothing was wrong with that. Just . . . well . . . everything was wrong with that. "He makes me really happy," she whined. Great, now she was whining.

"The bastard," said Bernie.

"I don't understand what's going on here. If he makes you happy, why are you crying?" Liam looked like he wanted to be anywhere but driving three emotional women off a mountain in West Virginia.

Becky shushed him.

Emma threw up her hands. "I haven't been happy in a long time."

"Oh, honey." Becky wrapped her in as

much of a hug as their seat belts would allow. "You're lucky, then."

"Yeah," Bernie added. "Who'd've thought you'd meet a great guy at a gay wedding?"

"No, it's not that *he* makes me happy. It's that . . . why haven't I been happy? I feel like I've been doing my life all wrong. I've been doing what I *thought* would make me happy and I think I was wrong."

"So, you should've been doing hot fiddlers the whole time?" Bernie asked.

"Are you talking about your dissertation?" Becky asked.

Emma shook her head. "I think so."

"I have no idea what's going on here," said Liam. "The hot fiddler makes you happy, so you're going to give up your PhD?"

"I think so."

"Hold on." Bernie looked like she was going to climb over the front seat. "I know he's hot and all, but you're *not* giving up years of work for him!"

Emma shook her head and took the tissue Becky offered her. "No, that's not it."

"It sure sounds like it."

"Bernie," Becky said. "She means that she forgot what it felt like to be happy, and the hot fiddler reminded her."

"He has a name!" Emma shouted. "He's not the hot fiddler! His name is Abe!"

"This airport seems farther away than last time," said Liam to the trees.

"Do you have plans to see the hot — Abe — again?" Becky asked.

"Wait, what about her PhD?"

Becky shushed Bernie and looked at Emma.

"We're going to try to see each other over New Year's."

"That's romantic," Bernie said. "A new beginning. Very appropriate. I like it."

"Thanks."

"And then what're you gonna do?" Bernie demanded.

"I don't know! That's why I'm crying!"

"Here's what she's gonna do," Liam said, with more force than they thought he had in him. "She's gonna stop crying so I can drive the car. Then she's gonna drive home, then bone the hell out of Abe the Fiddler, then she's gonna take some time to figure it out. You've always wanted to work in a library," Liam added, much more gently.

"You should have seen Granny Sue's library," Emma told them. "It's my dream."

"Well, there are plenty of Coral Bottoms in the world," Becky said. "Okay, that's probably not true. But there are plenty of Coral Bottomesque places in the world. It's worth looking into."

"Yeah," Emma agreed. "I'll look into it."

"Hey, Abe, I'm glad I caught you."

Abe was just tossing his backpack in his trunk when he turned to find Gary Loshe pulling up next to him, his front window rolled down.

"You sounded real good yesterday."

"Thanks, Gary."

"That one of yours?"

Abe knew Gary meant the song he'd written for Kevin and Daniel. Everyone was talking about it. "Yup."

"You plannin' on recording it?"

"I'd like to."

"Well, you remember what I said, will you? About you young people coming back? Making the traditional music scene a scene?"

"Sure."

"Abe, I'm not just blowin' smoke. You've got a gift, son. I remember what it's like in Nashville. It's hard to get a quiet voice like yours heard over all the shoutin'. You decide to come on home, we'll find a place for you."

Gary gave him a wave and drove off. Abe sat behind the wheel and thought about his long ride back to Nashville. He had New Year's to look forward to, when he was going to drive to Indiana to see Emma. Beyond that, well, he hadn't thought much beyond that, except that he was going to try to figure out how to spend as much time with her as possible. But Coral Bottom was about the same distance from Indiana as Nashville was, just in a different direction. He watched Gary's truck turn out of the parking lot. He'd definitely look into it.

CHAPTER NINETEEN

Just about one year later

When Emma finally dug her phone out of her purse, she saw that she had two voice mails. One was from Granny Sue, and it was short and sweet, just like her: *"Emma, I'm retiring. Call me."* The second was from Abe, and it was also sweet, but not short at all. In fact, he was cut off just as he was telling her how much he missed her and that he couldn't wait to see her again.

She sat down at her desk.

She knew what she had to do.

As Abe pulled into the parking lot of Emma's building, he couldn't stop the goofy smile from splitting his face. He knew he was doing it. Emma told him he always did it when he first saw her. Well, what did she expect? Sometimes they went weeks without seeing each other, and then he had that whole long drive to anticipate what it would be like to smell her hair again and hold her close — two things that Skype could not yet replicate — so by the time he saw her, she was lucky he was grinning. Otherwise he'd be panting like a dog, and who wants a boyfriend who can't keep his tongue in his mouth?

But after a year, this long-distance thing was getting old. Maybe he was just getting antsy because he was starting to feel like he knew where he was headed. It still felt funny, that he'd found his direction as soon as he turned right around and came back to Coral Bottom, but, as Granny Sue said, he'd just found where he belonged.

The problem was, he'd also found where he belonged with Emma, and she was very much not in Coral Bottom. He was starting to feel like it didn't much matter where she was, as long as he was with her. But he couldn't help but think about how much she liked visiting him (and not just for the anticipating-and-panting reasons). She loved Coral Bottom, strange little town that it was. She spent as much time with Granny Sue at the library as she did with him.

And now he had a surprise for her. To the surprise of everyone in town, Granny Sue was retiring. Ever since she'd announced it, people had been bugging Abe to get "that nice librarian gal of yours" to come down and take her spot. It's not that simple, he told them. Sure it is, they said. Heck, the mayor all but offered him the job on Emma's behalf.

So there was a job opening in Coral Bottom. And Gary Loshe was having his hip replaced, so Abe was going to step in as the first-ever guest host of *Up the Holler*. And his record was just about finished, and he was working on a video series with the Division of Tourism and he was going to be teaching traditional fiddle classes at the Heritage Center. He wouldn't have time to drive up to Indiana nearly as often.

The only thing for it was to bring Emma down to Coral Bottom. It might take some convincing. She loved to visit, sure, but it was still the middle of the middle of nowhere, especially for someone who was working so hard on her academic career. And even if Emma had been talkin' about how that might not be the direction she wanted her career to go in, that didn't mean she'd just drop everything for him and the mountains. Besides, Granny Sue would never forgive him if he just brought Emma down and left her to find her own way in town.

No, he'd have to make sure Emma understood how serious he was about it. How serious he was about her. He was seriously in love with her. And he had a ring burnin' a hole in his pocket to prove it.

All he had to do was ask.

Emma hung up the phone with Granny Sue, wishing her ears were farther apart so she could grin bigger. It felt right. A little scary, but right. Going into her PhD program had felt natural, like the next note in a totally boring, predictable piece of music. It felt like what she was supposed to be doing. No, it felt like what was expected of her. But she didn't want that. She didn't want a life in academia. She didn't want to be studying when she could be doing.

Bernie would probably kill her. Emma was officially ABD — all she had to do was write her dissertation, and defend it, and she would be Doctor Librarian, PhD, and spend the rest of her life scrambling to publish or perish. Trouble was, her heart just wasn't in it. And if there was one thing she'd learned at Kevin and Daniel's wedding, it was that you have to follow your heart. It had led her to Abe, hadn't it? And that was working out pretty well.

She smiled. She couldn't help it. Whenever she thought about him . . . well, there were some things that Skype just could not replicate. And now he was on his way here and she was gonna smooch on him till he couldn't breathe, and then she'd surprise him with the news.

She was going home with him, if he'd have her. Oh, she knew he'd have her. He had never made her doubt him for a second, not when he was uprooting his life in Nashville, not when he was figuring things out in Coral Bottom, not ever. And now he was doing so well for himself, like he'd really found his place.

Emma liked to think that she'd have found her way to Coral Bottom even if she and Abe hadn't worked out. And maybe that was true. Certainly Granny Sue would have kept in touch, and probably Emma would have had the courage to drop it all and move down there to manage that tiny little library of her dreams. But it didn't matter, did it? She did have him.

She was so moony that she almost didn't hear the knock at her door. She looked at the clock — Abe was early. But then, he was always early to see her, except when he got a speeding ticket. She opened the door, and there he was, her handsome, bearded fiddler with melty chocolate eyes, smiling that big smile of his, the one that was just for her.

She threw herself into his arms, and he caught her and spun her around and kissed her, and she forgot all about PhDs and Granny Sue and even the Christmas present she had waiting for him in her bedroom.

She forgot about everything but Abe.

He felt just like home.

■ ■ ■ ■

AN APPLE VALLEY
CHRISTMAS

SHIRLEE MCCOY

■ ■ ■ ■

CHAPTER ONE

He was dead, and Emma Baily wasn't sorry.

She wasn't sad.

She wasn't anything but empty and tired.

Four years devoted to caring for her father, four years of hearing him moan, complain, and curse the hand that was feeding him, and all she'd gotten for the effort was four years older.

Still single.

Still working in the same little town she'd grown up in.

Apple Valley, Washington.

Where young women became spinster and crotchety, mean-spirited old men lived the high life until they died.

She sounded bitter.

She *felt* bitter. Not about devoting years of her life to caring for a guy none of her siblings would even speak to. No. She wasn't bitter about that. She was bitter about the house. The one she'd inherited.

435

Everything to Emma. That's what her father's lawyer had said the will specified. Whatever money was left after her father's care, whatever assets were still there when he died, Emma would get them.

She didn't want them.

And, she especially didn't want the house.

Her father had known that. That was probably why he'd left the place to her.

Daniel Burns Baily was like that.

Mean.

Spiteful.

Dead.

The finality of that settled like lead in her stomach. She wasn't sad for the loss, but maybe she was a little sad for what had never been. For all the sweet childhood memories that her mother had tried to make. For all the wonderful holidays her mother had tried to create. For all the things Daniel had ruined with his drinking and his temper and his hate.

She moved past the freshly dug grave and the casket that would soon be lowered into it. Someone had dropped a handful of white daisies on top of it. Not Emma. She'd bought one of those edible arrangements and donated it to the local assisted living facility. The people there would appreciate it a lot more than her father ever could have.

He hadn't appreciated anything.

Not all the money he'd made in software development.

Not the wife who'd stuck by him until the day she'd died.

Not his ten kids.

He wouldn't even have appreciated the fifty people who'd stood in the freezing rain listening to the pastor of Apple Valley Community Church talk about life, legacies, and love. Daniel had despised them all. Small-town hicks was what he'd called them, and there wasn't one man or woman at the funeral who hadn't known that. They hadn't been there to pay their respects to Daniel. They'd been there for Emma.

Funny how that was.

She'd made friends in the past four years, made a decent life for herself with a decent job and people who cared. That was way more than Daniel had had when he'd died, and he'd lived in Apple Valley his entire life.

"You're fault, Dad," she muttered just in case Daniel's spirit happened to be hanging around listening. "You could have had a good life."

She kicked a pinecone, watched as it skittered across the graveyard, not quite sure what to do with herself now that her father was gone. No more growled demands, mumbled complaints, harsh criticisms. She was free. Finally.

Frozen grass crackled under her feet as she crossed the cemetery, walked through an old wrought-iron gate, and found her mother's grave. Unlike her husband, Sandra had been well liked by the community and well loved by her children. She'd been diagnosed with cancer when Emma was ten and had died six months later. *Her* will had only stipulated one thing — that she be buried in her family plot rather than the Bailys'.

Emma crouched near her mother's grave marker, swiping ice off the carved marble and placing the single rose she'd brought on top of it. Red. Not for romantic love. For Christmas. Sandra's favorite holiday.

Emma's least favorite.

Every memory she had of it was filled with disappointment, but that wasn't the reason she didn't like it. The way she saw things, Christmas should be about magic and miracles and love. Instead, it always seemed to be about glitter and glitz and excess.

"Merry Christmas, Mom," she said, because she didn't plan to be anywhere close to Apple Valley when December twenty-fifth rolled around. She'd put the house on the market, and then she'd go somewhere and spend Christmas alone planning what she wanted to do with the rest of her life.

"You've got to give this up, Em. You've got to start your life again. You're young, smart, driven. You could be living your dream. Instead, you're taking care of that old bastard, and it's wearing you out. I hate to see it."

Her brother, Adam, had told her that two days before he'd left on his third deployment with the Army. That had been six weeks ago. She'd sent him an e-mail the day their father died. She had no idea if he'd gotten it.

He'd been right, of course.

She needed to start her life again.

Too bad she wasn't sure what that meant.

The wind howled, spraying ice pellets into her face and down the collar of her wool coat. They melted, sliding into the V of the black dress she'd borrowed from a friend. She'd given up on dresses right around the time she'd realized Sunday morning church wasn't going to happen. Not while she was caring for her father. He'd hated church. Just like he'd hated everything else that was good and sweet and comfortable.

She stood, cold air biting through the thick stockings she'd purchased the previous night, wobbled on the heels she'd borrowed from another friend. Stilettos and they were sinking into the not-quite-frozen earth.

"Careful," someone said, and she turned, her ankle twisting as she whirled to face the speaker. Pain shot up her leg, and she stumbled, barely managing to stay on her feet.

"Darn-it!" she muttered, reaching down to rub the aching joint.

"You okay?" A man crouched beside her, probing at the ankle as if he had some business touching her.

"Fine. So, you can go ahead and back off," she responded, meeting his eyes.

Her heart stopped.

Literally. For about three beats, it froze, and then it started up again, beating frantically as she looked into a face she knew as well as she knew her own.

Jack McAllister. Adam's Army buddy.

And, Emma's ex-boyfriend.

They'd broken up so many years ago, she should have forgotten him by now.

Should have. Hadn't.

She frowned.

"What are you doing here?" she asked and heard a hint of her father in her voice, an edge of arrogance and disdain and discontent that made her stomach churn.

"Adam asked me to come. He got your

e-mail yesterday and contacted me. It looks like I missed the funeral. I'm sorry. The roads from the airport were a mess." He straightened, his body as lean and hard and beautiful as it had been when they were dating.

"You flew in from New Hampshire?"

"That *is* where I live." He shoved his hands deep into his pockets, watched her dispassionately.

"You traveled a long way for someone you haven't seen in years," she said and regretted it immediately.

He wasn't there for her.

She knew that.

"I saw Adam two months ago. Right before he deployed," he said, correcting her assumption without any meanness or spite. That was Jack. Always.

"And," he continued. "I told you when we broke up that I'd always be around if you needed me."

"That was a long time ago."

"Not that long." He took her arm, helped her off the grass and onto a paved path that wound through the cemetery. "How are you holding up?"

"Fine. He was my father, but we weren't close."

"That doesn't mean it's easy to say good-bye."

"Sometimes it means it's harder." More words that she regretted.

She pressed her lips together, staring out over the old marble headstones. Hundreds of lives that had begun and ended. Hopefully, most of them had been happier than Daniel's.

She shivered, wiping icy rain from her cheeks.

"You're cold. How about we go inside and warm up?"

"I need to get home." Not really. There was nothing there but memories. Most of them bad.

"Is there a reception at your place? A celebration of life?"

"No." Just that. She wasn't going to explain that she hadn't had the energy to plan one. Or the confidence to believe that people would attend.

"I'm sorry, Em," he said quietly, turning her toward the church, his hand still on her arm.

Emma didn't respond.

Jack hadn't really expected her to.

I'm sorry was the kind of platitude he tried to avoid. It didn't make a person feel any better. It sure as heck didn't solve any problems. He'd said it anyway, because he *was* sorry. Sorry that he'd found Emma alone in a cemetery that should have had at least a few people in it.

Obviously, they'd come and gone.

Either that, or they hadn't come at all.

From what Jack had heard, Daniel Baily was a mean-spirited, hate-filled bastard who hadn't had a friend in the world. Since Adam wasn't prone to exaggeration, and he was the one who'd offered the description, Jack believed it.

He also believed there was no excuse for not attending a parent's funeral. Daniel had ten kids. One of them was serving his country. One was walking silently beside Jack. The rest were MIA.

"What happened to the rest of your clan?" he asked, as they skirted the newly dug grave, the mahogany casket.

"What clan? We've been scattered since my mother died. You know that." She tucked a thick strand of hair behind her ear, her fingers white with cold. No hat. No gloves. Just a black coat and a black dress and shoes that were about three inches too high for this kind of weather.

"I thought maybe you'd all come together for this."

"I thought maybe we would, too, but I guess not." She shrugged, her shoulders narrower than he'd remembered. She looked skinny, her cheeks gaunt. He opted out of mentioning it.

"Are you disappointed?"

"I'm tired. That's about all I feel, right now."

"It's been a long few weeks, huh?"

"A long four years," she corrected. She didn't glance at the mahogany casket as they passed it. Didn't spare her father's final resting place even that quick of a look.

"And, now it's over. What's next?"

She laughed, but there was no humor in it. "I have no idea."

"You'll figure it out."

She stopped short, looked him straight in the eye. He could see the old Emma now, the one he'd fallen for the very first day they'd met — pretty and sweet-looking and full of all kinds of energy and fire. "Another platitude, Jack? I'm surprised. You're usually a lot more creative than that."

"Not a platitude. Just a statement."

She cocked her head to the side, studying him with dark gray eyes that always seen too much.

Maybe, she could see how much he didn't want to be there.

And, how much he absolutely did. Not just for Adam. For her.

"Fine," she finally said. "Not a platitude. So, how about we say good-bye, and I get on my way. You were right when you said it was cold. Thanks for coming, Jack. I really do appreciate it."

She walked away, moving across the parking lot in the too-high heels, her back straight, her head high. An old Ford was parked next to the SUV he'd rented, and she climbed into it, her dress shimmying up, revealing slim, muscular thighs.

He looked. Of course.

And, she noticed.

She tugged the dress back into place, offered a quick wave and closed the door. Seconds later, the engine sputtered to life, the windshield wipers came on, and she was driving away.

He didn't rush to follow.

Adam had provided the address, and he'd asked Jack to stay until Emma didn't need him any longer.

Jack wasn't sure she needed him at all, but he'd promised, and he was going to follow through on it. Whether she liked it or not.

CHAPTER TWO

She was shaking.

Literally.

Hands. Feet. Arms. Even Emma's hair seemed to be trembling.

From the cold.

That's what she was telling herself, but she thought it might also be from seeing Jack after all these years.

Jack.

She still couldn't quite believe that he was in Apple Valley, Washington. The next time she spoke with Adam, she was going to ask what the heck he'd been thinking sending her ex to the funeral. Adam knew how she'd felt when she and Jack had parted ways — devastated. He also knew that she'd never forgotten her first serious boyfriend.

Only serious boyfriend.

God! She'd been so young and naïve when she'd met Jack. A sophomore in college and filled with all kinds of wonderful dreams.

Three years older with four years of military service under his belt, Jack had already seen more of the world than she probably ever would.

She still wasn't sure what he'd seen in her.

She knew exactly what she'd seen in him — kindness, strength, intelligence. The fact that he was handsome as sin hadn't hurt.

She frowned, flicking the heat on high and hoping that hot air would pour out of the vent. She'd been meaning to bring the Ford in for a tune-up, but time had gotten away from her.

Four years of time.

She'd catch up on things now. Tune-up on the Ford. Haircut that was two years overdue. New clothes. And . . .

"What's next?"

Jack had asked a good question, and she'd had no answer.

She only knew that she had to move on. Just like her siblings had years ago. It wasn't a surprise that none of them had shown up for the funeral. They hadn't visited once in the four years since Daniel's Alzheimer's diagnosis. They'd called, of course. They'd sent cards. They'd asked if she needed anything, and she'd known that if she had, they'd have provided it. As long as *it* wasn't help with Daniel's care.

That was okay.

She was the one who'd made the promise to their mother, and she was the one who'd had to follow through.

Her hands tightened on the steering wheel, her body stiff with cold and nerves. No heat pumping out of the vents. That was for sure. At least she didn't have to worry about Jack anymore. He was probably on his way back to the airport, relieved to be freed of his obligation. Adam really shouldn't have asked him to come. The two were as close as brothers, and they'd do anything for each other, but flying all night to attend the funeral of a man he'd never met went above and beyond the call of duty.

At least, in Emma's opinion it did.

Not that she was one to talk. She'd devoted four years of her life to someone who despised her.

She turned onto the rutted country road that led to her father's house. *His* house. Not his family's. He'd made that clear to everyone who crossed the threshold and to everyone who'd lived inside the walls.

"This is my house, and if you don't like the way I run it, you can leave."

How many times had she heard him say that? To her? To her brothers and sisters? One sibling after another had done just

448

exactly that. Left. The big-family-sized house had emptied, the door of one bedroom after another closing for good.

Finally, it had been Emma's turn. She'd packed her bags and walked away and her father had barely even said good-bye. He hadn't kissed her on the cheek, hadn't wished her good luck at college, hadn't offered her money, a place to return, a simple "I'm proud of you."

Maybe he'd known that she'd be back.

Or — and this was more likely the case — he just hadn't cared. He'd been happy to have the big old house to himself, all the rooms empty. No one to bounce up the stairs or bound down them while he was hunched over his computer doing whatever it was he did. No one to interrupt his solitude. No one to worry about. No one to make him think of anything other than himself.

"You were a winner, Dad," she whispered as the old house came into view. Bright white against the steel-colored sky, the old farmhouse had the stately grace of bygone eras. For all his faults, Daniel had been good at maintaining his heritage. The place was nearly as perfect as it had been the day it was built. No faded paint or crumbling wood trim. No cracked windows or listing foundation. No expense had been spared when it came to maintaining the property, and it showed.

It wasn't that Daniel had loved it. It was simply that he'd taken pride in owning one of the most prestigious homes in the county. Just like he'd taken pride in having children who were always at the top of their classes. No grade lower than an A was tolerated. Anything less than that would bring on a full-out Daniel rage.

Emma shoved the thought away.

It was over.

The end of an era. An ugly era, but an era.

Up ahead, the road sloped up toward the circular drive, a thick layer of ice shimmering in the gray light. *This* was not going to be fun. The Ford's tires were nearly bald — another thing she'd been meaning to get to but hadn't — and the hill was steep. If she wasn't careful, she'd roll backward into one of the shallow ditches that edged both sides of the road.

"Come on, baby. You can do it," she cajoled, coaxing the old truck up the incline.

For a moment, she thought she was going to make it.

The truck chugged along smoothly, barely slipping on the icy pavement. Then, it happened. One split second of too much pressure on the accelerator, and she was spinning.

No hope for it.

She was going in the ditch.

A thud. A bump. And, she was there, nose down, bushes pressed against the windshield.

"For God's sake! Really?!" she growled, shoving the door open and stepping out of the truck. There didn't seem to be much damage. Maybe a scratch on the bumper, but it just added to the old beast's character. The axle looked good. There were no fluids leaking out.

Aside from the fact that it was stuck in the ditch, the truck seemed just fine.

She'd have to call for a tow. No way could she get it out herself.

Tomorrow would be soon enough for that.

For today, she was done.

Finished.

Over.

She yanked the keys from the ignition, told herself that a quarter-mile walk in the icy rain would be fun. A quarter-mile walk in the icy rain *wearing heels.*

Yeah. Real fun.

The collar of her coat was damp from melted ice, her hair lying in cold, limp strands on her cheeks. Her tights were soggy, the knit dress itchy. Her toes were frozen, her fingers blue with cold.

Yeah. Sure. This would be a blast.

There was nothing for it, though. She had to get to the house. Walking was the only way to do it. She started up the hill, slipping and sliding in her stupid borrowed shoes. She finally gave up on the pavement and stepped off the road, holding onto bushes and trees as she trudged along.

She made it to the front door in record time.

It was that or freeze to death.

The good news about being half-dead from cold?

She couldn't feel the throbbing pain in her twisted ankle.

She fished keys from her purse, cursing softly as they slipped from her frozen fingers and skittered across the porch. She dove for them, landing on her knees and skidding across the frozen whitewashed boards. Her fingers grazed the key, and it jumped away, slipping through a small knothole near the edge of the porch.

"I do not need this right now!"

She clamored off the porch, her stockings ripped at both knees, blood seeping out from torn flesh. She was so cold she couldn't feel it and so pissed she didn't care.

She just wanted the keys, so that she could go inside the house and get out of the dress, the coat, the shoes. Get back into her normal jeans and T-shirt. Sit for a few minutes and figure out what it meant to be in the house without her father in it.

Brick framing surrounded a lattice porch skirt. Emma used her cell phone light to peer into the darkness beyond it. There. About a foot from the edge of the latticework, the keys glinted against dark soil.

"All right, you little bugger," Emma growled, pulling at the porch skirt. "You're coming down, because I need that key."

She yanked, but the board didn't give.

She yanked again, rocking back on her stilettos and pulling so hard her fingers hurt. The dang thing still didn't give.

"Darn it! Can I just get one measly little break? One tiny little positive in this entire four years of negatives? Can I?" she shouted, the words mixing with the sound of a car engine.

Someone was coming. Probably one of the guys from the sheriff's department where she worked. Maybe Simon or Cade coming to check on her and make sure that she was okay.

She would be.

Once she got her keys.

She yanked harder and one of the boards gave so abruptly, she flew back, landing in a pile of slushy ice that soaked through the coat and dress and the already-torn tights.

She was up in a flash, shoving her arm through the opening, feeling around for the keys. No dice. Her arm was too short or the key was too far or some little demon had snatched the thing out from under her hand right before she could grasp it.

She grabbed another piece of the porch skirt, yanking at it with so much force, her shoulders ached.

Behind her, footsteps crunched on the icy ground.

Probably her boss. Sheriff Cade Cunningham approached most situations with quiet observation rather than boisterous greetings.

"Everything is fine," she called. "You can go back to the office or home or wherever you were headed before you stopped here."

Her voice sounded cheerful and light.

Just the way she'd planned it.

Hopefully, Cade would turn right back around and . . .

"Home is a long way from here, Emma," Jack said.

Jack.

Again.

And, this time she was coated with mud, her hair plastered to her head, her face probably splattered with dirt. Worse, she felt like crying, because it didn't seem as if anything in her life had gone right lately.

She didn't look at him.

Not when he stood beside her.

Not when he sighed.

Not when he crouched right next to her.

She was afraid if she did — if she looked into his dark green eyes, saw any kind of sympathy at all — she *would* cry.

"Problems?" he asked.

"My truck slid off the road."

"I saw that, but it doesn't explain why you're tearing your house apart."

"I dropped my keys."

"I see."

But, he didn't see. Not really.

Because Jack had no idea what tearing pieces off of the latticework porch skirt had to do with dropped keys.

"They fell through a hole in the porch," Emma continued, yanking at the wood again. It gave with a quick snap, and if he hadn't grabbed her waist, she would have gone flying.

Instead, she tumbled sideways, falling

against him in a shivery mass of wet fabric and frozen hair.

"You need to get inside," he said, grabbing her hand and pulling her to her feet.

Her teeth were chattering, and her skin was tinged blue.

He shrugged out of his coat, wrapped it around her shoulders, pulled the collar up around her ears.

"You're nearly frozen."

"You think?" she asked, and he smiled at the sarcasm in her voice.

"Obviously, you're not as close to death as I feared."

"No, but this darn porch will be if it doesn't give me back my keys." She reached for the wood again, but he nudged her out of the way.

"Let me." He took her cell phone, used the light to look under the porch, found the keys and snagged them with the edge of his pocket knife.

"Here you go," he said, dropping them into her hand.

"Figures," she muttered.

"What figures?"

"That you'd do in three seconds what it would have taken me four hours to accomplish."

"Is it a competition?" he asked gently,

because she looked miserable, her clothes ripped, her knees bleeding, her face flecked with melted ice and mud.

Her eyes were the same velvety gray they'd been six years ago. Now, though, they were red-rimmed and hollow, all the humor and vitality hidden by what looked like bone-deep fatigue.

She ran a hand over her soaked hair and shook her head. "I'm sorry. I'm in a mood. I shouldn't take it out on you."

"Because of your father?" he asked.

"Yes, but not for the reasons you might think." She headed up the porch stairs, her dress plastered to her legs, her calves splattered with mud.

"Are you going to tell me what reasons they are?"

"They're not important." She tried to unlock the front door, but her hand was shaking so much she missed the keyhole. Once. Twice. Three times.

He took the keys from her hand, unlocked it himself.

"Thanks," she said as she stepped inside.

He followed, stopping in the center of a two-story foyer. Mahogany trim and gleaming wood floors. Hand-carved banister. Wide, curved stairs. Not just a farmhouse. This place was a masterpiece.

He whistled softly, and Emma smiled.

"Impressive, huh?"

"Adam said I'd have a field day here. He was right."

"Field day doing what? Seeing it?" She turned to face him, his coat still around her shoulders. She was nearly drowning in it, the wool falling to her calves.

She looked small and a little fragile. She also looked suspicious. She had a right to be. Adam hadn't just asked him to make sure Emma was okay. He'd asked him to help organize the collections of antiques that filled the house. Generations' worth. That's what Adam had said. He hadn't been kidding. Everywhere Jack looked, there was something old, beautiful, valuable.

"You know my family owns an auction house, Emma." He sidestepped her question, because she was already upset. He didn't want to make things worse.

"Adam said you and your brother took over for your father." He shrugged out of his coat and hung it on a hook near the door. She removed hers, too, hanging it next to Jack's. She looked even thinner without the coat, her waist narrow, her hip bones and scapula jutting out.

He was worried, but saying it would get him nowhere fast, so he kept his own counsel and responded to her comment.

"We did. We've got three auction houses, now. The original one in New Hampshire. One in Maine and another near Boston."

"That's fantastic!" She sounded genuinely pleased. That didn't surprise Jack. One of the things he'd liked most about Emma was her enthusiasm for other people's dreams and accomplishments.

"We think so. New England is filled with history and antiquities. It's exciting to be part of giving old things new homes."

"I can imagine how satisfying that would be." She smiled, lifting an old piece of carnival glass from a built-in near the stairs. 1930s. Amethyst. He'd only ever seen one other like it.

"Not as satisfying as seeing you put that back on the shelf. It's worth a small fortune," he said, and she laughed.

"Afraid I'll drop it?"

"You *did* drop the keys."

"And destroy the porch skirt." She set the piece down, ran her hand through her drying hair. "And let my truck slide into a ditch."

"You've had a long four years," he said, repeating what she'd said earlier.

Her smile faded, and she shrugged. "Right, and you've had a very productive

459

one. You've got to be really busy, Jack, so I'm even sorrier that my brother asked you to come out here."

"I told you why I came. Adam was only part of the reason."

She looked like she wanted to say something. Her mouth opened. Closed. Finally, she sighed. "I'm so cold my brain isn't functioning properly. I need to get out of these clothes and warm up. You can look around if you want. If you have to leave before I come back down, thanks again. For everything."

She didn't give him a chance to respond. Just turned and ran up the stairs. She was assuming he would leave, of course. That was the way she'd always been — certain that what they'd had couldn't last. That had been the biggest reason why it hadn't.

"People don't stay, Jack. The kind of love all my friends are looking for? It's a fantasy. My mother spent years trying for it. She wasted her health and her youth, and she never got anything for it but tears."

She'd told him that a few weeks before they'd broken up.

He'd been annoyed. Not because he'd disagreed, but because he'd wanted to give it a shot, see if they could create something

460

that neither of them would ever walk away from.

Emma had wanted to take things a day at a time.

He'd wanted to talk about the future.

Maybe because he'd been twenty-four, a combat veteran, already wounded once. He'd seen men die, and he'd wanted proof that he was alive, that he had something to live for. Maybe, he'd wanted Emma to be that.

He didn't know.

He just knew that he hadn't been content to take things a day at a time. Eventually, he'd decided he didn't want to be with someone who didn't believe in what they had. He'd told Emma that.

That had been that. The end.

Except it hadn't really been.

When he'd told her that he'd be around if she ever needed him, he'd meant it.

He still meant it.

The floorboards above his head creaked, and old pipes groaned as Emma turned on the water. She must be taking a shower. He walked into the room to the left of the foyer, eyeing thousands and thousands of dollars' worth of antiques. Most of it looked to be in mint condition. Even the fireplace looked

461

unused. Not a smudge of soot on it. Too bad.

One of the things he'd learned from auctioning off estates: No one regretted living. Not one person he'd ever worked with had ever wished they hadn't used Aunt Gracie's fancy silver teapot or sat at Grandmother Maude's Chippendale table. Memories were built into things by the using of them. It made cleaning out estates bittersweet, but he figured the sweet outweighed the bitter for most people.

This house, though? He glanced around, taking in the Victorian settee and the Georgian couch, the gleaming fireplace mantel and the Limoges teacups and saucers that lined it. It didn't look like anyone had been in the room for decades.

A shame, because the large windows would have been the perfect frame for a Christmas tree, some glitter, a few lights.

He'd been in more than his fair share of old homes, and he knew how ones like this were set up. He walked through the parlor and into a formal dining room, opened pocket doors and stepped into what must have once been a library. It was empty now. Just an old desk and an older leather chair. Neither of them as fancy as what he'd seen in the other rooms. A small door opened

No way!

The last time there'd been a fire in one of the fireplaces, her mother had been alive.

That had been what? Eighteen years ago?

She inhaled deeply, confirmed what she'd already known — someone had definitely lit a fire.

Someone?

Jack. She knew it. Just like she knew that if she walked downstairs, she'd find him there. Maybe studying one of the hundreds of antiques that decorated the parlor or the sitting room.

She walked to the top of the stairs and stood there, breathing in the best childhood memories. Wood-burning fires on cold nights. Rocking in her mother's chair, staring into the crackling flames, imagining having a family of her own there one day, all of them living in the big old house that would always be part of the family.

She could remember her mother saying that.

Funny how that memory had been gone until now.

But, it was there again — the way her mother's voice had sounded, the way Emma had closed her eyes and imagined having a husband. Kids. Lots of noise and happiness and joy.

She couldn't remember the exact moment she'd stopped daydreaming about those things. Maybe the day she'd heard her father tell her mother that she was the worst mistake he'd ever made, that he wished to hell he didn't have to be burdened with the responsibility of a sick wife and lazy kids.

That had been a month before Sandra had been diagnosed with cancer. She'd been sick for a while, tired all the time, in pain from the tumor that was growing on her brain stem. Emma had been young, but she'd been old enough to see how sick her mother was. Adam had still been home. So had Michael and Jenna. The four of them had tried hard to make their mother's life easier. They'd cooked. They'd cleaned up after meals. They'd taken out the garbage and swept the floors, dusted every fancy vase and beautiful antique every single day. Just like their mother had always done. Just like their father had expected.

If Daniel had noticed, he hadn't said a word.

Then again, he'd never seemed to care who made his life comfortable, as long as someone did. And, of course, none of it was ever good enough anyway. There were always complaints, criticisms, harsh word that rang through the house.

No joy there.

No love.

Nothing but tension and fear mixed with shouts and slaps and slamming doors.

She frowned.

Water under the bridge, and there was no way to make it flow backward. Even if she could, there would be nothing she could do to change anything. Her mother had tried. God knew she had. She'd bent over backward to please her husband.

Daniel wouldn't be pleased.

Emma sure as heck knew that.

She'd spent years catering to his whims, and he'd never once thanked her for anything. He'd never complimented her. He'd never encouraged her. All he'd done was tear her efforts apart.

She hadn't thought it could be possible, but he'd been even meaner after his Alzheimer's diagnosis than he'd been before it.

But, now, it was over.

Time served.

And, there was a fire burning in one of the fireplaces, and something else in the air. Something fragrant and warm and . . .

Edible?

No way!

But . . . she was pretty sure she heard pans clanking in the kitchen as she walked down the stairs.

God! She hoped Jack wasn't cooking.

He could cook like a dream, and she could devour every bite of anything he made. She could also sit across the table from him and look in his eyes and remember just how good they'd been together.

Until they weren't.

Until she'd gotten scared.

That was the truth. She was old enough and mature enough to understand what she hadn't six years ago. She'd wanted Jack too much, and she'd been afraid of what that would do to her, how it would change her. How deeply it would hurt if it didn't work out.

She'd also been terrified of becoming her mother — a slave to her husband's discontent; an afterthought in the mind of a man who'd promised to love her forever.

"Poor, Mom," she murmured, walking into the parlor, the warmth of the room seeping into her bones.

A cheerful fire cast long shadows across the dark room. They danced over the throw rug and the gleaming hardwood floor, lapped against the cream-colored walls and the woodwork.

The sun had set, and the ice that had been falling all day had turned to snow, the flakes drifting silently outside the window. She could see them swirling through the dark-blue night, and she would have been tempted to walk out on the porch and get a better look if she hadn't been opposed to getting cold again.

She was.

She'd been cold enough for one day.

Cold enough for a lifetime, really.

She heard footsteps in the hall, and she turned, her breath catching as Jack walked into the room. His nearly black hair gleamed in the firelight, and his eyes glowed. He looked older, tougher, even more handsome than he had six years ago.

He held out a mug, smiled.

"Coffee?" he asked.

"I'm not a big coffee fan," she said, glad that he'd forgotten. Relieved, really, because she didn't want to think that he'd remembered that she almost never drank coffee and when she did . . .

"Four creams. Three sugars." He looked into the cup and frowned. "I'm not sure it can even be called coffee."

"I can't believe you remembered." She took the cup, sipped the scalding, sweet brew.

"How you liked your coffee? Why wouldn't I?"

"The last time we had coffee together . . ."

"Was the morning after your New Year's party. I remember." He walked to the fireplace, used the old poker to jab at the burning logs. The collar of his blue dress shirt was dark from melted ice. He'd rolled up the sleeves, and she could see the scar on his forearm. The one he'd gotten the day Adam had saved his life.

She knew the story just like she knew Jack, and for a moment it was as if nothing had changed between them. It was as if they'd been a couple for all the years they'd been apart. As if this moment, in this room with the snow blowing against the windows and the two of them standing close enough to touch, was just like any other moment of any other day.

Except, of course, that it wasn't.

They'd been out of each other's lives for six years.

She needed to remember that.

She sipped the coffee, trying really hard not to notice the way Jack's shirt clung to his broad chest and his muscular shoulders, the way his smile made her pulse jump.

Just how good it felt to have him there.

Okay.

Enough was enough.

She'd spent ten minutes with the man,

and she was already thinking things she shouldn't. Time to send him on his way.

"It's really starting to snow out there," she commented, walking to the window and trying to look casual and unconcerned. She didn't want him to think she was trying to kick him out. Even though she was.

"It is. We could have a few inches by morning."

"That will make travel difficult. If you've got a flight to catch —"

"I don't." He cut her off.

"You don't?"

"No." He looked up from the fire, the golden glow of the flames splashing across his face. He wasn't the kind of guy she'd ever thought she'd go for. She'd been hell-bent on finding a quiet, unassuming young man who would be as different from her father as the night was from the day. She hadn't wanted muscles. She hadn't wanted tough, rough, gruff. She hadn't wanted any of the things she'd found in Jack, but she'd wanted Jack.

Because of all those things?

On him, they'd added up to kindness, patience, compassion. The rough, gruff edges hid a heart of gold. She'd known it the minute she'd met him, and in all the years since, he'd never proven her wrong.

They might not have stayed together, but Jack had been as good a friend to Adam as anyone ever could be. She loved that about him.

Loved?

A strong word, and she'd better be very careful about applying it to her feelings for Jack!

"You do have plans to return to New Hampshire. Right?" she asked.

"Eventually." He replaced the poker, and turned so that they were face-to-face.

"What, exactly, does that mean?"

"It means, your brother asked me to help you settle your father's estate. I'll be here until that's done."

"No. You won't. I've got things under control here, and I don't need any help."

"That's a matter of opinion," he said calmly.

"The only opinion that matters is mine."

He smiled. Just . . . smiled, and she could feel the steam pouring from her head, all thoughts of love and friendship and what a good guy he was flying away.

"Are you hearing me?"

"Loud and clear."

"I don't need your help."

"Okay."

"You can go home."

"No. I can't."

"My brother —"

"Has your best interest at heart. He's worried. He doesn't want you to have to deal with this on your own. If he were here, he'd be helping you."

"He's not here."

"Exactly. Instead, he's in enemy territory. If he finds out you're on your own, working through all this yourself, he'll be distracted. That could get him killed."

"He's not going to find out."

"Want to bet?"

"You wouldn't dare tell him. You love him too much."

"I wouldn't lie to him, either. If he asked me flat-out, I'd have to tell him the truth. Would you want to risk the consequences of that?" He was dead serious. She could see it in his eyes.

"Do you always have to win, Jack?" she muttered.

"Only when I'm protecting people I care about."

People he cared about.

Not *a person*.

She noticed.

She didn't point it out, though.

Jack had figured Emma would put up more of an argument, but she seemed done.

She'd turned away, was looking out the window, sipping the sugary coffee he'd made for her.

She'd been right about the snow.

It was coming down hard.

If he'd planned to leave, he'd have been on the road by now, but he'd purchased a one-way ticket. He'd buy the return ticket once he figured out how long he was going to stay. Based on what he'd seen in the house — several weeks. Maybe longer. It just depended on what Emma wanted to do with the house and its contents.

"You hungry?" he asked, because she still looked skinny, her colorful leggings hugging slim thighs and calves, her oversized sweater sliding off a shoulder that seemed more bone than muscle.

"Did you cook?" she responded, turning to meet his eyes.

She was stunning in the firelight, her hair burnished gold, her skin glowing.

"I made chicken noodle soup."

"From scratch?" She raised one perfectly shaped brow.

"Will I win extra points if I did?"

"No." She laughed. "But, I might eat more of it."

"I'm sorry to say that I just opened a can and poured it into a pot. I did doctor it up a little."

"With what?"

"Minced onions. Diced carrots. A little thyme. Extra noodles."

"Extra noodles! I'm in!" She hooked her arm through his, nearly dragging him into the kitchen.

He'd left the soup on the burner, and she reached into a cupboard to grab bowls, her sweater sliding a little farther down her shoulder. If he'd wanted to, he could have leaned down and pressed a kiss to silky skin, let his lips linger there.

Who was he kidding?

He wanted to.

He didn't because Emma had had a rough day. A rough week. A rough few years. He didn't want to add to her stress, and he was pretty certain she'd be stressed if he tried to pick up where they'd left off six years ago.

She filled two bowls with soup, set both on the table and gestured for him to sit.

"Eat," she said, and then blushed. "Geeze! Sorry. I'm talking to you like you're my dad."

"You barked orders at him?"

"Unfortunately, it was the only kind of communication he responded to." She frowned, dropping into a chair and spooning up some soup. She didn't eat it. Just let it drop back into the bowl.

"Eat," he said in the same exact tone she'd used, and she smiled.

"Thanks, Jack."

"For the soup? You haven't even tried it yet."

"For trying to make me smile."

"I didn't try. I succeeded," he replied, knowing she'd smile again.

"Always the winner."

"Not always." He sat across from her, eyeing the bowl of canned garbage. He'd done the best he could with what he'd had. Her cupboards had been nearly bare, the refrigerator almost empty. No leftover turkey from Thanksgiving. No milk. No eggs. Just enough creamer to make her coffee, a lone carrot stick, an onion, and a tired stick of butter.

"You've never lost when you were around me."

"I lost you. That's a big one." He tasted the soup. Tin can with just a hint of thyme.

"You didn't lose me. We agreed to part ways." She scooped up soup and ate. Probably to avoid continuing the conversation.

That was fine.

He had other things he wanted to talk about. "What are your plans, Em? Now that your dad is gone?"

"Get this place ready to sell. He left it to me. Adam probably mentioned that in his e-mail."

"He did."

"I want to have it on the market before Christmas," she said. "So, I'll be really busy with that for the next few weeks."

"What about everything inside of the house?"

"Also mine. Also being sold."

"You're sure?" he asked, because the place was filled with treasures and family heirlooms. If it had been his, he'd have kept it.

"Of course."

"Then, I'll have an appraiser fly out. I'm pretty good at pricing certain things, but furniture, paintings, that kind of stuff? It's not my area of expertise. We can run the estate sale a week before you put the house on the market. That will get it cleaned out a little. Give potential buyers a better view of the bones of the house."

"Estate sale?"

"Isn't that what you planned?"

"I hadn't really planned anything." She carried her soup bowl to the sink.

"Then, it's good that I'm here. I can help you organize things."

"I should probably talk to my siblings first."

477

"Are they beneficiaries of the estate?"

"No, but they should be."

"Why?" He moved in next to her, setting his bowl in the sink and squirting dish soap into the water she was running.

"Because that's fair."

"From what Adam said, your father was never fair."

"True."

"But, he was just as abusive to you as he was to your siblings."

"Also true."

"So, why were you here while they were off living their lives?"

She'd been washing a bowl, and she stopped, water sloshing over her wrists as she met his eyes.

"The truth?"

"I always prefer that to a lie."

"I made a promise to my mother before she died. I told her that I'd make sure that he didn't die alone."

"She made you promise to stay with him?" He was shocked, and he was pissed. No way could Emma's mother not have known what she was asking her daughter to put up with.

"She didn't make me. She told me that she was worried about him. It was right after her diagnosis, and she knew she was going to die. One day we were talking, and she told me that if something happened to her, we'd all be fine. We were strong, but Daniel was weak, and she couldn't bear to think of him dying alone. She was sobbing, and I felt terrible —"

"So you told her that you'd make sure he didn't?"

"I didn't just tell her. I promised. If she'd have let me, I would have sworn a blood oath. Anything to keep her from crying."

"You were a kid, Em."

"It didn't matter then. It didn't matter when my father was diagnosed with Alzheimer's. It didn't matter during the four years I took care of him. I promised my mother, and I kept the promise, because I couldn't do anything else. She loved all of us. She held this family together. She deserved that." She washed the bowl quickly, set it in the drainer. "I'm tired. I'm going up to bed. My room's at the end of the upstairs hall. You can use any of the other ones."

That was it.

She was done, and she was gone, hurrying out of the kitchen, silent in her socked feet.

He wanted to go after her, but he'd lost that right years ago.

Maybe it was time to try and earn it back.

CHAPTER FOUR

She didn't sleep.

She couldn't.

Instead, she paced the room that she'd grown up in, the one where she'd hidden from all the chaos that her father caused. She'd been back for four years, and she hadn't changed any of it. Not the prissy pink comforter that her mother had bought when she was seven. Not the hanging basket of stuffed animals that swayed listlessly every time she opened the door. Not the white eyelet curtains, the dusty shades.

Like all the other bedrooms in the house, hers had a fireplace that hadn't been used in decades, the carved wood mantel painted white sometime in the middle of the last century, the paint so thick it nearly hid the details of the beautiful carved angels that decorated the mantel's wood. The same carpenter who'd carved the banister, laid the floors, and put in the kitchen cabinets had carved angels into one mantel, flowers into another, dogs in a third. Every mantel was different. As a kid, she'd loved sneaking into her siblings' rooms and studying the carvings.

That had been before, of course.

When her mother had still been alive, and they'd all still lived at home.

Years ago.

Decades.

A lifetime.

She pulled back the curtains and stared out into the snow. She needed to go to the grocery store in the morning, before things got too bad. She'd have to take her father's SUV. He'd bought it on a whim a few years back and had kept the keys from her and anyone else who'd wanted to borrow it. She'd found them, of course, but she hadn't wanted anything from her father. Not even a safer ride in the winter.

She let the curtains fall, wishing the flimsy fabric could block some of the cold air that seeped through cracks in the old window-pane. She'd been cold for months. Even in the summer, she'd felt chilled in the old house. If she'd had her way, they'd have put in new windows, added insulation into the attic, made the place a little more comfortable.

Too late now.

Outside the door, floorboards creaked, and she froze, terrified that Jack was wandering around outside the door, and that he'd knock if he thought she was awake. She didn't want to deal with Jack. Not now. Eventually, of course, she'd have to send him on his way, but she hadn't wanted to spend the night alone in the house that had never been empty. Not while she'd been in it.

Something thumped against the door, and every muscle in her body went tight. Another thump. Not a knock. Not a call to see if she was still awake. Just that soft little thump that could have been anything, but that she imagined was Jack trying to check on her but not wanting to wake her.

Thump.

"Fine. Okay," she muttered. "What do you . . . ?" She flung open the door, looked out into the hall. Dark. Not a hint of light seeping out from beneath any of the closed doors.

Was Jack asleep?

Or had he gone downstairs?

That had to be it. Someone had been at her door, and the only other person in the house was Jack.

She stepped into the hall. It was colder

there than in her room, the radiator heat doing little to warm the large area. The frigid wood floor only added to the chill. If she actually wanted to stay in the house instead of selling it — which she most definitely did not — she'd have paid to install heated floors. She'd seen them on one of the home improvement channels her father had liked to watch.

Not that he'd ever done any home improvement, but he'd hired people, and, thanks to DYI television, he'd been convinced that he knew more than anyone he was paying. He'd micromanaged every project he'd ever hired out. Until the last two years. Then, he hadn't been able to do much of anything but complain and ask where Sandra was. If a stroke hadn't taken him early, Daniel probably would have lived for years, slowly shrinking into the shell of what he'd always been.

She winced at the thought, moving through the hallway and listening for any sign that Jack was downstairs. She didn't want him to be. Not much anyway. She could admit there was a part of her that would have preferred to spend the sleepless night talking to someone rather than pacing her room, silently reliving a million old memories.

Her foot hit something. A ball? A bell? Whatever it was, it rattled across the floor, hit the top of the stairs, and bounced all the way down, jingling loudly as it went.

A bell for sure, but she had no idea where it had come from. Even with Christmas just a few weeks away, she had no decorations out. She had no intention of putting decorations out either. The holiday was for people who believed in miracles and magic and all the beautiful things that Christmas seemed to offer.

Emma? She believed in reality.

"Everything okay out here?" A door behind her opened, and she turned as Jack stepped out of Adam's old room.

"You're not downstairs," she responded, trying really hard not to notice that he didn't have a shirt on. Just loose flannel pajama bottoms that sat right on his hip bones. Acres of smooth, tan skin and rippling muscle, that's what she shouldn't have been looking at, but she couldn't quite help herself. She looked and looked some more.

"Not since midnight," he responded, walking past her open bedroom door. "Did you hear something out here?"

"I thought I did. Maybe it was just the wind or the house settling or —"

He flicked on the hallway light, and her

words fell away, because he looked even better with the warm yellow glow of the overhead light shining across his chest and abdomen.

"Or?" he prodded, taking a step closer.

He smelled like shampoo and soap and something dark and sensual and more appealing than a giant slice of chocolate cake with a scoop of vanilla ice cream on the side.

She swallowed hard and turned away, focusing on the stairs and the thing that she had kicked. "There was something on the floor. It sounded like a bell. Did you drop something when you brought your bags up?"

"Do you really think I carry bells with me?" he asked, his fingers sliding across her shoulders and settling on her nape.

She would have answered, but her brain was frozen, stuck on one simple thought — his hand? It felt as good as his body looked.

"I kicked something," she finally managed to say.

He smiled, and she knew that *he* knew exactly what she was feeling with his hand resting on her neck, and his nearly naked body just inches away.

"Where is it?" he murmured, leaning down so their heads were nearly touching. He was looking toward the stairs, but his hand was still right where he'd put it. Skin to skin, and there was a heck of a lot more skin less than an arm's length away.

"Emma?" he prodded, his thumb sliding across her collarbone.

God!

She needed to move away.

Now!

"At the bottom of the stairs," she finally responded, and then she did what she should have done the minute he'd stepped out of his room — she ran down the steps as fast as her shaking legs could carry her.

Jack wanted to grab her hand, pull her back into his arms, maybe kiss that soft spot where his hand had been. Right beneath the silky fall of her hair, where her skin was warm and velvety and tempting.

It would be a mistake.

Jack knew it, so he followed Emma downstairs, watched as she lifted a small metal object.

"This is it!" she announced. "The thing I kicked."

"Looks like a sleigh bell."

"It does." She frowned, holding it up to the light. "You're sure it's not yours?"

"Positive." It looked old, though. Like something he'd have found in an antique desk hidden away in a dilapidated barn. It certainly wasn't new, and he imagined that it had once hung from a horse's harness. More than likely, it had been repurposed in the years since then. Maybe used as a dinner bell or a Christmas decoration.

"Then where in the world did it come from?" she asked as if she really thought he would know.

"A dinner bell?"

"We've never had one."

"A Christmas ornament?"

She snorted at that, lifting the bell up toward the stairway light and eyeing it suspiciously. "The last time we had Christmas decorations out, I was ten, my mother was dying, and I was doing everything I could to make her happy for the holidays. My father was pissed that I walked to town and bought a Christmas tree with my allowance, but I didn't care. I just wanted Mom to smile."

"Your father didn't like Christmas?" he said as he took the bell from Emma's hand.

It was definitely old. Definitely handcrafted. A pretty little piece that had probably been used a century ago.

"He liked Christmas just fine. As long as he didn't have to go through any effort to make it a good one. My mother was the one who made it special. We did have a Christmas tree after she died. Stockings. A few presents." She shrugged. "But all the decorations and ornaments were tossed in boxes and shoved in the attic."

"Could this have been in one of the boxes? Maybe it fell out when your father brought everything to the attic."

"And lay on the floor undiscovered for nearly twenty years?" she responded.

"It might have fallen into a crack in the floor. Maybe rolled into a dark corner. This is a big house, Emma."

"And, it's always been meticulously maintained. While my father was here alone, he had a cleaning company come in twice a week to clean. Once I moved in, I did the work. I even have the checklist he made to prove it. I find it hard to believe that I, and every cleaning person who came, missed seeing that bell."

She raked a hand through her hair and sighed. She'd changed into pajamas. Nothing revealing about them. Just simple flannel bottoms and a cotton tank that showed off her narrow shoulders and her thin arms. Something about that smooth, creamy expanse of skin made his mind go in directions it shouldn't. Made him remember cold nights and rainy days, and the intoxicating taste of Emma's lips, the addictive feel of her satiny skin.

"Anyway," Emma continued, apparently completely unaware of what he was thinking, "it doesn't matter where it came from. I just thought it was strange. Hearing someone at my door and then finding the bell."

The words were like ice water in his veins. All thoughts of the past and Emma and the silky feel of her skin were gone, his body humming with a different kind of energy. He'd been awake, and he hadn't heard anything, but that didn't mean Emma was mistaken. The house was large and old. It creaked and groaned and made enough noise to mask an intruder's presence. "There was someone at your door?"

"Yes. No." She shrugged. "I heard something thump against it. I" — she blushed — "thought it was you."

Interesting, because he'd been lying in bed thinking about just how nice it would be to knock on her door. To take her in his arms. To kiss her until they were both breathless with want and need.

He shoved the thought away, focusing on the little bell and on the noise Emma had said she'd heard.

A thump.

Not a knock or a tap.

"Did you see anything when you left your room?"

"It was pitch-black."

"There's a back staircase that leads to the kitchen, right?"

"Yes. Why?"

"Because it's a lot better to be safe than sorry." He walked down the hall and into the kitchen, checked the back door and the windows. All of them were locked. He looked in the pantry closet, opened the door into the old library. Finally, he walked into the narrow stairwell that had once been used by servants. It was dark and cramped, the stairs steep and layered with dust.

"I don't think anyone has used these in years," Emma murmured. "When we were kids, we thought they were too creepy. Unless we were trying to get away from our father. Then, he was a lot creepier than this, and we used any escape route necessary."

A little hint into her past, but Jack was too focused on the dark stairs and the little bell that he was still holding to ask questions.

It could be that the bell was just a leftover decoration from a Christmas long ago, or it could be that it had been dropped and left by someone who had no business being inside the house.

"Stay in the kitchen. I'm going to check the second floor and the attic."

"For what?" she asked, completely ignoring his order to stay put.

She moved into the stairwell behind him, flicking on a light that barely illuminated the scuffed treads on the stairs. "You don't really think someone is in the house, do you?"

"No, but I also don't believe in taking chances."

He started up the stairs, and she was right behind him, so close he could feel the warmth of her chest against his back. So close he could have turned and taken her into his arms.

Another time.

When Emma wasn't so tired and overwhelmed. When they'd worked through her plans, figured out exactly how she was going to move forward.

That's when other things could happen.

Other plans could be made.

Plans that might include more than either of them had bargained for when they'd walked into the cemetery yesterday morning.

CHAPTER FIVE

The second floor was as empty as the first floor. Just like Emma had expected it to be. There was no way anyone from town had wandered all the way out here in the middle of a snowstorm. Even if someone had, they'd have rung the doorbell rather than thumping against her bedroom door. Sure, it was possible some drifter had come upon the house and decided to bunk there for the night, but it would have been easier to get to the town than to walk down the country road that led to the Baily property.

No. She didn't think anyone had been in the house.

She also didn't think the sleigh bell had been lying on the floor for years. She'd have seen it. Right?

She eyed the corners of the upstairs landing. No holes that she could see. No place for a shiny bell to hide.

"Does this lead to the attic?" Jack asked,

touching the door at the end of the hall. A skeleton key stuck out of the lock, the glass doorknob glistening in overhead light.

"Yes, but we'd have heard —" *someone if they'd walked up the stairs.*

Too late. He'd already opened the door and was heading up. She followed, the uneven steps icy under her feet.

"Any lights up here?" Jack asked as he reached the top.

"Hold on. I'll get it." Her arm brushed his shoulder.

His *bare* shoulder.

She'd kind of sort of almost forgotten about that.

Only now, she remembered.

God! Did she ever remember!

Heat swept up her arm and flooded through her blood. Her knees turned to jelly, a dozen butterflies came to life in her stomach, and she remembered every minute of every hour that she'd spent with Jack. She remembered all the reasons why he'd been the guy she'd almost spent a lifetime with.

She found the chord, yanked it so hard she was surprised it didn't break, and then she stepped around Jack. Tried to pretend that she hadn't felt anything. She probably would have been successful except that he was watching her, his eyes dark and simmering.

She wanted to say something.

She probably should have said something, but what could she say? I've missed you? You're the only guy that I've never been able to forget?

Wind whistled beneath the eaves, the mournful sound just enough to cut through the tension, and the moment was gone just as quickly as it had been there.

The heat died from Jack's eyes, and he glanced around the attic.

"There's a lot of stuff here," he said, and she nodded.

"Three generations' worth of stuff. Probably more. My great-great-great-grandmother's mother lived here at the end of her life. I'm sure some of her things are still here."

"That's a lot of greats," he muttered, glancing around the cavernous room.

"My father made sure we were aware of each and every one of them."

"What's this lead to?" He'd reached the door that led into the pretty little room that Annabelle Baily had once used as a personal retreat. Emma had found her diaries there along with photos and letters, a few half-finished sewing projects, some beautiful needlepoint.

"My great-great-great-grandmother's sewing room. Annabelle was ahead of her time. She understood the value of a woman cave."

"Isn't the term man cave?" he asked with a grin that made her heart flutter.

Fickle heart.

Fickle mind that kept thinking of how nice it would be to step into Jack's arms.

She walked into the small space. Unlike the rest of the attic, it was heated, a small radiator set against the wall. She'd been in the room less than a week ago, and she'd left a cup sitting on the edge of the sewing table. Her cardigan lay on the back of the chair, and a few photos were spread across a small sideboard that stood against one wall. She'd been organizing them, planning to sneak them out of the house and to the historic society.

She wouldn't have to sneak now.

The thought made her sadder than it should have.

Jack lifted the cup. "Looks like someone has been in here recently."

"That's mine."

"Spent a lot of time in here, did you?"

"There are journals and photos. Lots of historically significant things that I've been organizing." She pointed to three boxes that

495

sat against the wall.

"And no way for your father to get to you?"

"That too." She grabbed the cardigan and tried to put it on, but her hands were clumsy, her eyes burning from the tears that she seemed to keep wanting to shed.

"Let me." He took it from her hand, helped her into it, his fingers sliding under her hair as he pulled it out from the collar, and then she was looking into his eyes, seeing all the compassion and kindness and strength that she'd seen the first time she'd met him.

She didn't know how it happened.

Whether she leaned forward or he did. Maybe they moved at the same time, Emma levering up on her toes as he bent down, his hand cupping her nape, his lips brushing hers and hers brushing his. Heat and fire and beautiful gentleness that was nothing that Emma expected and everything that she needed.

She moved closer, her hands sliding along his firm waist and up his muscular back. She could feel the ridges of the scars that he'd gotten all those years ago, and she let her fingers trace the edges, let herself lean into the kiss just a little more.

Something dropped to the floor, clattering

along the old pine boards. Jingling like a sleigh bell at Christmas.

"Damn bell," Jack murmured against her lips, and she backed away, because of what they'd just shared? It was dangerous. Especially with the way she'd been feeling all day. A little sad. A little lonely. A lot upset.

"I guess we kind of lost sight of what we were up here for," she managed to say as he scooped the bell up again.

"I wouldn't mind forgetting for a while longer," he replied, and she laughed. A real laugh. The kind that she'd forgotten she knew how to do.

"You're still funny, Jack."

"I'm not trying to be funny. I'm being honest." He stepped out of the room, eyeing the huge attic. "Where do you keep all the Christmas stuff? I want to see if the boxes have been disturbed. It doesn't seem like anyone is up here, but something could be."

"Some*thing*?"

"Mice. Rats. Raccoon. Lots of critters need places to keep warm during the winter, and they can do a lot of damage if they're allowed to stay."

"I'm not all that worried about damage to the Christmas ornaments. Christmas is for people who like to spend money on stuff that's going to be forgotten in a closet somewhere. It's for people who —"

"Can it, Scrooge," he cut her off. "I'm trying to listen."

"I'm not a Scrooge."

"You hate Christmas," he pointed out. And, he'd known, because she'd mentioned it to him more than once when they were dating.

"Of all the things you could remember about me, that's one of the ones you choose?"

"Sweetheart, I remember everything about you." His gaze raked her from head to toe, and her cheeks went about ten shades of red. "But, for the record, it's not Christmas decorations that I'm worried about. Rats and mice are notorious for chewing wires. You could lose the whole house to a fire."

A few years ago, she'd have probably told him that she'd happily add kindling to the flames, but she'd spent a lot of time researching the old house, learning its history. Its real history. Not the stories her father liked to tell. The thought of all the hard work and craftsmanship being destroyed made her stomach hurt. "The Christmas stuff is over here."

She led him to a dark corner, eyed a pile of dust-covered boxes labeled CHRISTMAS.

He knelt beside them, studying the box tops, the floor beside them, brushing his hand through spiderwebs that clung to the beams in the wall. "Nothing," he finally said. "No sign of any animals anyway, but . . ." He pulled a box away from the wall. "It looks like this box is crumbling."

It did. The edge of the box had collapsed, and bits of glinting tinsel hung out of it. "Maybe the bell rolled out and fell through a crack in the floor?"

She knelt near the boxes, shivering as cold seeped through her pajama pants and speared through her cardigan.

The attic was freezing. She'd forgotten that.

Because of the kiss.

The kiss that she was absolutely not going to spend another second thinking about.

"It's too cold to figure it out now," Jack said, pulling her to her feet, his big hand dwarfing hers. "Go on downstairs. I'll bring the box."

"There's no nee—"

"You know what I do for a living, right?" he asked, one dark eyebrow raised. "I can't leave a crumbling box filled with old ornaments in an attic that isn't temperature controlled. They need to be stored properly."

"They've been up here for a long time."

"Hopefully, that hasn't ruined them," he replied. "A lot of craftsmanship went into the old bell, and I'm sure the same is true of everything in these boxes. They're meant to be used and enjoyed."

"I hope you're not thinking that I'm going to decorate this house for the holidays," she muttered. "Because, that isn't going to happen in this lifetime."

Jack figured she meant what she was saying, but her words gave him an idea. One that he thought might just be the key to getting the house out of Emma's hands and her life back to whatever she wanted it to be.

"You know," he said, lifting the box and following Emma out of the attic. "You might not like Christmas, but most people do."

"I'm well aware of that." She threw a scowl in his direction, her cheeks pink from cold, her lips red from their kiss. He could have kissed her again. He didn't think she'd protest, and he sure as hell wouldn't mind it.

But she was more vulnerable than she probably thought.

Sure, she'd despised her father. Sure, she hated the house she'd grown up in, but everything that had been her life for the past few years was over, and it had to be strange to say good-bye to all of it.

"And who doesn't love a Christmas Eve party?" he continued, and she sighed.

"Me."

"But you do love getting things done, Emma. And what better way to get people interested in this property than to open it up to the public?"

"What public? Do you know how small Apple Valley is?"

"I've done this kind of thing in smaller towns. We don't just pull guests locally, we contact businesses in other towns. Invite people who own antique shops, decorating companies. Even building contractors."

"Building contractors? For what?"

"Sometimes these old places get torn down to make room for other things. Doors. Windows. Old knobs. Fireplace mantels. They all can be sold and reused."

"I'm not letting the place be torn down." She touched the old newel post at the top of the stairs. "Too much went into it."

"I know, but that's not what the party is about. We won't be selling things. We'll just be giving people a look. Whet their appetites for an auction."

"You're ten steps ahead of me." She frowned. "I'm not even sure what I'm going to be doing in five minutes. I can't plan an auction."

"That's what I'm here for. Remember?" He moved past her and started down the stairs.

He expected her to protest.

When she didn't, he glanced over his shoulder, saw that she was running her hand along the banister.

He couldn't read her expression, had no idea what she was thinking, but he had a feeling she was remembering. Good times. Bad times. There were lifetimes of memories in the house. It was possible that Emma was finally realizing that. Maybe she was also realizing that she couldn't let all of that go.

One way or another, he was going to move forward with the plan for a Christmas party. Something fun that would fill the old house the way it had been in generations past.

"You okay?" he asked.

"Why wouldn't I be?"

"Because your father is dead, and your life has changed."

"*Again.* It's changed again, and I'm fine with that. I've known since I moved back to Apple Valley that I'd be leaving one day. As soon as I can sell the house and get rid of everything in it, I'm out of here." She said it as if she meant it, but her hand was still on the carved banister, her face still soft with whatever she'd been remembering.

"Then I'll move forward with the party. The more interest you have in the place, the more quickly you can unload it. We'll plan it for after Christmas Eve service, let it run until midnight."

"A party sounds like a lot of work. Couldn't we just advertise in local papers? Contact Realtors in other towns? Maybe bring some things to antique stores and see what we can get for them?"

"You don't think *that* sounds like a lot of work?" he asked, and she smiled.

"I guess it does, but I don't need you to handle all this for me."

"Adam needs me to," he responded.

"You know I can't argue when you bring my brother up."

"Exactly." He continued down the stairs. He thought she'd follow. Instead, he heard her walking away.

A door opened and then closed, and the house fell silent. Or as silent as an old house could get. The stairs creaked beneath his feet, the wind howled beneath the eaves. Somewhere, the old furnace was cranking on, the radiators clicking in response. The fire he'd banked in the parlor still tinged the air with the scent of wood and flames. It reminded him of his childhood, the times he'd spent with his grandfather on the old farmstead in New Hampshire. Granddad Jimmy had come from nothing, and he'd always wanted to remember that.

At least, that's what he'd told Jack and his brother when they'd complained about the cold floor or the drafty windows.

"It's good to remember where you've come from. Otherwise, you might find yourself back where you don't want to be."

True.

Most of the time, Jack had no desire to go back, revisit the places he'd been, the years he'd lived. Most of the time, he could do exactly what his grandfather had recommended — remember the past and be happy for the present.

Right now, though, with the taste of Emma's lips still on his, he couldn't help thinking he'd like a second chance at making things work with her.

CHAPTER SIX

Christmas had exploded all over the house.

Emma didn't know how. She didn't know why. But the evidence was right there, waiting at the end of the driveway when she got home from her first day of work since her father's stroke. Icicle-lights hung from the eaves. Wreaths hung in the windows. Another one hung on the front door. Christmas greenery had been draped over the porch railing and woven around the banister. Tiny white lights twinkled from the garland. More lights sparkled in the bushes that abutted the façade of the house. As if that weren't enough, there was a Christmas tree in the parlor. She could see it through the window.

Jack.

It had to be him.

No one else would have dared. Not even the well-meaning church ladies who'd been worrying about her spending Christmas alone. Not Emma's coworkers either, and they were the only ones who'd known that she planned to return to work. Three days after the funeral had seemed too soon to everyone except for Emma. She'd been ready to get out of the house, away from the memories, and, maybe, away from Jack.

One kiss, and everything she'd thought she'd understood about their relationship had been replaced by something she could only call longing. For what, she couldn't quite figure out. She didn't need a man in her life. She didn't want one. She'd spent years nursing a guy who gave nothing to anyone. That had sealed her desire to go it alone, but for the past three mornings, she'd woken up to the smell of coffee, the sound of silverware clinking in the sink, the feel of togetherness where there'd only been emptiness before. As if the house had suddenly begun to live again, and — she hated to admit it even to herself — she'd begun to live with it.

And now . . .

Christmas.

Staring her right in the face, defying everything she believed about the season, because the display wasn't gaudy. It wasn't over the top. It was simple and lovely and old-fashioned. Like a postcard from a bygone era or a Christmas card that came in a boxed set and had pretty little phrases about hope and renewal and love scrawled across the front.

The front door opened, and Jack stepped outside, a young woman beside him bundled up in a coat and hood and gloves. Emma's heart dropped, all the ooey-gooey feelings she'd been having gone as quickly as they'd come.

She got out of her father's SUV, pushing aside the strange hollow feeling that was filling her stomach.

"Emma," the woman called, the voice one Emma knew immediately. Tessa Cunningham. Her boss's wife and Emma's good friend. One of the few people who'd been able to put up with Daniel for any length of time, Tessa had visited every few weeks, helping Emma with whatever big project needed to be done around the house.

"Tess! What a great surprise!" Emma replied, running toward her, the hollow feeling gone because Tessa was Tessa. Not some new or old flame of Jack's.

Idiot, Emma's brain whispered, because she'd been jealous.

Jealous!

"A better surprise than me finding out you were going back to work today. When Cade told me that, I nearly bit his head off," Tessa said as Emma jogged up the porch stairs. "I couldn't believe he let you show up."

"He told me to take another few days, but I . . . needed some normalcy." Whatever that was. She pulled Tessa into a hug and did everything in her power to avoid Jack's gaze.

Somehow, he was there anyway. Right in her line of sight. He had no coat, no hood, no boots or gloves.

"You're going to freeze," she found herself saying.

"It's good to know you care," he responded.

"I don't," she lied, and he laughed.

"Well," Tessa broke in. "Isn't this interesting."

"No," Emma said at the same exact moment that Jack said yes.

Tessa grinned. "Here comes my ride. Right on time." She waved as the sheriff's car pulled into the driveway. "I'll leave you two to work out who cares about who, and I'll be back tomorrow with some fabric samples."

"Fabric samples for what?" Emma wanted to know, but Tessa was gone, and the only one left to answer was Jack.

"Drapes for the parlor and living room. The dining room has what I think are original. Or pretty close. I thought maybe I could find the ones for the other rooms, but I've been through every box in the attic, and they're not there."

"What's wrong with the drapes that are hanging?"

"Nothing, but they don't fit."

"Fit what?" She walked inside, felt the warmth of the house, inhaled cinnamon and pine and memories. The house had smelled like this an aeon ago. It had also rung with the laughter and giggles and teenage drama. Until her father got home from work. Then it had gone silent. Everyone scurrying to his or her room.

She shook the memories away, her fingers gliding over the garland that had been twined around the stair railing. Real pine. Real holly. Real everything.

"They don't fit the house," Jack said. "You want to bring it back to its original state, right?"

"I hadn't really thought about it."

Or, maybe, she had. She'd poured over Annabelle's old photo cache. She'd been to the historical society. She'd seen the original blueprints drawn up by the architect. She'd even copied newspaper articles written when the house was being constructed and added them to Annabelle's things.

She'd told herself that she was doing it to avoid Daniel, but she'd admit that she'd been fascinated. The house that she'd grown up in was way more than a hiding place from her father's rage. It was a heritage.

One that she'd be selling as soon as she could get it on the market and find a buyer.

"I need to call a Realtor," she murmured, more to herself than to Jack.

"I've got three coming to the party."

"The party . . ." She'd been trying not to think about that, trying not to imagine a bunch of gawkers coming to see all the things her family had accumulated over the years. "About that . . ."

"No," he said, and she turned to meet his eyes.

He was close. Closer than she'd expected, his dark green eyes nearly black, his jaw covered in a week's worth of stubble. Not really stubble anymore. He was growing a bona fide beard and mustache, and man! Did he ever wear it well!

"What do you mean 'no'?"

"I mean, we're not canceling the party."

"Who said I planned to cancel?"

"You've been thinking about it."

"Maybe."

There was no maybe about it. Jack had seen

the look on her face when she'd walked into the house. She'd looked surprised and a little uncomfortable. He couldn't blame her. He'd been moving quickly, lining things up, making calls, pulling boxes out of the attic, itemizing, organizing. All the things he did every time he worked an estate.

Only this wasn't just anyone's estate. This was Emma's, and he thought he might be moving a little too fast for her. He also thought she was making a mistake letting the property go. If it had been his, he'd have kept it in the family. But then that's the way he'd been raised. She seemed to have been raised with the idea that moving on was best, that letting go was what a person had to do.

So he was helping her do what she thought she had to and maybe what she wanted to, but he didn't want to force her into making decisions she wasn't ready to make.

"The party is just that, Em," he said. "A way to celebrate this house and all the things that are in it. Yes, the by-product will be interest in the property and the antiques it contains, but we're not going to auction things off until you're ready to do it."

"I'm ready."

"Yeah?" He moved closer, caught a hint of something flowery and light. Perfume?

That hadn't been Emma's style before, but she'd changed since they'd dated. He'd been noticing it these past few days. She was quieter, more introverted, less excited about what each new day would bring.

He wasn't sure how he felt about that.

A little worried, maybe.

Adam had said that the past few years had been tough on his sister, but he hadn't mentioned how much they'd affected her. Jack could only assume that Adam didn't know. He'd been deployed for six weeks, and as far as Jack had been able to figure, he hadn't been to Apple Valley in years.

"Yeah," Emma responded, shrugging out of her coat and hanging it from the hook. She wore a soft yellow sweater and dark jeans. Both were a size too large for her. She'd left the house with her hair in a ponytail, but at some point during the day, she'd taken it out. Static made it stand out in a dozen different directions, and he smoothed it down, his palms gliding over the soft strands.

She stilled, and he thought that if he wanted to, he could bend down, kiss her the way he had the first night he'd been in town.

The thing was, he wanted to.

It was possible he even needed to, but

Emma needed something different. She needed him to listen to what she was trying to say, to hear the words that maybe she wasn't capable of speaking. Like *"I know what I thought I wanted, but I'm not sure if that's changed, and there's no way I'm going to admit it."*

"Okay," he said, his hand dropping to his sides.

Her eyes narrowed. "Okay what?"

"Okay. You're ready. So, how about we take a look at the party invitations? I think you'll like them."

"Does it matter if I don't?" She sounded tired, and he knew she probably was. Near as he could tell, she'd barely slept the past few nights. He'd heard her pacing her room, the floorboards creaking under her feet. He'd thought about knocking on her door. He'd also thought about what might happen if she opened it. The last thing either of them needed was regrets, so he'd stayed away.

"It matters," he responded, taking her hand and leading her into the parlor. He didn't bother turning on the light. He'd built a fire earlier in the day, and it was still burning, the pile of logs he'd carried in stacked in the fuel box beside it. He'd brought in a tree, too, driving around town until he'd found a tiny Christmas tree stand at the corner of Main Street. Twenty bucks for a nice-sized spruce.

He could appreciate that the same way he'd appreciated the small-town vibe that Apple Valley offered. The place was a hidden gem. Sheltered in foothills of the Cascade Mountains, it had maintained all the charm of bygone eras and lost none of the homey feel of community.

He'd have spent more time exploring, but his brother had been calling nonstop. They had two big auctions coming up, and Ace wanted to take on a third. Fine by Jack, but he wouldn't be back to oversee any of them. He had a job to do here. Pro bono work, but it didn't matter. He'd told Adam he'd take care of things, and he would. No matter how long it took.

"Wow," Emma breathed, standing in the center of the room, her face painted gold by the firelight.

"You like it?"

"It looks like . . ."

"What?"

"All the best things about Christmas. Family and comfort and hope." She touched one of the ornaments he'd hung on the tree. "Were these all in the attic?"

"Yes."

"I'd forgotten how pretty they were. Mom got them out every year, and we all hung them together. Except for Dad. He sat in his office and grumbled." She smiled, a mixture of happy memories and sad ones in her eyes. "I can't believe how long it's been since I've seen them."

"That's a shame. I'm sure your mom would have wanted you to keep enjoying them after she was gone," he said, because he imagined that the woman who'd influenced Adam and Emma to be the people they were had to have had a big heart.

"Probably. Mom loved Christmas. She'd decorate the day after Thanksgiving, and the entire house would feel like a fairy tale. I'd sit on the couch in here, and I'd pretend that I lived in a home where the mother and father were always happy, and the kids . . ." Her voice trailed off, and she sighed. "That was a long time ago."

"That doesn't mean you can't still sit on the couch and pretend." He led Emma to the couch and sat, pulling her down beside him.

"Pretend what?" she said with a nervous laugh. "That I didn't give up years of my life and any hope I had of ever practicing law to help a man who hated me?"

"Still thinking about that dream?" he

asked. She'd talked about family law a lot when they were dating, telling him over and over again how determined she was to become a lawyer.

"Once in a while," she responded.

"You could still practice law," he reminded her, and she sighed.

"I've lost my momentum. I'd have to go back to school, finish my degree, take the bar exam. And right now, I don't even know if I'd be happy doing it."

"Should I ask what you would be happy doing?"

"Not unless you want to hear that I have absolutely no idea. I just know that I'm finally free of my responsibility, and that feels good and a little strange."

"You're working at the sheriff's department. Are you planning to continue?"

"Like I've said, I'm planning to leave town as soon as I sell the house. Now, how about instead of playing twenty questions, you show me the invitations?" she responded.

He'd left the box on the side table, and he took one out, handing it to her. Elegant and simple, the lettering a calligraphy style that mimicked old cards he'd found in the attic, the postcard-style invitation had watercolor birds and holly decorating its edges.

"What do you think?" he asked as she

turned the card over and smiled at the old photo he'd had scanned onto it — a winter scene of the house, a sleigh waiting in front of it, two horses ready to take passengers on a winter adventure.

"I think it's perfect," she said, handing it back and leaning her head against the high back of the couch. "The room is perfect. Even the tree that I should absolutely despise is perfect. All we need are some hand-knit stockings hung from the chimney with care."

He didn't laugh. He was too busy looking into her eyes and thinking that they should have been doing this for the last six years. Sitting together. Talking. Sharing quiet evenings.

"What?" she said, her hand going to her hair as if she thought he might be staring at a mess that could be fixed.

And maybe he was.

He'd made a mess of things their first go-round. She'd been young and filled with the kind of dreams most college students have. He'd been young, too, but he'd served in the military, he'd traveled the world, he'd been wounded, and he'd watched men die. All he'd dreamed about was returning home. He'd made it very clear that he wanted none of what Emma did. He didn't need the excitement of the city. He didn't want a high-stress career that would make him tons of money.

He'd wanted peace. He'd longed for security, safety, the knowledge that he didn't have to watch his back every second of every day.

He hadn't known how to tell her that.

Or maybe he'd just been too proud to.

Either way, he'd dug in his heels and refused to tell her the one thing she'd wanted to hear — that he was willing to think about living in the city. That, for her, he'd be willing to change his plans.

More importantly, that he could wait for her to be ready for forever. That they could keep on dating and enjoying each other without the pressure of having to think about their future.

Right now, with firelight dancing across her face, her eyes dark and filled with questions, he knew just how much of a fool he'd been.

"You're beautiful," he murmured, his hand sliding up her shoulder and cupping her jaw.

"So are you," she responded, and if he hadn't been so caught up in the need to taste her lips again, he would have laughed.

"What I am," he said, the scent of that

flowery perfume surrounding him, the warmth of the fire only adding to the heat flowing through his blood, "is a fool. I never should have let you walk out of my life, Emma. I don't even know why I did."

Then he did what he'd been wanting to for the past three days. He kissed her again. And he knew that once more would never be enough. He shifted his hold, pulled her into his lap, and she went, her arms twining around his neck, her fingers in his hair, all the years between them gone.

CHAPTER SEVEN

Emma didn't want it to end.

Ever.

Not the heated kiss, the harsh gasp of their breaths mixing. His hands sliding down her back, settling at the curve of her spine, finding their way beneath her T-shirt, his palms rasping across her skin.

She shuddered, edging closer, all the thoughts that had been haunting her for days — thoughts about the house, about letting it go, about heritage and family and all the things that she should have but didn't — sliding into the heat of that kiss, fading into nothing but feeling and desire and want.

She wove her fingers through Jack's hair, reveling in the silky feel of it against her palms.

God, she wanted this!

She wanted him.

She knew it was a mistake. She knew

they'd end up parting ways again, but right at that moment she didn't care. All she cared about was this moment.

He pulled back, his breath harsh, his eyes blazing, and she thought that he was going to give her a choice to continue or to stop. Which sucked, because as soon as he backed away, cool air replaced the heat, and her brain started moving again, clicking along and putting things into perspective.

The last thing she needed were memories that would leave her feeling like she'd missed out on something wonderful.

"Not the right time," Jack muttered, his forehead resting against hers. They were eye to eye, breath to breath, all that heat still between them, but there was something else there now — a gentleness as he cupped her cheeks, gave her a quick, hard kiss. "Much as I might want it to be."

He placed her back on her feet and stood, towering over her the way he always had. At six-foot-three, he was the kind of guy women noticed, and Emma couldn't help wondering how he'd spent the past few years.

Not alone. That much was for sure.

Not a guy like Jack.

"You're right. It's not the right time," she managed to say. "There probably will never be a right time, so it's better that we just shelve it."

She moved away, stood near the Christmas tree, and pretended that she was studying the ornaments. Truth? She couldn't actually see anything. All she could do was feel the hard edge of disappointment and regret.

"Shelve it?" he asked, and she thought she heard a hint of amusement in his voice.

"You know what I mean."

"No. I don't, so how about you explain it to me." He took her hand, pulled her closer, and she couldn't quite make herself move away again.

"Shelve it as in forget it," she offered. "Pretend it didn't happen."

"By *it,* I'm assuming you mean the kiss."

"I sure as heck don't mean our fireside chat," she responded.

"What if I tell you I don't want to forget it?" he asked, his words just kind of hanging there for a minute longer than they should have, because she wasn't sure what to say, didn't know how to respond.

"Because I don't, Em," he continued, filling the silence, filling her heart, too. She knew because it was slamming against the wall of her chest, galloping along and forcing her to take notice of it. "I wasn't kidding when I said I shouldn't have ever let you go."

"It's the firelight," she responded, the words rushing out and tangling all over themselves in their hurry to be said. "And the tree, and all the Christmas things. They make a person nostalgic."

"Do they also make a person want someone else more than he wants his next breath?" he retorted, his gaze hardening, his eyes narrowing.

She remembered that look.

She'd seen it the last day they'd spent together, when she'd told him that there was no way she was going to live in some Podunk town in New Hampshire when the entire world was there for her to explore. No way she was going to plot out a course for her future with someone she didn't know would be there in a week or a month or a year.

God! Had she really been so brash and foolish and insensitive? And was she really going to be that stupid again?

"Jack," she began, but she guessed he'd had enough, because he cut her off.

"Tell you what, how about you go through your address book and decide who you want to invite to the Christmas party? I figure the house can hold seventy-five comfortably, and I've got thirty businesspeople I'm inviting. You've got forty-five invitations you can send. Make a list. While you do that, I'm going out."

"Out where?"

"I have some work I need to do."

That was it. No further explanation.

One minute he was there, the next he was grabbing his coat and walking out the door. He closed it. Not with a loud slam. With a quiet click that was just as horrible.

She guessed she really was going to be as stupid as she'd been when she was in college, because she let him walk away, listening as his feet thudded on the porch stairs.

He fired up the engine of his SUV, and she didn't run outside to stop him. She just stood where she was, watching shadows dance on the parlor walls, listening to the crackle of the fire, and calling herself every kind of fool, because she wanted to run outside. She wanted to stop him. She wanted to tell him that the worst thing she'd ever done was let him walk out of her life the first time.

Only it wasn't the worst thing.

The worst thing was letting him walk away again, but she did, because she'd been through a lot the past few years, and she thought that maybe it had scrambled her brains, messed with her emotions, made her imagine something that wasn't really there.

Like a man who cared.

Like a chance at forever.

Like all the dreams that she'd put aside because she'd had a thankless father to care for and a job to do and no time to think about anything but getting through the next day.

"Idiot," she muttered, and she wasn't sure if she was an idiot for letting Jack leave or if she was an idiot for wishing that she'd asked him to stay.

Behind her, something clattered across the floor, and the soft sound of sleigh bells filled the room.

Surprised, she turned, saw something glimmering in the firelight. She scooped it up, holding it closer to the flames so that she could see it more clearly.

It looked like the bell she'd kicked the other night.

Surprised, she turned on the light, studying it more carefully. It definitely looked like the other bell, but if it was, how had it gotten in the parlor?

The last time she'd seen it, Jack had been holding it.

Had he dropped it?

She glanced around the room as if she could find the answer there. All she found were the beautiful decorations, the cheerful fire, the invitations. The mystery and magic of Christmas all packed into one room.

Jack had done that.

He'd seen what she couldn't. He'd known just how lovely the room would be.

She placed the bell in a bowl on the mantel and lifted one of the invitations. They really were pretty. Really perfect.

Just like Jack.

God! She was such a fool.

The doorbell rang, and she screamed, nearly dropping the invitation.

"Everything okay in there?" a woman called through the closed door.

"Fine," Emma responded.

She wasn't expecting anyone, but she assumed it was one of the blue-haired church ladies, bearing another load of casseroles. There'd been a steady stream of them since the funeral. She really needed to call the pastor and ask him to put a stop to it. The freezer was ready to burst at the seams, and there was no way she'd ever eat her way through all the food.

She yanked open the door and found a stranger with short gray hair, a pretty blue coat, and a broad smile.

"Can I help you?" she asked, surprised, because she knew just about everyone in

Apple Valley, but she didn't know the woman standing on the porch.

"You can if you're Emma Baily," the woman replied. She looked to be in her sixties, smile lines fanning out from her eyes, brackets framing her mouth. Something about her was familiar, but Emma couldn't quite place it.

"I'm Emma."

"I knew it. You look just like Sandra." The woman grabbed Emma's wrist, and the next thing she knew, she was being pulled into a bear hug.

"You're a friend of my mother's?" Emma asked, extracting herself from the hug as graciously as she could.

"A friend?" The woman's smile faltered, and she smoothed the front of her coat, her hand trembling. "I'm her sister-in-law. Leigh. Your father's younger sister."

"My father was an only child," she responded, but she knew, even before Leigh responded, that he wasn't, that everything he'd told her, all the stories about being the only child born to a couple late in life, had been a lie.

"Is that what he told you?"

"Yes."

"I should probably be surprised, but I'm not. Daniel and my father were cut from the same cloth." Her gaze shifted to a point beyond Emma's shoulders. "The house looks the same. At least, what I can see of it does."

She was fishing for an invitation.

Emma thought she probably shouldn't give one. After all, she didn't know the woman from Adam, but that familiar thing in Leigh's face? It was like a just-out-of-reach memory, niggling at the back of her mind and refusing to let her ignore it.

If she had another minute, she might be able to figure out exactly who Leigh looked like. Not Daniel. He'd had brown hair, brown eyes, and tan skin. Leigh was as fair as Emma, her eyes gray, her lashes light brown. She had a small frame rather than Daniel's large one, and she had a smile. Something that Emma couldn't remember ever seeing on her father's face.

Still, for all Emma knew, the woman was a serial killer. Or — and this was a much more likely scenario — an opportunistic thief who'd pretend to be a relative to get a piece of whatever pie Daniel had left.

Emma hadn't bothered checking all her father's bank account balances. There was a lot of money. She knew that. Plus whatever came from the sale of the house and its contents.

Her stomach twisted at the thought.

She ignored it.

She *was* going to sell the house. She *was* going to move on.

What she was *not* going to do was let Leigh into the house.

Except, somehow she found herself stepping aside, gesturing for the woman to enter.

"Come on in," she said, and it didn't even sound like her voice. It sounded like the voice of someone so worn down that she didn't care that she might be letting a fraudster into her house, didn't care that her father might have told her more lies than she'd ever imagined, didn't care about anything except getting on with the day so that she could close herself in her room and cry.

The Christmas lights were still on.

Jack could see them as he turned into Emma's driveway. He could also see a shiny Mustang parked behind Emma's truck. Texas plates. Whoever it was, they'd come a long way.

Maybe one of Emma's siblings?

That seemed like a long shot. As far as Jack knew, not one of them was even mildly interested in ever returning to Apple Valley. They sure as heck hadn't been interested enough to attend the funeral or to help Emma take care of their father. If one of them had shown up, it was probably for the inheritance. Hopefully, that wasn't going to mean a long, drawn-out legal battle. Emma had been through enough. He didn't want to see her go through more.

And *he* sure didn't want to cause her any trouble.

That's why he'd left. This wasn't the time for deep conversations about the past or talks about what the future could be. It wasn't time to try to force Emma into something she wasn't ready for, either.

They'd both regret that. Eventually.

He'd sure been tempted, though.

Tempted by her and by his own fierce need to make sure he didn't miss out this time around. He'd let her go before, but he wasn't planning to do it again.

He pulled up beside the Mustang and got out of his SUV. It was late. Just a little past midnight, the sky dark, the moon shrouded by clouds. The air smelled like snow and burning wood. Jack smelled like cigarette smoke and mediocre beer.

He'd spent an hour at the local dive bar, listening to locals talk about the weather and sports. He'd nursed a beer that tasted like crap, ate a couple of stale pretzels, and ignored the curious glances he'd gotten.

There was no one there he knew, and he wasn't in the mood to answer questions or to avoid them. He knew all about small-town life. He'd lived it when he was growing up, was living it again as an adult. He loved it, but news traveled fast, and he was certain everyone in Apple Valley knew about the Christmas party by now. He'd spoken to the local baker, who just happened to have old Victorian recipes for sponge cake, lemon pound cake, and hot chocolate that she'd been very excited to pull out. Charlotte was also going to set up tables with vintage doilies and pretty flowery arrangements.

Then there was Tessa. The owner of a little antique store. She was also an interior designer. She'd volunteered to come help with the house, because she'd been there on a couple of occasions, visiting Emma, and she'd loved it.

Yeah. He had plenty of local help, and he was certain that they were telling family all about his big plans. Family talked. People talked.

But tonight? He hadn't been in the mood for it, so he'd sipped his beer and kept his eyes focused on the oversized television. When he'd gotten tired of that, he'd driven through town and out into the countryside.

No doubt about it: Eastern Washington was beautiful. He could imagine spending time there. He could imagine spending that time with Emma.

He could imagine a lot of things.

Before any of them could have even a hope of happening, he needed to help Emma with this — the house, the stuff, her heritage . . . giving it up or keeping it.

He walked up the porch steps, the sound of jingling sleigh bells seeming to follow him. Surprised, he glanced over his shoulder, almost expecting to see a horse-drawn sleigh pulling up.

There was nothing, of course.

The front door opened, and Emma peered out.

"Jack?" she whispered as if she were afraid of waking whoever was visiting.

"Everything okay?" he responded.

"My aunt is visiting. I wanted to warn you before you came inside. She's in the room at the top of the stairs." She stepped outside, her body drowning in oversized flannel pajamas, a coat tossed over her shoulders.

"A surprise visit?" he asked, still listening for those bells to ring again.

"A surprise aunt," she replied. "She's my father's sister. They've been estranged for fifty years."

"And she just suddenly decided to come for a visit?"

"It's a long story."

"I have time, if you want to tell it."

"I wouldn't want to bore you."

"There's not a lot I can say for certain, Emma, but I can say that I have never found you boring."

She smiled wearily, tucking a loose strand of hair behind her ear. "I wish you weren't so perfect, Jack."

"I'm not even close to perfect."

"Maybe I meant that I wish you weren't so perfect for me." She walked to the porch railing, rested her elbows on the white crosspost, and stared out into the driveway.

"Why?"

"Because we don't work together. We established that years ago. Why revisit it?"

"Things change. People change. What didn't work before suddenly does." That was all he was going to say, because he wasn't going to argue for what he wanted. He'd just keep being there for her. Eventually she'd figure it out, or she wouldn't. Either way, he'd fight with his actions. Not his words.

The bell jingled again, the sound seeming to drift from somewhere behind the house.

Emma straightened. "Did you hear that? It sounds like one of those harness bells we found."

"I was thinking the same. It was ringing when I pulled into the driveway, too. I heard it as I got out of the SUV. Go on inside. I'm going to see if I can figure out where it's coming from."

She snorted. "That is not going to happen. I'm going with you."

"Put your coat on, then. It's cold." He helped her slide her arms in, the bell still jingling as if someone were shaking it over and over again. He tugged the zipper up, pulled the hood over Emma's hair, and she offered a sweet smile that he couldn't quite resist.

"If I'd realized how much I'd missed your smile, I'd have come for a visit a long time ago," he murmured, dropping a kiss to her lips, his hands wrapped around her slender biceps. He could have done a lot of things right then. He could have pulled her closer. He could have walked her back up the stairs and into the house. He could have shown her, in a dozen ways, just how well they worked, but she was Emma, and she needed a lot more than that from him.

He backed away, took her hand. "Ready?"

he said, and they walked around the side of the house together.

Chapter Eight

They followed the sound of jingling bells to the barn.

It had been years since Emma had been out there.

Maybe decades.

She hadn't been back during the time she'd been taking care of Daniel. She knew that. She did remember playing hide-and-seek in the shadowy interior of the barn. She remembered boxes filled with stuff. She remembered her mother taking her up into the loft once. Emma might have been six or seven, and they'd been looking for something.

She couldn't remember what.

She just remembered climbing the rickety ladder, her mother cheering her on, and then sitting in a pile of dry hay as Sandra dug through a leather trunk.

"This place is huge," Jack said as he used his free hand to open one of the large doors.

His other hand?

It was still holding hers.

She didn't pull away as they stepped into the barn together. The air seemed hushed there. No soft rustling of hay as mice or barn cats ran for cover. No whistling of air through open slats in the barn's side. The place was quiet as a tomb, the air just as still.

She edged closer to Jack, her heart thrumming with anxiety and a little bit of fear. She wasn't sure where it came from. Maybe old memories lingering at the back of her mind.

"It's quiet," she whispered, more to break the silence than to actually impart information. Jack could absolutely figure out for himself that the place was quiet.

"Is there a light?" he responded. "I'd think your father or grandfather would have run electricity out to the place at some point."

"There is, but I don't think the bulb has been changed in years." She slid her hand along the interior wall until she found the switch and hit it. To her surprise, dim light filtered from a bare bulb above their heads.

The place was exactly like she remembered — a huge empty room with stall doors lining it. Clean as a whistle except for a few pieces of dried hay that littered the floor.

No sign of a sleigh.

Or a harness.

Or bells.

And she realized that she'd really expected there to be. That she'd thought that maybe her father had purchased an old Victorian sleigh and left it out there.

"Looks pretty empty," Jack said.

"They used to host parties out here. I'm sure you saw the photos at town hall and at the local historical society."

"And the library," he added. "This used to be a fun place. I wonder when that changed."

"Probably my grandparents. From what I heard, they weren't very happy people."

"Who'd you hear that from? Your aunt?"

Her aunt . . .

She was still rolling that word around in her head, still trying to fit it into her life. Her entire childhood, she'd been told that there was no family left. That her mother and father had been only children, their parents dead.

She did have a few vague memories of her mother's mother, coming for Christmas when she was very young. She'd had a stroke the year Emma turned eight. Two years before Sandra's diagnosis.

"Some of my older siblings remember my father's father. He lived with us until he died, but that was before I was born."

"A mean bastard like your dad, huh?"

"Probably meaner. My dad had to come from somewhere, right? Mean doesn't just spring up onto the earth without someone watering and feeding it."

She walked to the first stall and peered inside, was surprised to see an ancient tractor. "Look at that. I guess it isn't as empty as I thought."

"It's in pretty good shape for its age. In the spring, you could set it out on the little hill that overlooks the road. People would love it."

"People never come out here. That's the thing about unhappy places. They get left behind. Besides . . ." *I'm not going to be here in the spring.* That's what she planned to say, but the bell jingled again, the sound coming from somewhere above.

"The loft." Jack strode toward the ladder that sat against the far wall. Above it, a square opening led into the upper level of the barn.

Years ago, hay had been stored there and tossed down into the yard through double-wide doors on the barn's north face. That had been when there were cows and horses and field hands who harvested food for the house and for the market.

"Be careful," she warned as Jack started up the ladder. "It might not be very sturdy."

"It's built to last," he responded, his voice muffled as he pulled himself through the hole.

She didn't really want to follow him, but she did, because this was her property, her barn, and whatever was in it, she was responsible for getting rid of it.

Getting rid of it?

She made it sound like the bell was possessed by some otherworldly being, jingling happily as it led them to their doom.

"Geez," she murmured as she clambered up the ladder. "Get a grip."

"Talking to yourself, Em?" Jack grabbed her hand, pulling her through the opening and setting her on her feet.

There was plenty of room to stand, but not a whole lot of room to move. The place was packed with boxes and trunks, all of them black shadows in the darkness.

"I don't know if there's a light up here," she said, but Jack was a step ahead of her, his phone in hand, a light suddenly illuminating the loft.

"Wow," he said with a quiet whistle. "Your

family packed this to the rafters."

"That bell could be anywhere," she replied. She still felt creeped out by the place — the sheer volume of stuff that filled it, all the dark shadows that anything could be hiding, and that endless jingling bell.

"One thing's for sure," Jack responded. "The bell has no reason to be ringing. There's no wind up here."

Okay. That made it even creepier.

"Well, it's ringing anyway." She pointed out the obvious.

"Let's figure out why. We can start at the far end. That seems to be where the sound is coming from." He seemed excited.

He probably was.

This was what he did, right?

Digging around old buildings looking for family treasures?

"I take it you've been in a lot of old barns?" she asked, as he stepped around several trunks and headed toward the doors. There was so much stuff, it was difficult to navigate, but he moved with ease, lifting a few items and shifting them out of his path.

"Old barns. Old houses. Old churches and schools and train depots. Look at that." He shone the light on a tarp that lay over something.

"What is it?"

"What I hope it is is that old sleigh. The one from the photo. With the way your father's family collected things, it doesn't seem possible they got rid of it." He shifted another box, and the bell stopped jingling, the loft going silent.

Surprised, she grabbed the back of his jacket, took a step closer, heard him chuckle. Which should have pissed her off, but she guessed he had a right to be amused. This was her barn, her property, her bell jingling and then not.

She had nothing to be afraid of.

"It's not really funny," she said anyway, and he took her hand, tugging into place beside him.

"Yeah. It is. Look." He flashed his light, and she saw it. Not some phantom sitting in an old rocking chair with the bell hanging from its bonelike fingers.

A kitten.

Fuzzy and gray with little white tufts poking out of its ears, it stood frozen in the light, one of the harness bells just a few inches away, dangling out from under the tarp.

She thought it was attached to a harness, but she was too busy looking at the kitten to pay much attention.

"What are you doing here?" she said,

kneeling down and patting the floor, trying to tempt it into coming closer. The kitten eyed her for about three seconds and then went back to batting the bell.

"He's obviously impressed by us," Jack said, a hint of laughter in his voice. He lifted the kitten by the scruff. "He's a scrawny little thing. We'll have to get some food in him."

"I'll go get some."

"Or," he suggested, handing her the fuzzy little bundle of warmth, "you could take him in the house and let him eat there."

"He's a stray." And her father would roll over in his grave if he knew she'd brought an animal into the home.

Which shouldn't matter.

Didn't matter?

But . . . *a kitten*?

She didn't have time, and she was planning to move. Probably into an apartment in Seattle or New York. Somewhere different and far away from Apple Valley.

The kitten purred, a little rumbling-motor sound that would have made the hardest heart melt. As much as Emma liked to pretend, she wasn't hard-hearted, and *her* heart had melted the second the fuzzy little guy got placed in her hands.

"I'm going to regret this," she said, and

Jack laughed.

"What's to regret about loving something that needs to be loved?"

There he went again.

Being absolutely perfect.

She might have commented on that, but he'd pulled the tarp away, and her heart just about jumped out of her chest, because, there it was — the old sleigh.

Pristine and beautiful.

Glossy old wood and red velvet seats, an old fur blanket hanging from the back, a leather harness trailing from the front.

She touched the wood, felt something odd and familiar welling up — a memory that she shouldn't have, of sitting in that velvet seat, looking out the wide doors that opened from the loft, seeing the fields and the farmhouses way beyond it.

"One day," her mother whispered in her ear, *"it's going to be yours, Sweet Pea. The house. The fields. The barn. The neighbors and town and memories. All of it, and you're going to make it happy again."*

She shuddered, not sure if the memory was real or some long-ago dream, or if the words had floated out of the dark shadows and drifted into her ears.

"You okay?" Jack asked, touching her free hand, his fingers rough and warm against her chilled skin.

"I just . . . thought I heard something."

As if her words had conjured it, a voice called from below. "Emma!"

She screamed, the kitten bolted, Jack muttered something, and all hell broke loose.

Years of combat had taught Jack everything he needed to know about quick and decisive action. He snagged the kitten before it could crawl into the barn walls, stepped between Emma and the ladder, and flashed his phone light down into the darkness below.

A woman was there.

Older. Pretty. Her eyes the same dove gray as Emma's.

"Emma?" she called again. "Is everything okay? I saw a light out here and got worried."

"Leigh? You nearly scared the life out of me," Emma responded.

"I'm sorry about that, dear. The mother in me just wouldn't allow sleep while you were wandering around outside." She headed up the ladder, and Jack grabbed her hand as she cleared the opening, helping her into the loft.

She was small. Light. Her build similar to Emma's. Other than that and the color of their eyes, they didn't look much alike.

Leigh had stronger features, a softer jaw-line, and thinner lips. She looked more haughty than cynical, more aristocratic than girl-next-door.

"You must be Jack," she said, brushing dust from her hands and glancing around the loft. "Emma has told me a lot about you."

"Hopefully good things," he responded, because he thought that was what she expected.

She smiled. "Are there other things that I should know?"

"Depends on who you ask."

She laughed, patting his shoulder.

"I'll ask Emma. Later. What are you two doing out here? And what in God's name is that doing here?" She pointed at the kitten. "In all the years I was here, a living creature never stepped foot in this barn. Human or otherwise. My father wouldn't allow it."

"Why not?" Emma asked, lifting the kitten from Jack's arms and cuddling it close.

"The truth?" Leigh walked to the old sleigh, her face soft with some distant memory. "Because, he was a bitter old man who'd nearly run the farm he'd inherited into the ground. Everything his grandfather had built and his father had maintained, he'd ruined it. So, of course, he took his anger out on things that were smaller and weaker than he was, and he held on to everything he had left with such tight-fisted zeal, that the neighbors pitied him. And us. Me, your father, and our mother. He'd married her for her money, you know."

"No. I didn't." Emma had moved closer to Jack, and he dropped an arm around her shoulder, tugged her into his side. She fit there perfectly. Just like she always had.

"Because your dad was cut from the same cloth, Emma. I don't want to speak ill of the dead, but it's the truth. Daniel clung to everything so hard he lost the things that were most important."

"I know."

"So, you'll understand when I say that my father was a bastard of the first order. He was an only child, and I think my grandparents must have spoiled him rotten. He thought the world revolved around him. He didn't know how to share, and he sure as heck didn't know how to love. Which is probably why he was single until he turned fifty. Right around that time, he realized that he was running out of cash. Gambling trips and boats and fancy cars . . . they cost money, and he'd bought a lot of all of them. So, he set out to find a woman who could bring something to the Baily family. Some-

547

thing, of course, being money. Enter my mother. Thirty-five. Still single. Desperate for love. The rest, as they say, is history."

"Your mother had an inheritance?" Jack asked, and Leigh nodded.

"She gave him every cent when they married, and he gave her two kids and a house. She always told me it was a fair trade. I don't know. I got pregnant at eighteen, and my father kicked me out. It was probably the best thing that ever happened to me. It forced me to grow up, get a degree, get a good job. I've lived a good life, but I'm not going to lie, there are things about this place that I've missed."

"Is that why you're here? Because you feel like it's your inheritance and you want it back?" he asked bluntly, and Emma stiffened.

"Jack —" she began, but Leigh raised her hand to stop the protest.

"It's a valid question, and if you weren't your mother's daughter, you'd have asked yourself. If I wanted this place, I'd buy it when it went on the market. I came here to meet my niece. My husband died three years ago. My kids are grown and living in other states. I have a couple of grandkids that I see a few times a year, and unlike my father and my brother, I value the people in my life. I want to get to know all of my nieces and nephews, but Emma's is the only address I had. Of course, there's also Apple Valley. There's just something about this place that makes me long for it." She shook her head, and Jack thought he understood what she meant.

Small towns called their people home.

No matter how far they went. No matter how long they were gone.

"I felt the same way about my hometown," he admitted, and Leigh smiled.

"There you go. Then you understand. My kids think I'm crazy, but I've been thinking about relocating."

"Back here?" Emma said. She sounded surprised, and Jack thought, pleased.

"Sure. Two of my kids ended up in Seattle. It's not too far for them to come visit, and I'd be back in a town I always loved. Of course, I thought that I'd have a niece here. I didn't realize you weren't intending to stay." She lifted the old fur from the back of the sleigh. "Your mother and I used to sneak in here when we were little. We'd sit in this old sleigh and look out into the fields, and she'd tell me how lucky I was. She came from nothing and no one. Just a girl born to a girl and raised in a little trailer on the farm behind ours. That was before either of us noticed boys, and my brother was just an annoying pest. We'd ring these old bells while he was out in the yard, but he never did figure out where the sound came from. He was too afraid to break the rules and explore the barn." She shook the harness and smiled.

"That was years ago, but I can still remember giggling with Sandra. I can still remember the way we'd huddle under this old fur in the winter and talk about how rich we'd be, how loved. I hope she got what she wanted. I really do, but my brother . . ." She sighed. "They're both gone now. I guess it doesn't matter anymore. And I'm an old lady. Too old to be out so late. I'm heading back to the house. I'll be out of your hair in the morning, Emma. I know you have a lot to do to get ready to sell the old place."

"If you want to buy the place —" Emma began.

"For what? For who? My kids have their own lives. This place is meant for someone who can value the legacy."

She eased through the opening and back down the ladder.

Gone as quickly as she'd arrived.

CHAPTER NINE

Leigh didn't leave in the morning.

Mostly because Emma had begged her not to go. She wasn't sure why she wanted her aunt to stay. Maybe she needed family more than she'd realized. Maybe she longed for connection more than she'd thought, but having an aunt felt good, and she wasn't ready to give it up.

She wasn't sure if she was ready to give up the house, either. All night, she'd lain in bed thinking about the barn, the sleigh, the dreamlike memory of her mother, whispering in her ear: *"One day, it's going to be yours, Sweet Pea. The house. The fields. The barn. The neighbors and town and memories. All of it, and you're going to make it happy again."*

The more she'd thought about it, the more she'd wondered if Sandra had known she was going to die. If she'd known . . . even then . . . that eventually Emma would come back to the house and the land and have the opportunity to make all the wrong things that had happened there right.

Was that why Sandra had made Emma promise to take care of her father? Because she'd thought that out of all of her children, Emma would value tradition the most?

And she did.

She hated to admit it. She wanted to deny it, but it was the truth. Emma loved the idea of continuity. She loved the thought of one family passing on a heritage from generation to generation.

That surprised her.

A lot of things had been surprising her lately.

After four years of the same old thing, the same routine, the same complaints and rudeness and hatred and unhappiness rolling off her father's tongue, Emma had thought she'd known what she wanted from life and what she could expect from it.

She'd been wrong.

Because there she was, standing in the local feed store, a kitten in her oversized purse. A kitten she should absolutely not be thinking about keeping.

So why was she there looking for food and cat litter?

"You're out and about early," Libby Mansfield called from behind the counter. "Can I help you find something, hun?"

"I need kitty litter. Some cat food."

"You have a kitten?" Libby hurried over. They'd gone to school together, but they hadn't reconnected these past few years. Libby was busy running her father's feed store and raising four kids while her husband, Craig, worked at the post office. Emma had been busy trying to keep her sanity.

"Sort of. I found him in my barn." She opened her purse and pulled the kitten out. Of course, he began purring immediately. The crazy little thing had spent the night in her bed, curled up on the pillow near her head, purring into her ear.

"Oh. My. Gosh. He's adorable. My little Alison has been begging for a kitten, and Craig just agreed to let her get one. If you're interested in finding this little guy a new home, I'd be happy to take him."

"Great. Go ahead and take him," is what she should have said.

The words were right there, for God's sake, just sitting on the tip of her tongue.

Only the kitten was sitting in her palm, warm and purring and sweet, and she shook her head instead. "Thanks. I think . . . I'll give keeping him a try."

"That's cool." Libby pulled a bag of cat litter from a shelf. "If you change your mind, you know where to find me." She set the litter on the front counter, grabbed a bag of kibble, and set it on top. "I hear you're having a huge Christmas Eve party at the house this year."

"That's right."

"Are you inviting friends?" She smiled a little sheepishly. "Because, I'm not going to lie, I could sure use a reason to get dressed up. The last time I went to anything fancy was so long ago I can't remember it."

"Of course you're invited," she said.

"You're a peach, Em. Now, tell me . . . it *is* going to be fancy, right?"

"It's going to be —"

The little bell above the door rang, and cold air rushed in, and she knew without even turning that Jack was there.

She could feel him the way she felt winter cold and summer heat, could sense him the way she'd sensed her mother in the barn last night. A breath of knowledge, a whisper of old memories, and the soul-deep feeling that she wasn't alone.

She turned, and sure enough, he was there. Tall and dark and masculine, his eyes that beautiful dark green.

"Jack," she said, and she heard a world of

longing in her voice, felt her cheeks heat and her heart pound. Everything in her that was saying that they could never work together shut up and let her think about what would happen, how wonderful it would be if they could.

"You left without saying good-bye," he responded.

"You were on the phone. I figured you were busy."

"I'll never be too busy for you," he said, and she smiled, because what else could she do?

"You need to stop saying such sweet things. I might get used to it."

"That's my plan." He grabbed the kitty litter and food.

"Are you working today?" he asked, and she nodded, her throat too tight to speak.

Everything she'd lost when she'd come back to take care of her father — her school plans, her career plans, her friends, her job — none of it was nearly as important as the man looking into her eyes.

She'd been a fool to let him go.

She wasn't going to be one again.

"Then I guess you can't help me," he continued, and she swallowed down the tightness in her throat and managed to speak.

"What do you need help with?"

"I've been thinking we should get that sleigh out of the barn, hire a team of horses, and offer rides to people at the party."

Libby squealed. "Oh. My. Gosh. That sounds perfect. All you need are some of those old fur rugs and some mulled wine, and it will be just like a Victorian Christmas."

"That's the plan," Jack said, and Libby sighed.

"Wow. Just . . . wow," she said. "I'm going to have to buy a dress for this. Something stunning and high-brow and fashionable. Who else is invited, Em? I don't want to brag to friends unless they're invited, too."

"Everyone," she said, and she saw Jack flinch, knew he was calculating in his head how many people that might be.

"Holy cow! That's fantastic. I've seen the pictures at the town hall — the parties the Bailys used to give. But I never thought there'd be another one. Or that I'd be invited to it. Excuse me. I've got to call my husband and tell him to pull out his tux. It's a tux kind of party, right?" she said, and Emma just nodded, because she really didn't know, but . . .

Why not everyone?

Why not tuxes?

Why not the biggest party Apple Valley had seen since Tessa and Cade Cunningham's wedding reception three years ago?

"Everyone is a whole hell of a lot of people," Jack said as Libby hurried into a back room.

"They won't all come."

"The house can't accommodate more than seventy-five. How many people live in town? Three hundred? Four?"

"We can open the barn, and . . ." She almost didn't say it, almost couldn't make herself, but there were some things in life that were more important than sticking to old ideas and old plans. There were some things that were worth taking chances on. "We could rent a couple of those big tents."

"That's still a lot of people to accommodate. Plus, we'll have folks coming from out of town. I'm sending out the invitations later today." They walked out into the gray morning. Thick clouds hid the rising sun and added a deeper chill to the winter air. There'd be snow before evening, and for the first time in longer than she could remember, Emma was happy about it.

If Jack could find a team of horses, they'd want lots of snow for the sleigh rides.

He dropped the kitty litter and food into her trunk. "If it's too crowded, the people we're trying to attract may be put off. I'm not trying to tell you what to do, Em. It's your place, but a more intimate Christmas party may get you more buyer interest than a bigger one."

"I've been thinking about that," she said, opening her purse and setting the kitten back inside. He purred his happiness, curling up into a fuzzy ball on the bed of towels she'd made him.

"About what?"

"Getting people's interest in the property."

"What about it?"

"I'm not sure I want to."

She thought he'd ask questions, try to convince her to do what she'd planned, but he just smiled.

"I was wondering how long it would take you to get there, Em," he said.

"Get where?"

"To the place where you realized what you had and what it could become."

He kissed her temple, her cheek, her lips.

"I've got to track down a team of horses. I'll see you at the house later."

Before she could respond, he was in his SUV, waving as he pulled out of the parking lot and onto the road that led into town.

She watched him drive away, the sound of his SUV fading into early-morning silence.

Then, she got in her car, set the purse on the passenger seat, and headed back toward home.

CHAPTER TEN

Everyone in town came to the party. Most of them driving straight from Christmas Eve service to Emma's place. Old friends. New ones. Acquaintances. Every member of Apple Valley Community Church. They were all there, milling around the house, the barn, and the two tents that had been rented and filled with long tables set with Victorian china and lush bouquets of winter flowers.

The first Christmas party at the Baily farm in nearly a hundred years, and no one wanted to miss out on it.

Emma couldn't blame them.

It was spectacular. Everything beautiful and simple and elegant. Every detail absolutely perfect. The food delicious. The sleigh and the horses and the driver all gussied up and looking Victorian.

Jack had arranged it all, and then he'd left. Some business he needed to take care of in New Hampshire.

That's what he'd told Emma before he'd gotten on the plane two days ago. She'd had no reason to doubt him. Except that he'd promised to be back in time for the party, and he hadn't shown. She'd gotten no text, no phone call. Nothing. When she'd tried to call him, she'd gotten no answer.

So, while everyone else ran around playing Victorian games or dancing in the barn or taking sleigh rides through the crisp white snow, Emma was wandering around feeling lost, a little lonely, and a lot pissed.

Because he'd promised, and because she'd believed him.

She grabbed a cup of cider from the sideboard, smiling as several friends walked by. She'd been putting on a show for so many years, it was second nature to do it now. Even when her heart was breaking.

The way she saw things, if Jack hadn't come, he wasn't planning on it. Which meant that he'd gone back to his life and his job and his home.

She couldn't blame him.

She knew how much it meant to him, how hard he'd worked to get into a position that would allow him to take over the family business. She would never have wanted him to give that up, never have expected him to.

But, God, she wished he'd told her face-to-face.

She wished that he'd come to the party and maybe given her the choice like he had so many years ago, because this time, she'd have gone with him. Wherever he planned to be.

The fact was, she loved him.

She'd never *stopped* loving him.

She wasn't sure why it had taken her so many years to realize it.

She walked into the kitchen, relieved to find it empty. The rest of the downstairs was bustling with life, but this room had been abandoned. She jogged up the servant stairs, the floorboards creaking under her feet. No one would miss her if she hid away for a few minutes.

She walked into her room, smiling as she saw Hemingway lying on her pillow. The kitten was smart enough to keep out of the way of the horde of children that were running around the front yard, eating chocolate and cake and playing tag.

"Hey, buddy," she cooed, scratching him under the chin.

He purred. Of course.

He, at least, was uncomplicated, his happiness secure as long as he had food and a warm place to sleep. Even Leigh liked him.

She'd started buying him cat toys and special treats. She'd even offered to watch him if Emma ever needed to go away for, say, a honeymoon trip.

Emma would have laughed if it hadn't been so sad.

She crossed the room, pulling back the curtains and looking out into the yard. A bonfire had been built, and several volunteer firefighters were manning it, warning children away and keeping the beautiful glow of the flames high and bright.

She could see Tessa standing near it, wearing a gorgeous Victorian gown, her hair in some classy updo, woven through with pearls and rhinestones. She had a baby on her shoulder and a smile on her face. When Cade walked up behind her and whispered something in her ear, she laughed.

Emma couldn't hear the sound, but she could see the joy, and for the first time in her life, she wanted that for herself. The husband. The kid. The secret words and shared laughter.

What she didn't want was to spend her entire life alone in the house her father had left her. She couldn't sell it. She knew that now, but she didn't want to walk the empty halls, measure the passing of years by the creaking and groaning of the settling house.

She wanted to fill the place with laughter and joy and contentment. Just like Annabelle and Micah had.

Someone knocked on the door. She opened it, wasn't surprised to see Leigh standing there. She'd dressed in a long, black skirt and a purple waistcoat, a long strand of pearls hanging around her neck.

"I saw you heading up the back stairs. What's wrong, hun?" she asked.

"Nothing that anyone can help me with."

"You won't know that for sure unless you let someone try. That someone," she said, walking into the room, "being me."

"I'm okay, Leigh."

"Are you worried that Jack isn't going to come through for you?"

"The party started two hours ago. He's still not here."

"In other words, he's already failed you?"

"I didn't say that."

"But you're thinking it. Along with a bunch of other things that probably aren't true." Leigh set her hands on Emma's shoulders, looked her straight in the eyes. "Don't call the game until the last play is made. My mother used to say that to me. It's still good advice."

"It would be. If this were a game."

"Maybe I should have put it another way.

564

Maybe what I should have said was do you really think that the man who planned this stunning Christmas party, the man who convinced you that this is the place where you belong, would break his promise without a good reason?"

"I've called and texted him. He hasn't responded."

"He could be sitting in the middle of a runway somewhere, waiting for the plane to take off. He could be driving from the airport and hasn't checked his phone. There are all kinds of things that might have happened, so I'm wondering why you're jumping to the worst conclusions about the man you love."

It was a good question, and Emma might have tried to answer it, but her aunt was already walking back into the hall and shutting the door. Firmly. Because she knew that she was right and that Emma was wrong.

The funny thing? Emma knew it too.

She had no reason to doubt Jack.

None at all.

"So, I'm *not* going to doubt him," she told Hemingway. The kitten meowed a response, then jumped down and scurried under the bed.

Emma fished her cell phone out of the pocket of the long velvet skirt she wore.

Gray and soft as butter, it floated around her ankles and feet as she moved across the room, peered outside again.

She dialed Jack's number. One last time. Waited until voice mail picked up.

"Hey, Jack," she said just like she had a half dozen times before. "It's Em. I'm worried sick about you. I hope you're okay. Wherever you are, I'll be there if you need me. Just call. I love you."

The last part? That was different.

That was the real Emma.

The deepest part of herself.

Jack deserved that more than anyone else ever could. She shoved the phone in her pocket, took a deep breath, and was absolutely sure she heard the sleigh bells jingling from somewhere inside the house.

She frowned.

They couldn't be inside. She was probably hearing the sleigh, making another pass across the snowy back field.

Instead of pacing the house, she'd take a ride, enjoy the cold air and the quiet hush of the winter night, sip some mulled wine, and wait a little longer for the man she loved to come home to her.

The Christmas lights were still on. Jack could see them even before he turned into

566

the driveway. He could see the bonfire, too, shooting sparks into the dark sky.

The party was well under way.

Not surprising since he was two hours late.

Actually, two hours and sixteen minutes.

He'd been counting every damn second of the time, because the only place he'd wanted to be was with Emma. He'd had some loose ends to tie up in New Hampshire, some papers to sign. One last auction to oversee. Everything else Ace could handle. They'd talked it all out, decided the best way to handle Jack's move.

And he *was* moving.

He loved his old hometown, but he loved Emma more.

His family?

He loved them, too, and they loved him enough to be happy with the decision he'd made. Besides, it wasn't as if he'd cut ties with the family business. He could do a lot of his work remotely. When he couldn't, he'd fly back to New Hampshire. Eventually, he'd open an auction house outside of Apple Valley, an extension of his family business and one he could pass down to his children when the time came.

He parked his SUV and stepped out into noise and laughter. People were everywhere, dressed in their holiday finest. Some wore old Victorian clothes. Others had opted for modern dress. All of them smiled and waved as Jack made his way toward the house. He hadn't had time to change, was still wearing the jeans and T-shirt he'd put on before he'd left for the airport that morning.

Two delayed flights and a hellish ride from the airport, and he'd finally arrived.

Thank God.

Now if he could just find Emma all would be right with the world.

"Jack!" Tessa hurried toward him, a baby on her shoulder, a smile on her face. "You finally made it! The party is flawless. The entire town is gushing. Except for Zimmerman Beck, but he can always be counted on to find fault."

"Should I ask what he's finding fault with?"

"What you should do," she responded, "is go find Emma."

"That's an even better idea. Have you seen her?"

"Ten minutes ago, she was climbing in the sleigh with two other people. They should be back soon."

"Thanks."

He headed around to the back of the house and walked across the field, a few flakes of snow drifting from the black sky.

Somewhere in the distance, sleigh bells rang, the sound mixing with the crackle of the bonfire and the music drifting from the barn. He'd hired a harpist and a violinist, had rented a piano from a Spokane company, and a young teen named Alex was playing that. "Silent Night." He could hear the beautiful strains of the old carol.

He stood for a moment and just took it all in, the music and the bells and crackle of the fire.

"Jack?" Someone touched his shoulder, and he turned, looked into Emma's gorgeous gray eyes. Flakes of snow dusted her hair, her cheeks were pink from cold, and she was the most beautiful woman he'd ever seen.

He didn't speak. Just pulled her into his arms, kissed her the way he'd wanted to every minute of every day that he'd been gone.

"I missed you," he murmured against her lips.

"I missed you, too. I've been worried."

"That I wouldn't come?"

"That something was wrong. I couldn't think of any other reason why you wouldn't call or send me a message."

"My battery died during the second delayed flight. My charger was in my luggage.

Which didn't make it to Spokane."

"Rough day?" she said, levering up on her toes and offering a soft, sweet kiss.

"Not anymore," he responded, and she smiled.

"I feel the same way."

"Did you enjoy your sleigh ride?"

"I opted out. I wanted to wait for you. How was the trip?"

"Successful. I let my family know that I'd be staying here."

"You did?"

"You sound surprised."

"Running your family business —"

"Means nothing without you," he cut in, because it was true, and because he wanted her to know it.

"I would have lived there with you, Jack. I want you to know that, and if you decide you don't like it here, we can move to New Hampshire, and I'll help you with the auction house."

"And give up your heritage? Our children's heritage?" he responded, and her eyes widened, her mouth dropped open.

"You're rushing the gun a little, aren't you? I'm barely used to having a kitten."

He laughed. "You'll make a great mom. When the time comes. How about for right now, though, we just take that sleigh ride together?"

"You know what?" she said as the sound of bells grew louder and the horse-drawn sleigh appeared, moving across the field and heading straight toward them. "I'd like that. I'd like it a lot."

He smiled, slipped his arm around her waist, felt her lean into his side, the beautiful sounds of Christmas and love enveloping them as they waited.

Dear Reader,

Writing *An Apple Valley Christmas* was like returning home after a long absence. I'd spent the previous year working on the first two books in my new Home Sweet Home series, and I'd missed the quirky little town of Apple Valley. Not to mention that I'd left poor Emma Baily hanging out, caring for her curmudgeon of a father and working at the local sheriff's department. She'd made her first appearance in *The House on Main Street* and returned again in the next two books in the series. *The Cottage on the Corner* and *The Orchard at the Edge of Town* gave deeper glimpses into Emma's life, but I hadn't written her story. It really did need to be told. After all, everyone deserves a happily-ever-after.

I hope you enjoy this peek into Apple Valley. You can meet all of the inhabitants in my Apple Valley novels. If you love small towns and quirky characters, and if you love chocolate, you may also want to visit Benevolence, Washington. Another tiny little town on the eastern edge of Washington, it was the perfect setting for Chocolate Haven — the Lamont family chocolate shop. You can read all about the little town and its inhabitants in my new series. *Sweet Haven* and *Sweet Surprises* were released in 2016, and

Bittersweet will follow in 2017.

This holiday season, I wish you joy and peace, family and love. I hope that wherever you are, home has followed. If it hasn't, I hope that you find your way back to the place where you belong.

I love to hear from readers. If you have time, drop me a line at shirlee@shirlee mccoy.com.

Merry Christmas and happy holidays,
Shirlee McCoy

ABOUT THE AUTHORS

Fern Michaels is the *USA Today* and *New York Times* bestselling author of over 150 novels and novellas, including *Fast and Loose, No Safe Secret, Double Down, In Plain Sight, Perfect Match, Eyes Only, Kiss and Tell, A Family Affair,* and *Blindsided.* There are over 160 million copies of her books in print. Visit her website at www.fernmichaels .com.

Sarah Title has worked as a barista, a secretary, a furniture painter, and once managed a team of giant walking beans. She currently leads a much more normal life as a librarian in West Virginia. Her first novel is *Kentucky Home.*

Shirlee McCoy is a busy mom of five. When she's not homeschooling her children or trying to keep up with endless piles of laundry, she enjoys losing herself in a good book. Armed with a laptop, ten fingers, and her God-given imagination, she overpowers bad guys, rights wrongs, and makes the world a better place for her characters.

Stacy Finz is an award-winning reporter for the *San Francisco Chronicle*. After more than twenty years covering notorious serial killers, naked-tractor-driving farmers, fanatical foodies, aging rock stars and weird Western towns, she figured she finally had enough material to launch a career writing fiction. In 2012 she won the Daphne du Maurier Award for unpublished single-title mystery/suspense. She lives in Berkeley, California with her husband.

LARGE TYPE

The most wonderful time